THE DISAPPEARANCE OF
STEPHANIE MAILER

Also by Joël Dicker in English translation

The Truth about the Harry Quebert Affair

The Baltimore Boys

THE DISAPPEARANCE OF STEPHANIE MAILER

JOËL DICKER

Translated from the French by
Howard Curtis

MACLEHOSE PRESS
QUERCUS · LONDON

First published in the French language as *La Disparition de Stephanie Mailer*
by Editions de Fallois in Paris, 2018
First published in Great Britain in 2021 by

MacLehose Press
An imprint of Quercus Publishing Ltd
Carmelite House
50 Victoria Embankment
London EC4Y 0DZ

An Hachette UK company

A CIP catalogue record for this book is available
from the British Library.

ISBN (HB) 978 0 85705 920 8
ISBN (TPB) 978 0 85705 925 3
ISBN (Ebook) 978 0 85705 927 7

10 9 8 7 6 5 4 3 2 1

Designed and typeset in Minion by Libanus Press Ltd
Printed and bound in Great Britain by Clays Ltd, Elcograf S.p.A.

Papers used by Quercus are from well-managed forests and other responsible sources.

For Constance

Concerning the events of July 30, 1994

Only those familiar with the Hamptons in New York State knew what happened on July 30, 1994, in a small, swanky oceanside resort called Orphea.

That evening, the town's very first theater festival was due to open, an event of more than local significance which had attracted large crowds. From late afternoon tourists and locals alike had gathered on Main Street for the many festivities organized by the town council. The residential neighborhoods had emptied of their inhabitants: no people strolling on the sidewalks, no couples on porches, no children on skateboards on the street, nobody in the gardens. Everybody was on Main Street.

Around eight o'clock, in the deserted neighborhood of Penfield, the only sign of life was a car slowly crisscrossing the abandoned streets. At the wheel, a man searching everywhere with panic in his eyes.

He had never felt so alone in the world. There was nobody around to help him. He was looking for his wife. She had left to go jogging and had not come home.

Samuel and Meghan Padalin were among the few inhabitants of the town who had decided not to go to the opening night of the festival. There had been such a demand for tickets that they had been unsuccessful, and they had no wish to watch the open-air activities on Main Street or at the marina.

At 6.30, as she did every day, Meghan had left home to go jogging. The only day she didn't go jogging was Sunday. She took the same route every evening. From their house, she went up Penfield Street as far as Penfield Crescent, which formed a semicircle around a little park. She would stop in the park to do an exercise routine—always the same—then run home by the same route. It took forty-five minutes, fifty if she extended the exercises, but never more.

At 7.30, Samuel Padalin was thinking it strange that his wife was not yet home.

At 7.45 he started to worry.

By 8.00 he was pacing up and down his living room.

At 8.10, unable to stand it anymore, he got into his car and set off to look around the neighborhood. The logical way to proceed was to follow Meghan's habitual route, which was what he did.

He drove along Penfield Street as far as Penfield Crescent, and there he turned. It was 8.20. Not a soul in sight. He stopped to look into the park, but there was nobody there. As he was starting the car again he noticed a shape on the sidewalk. At first he thought that it was a heap of clothes. Then he realized it was a body. He jumped out of the car, heart pounding. It was his wife.

Padalin would later tell the police that his first thought was that his wife had fainted from the heat. Then he was afraid that she had had a heart attack. But as he approached Meghan, he saw the blood and then the hole at the back of her skull.

He started screaming for help, unsure if he should stay with his wife or run to the nearby houses, ring the doorbells, and beg someone to call Emergency. His vision was blurred, and he felt as if his legs could no longer carry him. His cries finally alerted someone from a parallel street, and they called the emergency services.

Only minutes later, the police cordoned off the neighborhood.

One of the first officers on the scene noticed that the door of the mayor's house, close to where Meghan's body lay, was ajar. As he went closer he saw that the door had been kicked in. He took out his pistol, ran up the front steps and announced himself. There was no answer. He pushed the door open with his foot and saw a woman's body lying in the corridor. He at once called for backup, then slowly advanced into the house, pistol in hand. In a small room to his right he was horrified to discover the body of a young boy. And then in the kitchen he found the mayor, also dead, lying in a pool of blood.

All three had been shot dead.

PART ONE

In the Depths

-7

The Disappearance of a Reporter

MONDAY, JUNE 23 – TUESDAY, JULY 1, 2014

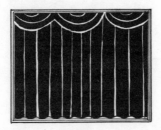

JESSE ROSENBERG

Monday, June 23, 2014

Thirty-three days to opening night of the 21st Orphea Theater Festival

The first and only time I saw Stephanie Mailer was when she gatecrashed the small reception organized in honor of my retirement from the New York State Police.

A host of police officers from all the squads had gathered in the noonday sun in front of the wooden platform erected for special occasions in the parking lot of troop headquarters. I was on that platform, next to my commander, Major McKenna. He had been my chief throughout my career and was now paying me a glowing tribute.

"Jesse Rosenberg is only a young captain, but he's clearly in a great hurry to leave," the major said to laughter from those present. "I would never have imagined he'd leave before me. Life really is a bummer. You'd all like me to leave, but I'm still here. You'd all like to keep Jesse, and Jesse's going."

I was forty-five years old and I felt good about leaving the force. After twenty-three years on the job, I had decided to take the pension to which I was by now entitled in order to realize a project that had been close to my heart for a long time. I still had a week to go before my leaving date of June 30. After that, a new chapter in my life would be starting.

"I still remember Jesse's first big case," the major was saying. "A horrible case, a quadruple murder, which he solved brilliantly, even though nobody in the squad thought he could. He was still a very young officer. From that moment on, we all realized what kind of man Jesse was. Anyone who's worked with him knows what an exceptional detective he is. I think I can safely say he was always the best among us. We call him Captain 100 Percent, because he's solved all the cases he's been involved in, and that makes him unique as a detective. An officer

15

admired by his colleagues, an expert everyone consults, and an instructor at the Academy for many years. Let me say this to you, Jesse: for twenty years, we've all been jealous of you!"

Another burst of laughter.

"We haven't quite figured out what this new project is that you're getting into, but we wish you good luck anyway. We're going to miss you, the police force is going to miss you, but it's our wives who are going to miss you the most, because they spent every police dance ogling you."

Thunderous applause. The major gave me a friendly hug, and then I got down off the stage so that I could say something to all those who had done me the kindness of being present before they rushed to the buffet.

Finding myself alone for a moment, I was approached by a very attractive woman, maybe in her thirties. I did not recall having seen her before.

"So you are the famous Captain 100 Percent?" she said in a seductive tone.

"Apparently," I said with a smile. "Do we know each other?"

"No. My name's Stephanie Mailer. I'm a reporter for the *Orphea Chronicle.*"

We shook hands.

"Do you mind if I call you Captain 99 Percent?"

I frowned. "Is there a case I didn't solve?"

By way of reply, she took from her bag a photocopy of a press clipping from the *Orphea Chronicle* of August 1, 1994, and handed it to me.

QUADRUPLE MURDER IN ORPHEA
MAYOR AND FAMILY SLAIN

On Saturday evening, the mayor of Orphea, Joseph Gordon, his wife Leslie, and their ten-year-old son Arthur were shot dead in their house. The fourth victim is Meghan Padalin, 32. The young woman, who was jogging at the time, must have been unfortunate enough to witness the scene. She was shot on the sidewalk close to the mayor's house.

There was a photograph of me and my then partner, Derek Scott, at the crime scene.

"What is this about?" I said.

"You didn't solve that case, Captain. You got the wrong man back in 1994. I thought you'd like to know that before leaving the force."

At first I thought that one of my colleagues was playing a practical joke on me, but soon I realized that the journalist was entirely serious.

"Are you conducting your own investigation?" I said.

"In a way, Captain."

"*In a way*? You're going to have to say more than that if you want me to believe you."

"I'm telling the truth, Captain. I have an appointment shortly that should allow me to obtain irrefutable evidence."

"An appointment with whom?"

"Captain," she said in an amused tone, "I'm not a beginner. This is the kind of scoop a reporter can't afford to pass up, but I promise you that whatever I find out I'll share with you when the time is right. Meanwhile, I have a favor to ask you. I'd like access to the State Police file on the case."

"You call it a favor, I call it blackmail," I said. "Start by showing me what you have. These are very serious allegations."

"I'm aware of that, Captain Rosenberg. That's why I don't want the State Police to get in ahead of me."

"Let me remind you that you have a duty to share with the police any information in your possession that has a bearing on this case. That's the law. I could also come to your newspaper office and search it."

The woman seemed disappointed. "Too bad, Captain 99 Percent," she said. "I assumed it would interest you, but I guess you're already thinking about your retirement and this new project the major mentioned in his speech. What is it? Repairing an old boat?"

"That's none of your business," I said curtly.

She shrugged and made to leave. I felt certain she was bluffing. But she stopped after a few steps and turned back. "The answer was right in front of your eyes, Captain Rosenberg. You just didn't see it."

I was both intrigued and irritated. "I'm not sure I follow you, Ms Mailer."

She raised her hand and placed it at the level of my eyes. "What do you see, Captain?"

"Your hand."

"I was showing you my fingers."

"But I see your hand," I said, not understanding.

"That's the problem right there," she said. "You saw what you wanted to see, not what you were being shown. That's what you missed twenty years ago."

She walked away, leaving me with her mystery, her business card, and the photocopy of the press clipping.

Spotting my former partner Derek Scott at the buffet—these days he was vegetating in a desk job—I hurried over to join him and showed him the clipping.

"You haven't changed a bit, Jesse," he said with a smile, amused to see a reference to that old case. "What did that girl want?"

"She's a reporter. According to her, we blew it back in '94. She claims we missed something in our investigation and ended up with the wrong man."

Derek choked. "That's crazy. What exactly did she say?"

"That the answer was right in front of our eyes and we didn't see it."

Derek was bewildered. He seemed troubled, too, but he was clearly going to dismiss the idea. "I don't believe it for a moment," he grunted. "It's just a two-bit reporter trying to make some cheap publicity for herself."

"Maybe," I said. "Maybe not."

Across the parking lot I saw Stephanie Mailer getting into her car. She waved to me and called out, "See you later, Captain Rosenberg."

But there was to be no "later". That was the day she disappeared.

DEREK SCOTT

I remember the day the whole thing started. It was Saturday, July 13, 1994.

Jesse and I were on duty that evening. We had stopped to have a meal at the Blue Lagoon, the fashionable restaurant where Darla and Natasha worked as waitresses.

Jesse and Natasha had been a couple for some years by that time. Darla was one of Natasha's best friends. They were planning to open a restaurant together and spent most of their time on the project. They had found a place and were in the process of obtaining the authorizations to start work. Evenings and weekends, they worked at the Blue Lagoon, putting aside half of what they earned to invest in their future establishment.

They could have managed the Blue Lagoon, or worked in the kitchen, but the owner said to them, "With your pretty faces and pretty asses, your place is out front. And don't complain, you make much more in tips than you'd earn in the kitchen." On that last point he wasn't wrong. Many customers came to the Blue Lagoon in the hopes of being served by them. They were beautiful, sweet, and friendly. They had everything going for them. Their own restaurant was going to be a resounding success and everyone was already talking about it.

Ever since I had met Darla she was all I could think about. I pestered Jesse to come to the Blue Lagoon whenever Natasha and Darla were there so we could have coffee with them. And when they met at Jesse's to work on their project, I was there as often as I could be, trying to charm Darla, who only half responded.

On that famous July evening, Jesse and I were having dinner at the

19

restaurant and chatting happily with the two of them as they went about their business. My pager and Jesse's went off simultaneously.

"For both of your pagers to go off at the same time," Natasha said, "it must be serious."

She pointed toward the phone booth as well as a phone on the counter. Jesse headed for the booth, I opted for the counter. The calls were brief.

"There's a general call out," I said as I hurried to the door. "There's been a quadruple killing."

Jesse was putting his jacket on.

"Hurry up," I teased him. "The first unit in the squad to reach the scene will get the case."

We were young and ambitious. This was a chance for us to do our first major investigation together. I was a more experienced officer than Jesse and had the rank of sergeant. The higher-ups liked me. Everyone said I had a great career ahead of me.

We ran to our car and bundled ourselves in.

I set off at speed and Jesse picked the flashing light up from the floor, switched it on, and reached through the open window to put it on the roof of our unmarked car, sending red flashes into the darkness.

That was how it started.

JESSE ROSENBERG

Thursday, June 26, 2014

Thirty days to opening night

I had assumed that I would spend my last week in the police hanging around the hallways, drinking coffee with my colleagues and saying leisurely goodbyes. But for the last three days I'd been in my office from morning to evening, absorbed in the file which I had taken out of records on the murders of 1994. My encounter with the journalist Stephanie Mailer had shaken me. I could think of nothing but that article, and her saying: "The answer was right in front of your eyes. You just didn't see it."

As far as I was concerned, we had seen everything there was to see. The more I went over the file, the more convinced I was that it was one of the most solid investigations I had conducted in my whole career. All of the pieces had fallen into place. The evidence against the man Derek and I had identified as the murderer was overwhelming. We had been meticulous. I could see no flaw in what we had done. How could we have gotten the wrong man?

That afternoon, Derek came to my office.

"What on earth are you doing, Jesse? Everyone's waiting for you in the cafeteria. The people in the administrative department have baked you a cake."

"I'll be right there, Derek. I'm sorry, my mind's on other things."

He looked at the documents spread out on my desk and picked one up. "Oh no, don't tell me you're swallowing the crap that reporter gave you?"

"Derek, I'd just like to make sure—"

He didn't let me finish. "Jesse, the case was rock solid! You know that as well as I do. Come on now, everyone's waiting."

"Give me a minute."

He sighed and left my office. I picked up the business card I had in front of me and dialed Ms Mailer's number. Her telephone was off. I had tried to call it the previous day, without success. She herself had not contacted me since our encounter on Monday, and I decided not to persist. She knew where to find me. Derek was right, I told myself. There was nothing to make us revisit the conclusions of the 1994 investigation. My mind at rest, I joined my colleagues in the canteen.

An hour later, when I got back to my office, I found a fax from the State Police in Riverdale in the Hamptons announcing the disappearance of a journalist named Stephanie Mailer, thirty-two years of age. She had apparently been missing for three days.

My heart skipped a beat. I tore the page from the machine and hurried to the telephone to contact the station in Riverdale. An officer there told me that Stephanie Mailer's parents had shown up early that afternoon, worried that they had not heard from their daughter since Monday.

"Why did her parents go to the State Police, not the local police?"

"They did, but the local police don't seem to have taken it seriously. So I told myself it might be best to pass it on to your squad. It may be nothing, but I thought you should know."

"You did the right thing. I'll take care of it."

I immediately telephoned Ms Mailer's mother. She had last spoken with her daughter on Monday morning. Since then, nothing. Her cell phone was off. The mother told me how worried she was. None of her daughter's friends had been able to reach her. Her mother had finally gone to her apartment with the local police, but there was nobody there.

I went straight to Derek in his office.

"The reporter who was here on Monday has disappeared."

"What are you talking about, Jesse?"

I handed him the missing persons report. "We have to go to Orphea and find out what's going on. This can't be a coincidence."

He sighed. "Jesse, aren't you supposed to be leaving?"

"I have four days more. During those days, I'm still a police officer. On Monday, when I saw her, she said she was meeting someone who would be able to supply something we had missed."

"Let someone else deal with it," he said.

"No way! That girl assured me that in 1994—"

He didn't let me finish. "We solved the case, Jesse! It's ancient history! What's gotten into you? Why are you so determined to go back to it? Do you really want to relive all that?"

I was irritated that he was not more supportive. "So you won't come to Orphea?"

"No, Jesse. I'm sorry, but I think you're crazy."

So I went to Orphea alone, twenty years after I had last set foot there. Twenty years since the murders.

It was an hour's drive from headquarters, but to gain time I put on the siren and the flashing lights so I did not have to obey the speed limits. I took Highway 27 as far as the fork to Riverhead, then 25 in a north-westerly direction. The last stretch of road passed through a gorgeous landscape, with luxuriant forests and ponds strewn with water lilies. Finally I got onto Route 17, which was straight and deserted, and which led to Orphea. I sped along it like an arrow. A huge billboard soon told me I had arrived.

WELCOME TO ORPHEA, NEW YORK
National Theater Festival, July 26 – August 9

It was five in the evening. Main Street was bright and verdant. I drove past stores, restaurants, coffee shops. There was an air of relaxation about the place. The lampposts were decorated with the Stars and Stripes in preparation for Independence Day, and billboards announced a firework display for the evening of the Fourth of July. Along the marina, lined with borders filled with flowers and neatly pruned bushes, people strolled between shacks offering excursions to look at the whales or bicycles for hire. It was a scene straight out of a movie.

*

My first stop was the police station.

Chief Ron Gulliver, head of the Orphea police department, invited me into his office. I did not need to remind him that we had already met.

"You haven't changed," he said, shaking my hand.

I could not have said the same of him. He had not aged well, and had become noticeably fatter. It was well past lunchtime and he was eating spaghetti out of a plastic container. In the time it took me to explain the reason for my visit, he gobbled down half the spaghetti in a disgusting manner.

"Stephanie Mailer?" he said, his mouth full. "We looked into that. She hasn't gone missing. I told her parents, but they're real pains in the ass. You can't get rid of them!"

"They may simply be parents worried about their daughter," I said. "They haven't heard from her for three days, which they say is quite unusual. I'm sure you'll understand that I'd like to treat it with due diligence."

"Stephanie Mailer is thirty-two, right? Old enough to do what she likes. Believe me, Captain Rosenberg, if I had parents like hers, I'd run away, too. Take it from me, the girl has taken off for a while, that's all."

"How can you be so sure?"

"Because of what her boss, the editor of the *Orphea Chronicle*, told me. She sent him a text message on Monday evening."

"The evening she disappeared."

"But I tell you: she hasn't disappeared!" Chief Gulliver growled at me.

Each of his exclamations was accompanied by a spray of tomato sauce. I took a step back.

"My deputy went to her place with her parents," Gulliver said, after swallowing. "They got in with their duplicate key and had a look around. Everything was neat and tidy. The text to her editor made it clear that there was no reason to worry. The girl doesn't have to justify herself to anybody. What she does with her life is no concern of ours. Nevertheless, we did our job. So please, don't come here and break my balls."

"But the parents are very worried," I said. "So, with your agreement, I'd like to check for myself that everything is fine."

"If you have time to waste, Captain, don't bother about me. You just have to wait for my deputy, Jasper Montagne, to come back from his patrol. He's the one who dealt with it."

When Deputy Jasper Montagne arrived, I was confronted with a huge wardrobe of a man, heavily muscled and formidable-looking. He told me he had accompanied Ms Mailer's parents to her apartment. They had gone in, she wasn't there. Nothing to report. No signs of struggle, nothing abnormal. Montagne had subsequently looked all over the neighboring streets in search of the journalist's car, but to no avail. He had even called the hospitals and police stations in the area. Nothing. Stephanie Mailer had evidently gone away.

Since I wanted to take a look at the apartment, he offered to go with me. She lived on Bendham Road, a quiet little street close to Main Street, in a narrow three-story block. A hardware store occupied the first floor, there was a single apartment on the second floor, and Ms Mailer's was on the third.

I rang her doorbell for a long time. I drummed on the door and called out, but it didn't get me anywhere.

"You can see for yourself, she isn't there," Montagne said.

I tried the handle. The door was locked.

"Can we go in?" I said.

"Do you have the key?"

"No."

"Nor me. Her parents opened the door the other day."

"So we can't go in?"

"No. And we're not going to start breaking people's doors down for no reason. If you want to set your mind at rest, go to the local paper and talk to the editor. He'll show you the text he got from Ms Mailer on Monday evening."

"What about the downstairs neighbor?" I said.

"Brad Melshaw? I talked to him yesterday. He didn't see or hear anything unusual. There's no point ringing his doorbell. He's a cook at Café Athena, the hip restaurant at the top of Main Street. That's where he'll be right now."

I wouldn't give in, though. I went one floor down and rang Brad Melshaw's bell. No response.

"I told you," Montagne sighed, going back downstairs, while I stood a little longer on the landing in the hope that someone would open the door.

By the time I decided to follow him, Montagne had left the building. When I got to the lobby, I took advantage of the fact that I was alone to inspect Ms Mailer's letterbox. Peering through the slit, I could see that there was a letter inside. I eased it out between my fingertips, folded it in half and slipped it into the back pocket of my pants.

Montagne drove me to the offices of the *Orphea Chronicle*, which were not far from Main Street, so that I could talk to Michael Bird, the editor.

The offices were in a redbrick building. The exterior was smart enough, but the interior was shabby-looking.

Michael Bird took us into his office. He had been in Orphea in 1994, but I did not remember meeting him then. He told me that, through a combination of circumstances, he had taken over the editorship of the *Orphea Chronicle* just three days after the murders, which was why he had spent most of that time drowning in paperwork rather than out in the field.

"How long has Stephanie Mailer been working for you?" I said.

"I hired her last December, so about seven months."

"Is she a good reporter?"

"She's very good. She's raised the level of the paper. That's important for us because it's hard to always have quality content. The paper isn't doing too well financially. We survive only because the premises are lent to us by the town council. People don't read local newspapers nowadays, so the advertisers have lost interest. This used to be an important

26

regional paper, widely read and respected. But now, why would you read the *Orphea Chronicle* when you can read the *New York Times* online? Not to mention those who don't read anything at all, just get their information from Facebook."

"When did you last see Stephanie?" I said.

"On Monday morning. At the weekly editorial meeting."

"Did you notice anything unusual? Was her behavior out of the ordinary?"

"No, nothing out of the ordinary. I know Stephanie's parents are worried, but as I told them and Deputy Montagne yesterday, she sent me a text message late on Monday, telling me she had to go away."

He took his cell phone from his pocket and showed me the text in question, which he had received at midnight on Monday.

I have to leave Orphea for a while. It's important. I'll explain later.

"And you have heard nothing from her since?"

"No. But to be honest, I'm not worried. Stephanie is the kind of reporter who likes to be independent. When she has something on she takes her time. I don't interfere too much with what she does."

"What's she working on right now?"

"The theater festival. Every year at the end of July, we have a theater festival here in Orphea."

"Yes, I know."

"Well, Stephanie wanted to write about the festival from the inside. She's preparing a whole series of articles about it. Right now, she's interviewing the volunteers who keep the festival going."

"Is it like her to disappear like this?"

"I'd say 'go away'. Yes, she goes away regularly. You know how it is, being a professional journalist requires you to leave your desk pretty frequently."

"Did she say anything about another investigation that she's conducting? She claimed she was meeting somebody about it on Monday night, somebody with information that was important to that story."

I was deliberately vague.

The editor shook his head. "No," he said. "She never mentioned anything like that."

On the way out of the newspaper offices, Montagne said, "Chief Gulliver wants to know if you're leaving now."

"Yes," I said. "I think I've done the tour."

Back in my car, I opened the envelope I had found in Stephanie Mailer's letterbox. It was a credit card statement. I examined it carefully.

Apart from her everyday expenses (gasoline, supermarket shopping, A.T.M. withdrawals, some purchases from the bookstore in Orphea), I noticed a fair number of tollbooth charges from rides into Manhattan. It seemed that she had been going to New York on a regular basis lately. In addition, she had bought a flight to Los Angeles. A quick round trip between June 10 and June 13. Payments while there—in particular, a hotel—confirmed that she had made the journey. Maybe she had a boyfriend in California. Whatever the case, she was a young woman who moved around a lot. There was nothing exceptional in the fact that she had gone away. I could understand the local police. None of these items pointed to a disappearance. Ms Mailer was an adult, she did not have to explain herself to anybody. So, since I did not have anything concrete to go on, I was on the verge of calling it a day when I was struck by one thing, one element that seemed out of place—the offices of the *Orphea Chronicle*. They did not correspond in any way to the image I had built up of Stephanie Mailer. I didn't know her, of course, but given the confidence with which she had approached me three days earlier, I could more easily imagine her at the *New York Times* than at a paper in a small resort town in the Hamptons. That one thing made me decide to look a little more deeply into the case. I would pay a visit to Ms Mailer's parents, who lived in Sag Harbor, twenty minutes' drive from where I was.

It was seven o'clock.

*   *   *

Around the same time, Betsy Kanner parked her car outside Café Athena on Orphea's Main Street, where she had arranged to meet her childhood friend Lauren and Lauren's husband Paul for dinner.

Lauren and Paul were the friends she had seen the most of since quitting New York to settle in Orphea. Paul's parents had a vacation home in Southampton, fifteen miles away, where they regularly spent long weekends.

Before Betsy got out of her car, she saw her friends already at a table on the terrace of the restaurant. What she mainly noticed was that there was a man with them. Immediately realizing what was happening, Betsy took out her cell phone and called Lauren.

"Have you set me up with a date?" she asked as soon as Lauren picked up.

There was a moment of embarrassed silence.

"I may have," Lauren said finally. "How did you know?"

"Instinct," Betsy lied. "Come on, Lauren, why did you do it?"

The only thing Betsy had against her friend was that she spent her time interfering in her personal life.

"You're going to love this one," Lauren assured her, having moved away from the table. "Trust me, Betsy."

"You know what, Lauren? It's not a good time for this right now. I'm still at the office and have a whole lot of paperwork to get through."

Betsy was amused to see Lauren becoming agitated.

"Betsy, I forbid you to stand me up! You're thirty-three years old, you need a guy! Tell me something. How long is it since you last got laid?"

That was the line of argument Lauren invariably used as a last resort. But Betsy was not in the mood to handle a blind date.

"I'm sorry, Lauren. Apart from anything else, I'm on duty."

"Oh, don't start with your duty! Nothing ever happens in this town. You're entitled to have a little fun, too!"

At that moment, a motorist sounded his horn and Lauren heard it both on the street and through the phone.

"Got you, girl!" she exclaimed, rushing out onto the sidewalk. "Where are you?"

Betsy didn't have time to get away.

"I see you!" Lauren cried. "If you think you're going to take off and dump me now . . . Do you realize you spend most of your evenings alone, like an old lady? You know, I wonder if you made the right choice, burying yourself here."

"Oh, for pity's sake, Lauren! I feel like I'm listening to my father!"

"If you carry on like this, Betsy, you're going to end up completely alone."

Betsy burst out laughing and got out of her car. If she'd been given a coin every time she heard people say that, she would be swimming in money by now. All the same, she had to admit that, given her situation, she couldn't blame Lauren. She was indeed living alone in Orphea, newly divorced and childless.

According to Lauren, there were two reasons for Betsy's successive failures in love. One was the fact that she did not show willing, the other her profession. "I never tell them in advance what you do for a living," Lauren had said a few times about the dates she arranged for her. "I think it intimidates them."

Betsy walked into the outdoor seating area of the restaurant. Today's candidate was named Josh. He had the air of a man who was too sure of himself. He greeted Betsy by giving her the eye in a frankly embarrassing manner and exhaling stale breath. This was not going to be the night she met Prince Charming.

*   *   *

"We're very worried, Captain Rosenberg," Trudy and Dennis Mailer said to me in unison in the living room of their beautiful house in Sag Harbor.

"I telephoned Stephanie on Monday morning," Mrs Mailer said. "She was in a meeting at the paper, she said, and would call me back. She never did."

"Stephanie always calls back," Mr Mailer said.

I could see from the start why the Mailers might have aggravated the police. With them, everything became a drama, even the fact that I had declined a coffee when I arrived.

"Don't you like coffee?" Mrs Mailer had said desperately.

"Perhaps you'd prefer tea?" her husband had said.

Managing at last to capture their attention, I had been able to ask them a few preliminary questions. Did Stephanie have any problems? No, they were categorical about that. Did she do drugs? No, definitely not. Did she have a boyfriend? Not as far as they knew. Was there any reason they could think of why she should drop out of sight? No, none.

Their daughter was not the kind of person to hide anything from them. But I soon discovered that this was not exactly the case.

"Why did Stephanie go to Los Angeles two weeks ago?"

"To Los Angeles?" Mrs Mailer said in surprise. "What do you mean?"

"Two weeks ago, Stephanie was in California for three days."

"We didn't know that," Mr Mailer said apologetically. "It's not like her to leave for Los Angeles without telling us. I guess it must have been in connection with the newspaper? She's very discreet about the articles she's working on."

I did not think that the *Orphea Chronicle* could afford to send its reporters to the other side of the country. And, in fact, it was her job at the paper that raised a number of further questions.

"When and how did Stephanie arrive in Orphea?"

"She had been living in Manhattan for the last few years," Mrs Mailer said. "She studied literature at Notre Dame. She's always wanted to be a writer, ever since she was young. She's had short stories published, two of them in the *New Yorker*. After her studies, she worked at the *New York Literary Review*, but she decided to leave in September."

"Did she give you a reason?"

"She quite soon found a job at the *Orphea Chronicle* and decided to come back to this area and settle here. She seemed pleased to be away from Manhattan and back in a calmer environment."

There was a moment's hesitation. Then Mr Mailer said:

"Captain Rosenberg, we're not the kind of people who trouble the police for no reason, believe me. We wouldn't have raised the alarm if we weren't both convinced that something was wrong. The police in Orphea made it very clear to us that there are no grounds for them to be involved. But even when she took a day trip to the city, Stephanie would send us a text or call us when she got back to let us know that everything was alright. Why text her editor and not her parents? If she had wanted us not to worry, she would have sent us a text, too."

"Speaking of which," I resumed, "why does Stephanie go so often to Manhattan?"

"I didn't say she went there often," Dennis said. "I was only giving an example."

"But she does go there often," I said. "Usually on the same days and at the same times. As if she had a regular appointment. What is it she does there?"

Again, the Mailers seemed not to know what I was talking about. Mrs Mailer, realizing she had not managed to convince me of the gravity of the situation, asked:

"Have you been to her apartment, Captain Rosenberg?"

"No, I'd have liked to, but I didn't have a key."

"Would you like to go take a look now? You may see something we didn't see."

I accepted, only so that I could close the case. A swift study of her apartment would surely convince me that the Orphea police were right and that there was nothing that pointed to the possibility that Stephanie's being missing was grounds for my being involved. She could go to Los Angeles or New York as often as she pleased. As for her work at the *Orphea Chronicle*, it was feasible that after losing her job in the city she had seized on the opportunity presented while waiting for something better to come along.

*

It was a little after eight o'clock when we got to Bendham Road. The three of us climbed the stairs to her apartment. Trudy handed me the key. I turned the key, but the door was not locked. I felt a powerful surge of adrenaline. There was someone inside. Was it Stephanie?

I signaled to Stephanie's parents to make no noise, say nothing, and gently pushed the door. It opened noiselessly. The shambles in the living room was appalling. Someone had been searching the place.

I whispered to the Mailers. "Go down the stairs. Wait for me in your car. I'll come and get you."

When they had gone, I took out my pistol and, looking left and right, stepped into the apartment. It had been turned upside down. I began by inspecting the living room. Its bookshelves had been pulled over, the cushions on the couch were ripped open. My attention was drawn to the objects scattered on the floor and I was unaware of a figure approaching me noiselessly from behind. It was when I turned to look in the other rooms that I found myself up against a shadowy apparition who sprayed tear gas in my face, burning my eyes and making it hard to breathe. Blinded, I bent double. I was struck on the back of my head.

A black curtain descended.

* * *

8.05 at Café Athena.

It is said that Cupid arrives without warning, but there was no doubt that Cupid had decided to stay home when he inflicted this dinner on Betsy. For a whole hour now, without a pause, Josh had been talking. Betsy, who had stopped listening to him, amused herself counting the number of "I"s in his monologue, trotting out like little cockroaches that repelled her a little more each time they appeared. Lauren, who did not know where to put herself, was on her fifth glass of white wine, while Betsy made do with alcohol-free cocktails.

At last, perhaps exhausted by his own eloquence, Josh reached for a glass of water and knocked it back in one go. After this welcome moment of silence, he turned to Betsy and asked her in a formal tone, "How about you, Betsy, what do you do for a living? Lauren wouldn't tell me." At that very moment, Betsy's cell phone rang. Seeing the number displayed on the screen, she knew at once it was an emergency.

"I'm sorry," she said, "I have to answer this call."

She got up from the table and walked away, then came back and told Lauren that, most unfortunately, she had to leave them.

"Already?" Josh said, disappointed. "We have hardly had time to get acquainted."

"But I know everything about you. It was . . . fascinating."

She kissed Lauren and her husband, waved at Josh, and quickly left. She must have taken the poor man's fancy, because he caught up with her on the sidewalk.

"Would you like me to drop you anywhere?" he said. "I have a—"

"A Mercedes Coupé," she said. "I know, you told me twice. It's very kind of you, but I'm parked just there."

She opened the trunk of her car, while Josh stood beside her.

"I'll get your number from Lauren," he said. "I'm often in the neighborhood. We could grab a coffee."

"Sure," Betsy said, as she opened a large canvas bag.

"You still haven't told me what you do."

Betsy lifted a bulletproof vest from the bag. Adjusting the straps around her body, she watched Josh's eyes open wide and stare at the shiny badge that bore in capital letters the word POLICE.

"I'm deputy police chief here in Orphea," she said, taking out the holster with her pistol in it and hooking it to her belt.

Josh kept staring, incredulous. She got into her car and set off at speed. The red and blue flashing lights shone through the dusk and her siren made everyone in the street turn to look.

According to the call from the switchboard, an officer from the State Police had been attacked in a nearby building. All available patrol cars as well as the officer on duty had been alerted.

She drove down Main Street. Pedestrians trying to cross turned back and took refuge on the sidewalks, and cars traveling both ways moved onto the curb to let her pass. She drove along the middle of the street, her foot down. She was used to taking emergency calls during rush hour in New York.

By the time she got to the building in Bendham Road, one patrol car was already on the scene. Entering the lobby, she ran into one of her colleagues coming down the stairs.

"The suspect ran out through the back door!" he cried.

Betsy went through the emergency exit at the rear of the building, and found herself in a deserted alleyway. There was an eerie silence. She stopped and listened, hoping for a sound that might point her in the right direction, then broke into a run and came to a little park. Again, total silence.

Thinking she heard a noise in the bushes, she took her gun from its holster and ran into the park. Nothing. Suddenly, she thought she saw a shadowy figure running. She set off in pursuit, but quickly lost sight of him. She finally stopped, disorientated and out of breath, blood hammering in her temples. She heard a noise behind a hedge. She approached slowly, heart pounding. She saw a dark figure advancing with muffled steps. She waited for the right moment, then leaped, pointing her gun at the man and ordering him to stop moving. It was Montagne, who was pointing a gun at her, too.

"Fuck, Betsy, are you crazy?"

She sighed and put her pistol back in its holster, bending double to regain her breath.

"Montagne, what the fuck are you doing here?" she said.

"I could ask you the same question! You aren't even on duty this evening!"

As head deputy, Montagne was technically her superior. She was only the second deputy.

"I'm on call," she said. "The switchboard called me."

"To think I'd almost cornered him!" Montagne said irritably.

"Cornered him? I was here before you. There was only one patrol car outside the building."

"I came from the street round the back. You should have radioed your position. That's what team players do. They communicate information, they don't act like desperados."

"I was on my own, I didn't have a radio."

"You have one in your car, don't you? You piss me off, Betsy! Since your first day here, you've been pissing everybody off!"

He spat on the ground and turned back toward the building. Betsy followed him. By now, Bendham Road had been invaded by emergency vehicles.

"Betsy! Montagne!" Chief Ron Gulliver called over to them.

"We lost him, Chief," Montagne said. "I could have had him if Betsy hadn't fucked up, like she always does."

"Go fuck yourself, Montagne!" she said.

"You go fuck yourself, Betsy!" Montagne retorted. "You can go home, this is my case!"

"No, it's my case! I was here before you."

"Do us all a favor and get out of here!"

Betsy turned to Gulliver for support. "What do you think, Chief?"

Gulliver could not abide conflict. "You're not on duty, Betsy," he said in a soothing voice.

"I'm on call!"

"Leave this case to Montagne," Gulliver said.

Montagne smiled and headed back to the building, leaving Betsy and Gulliver alone.

"That isn't fair, Chief!" she said. "Are you going to let Montagne talk to me like that?"

Gulliver did not want to hear. "Please, Betsy, don't make a scene. Everyone's looking at us. I don't need this now." Then he peered closely at her and said, "Did you have a date?"

"What makes you say that?"

"You're wearing lipstick."

"I often wear lipstick."

"This is different. You look like you're on a date. Why don't you go back to him? We'll talk tomorrow at the station."

Gulliver headed for the building, leaving her on her own. Suddenly hearing a voice calling to her, she turned. It was Michael Bird, the editor of the *Orphea Chronicle*.

"Betsy," he said, coming level with her, "what's going on?"

"No comment," she said. "I'm not in charge of anything."

"You will be soon," he said with a smile.

"What do you mean?"

"I mean when you take over as police chief. Is that why you were just quarreling with Deputy Montagne?"

"I don't know what you're talking about, Michael."

"Really?" he said, faking surprise. "Everyone knows you'll be the next chief."

Saying nothing, she walked back to her car. She took off her bullet-proof vest and threw it onto the back seat. She had absolutely no desire to go back to Café Athena. She drove home and sat on the porch with a drink and a cigarette to savor the mild evening weather.

BETSY KANNER

I arrived in Orphea on September 14, 2013, a Saturday.

It was only two hours from New York City, but it could have been on the other side of the world. I had moved from the skyscraper city of Manhattan to this quiet little town, bathed in soft, late-afternoon sunlight. I drove up Main Street and then through my new neighborhood to the house I had rented. I was driving slowly, looking at the people out strolling, the children crowding around an ice cream truck, the conscientious residents tending to their flower beds. Everything was calm and peaceful.

At last I came to the house. A new life was opening up in front of me. The only vestiges of my former existence were my furniture, which I had had brought from New York. I unlocked the front door, went inside, and switched on the light in the hall. To my surprise, I discovered that the floor was cluttered with my cardboard boxes. I quickly looked through the first floor. The furniture was all wrapped, nothing had been put together, my things were all in boxes piled up randomly around the rooms.

I immediately called the moving firm. The person who answered said, "I think you've made a mistake, Mrs Kanner. I have your file in front of me and you evidently ticked the wrong boxes. The service you signed for didn't include unpacking." She hung up.

I walked outside to get away from the mess and sat on the steps of the porch. I was angry. A figure appeared with a bottle of beer in each hand. It was my neighbor, Cody Springfield. I had met him twice before, once when I viewed the house, and again when I had signed the lease and came to prepare my move.

"I wanted to welcome you, Betsy."

"That's very kind," I said, making a face.

"You don't seem in a very good mood."

I shrugged. He handed me a beer and sat down next to me. I told him about my misadventure with the removers and he offered to help me unpack. Within a few minutes, we were carrying my bed up to what was going to be my bedroom.

"What should I do to fit in here?" I said.

"There's no need to worry on that score, Betsy. People will like you. You can always volunteer to help with the theater festival next summer. That's an event that always brings people together."

Cody was the first person I connected with in Orphea. He ran a wonderful bookstore on Main Street, which would soon become a kind of second home to me.

That evening, after Cody had left and I was still unpacking boxes of clothes, I had a call from my ex-husband.

"Are you kidding me?" he said when I picked up. "You left the city without saying goodbye to me."

"I said goodbye to you a long time ago, Mark."

"Ouch, that hurts!"

"Why are you calling me?"

"I wanted to talk to you, Betsy."

"Mark, I have no desire to 'talk'. We're not getting back together. It's over."

He ignored me. "I had dinner with your father this evening. It was great."

"Just leave my father alone, O.K.?"

"Is it my fault he loves me?"

"Why are you doing this to me, Mark? Is it revenge?"

"Are you in a bad mood, Betsy?"

"Yes," I said. "I *am* in a bad mood! I have furniture still needing to be assembled and I don't know how, which means I have better things to do than listen to you!"

I regretted saying this, because he immediately offered to come to my rescue.

"You need help? I'll get in my car and I'll be right there!"

"No, don't do that!"

"I can be there in two hours. We'll spend the night putting your furniture together and setting the world to rights. It'll be like the good old days."

"Mark, I forbid you to come."

I hung up and switched off my cell phone. The next morning, I had a nasty surprise. Mark had arrived.

"What are you doing here?"

He gave me a broad smile. "What a warm welcome! I'm here to help you."

"Who gave you my address?"

"Your mother."

"I don't believe it. I'll kill her!"

"Betsy, she's dying to see us back together. She wants grandchildren!"

"Goodbye, Mark."

He pushed against the door as I was shutting it. "Wait, Betsy. At least let me help you."

I was too much in need of a helping hand to refuse. And anyhow, he was already here. He put on his Mr Perfect act, carrying furniture, hanging pictures, installing a chandelier.

Between drilling holes, he said, "Are you planning to live here all alone?"

"Yes. This is where my new life starts."

*

The following Monday was my first day at the station. At eight in the morning I presented myself at the desk, in plain clothes.

"Are you here to make a complaint?" the officer asked me, without looking up from his newspaper.

"No," I said. "I'm your new colleague."

He looked up, gave me a friendly smile, and called out, "Hey, guys, the girl's here!"

A whole squad of officers appeared, gawping at me as if I was some kind of strange animal. Chief Gulliver came forward and held out his hand. "Nice to meet you, Betsy."

I was warmly welcomed. I greeted my new colleagues in turn. I was offered a coffee and asked lots of questions. Someone cried out cheerfully, "Guys, I'm going to start believing in Father Christmas. A shriveled old cop retires and we get a hot young babe as a replacement!" They all burst out laughing.

But the good-natured atmosphere was not to last.

JESSE ROSENBERG

Friday, June 27, 2014

Twenty-nine days to opening night

Early that morning I left for Orphea.

I absolutely had to figure out what had happened in Stephanie's apartment. As far as Chief Gulliver was concerned, it was a simple burglary, but I didn't believe that for a moment. My forensics colleagues had stayed there until late in the night looking for fingerprints, but they found none. For my part, judging by the force of the blow I had received, I inclined strongly to the idea that the intruder was a man.

I had to find Stephanie and I sensed that I did not have much time. Driving now along Route 17, I accelerated on the last straight stretch before getting to Orphea, without putting on either my flashing lights or my siren.

It was only when I passed the road sign marking the city limits that I noticed the unmarked police car concealed behind it, which immediately started following me. I pulled up onto the shoulder. In my rear-view mirror I saw a pretty young woman in a uniform get out of her vehicle and walk toward me. I was about to make the acquaintance of the first person who would agree to help me in unraveling this case: Betsy Kanner.

As she approached my open window, I showed my badge and smiled.

"Captain Jesse Rosenberg," she read. "I think I saw you briefly on Bendham Road yesterday." She introduced herself. "Deputy Betsy Kanner. How's your head, Captain?"

"My head's fine, thanks. But I'm a little disturbed by what happened in that apartment. Chief Gulliver thinks it was a burglary, but I don't hold with that. I wonder if I haven't gotten myself involved in a really weird case."

"Gulliver's a complete idiot," Betsy said. "But tell me about your case. I'm interested."

I realized then that Betsy might be a valuable ally in Orphea. And as I was subsequently to discover, she was also a terrific policewoman.

"Betsy, can I buy you a coffee? I'll tell you the whole story, as much as I know it."

A few minutes later, in a roadside diner, I was telling Betsy how everything had started, how Stephanie had come to see me at the beginning of the week and told me about an investigation she was conducting into the quadruple murder in Orphea in 1994.

"What quadruple murder in 1994?"

"The mayor of Orphea and his family were murdered, as well as a woman who was out jogging, who happened to pass by. It was the opening night of the first Orphea Theater Festival. And it was the first big case I worked on. My partner Derek Scott and I reckoned we had solved it. But on Monday, this woman, a journalist on the *Chronicle*, approached me at my retirement party to tell me she thought we had made a mistake. We had gotten the wrong man. And then she vanished. Last night, someone paid a visit to her apartment.

"According to the parents," I said to Betsy, "the only duplicate was the one in their possession. That means that whoever was in the apartment last night had Stephanie's keys."

I had already mentioned the text received by her editor Michael Bird, and now Betsy said, "If that person has Stephanie's keys, he or she may also have her cell phone."

"You mean she didn't send the text? Then who did?"

"Someone who was playing for time."

From the back pocket of my pants I took the envelope I'd slipped out of the letterbox the previous day and handed it to Betsy.

"This is Stephanie's credit card statement," I said. "She traveled to Los Angeles at the beginning of the month. We don't know what that was about. I've checked, and she hasn't taken a plane since. If she left of her own free will, she most likely left by car. I put out an A.P.B. on the license number. If she's on the road somewhere, the Highway Patrol will find her soon enough."

"You didn't waste any time," Betsy said.

"There is no time to waste," I said. "I also requested her telephone records and credit card statements for the last few months. I hope to have them by this evening."

Betsy quickly read the statement. "Her credit card was last used at 9.55 on Monday evening at the Kodiak Grill. That's on Main Street. We should go there. Someone may have seen something."

The Kodiak Grill was located at the top of Main Street. The manager consulted the week's roster for us and pointed out the members of staff there now who had also been on duty on Monday evening. One of the waitresses we questioned recognized Stephanie from the photograph Mrs Mailer had insisted I take with me when I was at their house yesterday.

"I remember her," she said. "She was here at the beginning of the week. A pretty girl, all on her own."

"How come you remember her out of all your customers? Was there something special about her?"

"It wasn't the first time she was here. She always asked for the same table. She'd say she was waiting for someone, but whoever it was never showed up."

"What happened on Monday?"

"She got here when my shift was starting, around six. And she waited. In the end she ordered a Caesar salad and a Coke, and then she left."

"Around ten."

"That's possible. I don't remember the time, but she was here for quite a while. She paid and left. That's all I remember."

Leaving the Kodiak Grill, we noticed that the building next door was a bank with an A.T.M. on the outside.

"There must be cameras," Betsy said. "Stephanie may have been filmed on Monday."

A few minutes later, we were in the cramped office of the bank's security officer, who showed us the angles from which the different cameras on the building recorded the scene. One of them was aimed at the sidewalk and we could see the outside seating area of the Kodiak Grill. He ran Monday's footage for us, from six o'clock onwards. Peering at the people passing on the screen, I suddenly saw her.

"Stop!" I said. "That's her."

The security officer froze the image.

"Now go back slowly, please," I said.

On the screen, Stephanie walked backward. The cigarette she was holding between her lips reconstructed itself, then she lit it with a gold lighter, took it between her fingers, and put it in a pack that she put into her bag. She moved back farther and veered off the sidewalk to a little blue car, in which she took her seat.

"A three-door blue Mazda. I saw her get into it on Monday, in the parking lot at troop headquarters."

I asked the security officer to play the sequence again, forward this time, and we watched Stephanie get out of the car, light a cigarette, smoke it as she took a few steps along the sidewalk, and head for the Kodiak Grill.

We moved the recording forward to 9.55, the time when Stephanie had paid for her dinner with her credit card. Two minutes later, we saw her come back out. She seemed nervous as she walked to her car. As she was about to get in, she took her cell phone from her bag. Someone had called her. The call was brief. She did not seem to be speaking, only listening. After hanging up, she got into the car and sat there motionless for a while. We could see her distinctly through the car window. She searched for a number in the phone's contacts and called it, but hung up again immediately, as if she had not been able to get through. She waited another five minutes, sitting behind the wheel. Then she made a second call. This time we saw her speaking. The exchange lasted perhaps twenty seconds. Finally, she started the car and drove away.

"That may be the last image of Stephanie Mailer," I said.

We spent half the afternoon questioning Stephanie's friends. Most lived in Sag Harbor, her hometown.

None of them had heard from Stephanie since Monday and they were all worried, especially since her parents had called them. They had tried to reach her by telephone, by e-mail, through social media, they had gone to her apartment and knocked at her door. But no-one had gotten hold of her.

It emerged from our conversations that Stephanie was a terrific young woman. She didn't do drugs, didn't drink to excess, and got along well with everyone. Her friends knew more than her parents did about her private life. One of them told us she knew Stephanie had had a boyfriend recently.

"Yes, there was a guy, his name was Sean. She came with him to a party. It was weird."

"In what way weird?"

"The chemistry between them. Something wasn't right."

Another friend told us that Stephanie had been up to her ears in work.

"We've hardly seen her lately. She said she had a lot going on."

"What was she working on?"

"I don't know."

A third friend told us about her trip to Los Angeles. "Yes, she did go to L.A. two weeks ago, but she told me not to talk about it."

"What was the purpose of the trip?"

"I don't know."

The last of her friends to have talked to her was Timothy Volt. He and Stephanie had seen each other the previous Sunday evening. "She came to my place," he said. "I was on my own, and we had a few drinks."

"Did she seem worried?" I said.

"I wouldn't say so."

"What kind of woman is Stephanie?"

"She's brilliant, but she's a tough cookie. She can be really stubborn. When she gets hold of something, she won't let go."

"Did she tell you what she was working on?"

"She said she was working on a really major project, but wouldn't go into any details."

"What kind of project?"

"A book. In fact that's why she came back to the area."

"How do you mean?"

"Stephanie's very ambitious. Her dream is to be a famous writer, and she'll make it. She was earning a living working for a literary magazine until last September. The name escapes me."

"The *New York Literary Review.*"

"That's it. But it was really only a sideline to pay her bills. When she was fired, she said she wanted to come back to the Hamptons so she could write in peace. I remember her saying to me one day, 'The only reason I'm here is to write a book.' I think she needed time, and she needed peace and quiet. She certainly found it here. Why else would she have accepted a job as a freelance reporter for a local paper? Like I said, she's ambitious. She aims for the moon. She must have had a good reason for settling in Orphea. Maybe she couldn't concentrate in all the excitement of the city. It's quite common to see writers moving out to the country, isn't it?"

"Where did she write?"

"At home, I guess."

"On a computer?"

"I don't know. Why?"

As we left Volt's place, I mentioned to Betsy that I had seen no computer in Stephanie's apartment.

We took advantage of being in Sag Harbor to go see Stephanie's parents. They had never heard of a boyfriend named Sean, and Stephanie had not left a laptop in their house. To set our minds at rest, we asked if we could take a look at Stephanie's room. She hadn't been in it since the end of high school and it had remained intact—the posters on the wall, the sporting trophies, the fluffy toys on the bed, the school books.

"It's years since Stephanie last slept here," Mrs Mailer said. "After high school, she went to college, and then she lived in Manhattan until she left the *New York Literary Review*."

"Was there a specific reason for Stephanie to move to Orphea?" I asked her, without revealing what Volt had told me.

"As I said yesterday, she'd left her job at the *Review* and wanted to come back to the Hamptons."

"But why Orphea?"

"Because it's the biggest town in the region, I guess."

"And in the city, Mrs Mailer," I ventured, "did Stephanie have enemies? Had she quarreled with anyone?"

"No, nothing like that."

"Did she live alone?"

"She had a roommate, a young woman who worked in publishing. We met her once when we helped Stephanie collect her few pieces of furniture after she'd decided to leave the city. She really had only a few things, we took everything straight to her apartment in Orphea."

Not having discovered anything in her apartment, or at her parents' house, we decided to go back to Orphea and check Stephanie's computer in the *Chronicle* offices.

It was five o'clock when we got there. The editor led us between his employees' desks. He pointed to Stephanie's tidy desk, on which stood a computer screen, a keyboard, a box of Kleenex, a mug with a prodigious number of identical pens, a notepad, and a few scattered papers. I looked through them quickly without finding anything very interesting.

"Could someone have had access to her computer since she's been away?"

As I spoke, I pressed the computer's ON button.

"No," the editor said. "The computers are protected by individual passwords."

48

The computer did not come on, so I pressed the button again.

"So there's no possibility that anyone could have had a look at Stephanie's computer without her knowing?"

"None at all," Bird assured us. "Only Stephanie has the password. Nobody else, not even the I.T. guy. In fact, I don't know how you'll be able to look at her computer if you don't have the password."

"We have specialists who can manage that. But I'd at least like to switch it on." I leaned down under the desk to make sure that the computer tower was properly connected, but there was no tower. There was nothing.

I looked up again and asked, "Where is Stephanie's computer?"

"It's under there, isn't it?"

"No, there's nothing there!"

Bird and Betsy immediately bent down to check. There was nothing there but cables hanging down.

"Someone stole Stephanie's computer!" Bird exclaimed, stunned.

By 6.30, the street outside the *Chronicle* building was a mass of vehicles from the Orphea police department and the State Police.

Inside, an officer from the forensics squad confirmed to us that someone had indeed broken in to the offices. Bird, Betsy and I followed him in procession to an electrical room in the basement that also served as a storeroom and as the emergency exit. At the end of the room, a door led out to a steep staircase that went back up to street level. Someone had smashed the window and had only needed to put his hand through it to turn the handle from the inside and open the door.

"Do you ever come to this room?" I asked the editor.

"Never. Nobody comes to the basement. There's nothing but the archives down here, and we very rarely look at them."

"No alarm, no cameras?" Betsy said.

"No, who'd pay for that? Believe me, if we had the money, it'd go on the plumbing first."

"We tried to find prints on the handles," the forensics officer explained, "but there are so many prints, mixed up with all kinds of filth, that they're unusable. We haven't found anything around Stephanie's desk either. In my opinion, the intruder came through that door, went upstairs, took the computer, and got out the same way."

We went back to the editorial office. "Mr Bird," I said, "could it be a member of your team who did this?"

"No way!" he said, offended. "I have complete confidence in my colleagues."

"So how do you explain how someone unfamiliar with this office could have known which one was Stephanie's computer?"

"I have no idea," he sighed.

"Who's first here in the morning?" Betsy said.

"Shirley. She opens the offices every morning."

We sent for Shirley.

"Over the last few mornings, have you noticed anything unusual when you got here?" I asked her.

Puzzled at first, Shirley searched in her memory. Suddenly, her eyes lit up.

"I didn't see anything myself. But on Tuesday morning, one of the reporters, Newton, told me his computer was on. He knew he'd switched it off the day before because he'd been the last to leave. He made a scene, saying that someone had switched on his computer without his permission, but I reckoned he'd simply forgotten to switch it off."

"Which is Newton's desk?"

"It's the one next to Stephanie's."

I pressed the button to switch on the computer, knowing there wouldn't be any usable prints on it because it had been used in the meantime. The screen lit up.

NEWTON'S COMPUTER
PASSWORD:

"He switched on the first computer," I said, "saw the name, and realized it wasn't the right one. Then he switched on the second one and Stephanie's name appeared. He didn't need to look any farther."

"Which tells us it was someone from outside who did this," Bird said, reassured.

"What it means more than anything is that the burglary took place on Monday night. In other words, the night Stephanie disappeared."

"Disappeared? What do you mean, disappeared?"

My only response was to ask him, "Mr Bird, could you print me all the articles Stephanie has written since she started here at the paper?"

"Of course. But aren't you going to tell me what's going on, Captain? Do you think something's happened to Stephanie?"

"Yes, I do. And I think it's serious."

I left Betsy in the offices and ran into Chief Gulliver and the mayor of Orphea, Alan Brown, discussing the situation on the sidewalk. The mayor recognized me immediately. It was as if he had seen a ghost.

"You are here?"

"I wish we were meeting again under different circumstances."

"What circumstances? What's going on? Since when do the State Police get involved in a simple burglary?"

"You have no authority to do anything here!" Chief Gulliver said.

"There's been a disappearance in this town, Chief Gulliver, and disappearances are the remit of the State Police."

"A disappearance?" Mayor Brown said in a choked voice.

"There's no disappearance!" Chief Gulliver cried in exasperation. "You don't have the slightest evidence, Captain Rosenberg! Have you called the D.A.'s office? That's what you should have done if you're so sure of yourself! Maybe I should give them a call."

I did not reply and left.

That night, at three in the morning, the Orphea fire department was called out to a blaze at 77 Bendham Road, Stephanie Mailer's address.

DEREK SCOTT

July 30, 1994, the evening of the quadruple murder.

It was 8.55 when we arrived in Orphea. We had driven across Long Island in record time.

Siren screaming, we got to the corner of Main Street, which was closed off due to the opening of the theater festival. A local police car was parked there and the officers let us through. The Penfield neighborhood was cordoned off. There were emergency vehicles from all the neighboring towns. Around Penfield Lane, police tape had been set up, behind which stood a mass of onlookers who had streamed there from Main Street, anxious not to miss a moment of the show.

Jesse and I were the first detectives on the scene. We were greeted by Kirk Hayward, Orphea's chief of police.

"I'm Sergeant Derek Scott, State Police," I said, showing my badge, "and this is my partner, Inspector Jesse Rosenberg."

"I'm Chief Kirk Hayward," he said, visibly relieved that he could pass this thing on to someone. "I won't bullshit you guys—I'm out of my depth here. We've never had to deal with anything like this. There are four people dead. It's a massacre."

Police officers were scurrying in all directions, shouting orders and counter-orders. It turned out that I was the highest-ranking officer on the scene.

"We have to close off all roads," I said to Chief Hayward, "and put roadblocks in place. I'm asking for backup from the Highway Patrol and all available units of the State Police."

Some twenty yards from us, in a pool of blood, lay the body of a woman in sports clothes. We slowly approached her. An officer was standing guard nearby, making an effort not to look.

"It was her husband who found her. He's in the ambulance, just over there, if you want to question him. But the most horrible thing is inside." He pointed. "A little boy and his mother . . . This is the mayor's house."

We headed immediately for the porch. As we tried to cut across the lawn, we found ourselves in an inch and a half of water.

"Goddammit," I cursed, "my feet are soaking, I'm going to get water everywhere. Why's there all this water here? It hasn't rained for weeks."

"A pipe burst in the automatic sprinkler system, sir," an officer outside the house said. "We're trying to turn the water off."

"The main thing is not to touch anything," I said. "We have to leave everything as it was until forensics arrive. And put tape on both sides of the lawn. I don't want the whole crime scene flooded."

I wiped my feet as best I could on the porch steps and we entered the house. The door had been kicked in. Right in front of us, in the hallway, a woman lay on the floor, several entry wounds visible. Next to her was an open suitcase, half filled. To the right, a small living room in which lay the body of a boy of about twelve, shot dead. He had collapsed into the curtains as if he had been cut down while trying to hide. In the kitchen, a man lying on his stomach in a pool of blood.

The smell of death and innards was unbearable. We quickly left the house, ashen-faced, shaken by what we had seen.

Before long, we were called into the mayor's garage. Some officers had found more suitcases in the trunk of the car. The mayor and his family had apparently been about to leave.

*

The night was hot and the young deputy mayor, Alan Brown, was sweating in his suit. He had come down Main Street as quickly as he could, pushing his way through the crowd. He had left the theater as soon as he had been informed of what had happened and had decided to get to Penfield Crescent on foot, convinced it would be quicker than going by car. He was right: the center of town, crowded with people as it was, was impassable. At the corner of Durham Street, the locals, having heard disturbing rumors, saw him and gathered around, asking for information. He did not reply and set off at a run. He veered right when he got to Bendham Road and went on as far as the residential area. At first he passed down deserted streets, with lights out in all the houses. Then he became aware of all the agitation in the distance. As he drew closer, he saw a halo of lights growing brighter, as well as the flashing lights on the emergency vehicles. The crowd of onlookers had grown. Some called to him, but he ignored them. He made his way through until he was up against the police tape. Spotting him, Deputy Chief Ron Gulliver let him through. Brown was overwhelmed by it all at first: the noise, the lights, a body covered in a white sheet on the sidewalk. He did not know where to turn until, to his relief, he saw the familiar face of Chief Hayward, with whom Jesse and I were talking.

"Kirk," Brown said to the chief, rushing toward him, "what's going on, for heaven's sake? Is the rumor true? Have Joseph and his family been murdered?"

"All three of them, Alan," Chief Hayward replied in a grave tone.

He nodded toward the house, where police officers were coming and going.

"All of them shot in the house."

Chief Hayward introduced us to the deputy mayor.

"Do you have a lead?" Brown asked us. "Any clues?"

"Nothing for the moment," I said. "What I can't get out of my head is that this should have happened on the opening night of the theater festival."

"You think there's a connection?"

"I can't even guess what the mayor was doing at home. Shouldn't he have been at the Grand Theater?"

"Yes, we'd arranged to meet at seven. When he didn't come, I tried to call him at home, but there was no answer. Since the play was about to start, I ad-libbed the opening speech in his place. His seat was empty all through the first act. It wasn't until the intermission that I was informed of what had happened."

"Alan," Chief Hayward said, "we found packed suitcases in Mayor Gordon's car. It looks like he and his family were going away."

"*Going away*? What do you mean? Going away where?"

"Your guess is as good as mine," I said. "Did you get the feeling the mayor was anxious about anything lately? Had he told you about any threats? Was he worried for his safety?"

"Threats? No, he never said anything like that. Can I . . . Can I look inside the house?"

"It's best to avoid contaminating the crime scene," Chief Hayward said. "And besides, it's not a pretty sight, Alan. A real slaughterhouse. The boy was killed in the living room, Leslie in the hallway, and Joseph in the kitchen."

Deputy Mayor Brown felt shaky. He suddenly had the impression that his legs were giving way and he sat down on the sidewalk. His gaze again came to rest on the white sheet a few dozen yards away.

"But if they all died in the house, then who's that?" he asked, pointing to the body.

"A young woman named Meghan Padalin," I said. "She was jogging. She may have run into the murderer as he was coming out of the house."

"It's not possible!" Brown said, covering his face with his hands. "This is a nightmare!"

Just then, Deputy Gulliver joined us. "The press are asking a lot of questions," he said to Brown. "Someone will have to make a statement."

"I . . . I don't know if I can face it," Brown stammered.

"Alan," Chief Hayward said, "you have to. You're the mayor of this town now."

JESSE ROSENBERG

Saturday, June 28, 2014
Twenty-eight days to opening night

It was eight in the morning. While Orphea slowly woke up, excitement was still high on Bendham Road, which was filled with fire engines. The building where Stephanie lived was a smoking, skeletal ruin.

Betsy and I stood on the sidewalk, watching the coming and going of the firefighters, who were busy rolling up their hoses and putting away their equipment. We were soon joined by the fire chief.

"It's arson," he said categorically. "Lucky that nobody was hurt. Only the second-floor tenant was in the building and he got out in time. He's the one who alerted us. Would you come with me? I'd like to show you something."

We followed him into the building, then up the black, soaked staircase. The air was smoky and acrid. When we got to the third floor, we discovered that the door to Stephanie's apartment was wide open. The lock looked intact.

"How did you get in without breaking the door down or damaging the lock?" Betsy said.

"That's what I wanted to show you," the fire chief replied. "The door was wide open when we arrived, just as you see it now."

"The arsonist had the keys," I said.

Betsy looked at me gravely. "Jesse, I think the person you surprised here on Thursday night came to finish the job."

I went closer and looked into the apartment. The furniture, the walls, the books—everything was charred. The person who had set fire to the apartment had had only one aim in mind: to destroy it.

*

Out on the street, Brad Melshaw, the man who had lived on the second floor, was sitting on the steps of a nearby building, wrapped in a blanket and drinking from a mug, contemplating the flame-blackened facade of the building.

He told us he had finished his shift at Café Athena at around 11.30.

"I came straight home," he said. "I didn't notice anything unusual. I took a shower, watched T.V. for a while, and fell asleep on my couch, as I often do. Around three in the morning, I woke up to find the apartment was filled with smoke. I quickly realized it was coming from the stairwell. When I opened my door I saw that the floor above was burning. I ran straight down to the street and called the fire department on my cell phone. Apparently, Stephanie wasn't at home. She's having problems, is that right?"

"Who told you that?"

"Everyone's talking about it. This is a small town, you know."

"Do you know Stephanie well?"

"No. Like neighbors who pass on the stairs, but not even that really. Our timetables are very different. She moved here late last year. She's nice."

"Did she tell you about a trip she had planned? Did she mention that she was going away?"

"No. Like I said, we weren't close enough for her to tell me that kind of thing."

"She might have asked you to water her plants or pick up her mail."

"She never asked me to do anything like that." Suddenly, Melshaw's eyes clouded over. "Wait! How could I have forgotten? She had an argument with a police officer the other night."

"Which night was this?"

"Last Saturday."

"What happened?"

"I was coming home from the restaurant. It was around midnight. There was a police car parked outside the building and Stephanie was talking to the driver. She was saying, 'You can't do that to me, I need you.' And he said something like, 'I don't want to hear from you again. If you keep calling me, I'll lodge a complaint.' Then he started the car and drove away. She stood there on the sidewalk for a while. She looked lost. I waited at the corner of the street, which was where I'd seen it all from, until she went up to her apartment. I didn't want to make her feel uncomfortable."

"What type of police car was it?" Betsy said. "From Orphea or another town? State Police? Highway Patrol?"

"I have no idea. I didn't pay attention. And it was dark."

We were interrupted by Mayor Brown. "I assume you've read today's paper, Captain Rosenberg?" he said angrily, unfolding a copy of the *Chronicle* in front of me.

On the front page was a photograph of Stephanie, and above it the headline:

HAVE YOU SEEN THIS WOMAN?

Stephanie Mailer, a reporter for the *Orphea Chronicle*, has been missing since Monday. A number of strange events have occurred in connection with her disappearance. The State Police are investigating.

"I didn't know anything about this article, Mr Mayor," I assured him.

"Whether you knew about it or not, Captain Rosenberg," Brown said crossly, "you're the one creating all this upset!"

I turned to the still-smoking building. "Are you saying that nothing out of the ordinary is happening in Orphea?"

"Nothing the local police can't deal with. So don't come here and create more chaos, O.K.? The town isn't in great shape financially, and everyone's counting on the summer season and the theater festival to put us back on our feet. If the tourists are scared, they won't come."

"I am sorry to insist, Mr Mayor, but I believe this may be something very serious."

"You don't have the first clue, Captain Rosenberg. Chief Gulliver told me yesterday that Stephanie's car hasn't been seen since Monday. What if she's simply taken off for a few days? And I made a few calls about you. I hear you're retiring on Monday."

Betsy gave me a strange look. "Jesse, are you quitting the police?"

"I'm not going anywhere until I get to the bottom of all this."

I understood the kind of reach Mayor Brown had when, after leaving Bendham Road, as Betsy and I were on our way back to the Orphea police station, I received a call from my commander, Major McKenna.

"Rosenberg," he said, "the mayor of Orphea is on my back. He says you're spreading panic in the town."

"A woman has disappeared, sir," I said, "and it may have something to do with the quadruple murder of 1994."

"That case is closed, Rosenberg. You should know that—you solved it."

"I know, sir. But I'm starting to wonder if we didn't miss something at the time."

"What the hell are you talking about?"

"The woman who's gone missing is a reporter who's been looking into the case. Maybe it's a sign we should dig deeper."

"Rosenberg, according to the local police chief, you don't have a single reason to be digging deeper," McKenna said impatiently. "Right now, you're spoiling my Saturday, and two days before you leave the force you're making a fool of yourself. Is that really what you want?"

I said nothing, and McKenna resumed, in a friendlier tone:

"Listen to me. I'm leaving with my family for Lake Champlain for the weekend, and when I do I'll make sure I leave my cell phone at home. I'll be unreachable until tomorrow evening and back in the office on Monday morning. You have until first thing on Monday to find something solid to show me. Otherwise, you come back nicely to the office, as if nothing has happened. We'll have a drink to celebrate your departure and I don't want to hear any more about this story. Is that clear?"

"Got it, sir. Thanks."

I didn't have much time. In Betsy's office, we started sticking the different elements of the case on a whiteboard.

"According to the other journalists," I said, "the theft of the computer from the editorial offices can only have taken place on Monday night. The break-in at the apartment took place on Thursday night, and finally there was the fire last night."

"What are you getting at?" Betsy said, handing me a cup of burning hot coffee.

"Well, this suggests that what this person was looking for wasn't on the office computer, and this forced him or her to search Stephanie Mailer's apartment. Obviously without success, since he took the risk of coming back the following night and setting fire to it. Why act this way unless he hoped to destroy the files if he couldn't get his hands on them?"

"So what we're looking for may still be out there."

"Exactly," I said. "But where?"

I had brought Stephanie's telephone and bank records with me, having picked them up the previous day from headquarters.

"Let's start by trying to find out who phoned Stephanie as she left the Kodiak Grill," I said, searching through the documents until I found the list of the last calls made and received.

Stephanie had received a call at 10.03. Then she had phoned the same person twice in a row, at 10.05 and 10.10. The first call lasted barely a second, the second lasted twenty seconds.

Betsy sat down at her computer. I read out the number of the call received by Stephanie at 10.03 and she looked in the search engine for the corresponding subscriber.

"My God, Jesse!" she exclaimed.

"What?" I said, rushing to the screen.

"The number is that of the phone booth in the Kodiak Grill!"

"Someone called Stephanie from the Kodiak Grill just after she left the place?"

"Someone was watching her," Betsy said. "All the time she was waiting, someone was watching her."

Going back to the records, I underlined the last number dialed by Stephanie. I read that one out and Betsy entered it into the system.

She was astonished at the name that appeared on her computer. "No, it must be a mistake!" she said, suddenly white. She asked me to repeat the number and tapped the keys frenetically as she once more entered the number.

I approached the screen and read the name. "Sean O'Donnell. What's the problem, Betsy? Do you know him?"

"I know him very well," she said, dismayed. "Sean O'Donnell is one of my officers."

*

Having been shown the phone records, Chief Gulliver could not refuse me permission to question Sean O'Donnell. He had him brought in from patrol and put in an interview room. When I walked in, accompanied by Betsy and Chief Gulliver, Sean half rose from his chair, as if his legs were giving way.

"Is anyone going to tell me what's going on?" he demanded anxiously.

"Sit down," Gulliver said. "Captain Rosenberg has some questions to ask you."

Gulliver and I sat down at the table, facing him. Betsy kept back, standing by the wall.

"Sean," I said, "I know Stephanie Mailer called you on Monday night. You're the last person she tried to contact. What are you hiding from us?"

Sean took his head in his hands. "Captain," he moaned, "I fucked up. I'm sorry. I should have told Chief Gulliver. I wanted to, I really did!"

"But you didn't, Sean. So now you have to tell us everything."

He spoke only after a long sigh. "Stephanie and I dated for a time. We met in a bar, a while back. I was the one who approached her and, to be honest with you, she didn't seem too crazy about the idea. But in the end, she let me buy her a drink, and we talked for a while. I didn't think it would go any farther. Until I told her I was a police officer here in Orphea—that seemed to grab her immediately. Right away her whole attitude changed, she suddenly seemed very interested in me. We exchanged numbers, and we went out a few times. No more than that. Then two weeks ago, things suddenly moved ahead. We slept together. Just once."

"Why only once?" I said.

"Because I realized it wasn't me she was interested in, it was the records room at the station."

"The records room?"

"Yes, Captain. It was really weird. She kept mentioning it. She absolutely wanted me to take her there. I thought she was joking and told her it was out of the question. But two weeks ago, when we were in bed together at her place, she woke me up and demanded that I drive her to the records room. As if I owed her something for spending the night with her. I was pretty hurt. I stormed out. I made it very clear to her that I didn't want to see her anymore."

"You weren't curious to know why she was so interested in the records room?" Chief Gulliver said.

"I was, of course. Part of me absolutely wanted to know. But I didn't want to show Stephanie that I was interested. I felt like I was being manipulated, and, since I really liked her, that hurt me."

"And did you see her again?" I asked.

"Just once. Last Saturday. She called me a few times that night, but I didn't pick up. I thought she'd give up, but she just kept calling. I was on duty, and I couldn't stand the way she wouldn't leave me alone. In the end, I was such a wreck that I told her to meet me outside her apartment building. I didn't even get out of my car, I told her that if she contacted me again I'd lodge a complaint for harassment. She told me she needed my help, but I didn't believe her."

"What was the help she needed?"

"She said she needed to take a look at a file connected to a murder committed here, something she had some information about. She said, 'The investigation was badly handled. There's a detail that nobody saw at the time even though it was really obvious.' To convince me, she showed me her hand and asked me what I saw. 'Your hand,' I said. 'It's my fingers you should have seen,' she said.

"All this about hands and fingers—I told myself she was playing with me. I left her standing there on the street and swore I'd never let her fool me again."

"And you didn't talk to her after that?" I said.

"No, Captain Rosenberg. That was the last time."

I paused for a moment, then played my trump card. "Sean, I know you talked to Stephanie on Monday night, the night she went missing."

"No, Captain! I swear I didn't talk to her!"

I waved the phone records and put them down in front of him. "Don't lie to me, it's written here. You talked to each other for twenty seconds."

"No, we didn't talk!" Sean cried. "She called me, that's true. Twice. But I didn't answer! The second time she called, she left me a message. Yes, our phones were connected, like the records say, but we didn't talk."

Sean wasn't lying. Checking his phone, we discovered a message received on Monday at 10.10, lasting twenty seconds. I pressed the button and Stephanie's voice suddenly emerged from the phone's speaker.

"Sean, it's me. I absolutely have to talk to you, it's urgent. Please . . . [Pause] Sean, I'm scared. I'm really scared."

There was panic in her voice.

"I didn't listen to the message at the time. I thought it was her whining again. I didn't listen to it until Wednesday, after her parents came to the station to report her missing. And I didn't know what to do."

"Why didn't you say anything?"

"I was scared, Captain. And I was ashamed."

"Do you think Stephanie felt threatened?"

"If she did, she never mentioned it. That was the first time she said she was scared."

Betsy, Chief Gulliver, and I exchanged glances. Then I asked Sean:

"I need to know where you were and what you were doing around ten o'clock on Monday night, when Stephanie tried to reach you."

"I was in a bar in East Hampton. A friend of mine is the manager. There was a group of us. We spent the whole evening there. I'll give you all the names, you can check."

Several witnesses did confirm O'Donnell's presence in the bar in question from seven o'clock until one in the morning on the night of Stephanie's disappearance. In Betsy's office, I wrote Stephanie's riddle on the whiteboard: *What was in front of our eyes and we didn't see in 1994?*

We were sure that Stephanie had wanted to get into the Orphea police records to gain access to the file on the investigation into the 1994 quadruple murder. So we went to the records room. It wasn't hard to locate the large box containing the file. But the box was empty. Inside, there was only a yellowing sheet of paper on which somebody had typewritten the words:

```
Here begins THE DARKEST NIGHT.
```

Like the start of a treasure hunt.

*

The only real lead we had was the telephone call from the Kodiak Grill immediately after Stephanie left. We went back there. The waitress we had questioned the previous evening was on duty.

"Can you tell me where your public phone is?" I said.

"You can use the one on the counter."

"That's kind of you, but I'd like to see your public phone."

She led us across the restaurant to the rear, where there were two rows of coat hooks fixed to the wall, a passage to the toilets, a coin machine, and, in a corner, a phone booth.

"Is there a camera?" Betsy asked, looking up at the ceiling.

"No, there's no camera in the restaurant."

"Is this booth often used?"

"Difficult to say. There's always a lot of coming and going. The toilets are reserved for the customers, but pretty often people come in and ask if there's a phone. We tell them yes. But we don't know if they really want to make a phone call or just need to take a leak. These days everyone has a cell phone, don't they?"

Just then, as if on cue, Betsy's cell phone rang. Stephanie's car had been found near the beach.

*

We sped along Ocean Road, which led from Main Street to Orphea's beach. The road ended in a parking lot consisting of a vast concrete circle, where bathers parked their cars any old how, with no time limit. In winter, there would always be a few scattered vehicles belonging to people walking on the beach, fathers flying kites with their children. It started to fill up on the fine days of spring. At the height of summer, it was besieged from early on the burning hot mornings, and the number of cars that managed to cram themselves in there was extraordinary.

About a hundred yards from the parking lot, a police car was parked at the side of the road. An officer waved to us and I drew up behind him. At this point on the road, a narrow hikers' trail plunged into the forest.

"It was some people out walking who saw the car," the officer told us. "Apparently, it's been there since Tuesday. It wasn't until they read the paper this morning that they made the connection. I checked the license number. It's definitely Ms Mailer's car."

We had to walk two hundred yards to get to the car, neatly parked in a nook. It was indeed the blue Mazda caught on the cameras at the bank. I put on a pair of latex gloves and walked around it, inspecting the interior through the windows. I tried to open the door, but it was locked. Betsy finally voiced the thought that was going through my head.

"Jesse, do you think she's in the trunk?"

"There's only one way to find out."

The officer brought us a crowbar. I plunged it into the groove. Betsy was standing right behind me, holding her breath. The lock gave easily and the trunk snapped open. I stepped back, then leaned forward to see inside. The trunk was empty. "Nothing here," I said, moving away from the car. "Let's call forensics before the scene gets contaminated. This time the mayor is going to agree that we have to dig deeper."

The discovery of Stephanie's car did indeed change things. Mayor Brown arrived on the scene with Chief Gulliver. Recognizing that a search operation had to be launched and that the local police would soon be overwhelmed by the situation, he called on police units from the neighboring towns for backup.

In one hour, Ocean Road was blocked off, from the halfway point to the beach parking lot. Police departments from all over the county had sent officers, supported by patrols from the State Police. Groups of onlookers had gathered beyond the police tape.

On the forest side, forensics officers were moving in white jumpsuits around Stephanie's car, going over it with a fine-toothed comb. Teams of sniffer dogs had also been dispatched.

Soon, the head of the dog team sent for us from the beach parking lot.

"All the dogs are following a single track," he said when we had joined him. "They set off from the car and take that little path that winds through the forest and arrives here."

He pointed to the path, which was a shortcut people out walking took to get from the beach to the hikers' trail.

"The dogs all stop here in the parking lot. Right where I'm standing. After that, they lose the scent."

The officer was standing literally in the middle of the parking lot.

"What does that mean?"

"That she got in a car here, Captain Rosenberg, and left in it."

The mayor turned to me. "What do you think, Captain?"

"I think there was a car waiting for her. She'd arranged to meet someone. That person was at the Kodiak Grill, sitting at a table at the far end from where she was, watching her. When she leaves the restaurant,

66

he calls her from the phone booth and arranges to meet her at the beach. Stephanie is worried: she's been expecting a meeting in a public place and now she finds she has to go to the beach, which is deserted at this hour. She telephones Sean, who doesn't answer. In the end, she decides to park her car on the forest path. Maybe to have a fallback solution. Or else to see the mystery person coming. Anyway, she locks her car, she walks down to the parking lot, and gets in her contact's vehicle. Where was she taken? God alone knows."

There was a chilling silence. Then Chief Gulliver, as if he was taking the measure of the situation, murmured:

"And that's when Stephanie Mailer disappears."

DEREK SCOTT

That evening, July 30, 1994, in Orphea, it took a while for the first of our colleagues from the squad to reach the scene, along with our commander, Major McKenna. Once we had updated them on the situation, the major took me aside.

"Derek, were you the first on the scene?"

"Yes, sir," I replied. "Jesse and I have been here for more than an hour. Being the highest-ranking officer, I had to make a few decisions. The main one was to set up roadblocks."

"You did the right thing. Everything seems to be well in hand. Do you think you're up to taking on this case?"

"Yes, sir. I'd be honored."

I sensed a hesitation on his part. "This would be your first big case," he said, "and Jesse is still an inexperienced inspector."

"Rosenberg has good instincts as a police officer," I assured him. "Trust us, sir. We won't disappoint you."

After a moment's reflection, he agreed. "I want to give you a chance. I like you and Jesse. Don't fuck up. When your colleagues find out that I entrusted a case as big as this to you, a lot of tongues will wag. Well, they should have been here! Where are they all, for fuck's sake? On vacation? Assholes."

The major called Jesse over, then announced so that our colleagues could all hear:

"Scott and Rosenberg, you're in charge of this case."

Jesse and I were determined not to make the major regret his decision. We spent the night in Orphea, putting together the first elements of

68

the investigation. It was almost seven in the morning when I dropped Jesse outside his home in Queens. He suggested I come in and have a coffee and I accepted. We were exhausted, but much too excited by the case to sleep. In the kitchen, while Jesse made the coffee, I started making notes.

"Who disliked the mayor enough to kill him, and his wife and son, too?" I asked out loud, writing this question on a piece of paper that he stuck to the refrigerator.

"We have to question those closest to him," Jesse said.

"What was the family doing at home on the opening night of the theater festival? They should have been at the Grand Theater. And what about those suitcases full of stuff in the car? It looked like they were about to leave."

"You mean they were running away? But why?"

"That," I said, "is what we have to find out."

I stuck a second piece of paper on the fridge, on which he wrote: *Did the mayor have enemies?*

Natasha, woken by our voices, appeared in the doorway, still half asleep.

"What happened last night?" she said, cuddling up against Jesse.

"Four killings," I said.

"'Murders at the theater festival'?" Natasha read on the fridge door before she opened it. "Sounds like a mystery novel."

"It could be one," Jesse said.

Natasha took out milk and eggs and flour and put them on the counter to make pancakes. She poured herself coffee, then looked again at the notes and asked us:

"So what are your first ideas?"

JESSE ROSENBERG

Sunday, June 29, 2014
Twenty-seven days to opening night

The search for Stephanie was getting nowhere.

For twenty-four hours the region had been on a state of high alert, but to no avail. Teams of officers and volunteers were combing the county. Dog teams, divers and a helicopter were also being held in readiness. Volunteers put up posters in supermarkets and went to stores and gas stations in the hope of finding a customer or an employee who might have seen Stephanie. The Mailer couple had given a statement to the press and the local T.V. channels, presenting a photograph of their daughter and calling on anyone who might have seen her to contact the police immediately.

Everyone wanted to participate in the effort. The Kodiak Grill offered free drinks to anyone who had taken part in the search. The Lake Palace, one of the most luxurious hotels in the region, located in the same county as Orphea, had put one of its reception rooms at the disposal of the police, who used it as a rallying point for the volunteers wishing to join in, and it was from there that they were directed toward one area or another of the search.

In Betsy's office at the police station, she and I pursued our investigation. Stephanie's trip to Los Angeles remained a mystery. It was on her return from California that she had suddenly become closer to Officer O'Donnell and pressed him to help her gain access to the police records room. What had she discovered in L.A.? We contacted the hotel where she had stayed, but it led us nowhere. On the other hand, by looking at her regular return trips to New York—revealed by her credit card payments at the tollbooths—we discovered that she had received fines for prolonged or illegal parking, and once even had her car towed away,

70

always on the same street. It was not hard for Betsy to dig up a list of the various establishments on that street: restaurants, doctors, lawyers, chiropractors, a laundry. But the most crucial one was the offices of the *New York Literary Review*.

"How is that possible?" I said. "Stephanie's mother told me her daughter left the *Review* in September and that was the reason she moved to Orphea. Why would she keep going back there? It doesn't make sense."

"Well," Betsy said to me, "the dates when she passed through the tollbooths certainly tally with the dates of the parking tickets. And from what I see here, the places where she was booked are in the immediate vicinity of the building where the offices of the *Review* are located. Let's call the editor and ask him if he can explain."

She picked up the receiver, but didn't have time to dial the number because just then there was a knock at the door of her office. It was the head of the forensics squad.

"These are the results from what was found in Stephanie Mailer's apartment and car," he said, waving a heavy envelope. "I think they'll interest you."

He sat on the edge of the desk.

"Let's start with the apartment," he said. "I can confirm that the fire was started deliberately. The place had been doused in accelerants. And in case you had any doubt, it wasn't Stephanie Mailer who did it."

"What makes you sure of that?"

He waved a plastic bag containing wads of banknotes. "We found $10,000 in cash in the apartment, hidden in the base of a cast-iron Italian coffee maker. The bills are intact."

"Right," Betsy said. "If I were Stephanie and had hidden $10,000 in cash in my apartment, I'd make damn sure I got it out before setting fire to the place."

"What about the car?" I said. "What did you find there?"

"Unfortunately, no D.N.A. apart from Stephanie's—we were able to make a comparison with a sample from her parents. On the other hand, we did find a rather mysterious handwritten note under the driver's seat. The handwriting seems to be Stephanie's."

The officer put his hand back in his envelope and took out a third plastic bag containing a sheet of paper torn from a school exercise book. On it was written:

Darkest Night → *Orphea Theater Festival*
Talk to Michael Bird

"Darkest Night!" Betsy cried. "The same as we found on the note left in the empty file."

"Let's talk to Michael Bird," I said. "He may know more than he was prepared to say last time."

*

We found Bird in his office. He had prepared for us a folder containing copies of all the articles written by Stephanie for the paper. Most of it was local news—a school fair, the Columbus Day parade, a community party for people on their own, the Halloween pumpkin competition, road accidents—all fairly trivial items. As I spread the articles out on the desk, I asked the editor:

"What's Stephanie's salary at the paper?"

"$1,500 dollars a month. Why do you ask?"

"It may be important for the investigation. I'll be honest with you—I'm still trying to figure out why Stephanie left New York to come to Orphea and write articles about Columbus Day and pumpkin contests. It makes no sense, as far as I'm concerned. Don't take this the wrong way, Mr Bird, but it doesn't fit with the ambitious picture of her I got from her parents and friends."

"I know exactly what you mean, Captain Rosenberg. In fact, I asked myself the same thing. Stephanie told me she had become weary of life in the city. She was looking for some kind of rebirth. She's an idealist, you know. She wants to change things. The challenge of working for a local paper doesn't faze her—quite the opposite, in fact."

"I think there's something else," I said, and showed Bird the piece of paper found in Stephanie's car.

"What is this?" he said.

"A note written by Stephanie. She mentions the theater festival, and says she needs to talk to you about it. What do you know that you're not telling us, Mr Bird?"

Bird sighed. "I promised her I wouldn't say anything. I gave my word."

"I wonder if you grasp the gravity of the situation . . ."

"You're the one who doesn't grasp it," he said. "There may be a good reason why Stephanie decided to drop out of sight for a while. And you're compromising everything by getting people worked up."

"What would be a good reason?"

"She may have known she was in danger and decided to hide. By turning the region upside down, you may be putting her life at risk. Her investigation is more important than you might imagine, and the people who are looking for her right now may be the very people she's hiding from."

"You mean police officers?"

"It's possible. She kept things very close to her chest. I kept asking her to tell me more, but she always refused."

"That's very much like the Stephanie I met the other day," I sighed. "But what's the connection with the theater festival?"

Although the editorial offices were deserted and the door of his office was closed, the editor lowered his voice again, as if fearful someone might overhear him. "Stephanie thought something was going on at the festival, and she needed to question the volunteers without anybody suspecting anything. I suggested she do a series of articles for the paper. It was the perfect cover."

"Phony interviews?" I said in surprise.

"Not really phony, because we did publish them. I told you about the paper's financial difficulties. Stephanie assured me that publishing the results of her investigation would make it possible to get things back on their feet. 'When this is published, people will fight to get hold of the *Chronicle*,' she told me one day."

Back at the station, we finally reached Stephanie's previous boss, the editor of the *New York Literary Review*. His name was Steven Bergdorf and he lived in Brooklyn. It was Betsy who called him. She put the phone on loudspeaker.

"Poor Stephanie," Bergdorf said after Betsy had informed him of the situation. "I hope nothing serious has happened to her. She's a very intelligent woman, a promising literary journalist, a fine writer. Always friendly to everyone. Not the kind of person to attract hard feelings or problems."

"If my information is correct, she left the magazine's staff last fall."

"I was very sorry to lose her. But we stayed on good terms. She told me later she was working for the *Orphea Chronicle* and she liked it a lot. I was pleased for her, I suppose, although I was a little surprised."

"Why surprised?"

"A girl like Stephanie Mailer should be writing for the *New York Times*. She's that good. What was she doing at a provincial paper?"

"Mr Bergdorf, has Stephanie been back to your offices since she left?"

"Not as far as I know. Why?"

"Because we've established that her car was parked close to your building on several occasions in the last two or three months."

*   *   *

For Betsy and me the money found in Stephanie's apartment was one of the leads we most needed to follow. $10,000 in cash. Stephanie earned $1,500 a month. Once she had paid her rent, her car insurance, and her general expenses, there could not have been much left. If these were her savings, why had she not put them in a bank?

We spent the rest of the day questioning Stephanie's parents and friends about that money. The Mailers said that their daughter had always gotten by on her own. She had won a scholarship to pay for her college studies and had subsequently lived on her salary. Her friends assured us that Stephanie often had difficulties in making ends meet. They found it hard to accept the idea that she might have put money aside.

As I was driving down Main Street on my way out of Orphea, instead of continuing toward Route 17 so as to get onto the highway, I veered almost without thinking into the Penfield neighborhood and came to Penfield Crescent. I drove round the little park and stopped outside the house that had been Mayor Gordon's twenty years earlier, the place where it had all started.

I sat there for a while, then, on the way back home, I couldn't stop myself from dropping by Derek and Darla's. I don't know if it was because I needed to see Derek, or because I didn't want to be alone. And apart from him I had nobody.

It was around eight o'clock when I reached their house. I stood for a while at the door, reluctant to ring the bell. From outside, I could hear cheerful conversation and yelling from the kitchen, where they were having dinner. Every Sunday, Derek and his family had pizza.

I approached the window discreetly and looked in at the meal. Derek's three children were still in high school. The eldest would be going to college the following year. Suddenly, one of them noticed I was there. They all turned toward the window and stared at me.

Derek came out of the house, still munching, his paper napkin in his hand.

"Jesse, what are you doing out here? Come in and eat with us."

"No, thanks. I'm not very hungry. Listen, strange things are happening in Orphea."

"Jesse," Derek sighed, "don't tell me you spent your weekend up there!"

I gave him a quick rundown.

"It's beyond doubt now," I said. "Stephanie did find out something new about the murders in 1994."

"That's just speculation, Jesse."

"What about the note saying 'Darkest Night' found in Stephanie's car, the same as the paper in the empty file? What about the link she made with the theater festival—which started in the summer of 1994, if you remember? Isn't that concrete enough for you?"

"You see the links you want to see, Jesse! Don't you realize what it would mean to reopen that case? It'd mean we screwed up."

"Well, maybe we did! Stephanie said we missed an obvious detail."

"But where did we go wrong?" Derek said. "Tell me where we went wrong, Jesse! You remember how hard we worked, how conscientious we were. We put together a cast-iron case. I think it's because you're leaving the force that you're brooding on these ugly memories. We can't turn the clock back, we can't undo what we did! So why are you doing this to us?"

"Because we have no choice!"

"No, Jesse, we don't have to do anything! Tomorrow's your last day as a police officer. Why do you want to stick your nose back in a pile of shit that's no concern of yours anymore?"

"I'm planning to postpone my departure. I can't leave the force like this. I can't live with this on my conscience!"

"Well, I can!"

He made to go back inside, as if trying to put an end to this conversation he didn't want to have.

"Help me, Derek!" I said. "If tomorrow I don't bring the major solid evidence of the link between Stephanie Mailer and the 1994 investigation, he'll force me to close the case for good."

He turned. "Why are you doing this, Jesse?" he said. "Why do you want to dig up all this crap?"

"Team up with me, Derek."

"Why are you trying to drag me back into this? I haven't been out in the field in twenty years, Jesse."

"Because you're the best I know, Derek. You were always better than me. You should have been captain of our unit, not me."

"Don't come here and judge me, Jesse, don't lecture me about how

I should have handled my career. You know perfectly well why I've spent the last twenty years behind a desk handling paperwork."

"I think this is an opportunity for us to put things right, Derek."

"There's nothing we can put right, Jesse. You're welcome to come inside and share our pizza, but I don't want to talk about that case anymore. It's over."

He opened the front door of his house.

"I envy you, Derek," I said.

He turned again.

"You envy me? What could you possibly envy?"

"The fact that you love and are loved."

He shook his head wearily. "Jesse, Natasha's been gone for twenty years. You should have rebuilt your life a long time ago. Sometimes, I get the feeling it's like you're waiting for her to come back."

"Every day, Derek. Every day, I tell myself she'll be back. Every time I walk through the door of my apartment I hope I'll find her there."

He sighed. "I don't know what to tell you. I'm sorry. You should see someone."

He went back inside, and I walked back to my car. As I was about to drive away, Darla came out of the house and ran toward me. She seemed angry and I knew why. I lowered my window.

"Don't do this to him, Jesse!" she cried. "Don't come here and awaken the ghosts of the past."

"Listen, Darla—"

"No, Jesse, *you* listen! Derek doesn't deserve you doing this to him. Leave him alone about that case. Don't do this to him. You're not welcome here if it's just to stir up the past. Do I need to remind you what happened twenty years ago?"

"No, Darla, you don't need to remind me. Nobody needs to remind me. I remember it every fucking day, Darla, do you hear me? Every fucking morning when I wake up and every night when I go to sleep."

She gave me a sad look and I saw that she regretted having brought up the subject.

"I'm sorry, Jesse. Come inside and eat, there's still pizza and I made a tiramisu."

"No, thanks. I'm going home."

I drove away.

Back home, I poured myself a drink and took out a folder I hadn't touched in a long time. Inside were press clippings from 1994, in no particular order. I looked through them for a long time until one of them caught my attention.

POLICE HAIL A HERO

Sergeant Derek Scott was decorated yesterday at a ceremony at the troop headquarters of the State Police for his bravery in saving the life of his partner, Inspector Jesse Rosenberg, while arresting a murderer for the killing of four people in the Hamptons during the summer.

The doorbell dragged me from my thoughts. I looked at my watch. Who could it be this late? I picked up my pistol, which I had put down on the table in front of me, and noiselessly approached the door. I peered through the peephole. It was Derek.

I opened the door and stared at him for a moment in silence. He noticed the weapon in my hand.

"You really think this is serious, huh?" he said.

I nodded.

"Show me what you have, Jesse."

I spread everything I had on the dining room table. Derek studied the photographs from the surveillance cameras, the lighter, the note, the cash, and the credit card records.

"It's obvious that Stephanie was spending more than she earned," I said. "The ticket to L.A. alone cost her $400. She must have had another source of income. We have to find out what it was."

Derek plunged into Stephanie's expenses. I caught a gleam in his eyes I had not seen there in quite a while. After spending a lot of time going through the credit card expenses, he took a pen and circled a monthly automatic debit of $60, starting the previous November.

"The payments are to a company called S.V.M.A.," he said. "Does that mean anything to you?"

"No, nothing."

He opened my laptop, which was on the table, and searched on the Internet.

"It's a self-storage company in Orphea," he announced, turning the screen toward me.

"Self-storage?" I said, remembering my conversation with Mrs Mailer. According to her, Stephanie had had only a few things in New York, which she had taken straight to her apartment in Orphea. So why would she have been using a self-storage facility since November?

The facility was open twenty-four hours a day, so we decided to go there at once. After I'd shown him my badge, the security guard on duty checked in his register and indicated to us the number of the unit rented by Stephanie.

We walked through a maze of corridors and lowered blinds and came to a metal shutter with a padlock on it. I had brought a pair of wire cutters, and I soon got through the lock. I rolled up the shutter and Derek shone a torch into the unit.

What we discovered there left us thunderstruck.

DEREK SCOTT

Early autumn 1994. One week had passed since the Gordon killings.

Jesse and I were putting all we had into the case, working on it day and night, all the hours we could, forgetting about sleep or time off.

We had taken up residence in Jesse and Natasha's apartment, which was more welcoming than the cold office at headquarters. We settled in the living room, in which we had put two camp beds, coming and going as we pleased. Natasha waited on us hand and foot. She sometimes got up in the middle of the night and made us something to eat. She said it was a good way to test the dishes she would be putting on the menu of her restaurant.

"Jesse," I would say with my mouth full, savoring what Natasha had cooked for us, "make sure you marry this woman."

"It's all planned," Jesse said one evening.

"For when?"

He smiled. "Very soon. Want to see the ring?"

"You bet!"

He disappeared for a moment and came back with a box containing a magnificent diamond.

"My God, Jesse, it's beautiful!"

"It was my grandmother's," he said, hurriedly putting it back in his pocket because Natasha was coming in.

*

The ballistics analysis was categorical: one weapon had been used, a Beretta. Only one person had been involved in the murders—probably a man, according to the experts. Not only because of the violence of the crime, but because the door of the house—which had not been locked—had been kicked in.

At the request of the D.A.'s office, a reconstruction was conducted, which established the following chain of events: having kicked in the door of the Gordon family's house, the murderer had first come across Leslie Gordon in the entrance hall and had shot her four times from the front, in the chest, at almost point-blank range. Then he had seen the boy in the living room and had shot him dead with two bullets in the back, fired from the hallway. He had then headed to the kitchen, presumably because he had heard noises from there. Mayor Joseph Gordon was trying to escape into the garden through the French windows in the kitchen. He had shot him four times in the back then, retraced his steps and left through the front door. Not one of the bullets had missed their target, which meant he was an experienced shooter.

Coming out of the house through the front door, he had come slap-bang up against Meghan Padalin, who was out jogging. She had tried to run away and he had shot her twice in the back. His face had probably been uncovered, because he had subsequently fired a bullet at point-blank range into Meghan's head, to make sure she was truly dead.

A further difficulty was that, although we had two indirect witnesses, they were not in a position to help us with our investigation.

At the time of the murders, Penfield Crescent was almost empty. Of the eight houses on the street, one was for sale, and the occupants of five others were at the Grand Theater. The last house was occupied by the Bellamy family, of whom only Lena Bellamy, a young mother of three children, had been in the house that evening with her youngest child, who was not yet three. Her husband Terrence was at the marina with the two older children.

Lena Bellamy had, of course, heard the shots, but she had thought they were fireworks going up from the marina to celebrate the opening of the festival. Just before the shots, though, she had seen a van with a big logo on the rear window, a logo she could not describe. It was some kind of drawing, she remembered, but she had not paid enough attention to recall what it depicted.

The second witness was a man named Albert Plant, who lived alone in a single-story house on a parallel street. Confined to a wheelchair since an accident, he had been at home that evening. He had heard the shots as he was having dinner, and they had attracted his attention sufficiently for him to go out onto his porch, curious about what was going on in the neighborhood. He had the presence of mind to check the time: 7.10. By then silence had returned and he assumed someone must have been letting off firecrackers. He stayed out on the porch, enjoying the mild evening until, just over an hour later, around 8.20, he heard a man screaming for help. Mr Plant immediately called the police.

One of our first difficulties was the absence of motive. To discover who had killed the mayor and his family, we needed to know who had a good reason to do so. But no line of questioning seemed to lead any-where. We talked to many townspeople, to municipal employees, to the families and friends of the mayor and of his wife, all without success. The Gordons seemed to have led a perfectly unobtrusive life. No known enemies, no debts, no drama, no dubious past. An ordinary family. Leslie Gordon, the mayor's wife, was a much-loved teacher at Orphea's elemen-tary school. As for the mayor himself, although nobody was fulsome in their praise of him, he was well enough liked by his fellow citizens, and everyone assumed he would be re-elected in the elections in September, in which his deputy, Alan Brown, would be standing against him.

One afternoon, as we were yet again going through the case file, I said to Jesse:

"What if the Gordons weren't running away? What if we've been getting it wrong from the start?"

"Wrong in which way?"

"Well, we've focused on the fact that Gordon was at home, not at the Grand Theater, and that they had packed their cases."

"You have to admit that it's odd for the mayor not to show up on the opening night of a festival he was responsible for."

"Maybe he was late," I said. "Maybe he was just about to set off. The official ceremony wasn't due to kick off until 7.30. He still had time to get to the Grand Theater. It's only a ten-minute drive. As for the cases, maybe the Gordons had planned to go on vacation. The wife and son had the whole summer off. It's perfectly logical. They were planning to leave early the next day and they wanted to have their cases packed before going to the theater because they knew they'd be late back."

"So why were they killed?" Jesse said.

"A burglary that went wrong," I suggested. "Someone who assumed that the Gordons would be at the Grand Theater by then and they'd easily get into their house."

"Except that the supposed burglar didn't take anything—apart from their lives. And would you have kicked the door down to get in? Not very discreet as a method. Besides, none of the municipal employees we spoke to mentioned anything about the mayor having said he was going on vacation. No, Derek, it's something else. Whoever killed them wanted to get rid of them. The violence of it is indication enough."

From the file, Jesse took a photograph of the mayor's body taken in the house and stared at it for a long time.

"Is there anything that surprises you in this photograph?"

"You mean apart from the fact that the mayor is lying in a pool of blood?"

"He wasn't wearing a suit and tie," Jesse said. "He was wearing casual clothes. What mayor would launch a festival in an outfit like that? It makes no sense. I reckon the mayor never had any intention of going to the theater."

In the photographs of the open suitcase beside Leslie Gordon, some of the contents were visible. Photograph albums, a trinket.

"Look at this," Jesse went on. "When she was killed, Leslie Gordon was filling her suitcase with personal objects. Who takes photograph albums with them on vacation? They were running away, probably from the person who killed them. Someone who knew that they wouldn't be at the theater."

Natasha came into the room just as Jesse was finishing his sentence.

"Well, guys," she said with a smile, "do you have a lead?"

"No," I said. "We don't have a damn thing apart from a black van with a design on the rear window, which the witness cannot describe."

We were interrupted by the doorbell.

"Who's that?"

"Darla," Natasha said. "She's come to look at the plans for the decor of the restaurant."

I scooped up the documents and put them in a cardboard file.

"Don't talk to her about the case," I said to Natasha as she was on her way to the door.

"O.K., Derek," she said nonchalantly.

"This is serious, Nat. We're sworn to secrecy. We shouldn't be here, you shouldn't be seeing all this. Jesse and I could get in trouble."

"Word of honor."

Natasha opened the door. Coming into the apartment, Darla immediately noticed the file I was holding.

"So, how's the case going?" she said.

"Fine," I said.

"Come on, is that all you can say?"

I used the same words as I'd used with Natasha, rather more curtly than I had planned. "We're sworn to secrecy."

"Sworn to secrecy?" Darla retorted. "That's bullshit! I bet Natasha knows the whole story."

JESSE ROSENBERG

Monday, June 30, 2014
Twenty-six days to opening night

I woke Betsy at 1.30 in the morning and asked her to join Derek and me at the self-storage facility. She knew where it was, and was there twenty minutes later. We met her in the parking lot. It was a hot night and the sky was studded with stars.

Introducing Derek, I said to Betsy:

"It's Derek who found out where Stephanie was conducting her investigation."

"In a self-storage facility?"

Derek and I nodded in unison and led Betsy along the rows of metal shutters. We stopped when we came to 234-A. I raised the shutter and switched on the light to reveal a small room, six feet by ten, lined top to bottom with folders of documents, all devoted to the quadruple murder of 1994. There were clippings from various regional daily papers of the time, notably a series of articles in the *Orphea Chronicle*. There were enlargements of photographs of each of the victims and a photograph of Mayor Gordon's house taken on the night of the murder, also cut from a newspaper. There I was, with Derek and a group of police officers, standing next to a white sheet covering the body of Meghan Padalin. Stephanie had written on the photograph with a marker pen:

What nobody saw

The only furniture was one small table and one chair. It was easy to imagine Stephanie spending hours here.

On that makeshift desk were paper and pens. And there was a sheet of paper stuck to the wall, on which she had written:

"Who's Kirk Hayward?" Betsy said.

"He was Orphea's police chief at the time of the murders," I said. "He worked on the case with us."

"And where is he now?"

"I have no idea. He must have retired. We need to contact him. He may have talked to Stephanie."

Searching among the notes in little heaps on the table, I made another discovery.

"Betsy, look at this," I said, handing her Stephanie's airline ticket to Los Angeles. On it, she had written:

Darkest Night → *Police records*

"'Darkest Night' again," Betsy said. "What the hell does it mean?"

"It means her trip to L.A. was connected with her investigation," I said. "And now we know for certain that Stephanie really was investigating the Gordon killings."

On the wall was a photograph of Mayor Brown, taken at least twenty years earlier. It looked like a frame from a video. Brown was standing at the microphone with a sheet of paper in his hand, as if he were making a speech. The sheet of paper had been circled in felt-tip. The background suggested the stage of the Grand Theater.

"It could be a picture of Mayor Brown giving the opening speech of the festival on the night of the murders," Derek said.

"How do you know it's the night of the murders?" I said. "Do you remember what he was wearing that night?"

Derek picked up the press photograph in which Brown also appeared. "He seems to be wearing the same clothes."

We spent all night in the self-storage facility. There were no security cameras and the guard told us he was there only in case there were any problems, but there never were. Customers came and went as they pleased, at all hours, without being checked and without having to answer any questions.

The forensics team from the State Police was sent to inspect the place, and their meticulous search uncovered Stephanie's laptop, hidden in the false bottom of a cardboard box they had supposed was empty until the officer who lifted it to move it expressed surprise at the weight.

"This is what whoever set fire to the apartment and burglarized the newspaper offices was looking for," I said.

The computer was taken away by the forensics team for analysis, while Betsy, Derek and I removed the items from the wall and put them back together in the same order in Betsy's office. At 6.30 in the morning, eyes swollen by lack of sleep, Derek pinned up the photograph of Mayor Gordon's house, stared at it for a long while and read again out loud what Stephanie had written on it: *What nobody saw.* He moved his face to within a few inches of the picture and studied the faces of the people in it. "So, let's see. This is Mayor Brown," he said, pointing to a man in a light-colored suit. "And this," he said, pointing to a tiny head, "is Chief Kirk Hayward."

I was due back at troop headquarters to inform Major McKenna of whatever progress I had made. Derek came with me. As we were leaving Orphea, going back down Main Street in the morning sunshine, Derek, who was seeing Orphea again after a gap of twenty years, said:

"Nothing's changed. It's like time stood still."

An hour later, we were in Major McKenna's office. He listened in amazement to my account of the weekend. With the discovery of the unit in the self-storage facility, we now had proof that Stephanie had been investigating the 1994 murders.

"Goddammit, Jesse," McKenna said, "is this case going to follow us around our whole lives?"

"I hope not, sir. But we can't give up on the investigation now."

"Do you realize what it means if you screwed up at the time?"

"Yes, I do. That's why I'd like you to keep me on the force for as long as it takes me to see this thing through."

He sighed. "You know, Jesse, it's going to cost me a hell of a lot of time in paperwork and explanations to the top brass."

"I'm aware of that, sir, and I'm sorry."

"And what about this famous project of yours, the one that persuaded you to quit the force?"

"That can wait until I've closed this case, sir."

Grunting, McKenna took some forms from a drawer. "I'm doing this for you, Jesse, because you're the best police officer I've ever known."

"I'm very grateful, sir."

"I'm afraid I already assigned your office to someone else, starting from tomorrow."

"I don't need an office, sir. I'll go pick up my things."

"And I don't want you to investigate on your own. I'm assigning you a partner. Unfortunately, the other teams in your unit are already fixed up, since you were supposed to be leaving today, but don't worry, I'll find you someone."

Derek, who had been sitting beside me, now broke his silence.

"I'm ready to back up Jesse, sir. That's why I'm here."

"You, Derek? How long is it since you were last in the field?"

"Twenty years."

"It's thanks to Derek that we found the self-storage facility," I said.

The major sighed again. I could see how troubled he was.

"Derek, are you telling me you want to throw yourself back into a case that was the reason you're behind a desk now?"

"Yes, sir," Derek said, determination in his voice.

The major stared at us for a long time. "Where's your service pistol, Derek?" he said at last.

"In my desk drawer."

"Do you still know how to use it?"

"Yes, sir."

"Well, at least do me the kindness of firing off a couple of rounds at the range before walking around with that thing on your belt. Gentlemen, tie this thing up quickly and tie it up well. I really don't want the sky to come crashing down on our heads."

*   *   *

While Derek and I were at headquarters, Betsy did not waste her time. She had gotten it into her head to track down Kirk Hayward, but this would prove more difficult than she had imagined. She spent hours without any success searching for traces of the former chief. He had dropped clean out of circulation. He had, apparently, neither an address nor a telephone number. Lacking sources, she turned to the one person she could trust in Orphea: her neighbor Cody Springfield. She went to see him in his bookstore, which was right next door to the offices of the *Chronicle*.

"There's not a soul about today," Springfield said wearily on seeing her.

Betsy realized he had hoped she was a customer when he heard the door open.

"I hope the fireworks on the Fourth of July will attract a few people," he went on. "This has been a lousy June."

Betsy took a novel from one of the displays. "Any good?"

"Not bad."

"I'll buy it."

"Betsy, you're not obliged to do that."

"I've run out of things to read. It's perfect timing."

"But I don't suppose that's what you came in here for."

"I didn't come here *only* for that," she said with a smile, handing him a fifty-dollar bill. "What can you tell me about those murders back in 1994?"

He frowned. "Nobody's mentioned that in a long time. What do you want to know?"

"I'm just curious to know what the atmosphere was like in the town at the time."

"It was terrible," Springfield said. "Obviously, people were shocked. Can you imagine? A whole family wiped out, including the young boy. And Meghan, who was the sweetest girl you could imagine. Everyone here loved her."

"Did you know her well?"

"Did I know her well? She worked right here. The store was doing really well in those days, and a lot of it was down to her. She was young, pretty, passionate, delightful, brilliant. People came from the whole of Long Island just for her. How unfair it was! To me, it was a terrible shock. For a while, I even thought about dropping everything and getting out. But where would I have gone? All my ties are here. You know, Betsy, the worst of it is that everyone assumed from the start that the reason Meghan died was that she had recognized the Gordons' killer. That meant it was one of us. Someone we knew. Someone we saw at the supermarket, on the beach, even here in the bookstore. And unfortunately, we discovered we were right when the killer was identified."

"Who was it?"

"Ted Tennenbaum, a pleasant, friendly guy from a good family. A model citizen. Restaurant owner by trade. Member of the volunteer fire service. He'd contributed toward organizing the first festival." Springfield sighed. "I don't like talking about all this, Betsy, it gets me too stirred up."

"I'm sorry, Cody. One last question. Does the name Kirk Hayward mean anything to you?"

"Sure, he used to be police chief. Before Gulliver."

"And what happened to him? I'm trying to discover his whereabouts."

Cody stared at her curiously. "He vanished into thin air," he said, handing over her change and slipping the book into a paper bag. "Nobody's seen hide nor hair of him since."

"What happened?"

"Nobody knows. He vanished one fine day in the fall of 1994."

"You mean the same year as the murders?"

"Yes, three months later. That's why I remember it. It was a weird summer. Most people here would rather forget all about it."

As she spoke, he picked up his keys and stuffed his cell phone, which had been on the counter, into his pocket.

"Are you leaving?" Betsy said.

"Yes, I'm going to take advantage of the fact that there's nobody here to drop by the theater and work a little with the other volunteers. As a matter of fact, we haven't seen you there in a while."

"I know. I've been a bit snowed under lately. Can I give you a ride? As it happens, I've been planning to go to the theater to talk to the volunteers about Stephanie."

Orphea's Grand Theater was next to Café Athena, at the top of Main Street, almost opposite the entrance to the marina.

As in all quiet towns, there was not much surveillance of the public buildings. Betsy and Cody had only to push open the front door to get into the theater. They crossed the lobby to the auditorium, went in, and walked down the central aisle between the rows of red velvet seats.

"Imagine this place in a month, filled with people," Springfield said proudly. "All that thanks to the work of the volunteers."

He climbed the steps leading up to the stage and Betsy followed him. They went behind the curtains into the backstage area. They opened a door to where the volunteers worked. It was a hive of activity. There were people everywhere, some running the box office, others the logistical aspects. In one room, they were preparing to stick up posters and were proofreading programs which would soon be sent back to the printers. In the workshop, a team was putting together the framework for a set.

Betsy took the time to talk to each one of the volunteers. Many had abandoned the Grand Theater the day before to take part in the search operations for Stephanie and they came spontaneously to ask if the investigation was making any progress.

"Not as much as I would have liked," she told them. "But I know she came to the Grand Theater a lot. I even met her here a few times."

"Yes," said a short man who was in charge of the box office, "it was for her articles about the volunteers. Didn't she ask you any questions, Betsy?"

"No," Betsy said. It had not even occurred to her.

"Me neither," said a man who had only recently arrived in Orphea.

"That must be because you're both new here," someone said.

"That's right," someone else piped up. "And you weren't here in 1994."

"1994?" Betsy said in surprise. "Stephanie asked you about 1994?"

"Yes. She was mainly interested in the very first festival."

"What kind of thing did she ask?"

To this question, Betsy obtained a variety of answers, but one cropped up frequently: Stephanie had systematically asked questions about the fire officer on duty in the theater on opening night. In gathering the volunteers' testimonies, she appeared to have been trying to reconstruct in detail what had happened in the theater that evening.

Betsy finally went to see Springfield in the tiny room that served as his office. He was sitting behind a makeshift table, on which were an old computer and untidy piles of paper.

"Have you finished disturbing my volunteers, Betsy?" he said good-humoredly.

"Cody, do you by any chance remember who was on duty as fire officer on the opening night of the festival in 1994 and if he's still living in Orphea?"

Springfield's eyes opened wide. "Do I remember? Hell, Betsy, this is really a day for ghosts. It was Ted Tennenbaum, the man who committed all those murders. And you won't be able to find him, because he's dead."

The friendly atmosphere there had been in the station when I arrived lasted barely two days before the difficulties started. The first one involved a question of organization: what to do about the toilets. In the part of the station where the public didn't go, there were toilets on every floor, all designed for men, with rows of urinals and individual cubicles.

"One of the toilets will have to be for women only," one of the officers suggested.

"Yes, but that gets complicated if you have to change floors to take a leak," someone else retorted.

"We could make all the toilets unisex," I proposed, trying not to complicate matters. "Unless anyone has a problem with that."

"I'd find it tricky to be taking a leak with a woman doing whatever she'd be doing in the cubicle behind me," said another of my new colleagues, putting his hand up like an elementary school pupil.

"Wouldn't you be able to get it out?" someone said, and everybody laughed.

It so happened that in the visitors' section, just beside the front desk, there were separate toilets for men and women. It was decided that I would use the female visitors' toilet, and that suited me perfectly. The fact that I had to cross the reception area of the station every time I wanted to go to the toilet would not have bothered me if I hadn't one day heard the desk sergeant sniggering as he counted my comings and goings.

"My God, she certainly takes a lot of leaks," he said to the officer he was talking to.

"Or else she's thinking about Gulliver and touching herself up," the other man said.

The next difficulty brought about by the new mixed-sex situation was the locker room. The station had one large locker room, with adjoining showers, where the officers could change at the beginning and end of their shift. As a consequence of my arrival, and without my asking anyone for anything, access to the locker room was forbidden to all male staff. On the door, beneath the metal plate bearing the words LOCKER ROOM, Chief Gulliver put a piece of paper with the word WOMAN, in the singular. "The two sexes have to have separate locker rooms, that's the law," Gulliver told his men as they stood watching him do this, dumbfounded. "Mayor Brown has insisted on Betsy having a locker room to get changed in. So, gentlemen, from now on you have to change in your offices." The officers present started grumbling. We finally decided on a compromise. I would change at home and come to the station in my uniform. Everyone was happy. But the next day, seeing me get out of my car in the station's parking lot, Chief Gulliver summoned me to his office.

"Betsy," he said, "I don't like you driving your own car in your uniform."

"But I don't have anywhere to change in the station," I said.

"I know. That's why I'm going to let you have one of our unmarked cars. I want you to use it to move around between your house and the station when you're in uniform."

And so I found myself with a vehicle from the motor pool, a black S.U.V. with tinted windows. The revolving lights were hidden at the top of the windshield and the radiator grille.

What I did not at first know was that there were only two unmarked cars in the pool. Chief Gulliver had allocated himself one for his personal use. The second one, which had been sitting there in the parking lot, was a treasure coveted by all my colleagues and now it had been given to me, and that inevitably aroused a certain indignation in the other officers.

"That's a privilege!" they complained during a hastily called meeting. "She just got here and already she's getting privileges."

"You have to choose, guys," I said to them when they opened up to me. "Share the car between yourselves and leave me the locker room if you prefer. I'd be fine with that, too."

The episode of the car was the first unwitting insult to Montagne on my part. He'd had his eyes on that unmarked car for a long time.

"It should have been me," he moaned to Gulliver. "I am the deputy, after all! How does this make me look?"

But Gulliver turned him down point-blank. "Listen, Jasper," he said, "I know the situation is complicated. It's complicated for everyone, especially me. Believe me, I'd happily have done without it. Women always create tension in a team. They have too much to prove. And of course when she gets pregnant, we'll all have to do overtime!"

One drama followed another. Once the logistics had been fixed, the next questions that came up concerned my legitimacy and my competence. I had arrived with the rank of second deputy, a rank created specially for me. The official reason was that over the years, as the town had developed, the Orphea police department had seen a significant increase in its workload and its manpower, and the arrival of a third commanding officer was meant to allow Chief Gulliver and Deputy Montagne to breathe more easily.

First I was asked, "Why did they need to create a position for you? Is it because you're a woman?"

"No," I said, "the post was created first, and then they tried to fill it."

The next question was:

"What happens if you have to fight a man? I mean, you're just a woman alone in a car. Can you arrest a guy all on your own?"

"Can you?" I said.

"Sure."

"So why not me?"

Finally, trying to take my measure:

"Do you have experience in the field?"

"I have experience of the streets of New York."

"It's not the same. What kind of thing did you do in New York?"

I hoped that my résumé would impress them. "I was a crisis negotiator. I was constantly on call. I dealt with hostage situations, domestic incidents, suicide threats."

My colleagues shrugged. "It's not the same."

*

I spent the first month partnered up with Lewis Erban, an old, worn-out officer. He was on the verge of retirement, and I would be replacing him. I soon learned the ropes: night-time patrols on the beach and in the municipal park, taking down statements on traffic violations, breaking up fights when the bars were closing.

While I may have proved myself in the field, both as a superior officer and when I was on call, everyday relations remained tense. The established hierarchy had been shaken up. For years, Chief Ron Gulliver and Deputy Montagne had laid down the law, two wolves at the head of their pack. Gulliver was due to retire on October 1 the following year and it was taken for granted that Montagne would succeed him. In any case, it was Montagne who already ruled the roost in the station, with Gulliver only pretending to give the orders. When it came down to it, Gulliver was quite a pleasant man but not a good chief. He was manipulated by Montagne who had long taken over as head of the chain of command. But this had changed. With my arrival in the post of second deputy, there were now three of us in command.

It did not take much more for Montagne to launch a ferocious smear campaign. He made it clear to all the other officers that it was best for them if they didn't team up with me. Nobody in the station wanted to be in Montagne's bad books and my colleagues avoided contact with me outside our professional exchanges. I knew that in the locker room, when the guys at the end of their shift mentioned going for a beer, he would lecture them: "Don't even think of asking that bimbo to go with you. Unless you want to scour the toilets for the next ten years."

This campaign of Montagne's did not make my integration into the town of Orphea any easier. My colleagues were not inclined to see me when we were off duty, and my dinner invitations to them and their wives resulted either in refusals, last-minute cancellations, or even no-shows. I lost count of the number of Sunday brunches I spent alone at a table set for five or more with a kitchen full of food. My social activities were very limited. I sometimes went out with the mayor's wife, Charlotte Brown, and since I was particularly fond of Café Athena on Main Street, I hit it off with the owner, Sylvia Tennenbaum. We would regularly chat, though I could not say we were friends. The person I saw most of was my neighbor, Cody Springfield. Whenever I felt bored, I would drop by his bookstore. Sometimes I would even help out there. I finally joined his volunteers' organization that handled the theater festival at the beginning of summer, which gave me at least one evening a week when I was busy, preparing for the festival that was due to open at the end of July.

At the station, as soon as I had the impression I was beginning to be accepted, Montagne struck back. He moved up a gear, searching in my past and starting to give me suggestive nicknames like "Betsy the trigger-happy" or "the killer," or saying to my colleagues: "Better be careful, guys. Betsy's quick on the draw." He would laugh like an idiot, then say, "Betsy, does everyone know why you left New York?"

One morning I found a press clipping stuck to the door of my office, with the headline:

MANHATTAN: HOSTAGE KILLED BY POLICE IN JEWELRY STORE

I went straight to Gulliver's office, brandishing the clipping. "Did you tell him, Chief? Was it you who told Montagne?"

"It was nothing to do with me, Betsy," he said.

"Then how the hell did he find out?"

"It's in your file. He could have had access to it one way or another."

Determined to get rid of me, Montagne made sure I was sent out on the most most boring or thankless assignments. When I was alone on patrol in the town or its surroundings, I would frequently receive a radio call from the station: "Kanner, switchboard here. I need you to answer an emergency call." I would go to the address indicated, with sirens blaring and lights flashing, not realizing until I arrived that it was a minor incident.

Wild geese blocking Route 17? That was for me.

A cat stuck up a tree? That was for me.

An old, slightly senile lady who frequently heard suspicious noises and called three times in one night? That would be for me, too.

I even got my photograph in the *Chronicle* in an item about cows that had escaped from a pen. There I was, looking ridiculous, covered in mud and trying to retrieve a cow by pulling its tail. The headline read:

THE POLICE IN ACTION

That article earned me a lot of teasing from my colleagues, some of it funny, some of it less so. I found a clipping under the windshield wiper of my car, on which an anonymous fan had written with a black Sharpie: *Two Cows in Orphea*. And as if that wasn't enough, my parents came from New York to visit me that weekend.

"Is that why you moved here?" my father asked as soon as he arrived, waving a copy of the *Chronicle* in front of me. "You screwed up your marriage to become a cowherd?"

"Daddy, are we going to start arguing?"

"I just think you would have made a good lawyer."

"I know, Daddy, you've been telling me that for the last fifteen years."

"When I think you studied law for so long only to end up a police officer in a little town! What a waste!"

"I'm doing what I like, that's the most important thing, isn't it?"

"I'm taking Mark as my partner," he announced.

"Dammit, do you really need to work with my ex-husband?"

"He's a good man, you know."

"Don't start, please!"

"He's prepared to forgive you. You could get back together again, and you could come back to the firm."

"I'm proud of working for the police."

JESSE ROSENBERG
Tuesday, July 1, 2014
Twenty-five days to opening night

Stephanie had been missing for a week.

In the area, it was the only topic of conversation. A handful of people were convinced she had orchestrated her escape. Most thought that something had happened to her and were worried about who would be the next victim. A housewife out shopping? A girl on her way to the beach?

That morning, July 1, Derek and I joined Betsy at Café Athena for breakfast. She told us about the strange disappearance of Kirk Hayward, something neither Derek nor I had known about at the time, which meant it had happened after we had solved the Gordon killings.

"I had a look at the archives of the *Chronicle*," Betsy said. "And this is what I found, searching for articles about the first festival in 1994 . . ."

She showed us a photocopy of an article with the headline:

THE GREAT CRITIC OSTROVSKI
ON THE FESTIVAL

I skimmed the beginning of the article, an interview with Meta Ostrovski, a famous New York critic, about that first festival. My eyes were drawn to a particular section.

"Listen to this," I said to Derek. "The interviewer asks Ostrovski about his highlights and disappointments from the festival, and Ostrovski replies: 'The highlight—and I think everyone will agree—was definitely the wonderful production of "Uncle Vanya", above all Charlotte Carrell's superb performance as Yelena. As for the disappointments, I was surprised to find there was no play by Kirk Hayward on the program, as

I had been led to believe. I had heard good things about his recent production in Albany."'

"Did he say *Kirk Hayward*?" Derek said, incredulous.

"That's right, Kirk Hayward," Betsy said, proud of her discovery.

"What's that all about?" I said in astonishment. "Orphea's police chief had a connection with the festival?"

"What's more," Derek added, "Hayward investigated the Gordon murders. So he was linked both to the murders and to the festival."

"That must be why Stephanie wanted to find him." I said. "We must absolutely track him down."

One man could help us in our search: Lewis Erban, the officer Betsy had replaced in Orphea. He had spent his whole career in the Orphea police department, which meant he had definitely been around at the same time as Chief Hayward.

Betsy, Derek and I paid him a visit. We found him tending a flower bed in front of his house. Seeing Betsy, his face lit up with a friendly smile.

"Betsy," he said, "what a pleasure! You're the first of my colleagues to come calling."

"I'm sorry that this is more than a social visit," Betsy said. "These two officers are from the State Police. You may remember them from the 1994 investigation. We'd like to talk to you about Chief Hayward."

Sitting in his kitchen, where he insisted on offering us a homemade cookie, Erban told us he had no idea what had become of Kirk Hayward.

"Could he be dead?" Betsy said.

"I doubt it. How old would he be today? Around fifty-five."

"He disappeared in October 1994, soon after the murders of Mayor Gordon and his family were solved, is that right?"

"That's right. One day he was there, the next day he was gone. He left a strange letter of resignation. We never could figure it out."

"Was there an investigation?"

"Not really," Lewis said with a slightly shamefaced air.

"How do you mean? Your police chief walks out on you and no-one tries to find out why?"

"The truth of it is, everyone disliked him," Erban said. "By the time he disappeared, he wasn't really in control anymore. His deputy, Ron Gulliver, had taken over, more or less. We'd lost all patience with Hayward. We called him Chief Loner."

"Then why was he ever appointed chief?" Derek said.

"Well, we liked him at first. He was charismatic and highly intelligent. A good commander, too. Crazy about the theater. You know what he did during his spare time? He wrote plays! He'd spend his vacations in New York, seeing all the plays that were on. He even put on a play with a student company from the University of Albany, and it was quite successful. Got talked about in the paper and everything. He had found himself a girlfriend, a student who was in the cast, a really pretty girl. He had the works. The guy had everything going for him."

"What went wrong?" Derek said.

"His sudden fame didn't last more than a year, if that. He wrote a second play. When the theater festival was created, he moved heaven and earth to get his play put on as the opening show, but Mayor Gordon said no. They had arguments about it. And, at about that time Hayward's girlfriend left him, so his life took a turn for the worse . . ."

"Was it because of his play that Hayward's colleagues in the force turned against him?"

"Yes and no," Erban replied. "As I said, after his girlfriend broke up with him, he lost his way. In short, he was falling apart. There were rumors that he was spending his time following her around town rather than doing his job. You're police officers, you know what it's like. When there's something wrong at the top it affects everyone. Hayward was still coming into the station, but for all intents and purposes we had no chief."

"When did all this happen?"

"We found out all about it in June 1994."

"But how were the police able to function without a chief from June to October?"

"Gulliver stepped up. He became de facto chief. The guys respected him, and everything went well. There was nothing official about the situation, but nobody minded. Then Mayor Gordon was killed, and in the months that followed, Mayor Brown had his hands full of administrative problems."

"And yet," Derek said, "we worked with Hayward when we were investigating the Gordon killings."

"Who else from the station did you see a lot of?" Erban wanted to know.

"Nobody else," Derek said.

"Didn't you think it was strange that you only had dealings with Hayward?"

"I didn't think about it at the time."

"Look, it doesn't mean we neglected our jobs. Four people had been killed. We took every call from the public seriously, every request from the State Police, too. But outside that, Hayward conducted his own investigation. He was obsessed by the case."

"So he had his own file?"

"Of course. It's probably still in the records room."

"There's nothing there," Betsy said. "It's an empty box."

"Maybe it's in his office in the basement," Erban said.

"What office in the basement?"

"In 1994, a group of us went into Hayward's office, hoping he'd explain himself. He wasn't there, so we started searching and we realized he'd been spending more time working on his play than doing his job. There were all kinds of scripts and notes there. We decided to do a thorough clean. All the things that had nothing to do with his police work we put through the shredder. Let me tell you, there wasn't much left. After that, we unplugged his computer, took his chair and his desk, and moved everything into a room in the basement that had been used as an equipment store. The place was a mess, no windows, no fresh air. From that day on, when he got to the station, Hayward went straight down to his new office. We didn't think he'd hold out for a week, but he managed to survive in that basement for three months, until one day in October he was gone."

The mutiny described by Erban left us astonished. Finally, I said:

"Without warning anyone, he went missing?"

"That's right, Captain. I remember it very well, because the day before he left he tried to talk to me about his case."

*   *   *

Orphea, late October 1994

Erban walked into the toilets and there was Hayward, washing his hands.

"Lewis, we need to talk," he said.

Erban pretended at first not to have heard him. But Hayward kept looking at him, so he said:

"Kirk, I don't want to be roasted by the others . . ."

"Listen, Lewis, you can hate me all you want. But I need your help."

"Forget it. If the guys find out I've even been talking to you, I'm going to end up in the basement like you."

"Then let's meet somewhere else. How about the marina parking lot at eight tonight? I'll tell you everything I've been working on. It's important. It's about Ted Tennenbaum."

*   *   *

"Ted Tennenbaum?" I echoed.

"That's right, Captain Rosenberg," Erban said. "Obviously, I didn't go. Being seen with Hayward was like having scabies. That conversation was the last I ever had with him. The next day, when I got to the station, I heard that Gulliver had found a letter from Hayward on his desk, saying he had left and would not be coming back."

"What was your reaction?" Derek said.

"Good riddance, I thought. Honestly, it was better for everyone."

Leaving Erban's house, Betsy said to us:

"At the Grand Theater, Stephanie asked the volunteers about Ted Tennenbaum's movements on the night of the murders."

"Shit," Derek said under his breath. "Tennenbaum was the man who—"

". . . committed those murders, I know," Betsy cut in.

"At least that's what we've been thinking these twenty years. What had Kirk Hayward found out about him, and why didn't he tell us?"

That same day we received from forensics an analysis of the contents of Stephanie's computer. There was only one file on the hard drive, a Word document, protected by a code the I.T. people had easily been able to get around.

The three of us gathered in front of Stephanie's computer and opened the file. "Maybe it's her article," Derek said.

"Looks more like a book," Betsy said.

She was right. Reading the file, we discovered that Stephanie had been devoting a whole book to the case. This was the start of it:

NOT GUILTY

by

Stephanie Mailer

The ad was in between one for a shoe repairer and another for a Chinese restaurant offering an all-you-can-eat buffet for less than $20.

DO YOU WANT TO WRITE A BESTSELLER?
MAN OF LETTERS SEEKS AMBITIOUS WRITER FOR
SERIOUS WORK. REFERENCES ESSENTIAL.

I didn't take it seriously at first. But I was intrigued enough to dial the number. A man answered. I didn't recognize his voice. It wasn't until the next day, when I saw him in the café in SoHo where we had arranged to meet, that I realized who it was.

"You?" I said in surprise.

He seemed as surprised as I was. He explained that he needed someone to write a book that had been going around in his head for a long time.

"I've been placing that ad for nearly twenty years, Stephanie," he said. "A lot of people have replied to it over the years, but they were all pitiful."

"Why are you looking for someone to write it instead of you?"

"Not instead of me. For me. I give you the subject, you write it."

"But why not write it yourself?"

"Me? Impossible! What would people say? Can you imagine . . .? Anyway, I know your work on the *Literary Review* and how good you are, I'll pay all your expenses while you're writing. And when the book comes out you'll be a rich and famous writer, and I'll be a calmer man. I'll finally have the satisfaction of knowing the answers to questions that have been haunting me for twenty years. And the pleasure of seeing this book actually out there. If you solve the mystery, it'll make a wonderful detective story. The readers will love it."

It has to be admitted, the story did make for a fascinating read. Stephanie told how she had gotten herself hired by the *Orphea Chronicle* as a cover to allow her to investigate the 1994 murders at her leisure.

It was difficult, though, to distinguish what was true from what was fiction. If she was only telling the truth of what had happened, then who was this mysterious sponsor who had asked her to write the book? And why? She did not give his name, but she did make clear that it was someone she knew, someone who had, apparently, been in the Grand Theater on the night of the murders.

"That may be why I'm so obsessed by what happened. I was in the theater, watching the play. A very ordinary production of 'Uncle Vanya'. The real drama, a fascinating one, was taking place a few streets away, in the Penfield neighborhood. Every day since then, I have been wondering what exactly happened, and every day I have been telling myself that this story would make a wonderful mystery novel."

"But from what I heard, the murderer was found. It was a man named Ted Tennenbaum, who owned a restaurant in Orphea."

"I know, Stephanie. I also know that everything points to his guilt. But I'm not convinced. He was the fire officer on duty in the theater that night. Just before seven, I went out onto the street to get a breath of fresh air and saw a van drive by. It was easy to recognize because of the unusual sticker on the rear window. Sometime afterward, reading the newspapers, I realized it was Ted Tennenbaum's vehicle. The problem is, it wasn't him at the wheel."

"What's all this about a van?" Betsy said.

"Tennenbaum's van was one of the principal things that led to his arrest," Derek said. "A witness stated categorically that it was parked outside the mayor's house just before the murders."

"So it was his van, but he wasn't at the wheel?" Betsy said.

"That's what this guy seems to be saying," I said. "And why Stephanie told me we had nailed the wrong man."

"So someone doubted his guilt but never said anything in all this time?" Derek said.

It was clear to all three of us that if Stephanie had disappeared of her own free will, she would never have left without her computer.

Unhappily, this conviction of ours was to prove correct. The following morning, Wednesday, July 2, an amateur birder walking on the shore of Stag Lake noticed a mass floating in the distance, in among rushes and water lilies. Intrigued, she looked through her binoculars. It took her only a few moments to realize it was a human body.

DEREK SCOTT

August 1994. Our investigation was going nowhere. We had neither a suspect nor a motive. If Mayor Gordon and his family had indeed been meaning to flee Orphea, we had no idea of their intended destination or of the reason. We did not have a single clue, a single lead. Nothing in the behavior of Leslie or Joseph Gordon had alarmed their nearest and dearest, and their bank accounts indicated nothing abnormal.

To retrace the killer's steps, even if we did not yet understand his motive, we needed something specific to go on. Thanks to the ballistics experts, we knew that the weapon used for the murders was a Beretta pistol, and, to judge by the accuracy of the shooting, the murderer was well trained. We were drowning in weapons registrations and membership lists from shooting clubs.

We did have one thing, though, which might change the course of the investigation: the vehicle spotted on the street by Lena Bellamy just before the murders. She vaguely remembered a black van, with an impressive drawing on the rear window.

Jesse and I spent hours with her, showing her images of every possible vehicle.

"How about this one?" we would ask her.

She would look closely at the photographs propped up in front of her and reply, "It's really hard to say."

"When you say a van, do you mean a van or a pickup?"

"What's the difference? You know, the more vehicles you show me, the more confused I am."

For all Lena Bellamy's goodwill, we were going round in circles. And time was not on our side. Major McKenna was putting a lot of pressure on us.

"Well?" he would repeat. "Tell me you have something, guys."

"Nothing yet, sir. It's a real puzzle."

"Dammit, you really have to make some progress. Don't tell me I made a mistake about you. This is a big case and everyone in the squad is waiting to see you screw up. You know what they're saying about you around the coffee machine? That you're amateurs. You're going to look like idiots, I'm going to look like an idiot, and all this is going to be very unpleasant for everyone. So I need you to think about nothing but this case. Four people dead in broad daylight—there has to be a lead somewhere."

We were living and breathing the case. Twenty hours a day, seven days a week. I was practically living with Jesse and Natasha. There were three toothbrushes in their bathroom now.

It was thanks to Lena Bellamy that the investigation took a dramatic new turn.

Ten days after the murders, her husband took her out for dinner. Since that terrible night of July 30, Lena had been so worried and nervous that she had barely left home. She had stopped letting her children play in the park in front of the house. She preferred them to play farther away, even if that meant a car ride. She even thought about moving. Her husband Terrence, anxious to get her out of this mood, finally got her to agree to an evening out together. He wanted to try the hip new restaurant everyone was talking about, Café Athena on Main Street. It had opened just in time for the festival and was already heavily booked.

It was a mild evening. Terrence parked in the marina parking lot and they strolled to the restaurant. The place was wonderful, with an outdoor seating area, entirely candlelit and surrounded by banks of flowers. The front of the restaurant was a large picture window, on which a series of lines and dots had been etched, which at first glance looked like a Native American motif, until it became clear that it was an owl.

Seeing that design, Lena Bellamy began shaking. "That's it!" she said to her husband.

"What?"

"That's the logo I saw on the back of the van."

Bellamy called us from a phone booth. Jesse and I drove straight to Orphea and found the Bellamys lying low in their car at the marina. Lena was in tears. In the meantime, the famous black van had drawn up outside Café Athena. The logo on the rear window was indeed identical to the one on the front of the restaurant. Its driver was a man of imposing build whom the Bellamys had seen entering the establishment. We were able to identify him thanks to the van's license plates. It was Ted Tennenbaum, the owner of Café Athena.

We decided not to rush in and arrest Tennenbaum. We would start by making inquiries. It did not take us long to realize that he corresponded to the profile we had of the killer. He had bought a handgun a year earlier—although it was not a Beretta—and he practiced regularly in a local shooting range, whose owner told us he was a pretty good shot.

Tennenbaum came from a well-to-do Manhattan family, the kind of impulsive rich kid who liked to use his fists. It was because of his propensity for getting into fights that he had been dismissed from Stanford University. He had even done a few months' jail time—although that had not prevented him from later buying a weapon. He had been living in Orphea for a few years, and had, apparently, kept out of trouble. He had worked at the Lake Palace before launching out on his own with Café Athena. And it was his restaurant that had landed him in a dispute with the mayor.

Tennenbaum had bought a building that was ideally situated, bang on Main Street. The high price asked by the owner had put off other purchasers, but Tennenbaum was confident his restaurant would be a success. There was just one big problem: the zoning regulations did not allow for a restaurant in that location. Tennenbaum was somehow persuaded that the town council would grant him favorable treatment, but Mayor Gordon did not see things that way. He was fiercely opposed to the plans for Café Athena. Tennenbaum planned to make it a happening spot, the kind of place you might find in Manhattan, and Gordon claimed to see no benefit for Orphea. He refused any exemption from the zoning regulations. A number of municipal employees told us there had been heated arguments between the two men.

The next thing we discovered was that one night in February the building had been devastated by fire. That turned out to be a lucky break for Tennenbaum. The need for a total rebuild meant that the zoning regulation was changed. It was Chief Hayward who told us about this episode.

"So it was thanks to the fire that Tennenbaum was able to open his restaurant," I said. "And the fire was caused deliberately, I imagine."

"Obviously. But we found nothing that could prove that Tennenbaum was responsible. In any case, as luck would have it, the fire took place just in time for Tennenbaum to complete the work and open the restaurant before the start of the festival. Since then, it's been pretty much full all the time. It wouldn't have worked out if there had been the slightest delay."

That was the point that would prove crucial. Several witnesses asserted that Gordon had implicitly threatened Tennenbaum with a delay to the work. We even heard from Deputy Gulliver about an incident when he had had to step in to stop the two men coming to blows in the street.

"Why did nobody tell us about this disagreement with Tennenbaum?" I asked.

"Because it happened back in March," Gulliver said. "I'd forgotten about it. You know, when it comes to politics, people are always getting worked up. I have heaps of stories like that. You should go to a council meeting. The guys are forever going at each other hammer and tongs. That doesn't mean they end up shooting each other."

But for Jesse and me, that was enough. Tennenbaum had a motive to kill the mayor, he was a trained marksman, and his van had been formally identified as being parked outside the Gordons' house a short time before the murders. At dawn on August 12, 1994, we arrested Tennenbaum at his home for the murders of Joseph, Leslie, and Arthur Gordon, and Meghan Padalin.

We arrived triumphantly at troop headquarters and escorted Tennenbaum to the cells while our colleagues and Major McKenna looked on admiringly.

Our blaze of glory lasted just a few hours. Long enough for Tennenbaum to call Robin Starr, a top-flight New York lawyer, who made the journey from Manhattan as soon as Tennenbaum's sister paid him a $100,000 retainer.

In the interrogation room, Starr simply tore us to pieces, while the major and the rest of our colleagues could only watch behind a two-way mirror, doubled up with laughter.

"I've seen some incompetent police officers in my time," Starr said, "but you two really are the last straw. Would you mind telling me your story again, Sergeant Scott?"

"There's no need to treat us like fools," I retorted. "We know your client was in a dispute with Mayor Gordon for several months about the work on Café Athena."

Starr looked at me, intrigued. "The work has already been completed, it seems to me. So, Sergeant Scott, where is the problem?"

"Construction on Café Athena could not be delayed, and I know Mayor Gordon threatened to hold it up. After one final quarrel, Mr Tennenbaum ended up killing the mayor, his family, and that unfortunate jogger who was passing the house. Because, as I'm sure you know, Mr Starr, your client is a trained marksman."

Starr nodded ironically. "That's quite a tangled web, Sergeant, I'm really impressed."

Tennenbaum did not react. He was content to let his lawyer talk for him, which had worked well so far. Starr continued:

"If you've finished with this tall story of yours, please allow me to reply to it. My client couldn't have been at Mayor Gordon's house at seven o'clock on July 30 for the perfectly good reason that he was the fire officer on duty at the Grand Theater. You can ask anyone who was backstage that night, they'll tell you they saw Ted."

"There was a lot of coming and going that night," I said. "Mr Tennenbaum had time to slip out. It's only a few minutes' drive to the mayor's house."

"Oh, I see, Sergeant! So your theory is that my client jumped into his van, drove over to the mayor's house, killed everyone who he happened to run across, and then calmly returned to his post at the Grand Theater."

I decided to play my trump card. After leaving a moment's silence, I said:

"Your client's van has been formally identified as having been parked outside the Gordon family's house a few minutes before the murders. That's why your client is here, and it's why he won't leave here except to go to a federal prison while awaiting trial."

Starr looked me up and down severely. I had the feeling I had hit the target. He started clapping. "Congratulations, Sergeant. And thank you. I haven't had such a good laugh in years. So, your whole house of cards rests on this preposterous story of the van, which your witness was apparently unable to identify for ten days until she suddenly got her memory back?"

"How do you know that?"

"Because, unlike you, I do my job. I'm sorry to tell you this, but no judge would accept such an absurd testimony! You have no tangible evidence. Your case is worthy of a Boy Scout. You should be ashamed, Sergeant. If you have nothing to add, my client and I will now take our leave of you."

The door of the room opened. It was the major, glaring at us. He let Starr and Tennenbaum go, and when they had left he came back in. With an angry kick, he sent a chair flying. I had never seen him so furious.

"So this is your great investigation?" he shouted.

Jesse and I lowered our eyes. We did not dare say a word, we knew it would only have reinforced the major's fury.

"Well? What do you have to say for yourselves?"

"I'm convinced Tennenbaum did it, sir," I said.

"How convinced, Scott? So convinced that you won't sleep or eat until you've closed this case?"

"Yes, sir."

"Then get on with it! Get the hell out of here, the two of you, and solve the case!"

-6

Death of a Reporter

WEDNESDAY, JULY 2 – TUESDAY, JULY 8, 2014

JESSE ROSENBERG

Wednesday, July 2, 2014
Twenty-four days to opening night

On Route 117 an armada of emergency vehicles—fire engines, ambulances and police cars from all over the region—blocked access to Stag Lake. Traffic had been diverted by the Highway Patrol. Tape had been strung across the surrounding meadows, from one part of the forest to another, and behind them officers kept guard, stopping onlookers from getting in, as well as the reporters who had come running.

A few dozen yards away, at the foot of a gentle slope, in the middle of the high grass and cherry bushes, Betsy, Derek and I, as well as Chief Gulliver and a handful of officers, were gazing in silence at the fairy-tale setting of a vast stretch of water, covered in aquatic plants. Right in the middle of the lake, a patch of color was clearly visible in the vegetation. A little mound of white flesh. A human body caught among the water lilies.

It was impossible to say from that distance if it was Stephanie. We were waiting for frogmen from the State Police. As we waited, powerless and speechless, we looked at the calm stretch of water.

On one of the opposite shores, police officers trying to approach had become bogged down in the mud.

"Wasn't this area searched?" I asked Chief Gulliver.

"We didn't get as far as here. The place isn't easily accessible. And the shore's impassable, what with the mud and the reeds."

We heard sirens in the distance. Backup was coming. Then Mayor Brown arrived, escorted by Montagne, who had gone to collect him from the town hall. At last, the State Police units arrived, and things moved into higher gear: police officers and firefighters unloading rubber dinghies, followed by frogmen carrying crates of heavy equipment.

"What's going on in this town?" the mayor said as he joined us, staring out at the expanses of water lilies.

The frogmen rapidly got to work, and the dinghies were launched on the water. Chief Gulliver and I got into one of them. We set out across the lake, followed by a second dinghy carrying the frogmen. The frogs and the birds suddenly broke off their cries, and when the engines were turned off, the silence that ensued was nerve-wracking. The dinghies continued moving through the carpets of flowering water lilies and soon came level with the body. The divers slipped into the water and disappeared in a cloud of bubbles. I crouched in the stern of the dinghy and leaned over the side to get a better view of the body as it was freed by the frogmen. When finally they managed to turn it over, I recoiled. The face I saw, distorted by the water, was Stephanie Mailer's.

The announcement that Stephanie Mailer's drowned body had been found in Stag Lake caused a great stir in the area. Onlookers massed beyond the police barriers. The local media were there in numbers. The whole side of Route 17 was one huge, noisy carnival.

On the shore, where the body now lay, the medical examiner, Dr Ranjit Singh, proceeded with an initial examination, then joined us—Betsy, Derek, Mayor Brown, Chief Gulliver, and me—to let us know his observations.

"I think Stephanie Mailer was strangled," he said.

Mayor Brown hid his face in his hands.

"We'll have to wait for the results of the postmortem to know beyond doubt what happened," Dr Singh went on, "but I've already noticed big bruises on the neck as well as signs of major cyanosis. There are also scratches on the arms and face, and grazes on the elbows and knees."

"Why didn't anyone see her before?" Gulliver said.

"It takes time for drowned bodies to come back to the surface. Judging by the condition of the body, death occurred eight or nine days ago. More than a week anyway."

"Which would take us back to the night she went missing," Jesse said. "Stephanie was kidnapped and then murdered."

"Oh, my God!" Brown said, passing a hand through his hair. "How is it possible? Who could have done this to that poor girl?"

"That's what we're going to have to find out," Derek said. "You're facing a very serious situation, Mr Mayor. There's a killer in the area, maybe in your town. We don't know anything about his or her motives and we can't rule out the possibility that they may strike again. Until we catch whoever is responsible, we have to be even more careful. We may need to put security measures in place, with the State Police supporting the local force."

"Security measures?" Brown said anxiously. "Don't even think about it, you're going to scare everyone! You don't seem to realize, Orphea is a resort town. All we need is a rumor that there's a murderer on the loose and the summer season is screwed! Do you know what that means for us?" He turned to Chief Gulliver and Betsy. "How long can you stop this from getting out?"

"It's already out, Alan," Gulliver said. "It's spreading like wildfire. Look for yourself, up there on the side of the road."

We were suddenly interrupted by a commotion: the Mailers had just arrived. They appeared at the top of the slope leading down to the shore. "Stephanie!" Mrs Mailer cried as she approached, followed by her husband. Derek and I, seeing them hurrying down the slope, rushed to stop them coming any farther and spare them the sight of their daughter lying on the shore, ready to be loaded into a body bag.

"You really shouldn't look," I said to Mrs Mailer, who huddled against me, screaming and weeping. We led the Mailers to a police van, where a counsellor would soon join them.

A statement had to be made to the media. I preferred to let the mayor deal with that. Gulliver, who seemed not to want to miss an opportunity to appear on T.V., insisted on going with him.

They climbed back up to the security cordon, behind which reporters were kicking their heels. There were regional T.V. channels, photographers, and the printed press, too. When Mayor Brown and Gulliver appeared, a little forest of microphones and lenses turned in their direction. In a voice that stood out from those of his colleagues, Michael Bird asked the first question:

"Was Stephanie Mailer murdered?"

There was a brief, icy silence.

"We have to wait for the results of the investigation," Mayor Brown said. "Please let's not jump to conclusions. A press release will be issued in due course."

"But it was Stephanie Mailer who was found in the lake?" Bird persisted.

"I can't tell you anything more."

"We all saw her parents arrive, Mr Mayor."

"Yes, it does seem to be Stephanie Mailer," Brown was forced to confirm. "But her parents have not yet formally identified her."

He was at once bombarded by questions from the other reporters present. Bird's voice again rose above the mass:

"So Stephanie was murdered," he said. "Which means there's no way the fire in her apartment was a coincidence. What's going on in Orphea? What are you hiding from the townspeople, Mr Mayor?"

Keeping his composure, Brown replied in a calm voice, "I understand your questions, but it's important that you let the detectives do their job. I won't be making any comment for the moment, I don't want to risk hampering the work of the police."

Bird, visibly upset, now cried:

"Mr Mayor, are you planning to continue with the Fourth of July celebrations when your town is in mourning?"

Mayor Brown, caught unawares, had only a fraction of a second in which to consider his reply.

"For the moment, I'm announcing that the firework display on the Fourth of July is canceled."

A murmur ran through the reporters and the onlookers.

*

For our part, Betsy, Derek and I were examining the shores of the lake, trying to figure out how Stephanie could have ended up here. In Derek's opinion, it had to have been an unpremeditated murder.

"Any murderer with the slightest sense would have weighed down the body to stop it coming back to the surface so soon. The person who did this had not planned to kill her here or in this way."

Covered as it was with a vast, dense reed bed, which rose like a wall, most of the shoreline of Stag Lake was inaccessible on foot, making it a paradise for birds. It was like virgin forest, within which dozens of species of birds nested and lived in peace. Another part was edged with a real forest, of thick pines, which ran alongside Route 17 all the way to the ocean.

Our first thought was that it was only possible to access this area on foot if you came along the shore, as we had done. But carefully examining the surroundings, we noticed that a swathe of tall grass on the forest side had recently been flattened. With difficulty we reached the spot and found that the soil was soft and mushy. We then discovered a flat expanse emerging from the forest, where the mud had been shifted. It was impossible to say for certain, but we thought there were footprints.

"Something happened here," Derek said. "But I doubt that Stephanie came the same way we did. It's much too steep. I think the only way to reach this place . . ."

"Is to come through the forest?" Betsy said.

"Precisely."

Assisted by a handful of police officers from Orphea, we undertook a search of the strip of forest. There were clear indications that someone had been this way: broken branches, a piece of cloth hanging from a bush.

"This could be from the T-shirt Stephanie was wearing on Monday," I said, lifting the cloth with latex gloves.

When I had seen her in the water, Stephanie had been wearing only one shoe, on her right foot. We found the left shoe in the forest, behind a stump.

"She was running through the forest, trying to escape from someone," Derek said. "Otherwise, she would have taken the time to put her shoe back on."

"And her pursuer caught up with her by the lake and drowned her," Betsy said.

"That sounds right. But could she have run all the way here from the beach?"

It was more than five miles.

Going back through the forest, following the traces, we came out onto the road, some two hundred yards from the police barriers.

"She must have come in this way," Derek said.

It was around here that we spotted tire tracks at the roadside. Most likely her pursuer had been in a car.

*   *   *

Meanwhile, in New York

In the offices of the *New York Literary Review*, Meta Ostrovski was gazing through the window of his office at a squirrel bounding across the lawn of a park. In almost perfect French, he was giving an interview by telephone to an obscure Parisian intellectual magazine curious to know what he thought was the perception of European literature in the United States.

Ostrovski was in an expansive mood. "The reason I'm one of the most eminent critics in the world today, of course, is that for the past thirty years," he was saying, "I have never compromised my standards. Discipline and steadfastness of mind, that's my secret. Above all, never love. To love is to be weak!"

"All the same," the journalist at the other end objected, "some people claim that literary critics are generally failed writers."

Ostrovski replied with a laugh. "That's utter nonsense, madame. I've never, and I mean *never*, met a critic who dreamed of being a writer.

Critics are above that. Writing is a minor art. Writing is putting together words that then form sentences. Even a monkey can do that with a little training!"

"So what is the role of the critic?"

"To establish the truth. To make it possible for the masses to distinguish what is good from what is worthless. You know, only a small part of the population has the ability to judge for itself what is good. Unfortunately, since these days everybody wants to give his opinion about everything and we've seen utter nonentities praised to the skies, we critics are obliged to put a little order into this chaos. We're the intellectual truth police. That's all."

The interview was over. A secretary opened the door to Ostrovski's untidy office without knocking.

"Today's mail," she said, putting an envelope down on a pile of books waiting to be read.

Ostrovski was disappointed. "One letter, is that all?"

"That's all," the secretary said, and left.

How dismal that his mail had become so meager! In the days when he worked for the *New York Times*, he would receive bundles of impassioned letters from readers who seemed never to miss any of his reviews or columns. But that was before. The days when he had been all-powerful—a bygone time. These days nobody wrote to him, he was no longer recognized in the street, in theaters there was no longer a murmur when he passed along a row, authors no longer hung around outside his building to give him their books. The number of careers he had launched with his reviews! The number of would-be writers he had destroyed. But today he was no longer feared the way he had been. What he wrote now was followed only by readers of the *Review*, which was highly regarded, of course, but much less widely read.

Waking up that morning, Ostrovski had had a premonition. Something was going to happen, something that would relaunch his career. He realized that it was this letter. His instinct never betrayed him. What could be in this letter? He did not want to open it too quickly. Why a letter and not a telephone call? Having gazed again at the envelope, he cut it open and took out the sheet of paper it contained. He looked first to see who was the sender: Alan Brown, Mayor of Orphea.

> Dear Mr Ostrovski,
>
> We would be delighted if you could this year attend the 21st National Theater Festival in Orphea, New York State. Your reputation as a critic is so well established that your presence at the festival would be an honor for us. You graced us with your presence at the very first festival. It would give us great pleasure if you would celebrate our twentieth birthday with us. We would take care of all your expenses during your stay and would provide you with the best accommodation.

What a disappointment! He threw the letter into the wastepaper basket.

To clear his mind, he took up the latest list of bestsellers in New York, confirmed which was now the number one bestseller, and then set about writing a devastating review of this shockingly bad novel. He was interrupted by a knock at the door, and, a moment later Steven Bergdorf, the editor of the *Review*, entered his office. Ostrovski reached out to remove a file from a chair so Bergdorf could sit, but the other shook his head.

"Not to worry, Meta," he said. "I won't keep you long, but . . ." He hesitated a moment before continuing. "But I'm afraid I have some unwelcome news. The *Review* is only too conscious of the debt we owe you, the renown you bring to it, the readers who are devoted to you, but the fact is that our level of subscribers is not rising, our finances are in a perilous state, and I have been instructed by our owners to reduce costs. Believe me, I do this with great professional and personal regret, but I have no option but to bring our relationship with you to an end."

Ostrovski stared open-mouthed at Bergdorf. He stifled the sob that was rising in his throat.

"Very well, Steven," he said, with all the dignity he could muster. "Thank you for coming to tell me in person. I assume you will be able to have my books and files sent to my apartment?"

Bergdorf nodded. "Of course, Meta. Of course. I am so very sorry," he said, before backing out and closing the door very softly behind him.

*   *   *

Orphea was in a restless state. What with the discovery of Stephanie Mailer's body and the announcement by the mayor that the fireworks display was being canceled, the town was in turmoil. While Derek and I pursued our inquiries on the shores of Stag Lake, Betsy was called to the town hall as backup. Outside the building, a group of demonstrators, all local storekeepers and traders, had gathered, waving placards, to demand that the firework display go ahead.

"If there's no firework display on Friday night, I might as well close down," protested a bald little man who ran a Mexican food stand. "It's my biggest night of the season."

"I spent a lot of money renting a spot at the marina and hiring staff," another said. "Will the council reimburse me if the fireworks are canceled?"

"What happened to the Mailer girl is terrible, but why should that affect the Fourth of July? Thousands of people come to the marina to see the fireworks. They get there early, they go shopping on Main Street, then eat in the town's restaurants. If it doesn't go ahead, people won't come at all!"

The demonstration was peaceful. Betsy decided to see Mayor Brown in his office on the third floor. She found him standing looking out of the window. He waved to her, still looking out at the demonstrators.

"The joys of politics, Betsy," he said. "With this murder shaking the town, if I let the celebrations go ahead I'm heartless, and if I cancel them, I'm reckless and driving everyone to ruin."

There was a moment's silence.

"People here really like you, Alan," Betsy said.

"Unfortunately, there's a good chance I won't be re-elected in September. Orphea isn't the town it used to be and the inhabitants are demanding change. I need a coffee. You want a coffee?"

"I'd love one," she said. She thought the mayor was going to ask his assistant to bring them two coffees, but he drew her out into the corridor, at the end of which stood a hot drinks dispenser. He put a coin in the machine and a blackish liquid ran down into a paper cup.

Brown was a fine figure of a man, with deep eyes and an actor's good looks. He was always dressed to the nines, and his salt-and-pepper hair was impeccably groomed. When the first coffee was ready, he handed it to Betsy, then repeated the operation.

"And if you aren't re-elected," Betsy said after taking a sip of the awful coffee, "would that be so terrible?"

"Betsy, you know what I liked most about you the first time I saw you at the marina last summer?"

"No . . ."

"We share strong ideals, similar ambitions for our society. You could have made a terrific career for yourself in the N.Y.P.D. I could long ago have yielded to the siren call of politics and stood for the Senate or the House. But when it comes down to it, that's not what we're interested in, because what we can achieve here in Orphea we'd never be able to achieve in New York, Washington, or L.A., in other words, the idea of a fair town, a society that works, without too many inequalities. When Mayor Gordon asked me to become his deputy, in 1992, there was a lot that needed doing. This town was like a blank page. I've been able to mold it more or less to my beliefs, always trying to think of what was *right*, what was the best for the good of our community. Since I've been mayor, people's standard of living has improved, they've seen their daily lives get better thanks to top-quality services, better social services, and all that without any tax hikes."

"So why do you think the citizens of Orphea won't re-elect you this year?"

128

"Because time has passed and they've forgotten. Almost a whole generation has been and gone since my first term. Today, people's demands have changed because they take everything for granted. Now that Orphea is prosperous, people's appetites are keener, and there's a whole bunch of ambitious young people greedy for a little power who can easily see themselves as mayor. The next election may mark the end of this town. My successor's selfish hunger for power could well ruin it."

"Your successor? Who will that be?"

"I have no idea yet. He'll come out of the woodwork, you'll see. People have until the end of the month to announce their candidacy."

Mayor Brown had an impressive ability to get back in the saddle. Betsy realized that when the two of them went to see Stephanie's parents in Sag Harbor late that afternoon.

Outside the Mailers' house, protected by a police presence, the atmosphere was electric. A crowd had gathered on the street. Some were bystanders attracted by all the excitement, but others wanted to demonstrate their support for the family. Many among those present were holding candles. A makeshift altar had been set up against a lamppost, around which flowers, messages, and cuddly toys were strewn. Some people were singing, others praying, others taking photographs. There were reporters, too, and part of the sidewalk had been invaded by the vans of the local T.V. channels. Immediately Mayor Brown appeared, the reporters rushed up to him and asked him about the cancellation of the fireworks. Betsy tried to push them aside to let him get by without having to reply, but he restrained her. He wanted to speak to the media. Whereas earlier, in his office, he had seemed cornered, now he was bristling with self-confidence.

"I've listened to the town's tradespeople," he declared. "I understand their anxieties, and I'm well aware that canceling the Fourth of July celebrations could endanger the local economy, which is certainly fragile. So, having consulted my council, I have decided to go ahead with the fireworks and to dedicate them to the memory of Stephanie Mailer."

Pleased with the effect the annoucement had created, the mayor took no more questions.

That evening, after dropping Brown at his house, Betsy stopped in the marina parking lot, facing the ocean. It was eight o'clock. The delightful warmth of the evening invaded the car. She had no desire to be home on her own, still less to have dinner alone in a restaurant.

She phoned her friend Lauren, but Lauren was in New York.

"I don't get it, Betsy," she said. "When we have dinner together you take off at the first opportunity, and when I'm in New York you call and suggest we have dinner."

Betsy was in no mood to get into a debate. She hung up and went and bought a take-out meal from a snack bar at the marina. Then she went to her office at the station and ate her meal while gazing at the board where the elements of the investigation were displayed. As she was staring at the name *Kirk Hayward*, she thought again about what Lewis Erban had said the previous day—how the former police chief had been forced to move down to the basement. She remembered the storeroom, and decided to go down there. As she opened the door, she was seized with a strange feeling of unease. She could imagine Chief Hayward, in this very place, twenty years earlier.

Since the light did not work, she had to switch on her torch. The space was cluttered with chairs, filing cabinets, rickety tables, and cardboard boxes. She made her way through this graveyard of furniture until she came to a desk in lacquered wood, dust-covered and strewn with various objects, among which she noticed a metal stand engraved with the name Chief K. Hayward. She opened the four drawers. Three were empty, the fourth resisted. It was locked. She found a narrow crowbar in the workshop next door and prised open the lock, which yielded easily. Inside, there was a single yellowing sheet of paper bearing the handwritten words:

The Darkest Night

BETSY KANNER

There's nothing I like more than patrolling at night in Orphea.

There's nothing I like more than the quiet streets of the town bathed in the warmth of summer nights, the navy blue sky strewn with stars. Driving slowly through peacefully sleeping neighborhoods where all the shutters are closed. Passing a lone walker who can't sleep or happy townspeople who are taking advantage of these night hours to sit out on their porches and who give you a friendly wave as you pass.

There's nothing I like more than the streets downtown on winter nights, when suddenly it starts snowing and the ground is soon covered in a layer of white powder. That moment when you're the only person awake, when the snowplows have not yet gone to work, and when you're the first to make a mark in the virgin snow. Getting out of the car, patrolling on foot in the park, hearing the snow creak beneath your boots, happily filling your lungs with that dry, invigoratingly cold air.

There's nothing I like more than catching sight of a fox walking all the way up Main Street in the early hours of the morning.

There's nothing I like more than sunrise, in all seasons, over the marina. Seeing the inky horizon tinged with bright pink, then orange, and seeing that ball of fire rise slowly above the waves.

I moved to Orphea just a few months after signing my divorce papers.

I got married too early, to a wonderful man who wasn't the right one for me. I think I got married too early because of my father.

I have always had a very strong, very close relationship with my father. He and I have been like two fingers of the same hand since my early childhood. Whatever my father did, I wanted to do. Whatever my father said, I repeated. Wherever he went, I followed.

My father loves tennis. I played tennis, too, in the same club as him. On Sundays we often played each other, and, as the years passed, the closer our games became.

My father loves playing Scrabble. By the greatest of coincidences I, too, love the game. For a long time we spent our winter vacations skiing in Whistler, British Columbia. Every evening after dinner, we would settle down in the main room of our hotel and play a game of Scrabble, scrupulously noting down, game after game, who had won and by how many points.

My father is a lawyer, a Harvard graduate, and it was quite natural—I didn't even question it—that I should also study law at Harvard. I always believed it was what I wanted.

My father was very proud of me. At tennis, at Scrabble, at Harvard. In every situation. He never wearied of being congratulated about me. More than anything he loved it when people told him how beautiful and intelligent I was. I know how proud he was to see all eyes turn toward me whenever I arrived somewhere, at a party we went to together, on the tennis courts, or in the public rooms of our hotel in Whistler. But at the same time, my father could never stand any of my boyfriends. Not one of the boys I date from the age of sixteen or seventeen was, as far as my father was concerned, respectable enough, good enough, handsome enough, or intelligent enough for me.

"Come on now, Betsy," he would say, "you can do better than that!"

"I like him, Daddy, that's the main thing, isn't it?"

"But can you imagine yourself married to him?"

"Daddy, I'm seventeen! I'm not thinking about that yet!"

The longer the relationship lasted, the more impatient my father's campaign of obstruction. It was never head-on, but it was insidious. Whenever he could, through a detail he mentioned, an observation he slipped in, he would demolish, slowly but surely, the image I had of my boyfriend of the moment. I would invariably break up with him in the end, sure that the breakup was initiated by me—at least that's what I wanted to think. And the worst of it was that, with each of these new relationships, my father would say: "You know, the last one was a really nice boy—it's a pity you broke up—but this one, well, I really don't know what you see in him." And each time, I was taken in. But was I really taken in to the point that my father could cause my breakups without my knowing it? Or wasn't it rather that I was the one who broke up, not for specific reasons, but simply because I couldn't make up my mind to love a man my father disapproved of?

After graduating from Harvard and passing the New York bar exams, I became a lawyer in my father's firm. That lasted a year, at the end of which I discovered that the law, sublime as it might be in principle, was a machine that took a lot of time and money to keep going, over-burdened with rules and procedures, from which, when it came down to it, even the victors did not emerge unscathed. I soon acquired the belief that justice might be better served if I could apply it earlier in the process and that working on the streets would have more impact. I enrolled in the N.Y.P.D.'s Police Academy, to the dismay of my parents, especially my father, who wasn't pleased about my leaving his firm, but liked to believe that this was just a passing fancy, that I wasn't giving up on the law and might drop out of my course halfway. I left the Academy a year later, valedictorian of my year, praised by all my instructors, and I became a detective in the 55th precinct.

I immediately loved the job, especially for all those tiny everyday victories that made me aware that, faced with the fury of life, a good police officer could actually fix things.

The place I had left free in my father's firm was offered to an experienced lawyer, Mark, who was a few years older than me.

The first time I heard about Mark was at a family dinner. My father was in awe of him. "A brilliant, gifted, handsome man," he said. "He has it all. He even plays tennis." Then suddenly he said something else— words I heard uttered for the first time in my life: "I'm sure you'd like him. I'd like you to meet him."

I was at a time in my life when I really did want to meet someone. But the encounters that I had never ended up being anything serious.

After police academy, my relationships lasted no longer than a first dinner or a first excursion with third parties. Learning I was with the police—a detective, no less—people became fascinated and bombarded me with questions. I monopolized all the attention despite myself, captured all the light. And often the relationship ended with words along the lines of: "It's hard to be with you, Betsy, people are only interested in you, I have the feeling I don't exist. I think I need to be with someone who leaves me more space."

I met the famous Mark one afternoon when I went to see my father in his office, and I was pleased to discover that he didn't suffer from those complexes. With his natural charm, he was always the center of attention and had no problem engaging in conversation. He knew everything about everything, could do almost everything, and when he couldn't, he admired those who could. I looked at him as I had never looked at anybody before, perhaps because my father looked at him with such obvious admiration. Mark was his blue-eyed boy, and they even started playing tennis together. My father went into ecstasies every time he talked to me about him.

Mark invited me for a coffee. The chemistry was immediate, perfect, a swift current of mad energy. After the third coffee, we went to bed together. Neither he nor I mentioned our meetups to my father, but one evening, when we were having dinner, he said to me:

"I'd really like things to become more serious between us . . ."

"But . . . ?" I said apprehensively.

"I know how much your father admires you, Betsy. He's placed the bar very high. I don't know if he likes me enough."

When I reported these words to my father, he loved Mark even more, if that was possible. He called him to his office and opened a bottle of champagne.

When Mark told me about this, I couldn't stop giggling for several minutes. I grabbed a glass, raised it in the air and, imitating my father's deep voice and paternalistic gestures, declared, "To the man who's fucking my daughter!"

134

That was the beginning of a passionate affair between Mark and me, which turned into a genuinely romantic relationship in the best sense of the word. We turned a first real corner when we had dinner with my parents. And for the first time, in contrast to the last fifteen years, my father was radiant, affable and considerate with a man I was with. Having dismissed all the previous ones, now he was in a state of awe.

"What a guy!" my father said to me on the telephone the day after the dinner.

"He's amazing!" my mother said in the background.

My father had the nerve to add, "Try not to scare him away, like you did with the others!"

"Yes, this one's precious," my mother said.

The celebration of our first year together coincided with the traditional skiing vacation. My father suggested we go to Whistler together and Mark gladly accepted.

"If you can survive five evenings in a row with my father, especially the Scrabble contests, you'll deserve a medal."

Not only did he survive, he won three times. Added to that, he skied like a god. The last evening, as we were having dinner in a restaurant, a customer at the next table suddenly had a heart attack. Mark called Emergency, then gave first aid to the victim.

The man's life was saved and he was taken to the hospital. While the paramedics were taking him away on a stretcher, the doctor who was with them shook Mark's hand admiringly. "You saved that man, sir. You're a hero." The whole restaurant applauded him and the owner wouldn't allow us to pay for our dinner.

My father mentioned this in his speech at our wedding, a year and a half later, as an example of how exceptional Mark was. I was radiant, unable to take my eyes off my husband.

Our marriage would last less than a year.

Front page of the *Orphea Chronicle*:

IS THERE A CONNECTION BETWEEN THE MURDER OF STEPHANIE MAILER AND THE THEATER FESTIVAL?

The murder of Stephanie Mailer, a young reporter on the *Orphea Chronicle* whose body was found in Stag Lake, has left the town reeling. There is a great deal of anxiety among townspeople, putting the council under pressure just as the summer season is getting underway. Is a killer at large among us?

A note found in Ms Mailer's car mentioning the Orphea Theater Festival suggests she may have paid with her life for the investigation she was conducting for this newspaper into the murder in 1994 of Mayor Gordon, founder of the festival.

Betsy showed the newspaper to Derek and me when we met up that morning at troop headquarters.

"That was all we needed!" Derek said.

"It was stupid of me to mention that note to Bird," I said. "I saw him at Café Athena before coming here, I think he's taking Stephanie's death quite badly. He says he feels partly responsible. So what does the forensic analysis show?"

"Unfortunately, the tire tracks at the side of Route 17 are going to yield nothing. But the shoe is definitely Stephanie's and the piece of cloth comes from the T-shirt she was wearing. They also found a print of her shoe at the side of the road."

"Which confirms that she went into the forest at that point," Betsy said.

We were interrupted by the arrival of Dr Ranjit Singh who had come with the first results of the postmortem.

"Thanks for working so fast," Derek said.

"I wanted you to get ahead before the Fourth of July break."

Dr Singh was an elegant, affable man. He put his glasses on to read us the main points of his report.

"I found a few fairly unusual things. Stephanie Mailer died by drowning. There was a great deal of water in her lungs and in her stomach, as well as silt in her trachea. There are major signs of cyanosis and respiratory distress, which suggests that she struggled with her attacker. I discovered bruises on the back of her neck, left by a broad hand, which would mean that her neck was gripped firmly in order to push her head into the water. In addition to the traces of silt in the trachea, there are also some on her lips and teeth as well as on the top of her hair, which suggests that her head was kept under the water, at a shallow depth."

"Was she physically assaulted before she was drowned?" Derek said.

"There is no trace of violent blows, by which I mean that Stephanie was not knocked out or beaten. Nor was there any sexual assault. I think Stephanie was running away from her killer and that he caught up with her."

"He?" Derek said. "You think it was a man?"

"Judging by the strength necessary to keep someone under the water, I'd say a man, yes. But it could have been a strong woman."

"So she was running through the forest?" Betsy said.

Singh nodded. "I found a large number of contusions and marks on the face and arms, caused by scratches from branches. There were marks on the underside of the bare foot. She must have been running fast through the forest and grazed the sole of her foot with branches and stones. There were traces of earth under her nails. I think she probably fell on the shore of the lake and the killer only had to push her head into the water."

"Which might make it an unpremeditated crime," I said. "Whoever did that had not planned to kill her."

"I was getting to that, Captain," Singh said, showing us close-up photographs of Stephanie's shoulders, elbows, hands, and knees.

Dirty, reddish wounds were visible.

"They look like burns," Betsy said.

"Indeed," Singh said. "They're relatively superficial abrasions in which I found pieces of asphalt and gravel."

"Asphalt?" Derek said. "I'm not sure I follow you, doctor."

"Well, judging by the location of the wounds, they're due to a forward roll on asphalt, in other words, on a road. Which might mean that Stephanie threw herself from a moving car before escaping into the forest."

Singh's conclusions would be backed up by two crucial testimonies. The first was the account of a teenager on vacation with his parents who every evening met up with a group of friends on the beach near which we had found Stephanie's car. It was Betsy who questioned him after his parents, alerted by the media storm, contacted us, thinking their son might have seen something important. They were right.

According to Dr Singh, Stephanie's death occurred on the Monday night. The teenager told Betsy that on Monday, June 26, he had walked away from the group for a quiet phone call to his girlfriend, who had stayed behind in New York.

"I sat down on a rock," the boy said. "From there, I had a view of the parking lot. I remember it was deserted. Suddenly, I saw a woman coming along the path from the forest. She waited for a while, until 10.30. I know that because that's when I finished my call. I checked on my phone. Just then, a car drove into the parking lot. I saw the woman in the headlights. She was wearing a white T-shirt. The window on the passenger side was rolled down and the woman said something to the person at the wheel, then got in next to him and the car drove off. Was it the woman who died?"

"I'll check it out," Betsy said, not wanting to shock him needlessly. "Could you describe the car for me? Did you notice anything you remember? Maybe you saw the license plates? Even part of them? Or the name of the state?"

"No, I'm sorry."

"Was the driver a man or a woman?"

"I couldn't say. It was pretty dark and it happened quickly. I didn't really pay that much attention. If I'd known . . ."

"You've already helped me a lot. You can confirm that the girl got in the car voluntarily?"

"Oh, yes! She was waiting for that car, I'm sure of it."

So the teenager was the last person apart from the murderer to have seen Stephanie alive. The second testimony was provided by a traveling salesman from Hicksville who showed up at troop headquarters. He told us he had come to Orphea on Monday, June 26, to see some customers.

"I left town around 10.30 in the evening. I took Route 17 to get back on the highway. As I passed Stag Lake, I saw a car parked at the side of the road with its engine running and both front doors open. I thought that was odd, obviously, so I slowed down. I thought someone might be in trouble. It does happen."

"What time was this?"

"Around 10.50. Shortly before 11, anyway."

"So, you slowed down, and . . . ?"

"I slowed down, because I thought it was strange this car should have stopped there. I looked around, and saw someone climbing back up from the lake. I thought it was probably someone who'd stopped to take a leak. I didn't think further than that. If this person had needed help, he'd have signaled to me. I started my car again and drove home, didn't think about it anymore. It was only when I heard about a murder on the shore of the lake on Monday night that I made the connection with what I'd seen and figured it might be important."

"The person you saw—was it a man or a woman?"

"I'd say more likely a man. But it was quite dark."

"How about the car?"

"My recollection is only of the doors being open and the engine. But nothing else."

In Betsy's office at the Orphea police station, we were able to put together these different elements and reconstruct a timeline of Stephanie's last night.

"At 6.00 she arrives at the Kodiak Grill," I said. "She waits for someone—probably the killer—who doesn't show himself, but is in fact watching her in the restaurant without her knowing it. At 10.00 she leaves the restaurant. Her possible killer calls her from the booth in the restaurant and arranges to meet her on the beach. Stephanie is worried and calls Sean, the police officer, but he doesn't answer. So she goes to the place they agreed on. At 10.30, the killer arrives in his car. She gets in. Which means she must trust him, or maybe that she actually knows him."

With the help of a huge wall map of the region, Betsy traced in red marker the route the car must have taken. From the beach, along Ocean Road, then along Route 17 in a north-easterly direction, beside the lake. From the beach to Stag Lake was five miles, in other words, about fifteen minutes by car.

"Around 10.45," I went on, "realizing she's in danger, Stephanie throws herself out of the car and runs off through the forest, before the driver catches up with her and drowns her. At some point he takes her keys and goes to her apartment, probably that same Monday night. Not finding what he is looking for there, he burglarizes the newspaper offices and leaves with Stephanie's computer, but there, too, he draws a blank. Stephanie has been too careful. Playing for time, he sends a text at midnight to Michael Bird, knowing he's her editor and still hoping to get his hands on Stephanie's investigative work. But when he realizes that the State Police are starting to think that Stephanie's disappearance is suspicious, things move quickly. He goes back to Stephanie's apartment, but I show up. He knocks me out and comes back the following night to set fire to it, hoping at least to destroy whatever it was he never found."

For the first time since the beginning of the case, we had a clearer idea of what had happened. But where we felt that the vise was starting to close in, the townspeople were getting increasingly paranoid, and the front page of that day's *Chronicle* certainly did not improve matters. I became aware of that when Betsy received a call from Springfield.

"Have you read the paper?" he said. "Stephanie's murder is being linked to the festival. I'm calling a meeting of the volunteers today at five o'clock at Café Athena to vote for a strike. We aren't safe anymore. There may not even be a festival this year."

* * *

Meanwhile, in New York

In a conference room on the 53rd floor of the glass tower that housed the headquarters of Channel 14, the prestigious private T.V. station, the C.E.O., Jerry Eden, had summoned the principal members of the board.

"As you know," he told them, "the early summer ratings are bad, disastrous even, and that is why I've asked you all here. We need to fix something, and fix it fast."

"Which is the main problem?" one of the creative heads said.

"The six o'clock slot. We've been left behind by 'Look!'"

"Look!" was Channel 14's direct competitor. Similar audience, similar content. The two channels had been waging a fierce battle, with record advertising contracts for the flagship shows at stake.

"'Look!' has a reality show that's a big hit," the marketing director said.

"What's the pitch?" Eden said.

"That's just it. It doesn't have one. There's this group of three sisters. They have lunch, they shop, they go to the gym, they argue, they make up. We follow their typical day."

"And what kind of jobs do they do?"

"They don't have jobs, sir," the deputy director of programming said. "They're paid to do nothing."

"That's where we could do better than them!" Eden said. "By making a reality show that's truer to life."

"But, sir," the director in charge of reality shows objected, "the target audience for these shows is generally less well-off financially and poorly educated. They want to dream when they switch on their T.V.s."

"Exactly," Eden said. "We need a concept that brings viewers face to face with themselves and their ambitions. A reality show that shows them the way forward! We have to do something big for the fall season! I can see the slogan: CHANNEL 14. THE DREAM IS INSIDE YOU!"

This suggestion unleashed a wave of enthusiasm.

"That's really good!" the marketing director said.

"I want a show for the fall that makes a big impact. I want to shake everything up. In September, I want to launch a brilliant concept that grabs the viewers. By Monday, July 14, I want a plan for a flagship show for the fall. That's ten days."

As his colleagues were leaving the conference room, Eden's cell phone rang. It was his wife.

"Jerry," Cynthia said, "I've been trying to reach you for hours."

"Sorry, I was in a meeting. You know we're planning next season's shows and things are tense here right now. What's going on?"

"Carolina got home at eleven this morning. She was drunk again."

Eden sighed, overcome with a sense of powerlessness. "What do you want me to do, Cynthia?"

"Come on, Jerry, she's our daughter! You heard what Dr Lern said. We have to get her away from New York."

"Get her away from New York, as if that's going to make any difference!"

"Stop being such a fatalist! She's only nineteen. She needs help."

"Are you telling me we're not trying to help her?"

"You don't realize what she's going through, Jerry!"

"What I mainly realize is that I have a nineteen-year-old daughter who gets drunk and does drugs!" In spite of his irritation, he lowered his voice to a whisper to avoid being overheard.

"We'll talk about it face to face," Cynthia said. "Where are you?"

"*Where am I?*"

"Yes. The session with Dr Lern is at five. Don't tell me you forgot?"

Eden opened his eyes wide. He had indeed forgotten. He ran out of his office and hurried to the elevator.

Miraculously, he got to Dr Lern's office on Madison Avenue in time. For six months, Eden had been at family therapy sessions every week with his wife Cynthia and their nineteen-year-old daughter Carolina.

The Edens took their seats on a couch opposite the therapist, who was in his usual armchair.

"Well?" Dr Lern said. "What's happened since our last session?"

"You mean two weeks ago," Carolina said, "since my father forgot to show up last week?"

"Forgive me for working to pay this family's insane expenses!" Eden said.

"Jerry, please don't start!" his wife said.

"I only said *last session*," Dr Lern reminded them in a neutral voice.

Cynthia made an effort to steer the discussion in a constructive manner. "I've told Jerry he should spend more time with Carolina."

"And what do you think of that, Jerry?"

"I think it's going to be hard this summer. My company has run into tough competition, and we really need to develop a new show by the fall."

"Jerry!" Cynthia said crossly. "There must be someone who can take your place for the summer. You never have time for anything except your work!"

"I have a family and a psychiatrist to support," Eden said mildly.

Dr Lern did not react to that.

"Anyway, Daddy," Carolina said, "you only ever think about your fucking job."

"Do not use that kind of language," Eden said to his daughter.

"Jerry," Dr Lern said, "what do you think Carolina is trying to tell you when she uses those words?"

"That this *fucking job* pays her phone bill, pays for her clothes, her fucking car, and everything she stuffs up her nose!"

"Carolina, is that what you're trying to tell your father?" Lern said.

"No," Carolina said. "But I want a dog."

"Always something new," Eden said. "First of all, you want a computer, now you want a dog ..."

"Stop talking about that computer! I never want to hear about it again!"

"Was the computer a request from Carolina?" Lern said.

"Yes," Cynthia said. "She really liked to write."

"And why not a dog?"

"Very simply, because she's not a responsible person," Eden said.

"How do you know if you don't let me try?" Carolina protested.

"I see how you take care of yourself, and that's enough for me!"

"Jerry!" Cynthia wailed.

"Anyhow," Eden said, "she only wants a dog because her friend Neila bought a dog."

"It's *Leyla*, not *Neila*! You don't even know my best friend's name!"

"That girl's your best friend? She called her dog Marijuana."

"Well, Marijuana is very sweet! He's four months old and he's already housebroken!"

"That's not the problem, dammit!"

"What is the problem, then?" Dr Lern said.

"The problem is that this Leyla girl is a bad influence on my daughter. Whenever they get together, they do something stupid. If you want my opinion, everything that happened isn't the fault of the computer, it's the fault of that Leyla!"

"No, Daddy, you're the problem," Carolina protested, "because you're dumb and you just don't get it!"

She got up from the couch and walked out of the room. The session had lasted only fifteen minutes.

*   *   *

At 5.15, Betsy, Derek and I got to Café Athena. We found a table at the far end. The establishment was filled by the volunteers and onlookers who had come to witness the strange meeting that was taking place. Springfield, taking his function as president of the volunteers very seriously, was standing on a chair, hammering out words that the crowd took up in unison.

"We're in danger!" he cried.

"*Yes, in danger!*" the volunteers repeated.

"Mayor Brown is hiding the truth about Stephanie Mailer's death. Do you know why she was killed?"

"*Why?*" the chorus responded.

"Because of the theater festival!"

"*The theater festival!*" the volunteers sang out.

"Did we give our time in order to be murdered?"

"*Noooooooo!*" the crowd chanted.

A waiter came with coffee and the menu. I had already seen him in the restaurant. He looked Native American, with shoulder-length grizzled hair, and I had been struck by his first name, Massachusetts.

The volunteers took turns to speak. Many of them were worried by what they had read in the *Chronicle* and were afraid they would be the killer's next victims. Mayor Brown, who was also there, listened to all the grievances and tried to respond reassuringly, hoping to make the volunteers see reason.

"There is no serial killer in Orphea," he said.

"But there is a killer," a wiry, silver-haired man observed. "Stephanie Mailer is dead."

"Listen, that was a very tragic thing that happened, I agree. But it has nothing to do with you or the festival. You don't have the slightest reason to worry."

Still standing on his chair, Springfield called out, "Mr Mayor, we're not going to put ourselves in the way of being killed because of a theater festival!"

"I'll say it again, for the hundredth time, if necessary," Brown said, "this tragedy, terrible as it is, has absolutely no connection with the festival! Your argument is absurd! And the fact is, as you must realize, that without you the festival cannot take place."

"So that's all that worries you, is it, Mr Mayor?" Springfield said. "Your lousy festival rather than the safety of your citizens?"

"I'm just pointing out the consequences of making an irrational decision. If the festival does not take place, this town will not get back on its feet."

"It's the sign!" a woman suddenly cried out.

"What sign?" a young man asked.

"It's 'The Darkest Night'!" the woman screamed.

Derek, Betsy and I looked at each other in astonishment, while at the mention of those words Café Athena came alive with a loud, anxious murmur. Springfield struggled to regain control of the gathering. When silence was finally restored he suggested they take a vote.

"Who among you is in favor of an all-out strike until Stephanie's murderer is arrested?" he said.

A forest of hands went up. Almost all the volunteers.

"An all-out strike has been approved," Springfield announced, "until Stephanie Mailer's murderer is arrested and our safety is guaranteed."

The session having been brought to an end, the crowd trooped noisily out of the establishment and into the hot late-afternoon sun. Derek hurried to catch up with the woman who had mentioned "The Darkest Night".

"What is 'The Darkest Night'?" he asked her.

She stared at him fearfully. "You're not from around here, are you?"

"No, I'm not," he said, showing her his badge. "I'm with the State Police."

"'The Darkest Night' is the worst thing that can happen. It's already happened once and it'll happen again."

"I'm not sure I understand."

"Don't you know anything? Summer 1994, the summer of 'The Darkest Night'!"

"You mean the murders?"

She nodded nervously. "Those murders were 'The Darkest Night'! And it's going to happen again this summer! Get away from here, leave before it comes back and hits the town. This festival is cursed!"

She hurried away from the restaurant and disappeared along with the last volunteers, leaving Café Athena all but empty. Derek came back to our table. The only other person left inside was Mayor Brown.

"That woman seemed really scared about 'The Darkest Night,'" I said to the mayor.

He shrugged. "Don't take any notice of her, Captain Rosenberg. 'The Darkest Night' is nothing but a silly legend. That woman has a screw loose."

Mayor Brown now also left. Massachusetts hurried to our table to pour more coffee into our cups, even though we had barely touched them. I understood that it was just an excuse to talk to us.

"The mayor didn't tell you the truth," he said. "'The Darkest Night' is more than an urban legend. A lot of people here believe in it and see it as a prediction that came true already in 1994."

"What kind of prediction?" Derek said.

"That on a certain day, because of a play, there'll be chaos in this town for one whole night—the famous 'Darkest Night.'"

"Is that what happened in 1994?" I said.

"I do remember that just after Mayor Gordon announced there was going to be a theater festival here, strange things started happening."

"What kind of things?"

Massachusetts couldn't tell us more because right then the owner of Café Athena walked in. I immediately recognized her as Ted Tennenbaum's sister Sylvia. She must have been sixty, but she had barely changed physically since 1994. She was still the sophisticated woman I had met in the course of the investigation. When she saw us, she was unable to hold back an expression of dismay.

"They told me you were back in town," she said, her voice hard.

"Hello, Ms Tennenbaum," I said. "I didn't know you took over this place."

"Somebody had to do it, after you killed my brother."

"We didn't kill your brother," Derek said.

"You're not welcome here. Pay and get out."

"Alright," I said. "We didn't come here looking for trouble."

We asked Massachusetts for the check, which he brought in no time at all. At the bottom of the receipt, he had written in ballpoint:

Check out what happened on the night of February 11, 1994.

*

"I hadn't made the connection between Sylvia and Ted Tennenbaum," Betsy said once we were out of Café Athena. "What happened to her brother?"

Neither Derek nor I wanted to talk about it. There was a silence, and then Derek changed the subject.

"Let's start by clearing up this business of 'The Darkest Night' and this note from Massachusetts."

There was one person who could certainly help us with that: Michael Bird. We went straight to the offices of the *Chronicle*. Seeing us walk into his office, Bird asked:

"Have you come because of today's front page?"

"No," I said, "but since you mention it I'd certainly like to know why you did that. When I told you about the note found in Stephanie's car, it was part of a friendly conversation. I had no wish for it to end up on the front page of your newspaper."

"Stephanie was a very brave woman and an exceptional reporter," Bird said. "I'd hate to think she might have died in vain. Everyone should know what work she was doing."

"Which means the best way to pay tribute to her is to finish her investigation, not spread panic in the town by revealing the leads she was following."

"I'm sorry, Captain. I feel like I should have protected Stephanie and I failed. I wish I could turn the clock back. And to think I believed that damned text message! That was why I told you a week ago that there was no reason to worry."

"You weren't to know. Don't torture yourself needlessly. In any case, she was already dead by then. There was nothing more we could have done."

Bird collapsed onto his chair.

"But you can still help us find whoever did it," I said.

"I'm at your disposal."

"Stephanie was intrigued by a phrase we're finding it hard to make sense of: 'The Darkest Night.'"

He gave an amused smile. "I saw those words on the note you showed me, and I, too, was intrigued. So I did a bit of research in the archives."

He took a file from his drawer and passed it over his desk. Inside was a series of articles that had appeared between the fall of 1993 and the summer of 1994, reporting the appearance of graffiti as disturbing as it was mysterious. First on the wall of the post office—*Coming soon: The Darkest Night*—then all across town.

One night in November 1993, a note was slipped inside the windshield wipers of some hundreds of cars, saying: *The Darkest Night is coming.*

In January 1994, on the front door of the town hall, the start of a countdown: *In six months: The Darkest Night.*

In February 1994, after someone had set fire to a disused building on Main Street, the firefighters discovered more graffiti: *The Darkest Night will be here soon.*

And so on until the beginning of June 1994, when it was the turn of the Grand Theater to have its facade vandalized: *The theater festival will be starting soon. So will The Darkest Night.*

"So 'The Darkest Night' did have a connection with the festival," Derek said.

"The police never did find out who was responsible for the graffiti," Bird said.

I resumed: "Betsy found those same words in police records where the file on the 1994 murders should have been, and also in a drawer of Chief Hayward's desk at the station."

Did Chief Hayward know something? Could this have had a connection with his disappearance? We were also anxious to know what happened in Orphea on the night of February 11, 1994. In the newspaper's archives, we found, in the February 13 issue, an article about a building on Main Street being burned down, a building belonging to Ted Tennenbaum, who was trying to turn it into a restaurant against the wishes of Mayor Gordon.

Derek and I had known of this episode during the 1994 investigation. But for Betsy, this information was news.

"This was before Café Athena," Derek told her. "Actually it was because of the fire that it was possible to alter the legal use of the building, allow it to become a restaurant."

"Could Ted Tennenbaum have set fire to it himself?" Betsy said.

"We never did get to the bottom of that," Derek said. "But the story's common knowledge. There must be another reason why the waiter in Café Athena told us to look into it."

"What if this thing about 'The Darkest Night' has substance?" Betsy said. "What if, because of a play, there really is going to be chaos in the town for one whole night? What if, on July 26, on the opening night of the festival, there's going to be another murder or murders similar to the ones in 1994? What if the murder of Stephanie is only the prelude to something even more catastrophic?"

DEREK SCOTT

On the evening after we had been humiliated by Tennenbaum's lawyer, in mid-August 1994, Jesse and I drove to Queens at the invitation of Darla and Natasha, who were determined to take our minds off things. They had given us an address in Rego Park. It was a single-story building still under construction, its sign covered with a sheet. Darla and Natasha were waiting for us outside. They were radiant.

"Where are we?" I said.

Darla smiled. "Outside our future restaurant."

Jesse and I stood there amazed, immediately forgetting all about Orphea, the murders, and Ted Tennenbaum. Their plans for a restaurant were about to come to fruition. All those hours of unrelenting work were going to pay off. They would soon be able to leave the Blue Lagoon and live their dream.

"When are you planning to open?" Jesse said.

"By the end of the year," Natasha said. "There's a lot to do inside."

We knew they would be a great success. People would queue around the block waiting for a table.

"By the way," Jesse asked, "what's your restaurant going to be called?"

"That's why we wanted you here," Darla said. "We've just had the sign put up. We were sure of the name and we told ourselves that, this way, people in the neighborhood would already be talking about it."

"Isn't it bad luck to reveal a restaurant's sign before it opens?" I said.

Natasha laughed. "Don't talk bullshit, Derek."

She took a bottle of vodka and four small glasses from a bag, handed them around, and filled them to the brim. Darla grabbed a small rope tied to the sheet covering the sign and, after agreeing on a signal, they both yanked on it. The sheet floated to the ground like a parachute, and the name of the restaurant glowed in the dark:

LITTLE RUSSIA

We raised our glasses to Little Russia. We drank a few more vodkas, then took a tour of the premises. Darla and Natasha showed us the plan so that we could imagine the place as it would be. There was a cramped little mezzanine, where they planned to set up an office. A ladder gave access to the roof, and it was there that we spent most of that burning hot summer night, drinking vodka and dining by candlelight from a picnic hamper the girls had prepared, gazing at the Manhattan skyline in the distance.

I looked at Jesse and Natasha embracing. They were so beautiful together, they looked so happy. They were the kind of couple who made you believe that nothing would ever separate them. It was when I saw them as they were then that I knew I needed something very similar in my life. Darla was beside me. I looked into her eyes. She moved her hand forward to lightly touch mine. And I kissed her.

The following day, we were back in business, on a stakeout outside Café Athena. We were heavily hungover.

"So," Jesse said, "did you sleep over at Darla's?"

My only response was to smile. He burst out laughing. But we weren't in a laughing mood. We had to start our investigation all over again.

We were certain that it was Tennenbaum's van that Lena Bellamy had seen out on the street just before the murders. The Café Athena logo was a unique creation, which Tennenbaum had put on the rear window of his vehicle to advertise his restaurant. But it was Mrs Bellamy's word against his. We needed more.

We were going round in circles. At the town hall, we were told that Mayor Gordon had been furious about the fire in Tennenbaum's building and was convinced that Tennenbaum had started the fire himself.

So did the Orphea police. But there was nothing to prove it. Tennenbaum clearly had a gift for covering his tracks. Our only hope was to refute his alibi by proving that he had left the Grand Theater at a particular time on the evening of the murders. His shift had lasted from 5.00 to 11.00. He would have needed only twenty minutes to drive to the mayor's house and back. Twenty short minutes. We questioned all the volunteers who had been in the backstage area on opening night. They all stated that they had seen Tennenbaum several times that evening. But had he been there between 5.40 and 6.00? And, of course, nobody could confirm that. He had been seen near the dressing rooms, in the workshop, even in the bar, grabbing a sandwich. He had been seen everywhere and nowhere.

We were bogged down, almost losing hope, when one morning we received a call from a woman working at a bank in Hicksville that would change the course of the investigation.

JESSE ROSENBERG

Friday, July 4 and Saturday, July 5, 2014
Twenty-two days to opening night

Every year, Derek and Darla had a big barbecue in their garden to celebrate the Fourth of July. This year they invited Betsy and me. I declined the invitation, saying I'd been invited somewhere else. In fact, I spent the day alone, shut up in my kitchen, trying desperately to reproduce a hamburger sauce that had been a secret of Natasha's in the old days. But none of my many attempts succeeded. I didn't have all the ingredients, and I had no way of distinguishing which ones were missing. Natasha had created the sauce for roast beef sandwiches. I had suggested using it on hamburgers, too, which had proved to be a great idea. But none of the dozens of versions I put together that day were anything like the one that Natasha made.

As for Betsy, she went to her parents' house in Worcester, a comfortable suburb located not far from New York City, for a traditional family celebration. She was almost there when she received a panicky call from her sister.

"Betsy, where are you?"

"Almost there. What's going on?"

"The barbecue's been organized by Mommy and Daddy's new neighbor."

"So the house next door was finally sold?"

"Yes, Betsy. And you'll never guess who bought it. Mark. Mark, your ex-husband."

Aghast, Betsy stepped hard on the brake. She could hear her sister over the phone: "Betsy? Are you there?" As luck would have it, she had stopped just outside the house in question. She had always thought it was quite pretty, but now it struck her as horribly flashy. She looked at the ridiculous Fourth of July decorations hanging from the windows.

Anyone would have thought it was the White House. Mark was over-doing it, as usual. Not sure anymore if she would stay or simply drive away, Betsy decided to lock herself in her car. On a neighboring lawn, she saw children playing, happy parents. Of all her ambitions, her most cherished was to start a family. She envied her happy friends who were in couples. She envied her friends who were contented mothers.

A knocking on her car window made her jump. It was her mother.

"Betsy, I beg you, don't embarrass me, please come out. Everyone knows you're here."

"Why didn't you warn me?" Betsy said. "I wouldn't have come all this way."

"That's why I didn't tell you."

"Have you both gone crazy? You're celebrating the Fourth of July in my ex-husband's house?"

"We're celebrating the Fourth of July with our neighbor."

"Oh, please, don't play with words!"

Gradually, the guests gathered on the lawn to observe the scene. Among them was Mark, sporting his best hangdog look.

"It's my fault," he said. "I should have talked to Betsy first. We ought to cancel."

"We're not canceling anything, Mark!" Betsy's mother said. "You don't have to justify yourself to my daughter!"

Betsy heard someone murmur: "Poor Mark, being humiliated like this when he was kind enough to invite us."

Betsy felt all eyes on her, heavy with disapproval. She didn't want to give Mark a reason to unite her own family against her. She got out of the car and joined the party, which was taking place in the rear part of the garden, by the swimming pool.

Mark and Betsy's father, wearing identical aprons, were bustling around the barbecue. Everyone was in ecstasy over Mark's new house and the quality of his hamburgers. Betsy grabbed a bottle of white wine and sat down in a corner, resolved to remain polite and not cause a scandal.

*

A few dozen miles away, in Manhattan, in the study of his apartment on Central Park West, Meta Ostrovski was looking sadly through the window. He had thought at first that his dismissal from the *New York Literary Review* was merely a passing whim and that Bergdorf would call him back the next day to tell him how indispensable he was. But Bergdorf had not called back. Ostrovski had gone to the offices and discovered that his desk had been emptied, his books piled up in cardboard boxes, ready, presumably, to be shipped to his home.

What was to become of him?

His cleaning woman came into the room, bringing him a cup of tea.

"I'll be off now, Mr Ostrovski," she said softly. "I'm going to my son's for the Fourth of July."

"That's fine, Erika," Ostrovski said.

"Is there anything I can do for you before I go?"

"Would you be so kind as to take a cushion and stifle me with it?"

"No, sir, I can't do that."

Ostrovski sighed. "Then you may as well go."

On the other side of the park, in their apartment on Fifth Avenue, Jerry and Cynthia Eden were getting ready to celebrate the Fourth of July with friends.

Carolina said she preferred to stay home because she had a migraine. They raised no objection. They preferred to know she was at home. When they left, she was in the living room, watching T.V. A few hours went by. Weary and alone in that vast apartment, she eventually rolled a joint, took a bottle of vodka from her father's bar—she knew where he hid the key—and sat down under the fan in the kitchen to drink and smoke. Once she had finished her joint, slightly high and a little drunk, she went to her room. She took out her high school yearbook, found the page she was looking for, and went back into the kitchen. She rolled another joint, drank some more, and ran her fingertip over one of the photographs. Tara Scalini.

She spoke the name out loud. *Tara.* She started laughing, but then tears ran from her eyes and she burst into uncontrollable sobs. She slid to the ground, weeping in silence. She stayed like that until her cell phone rang. It was Leyla.

"Hi, Leyl," Carolina said, picking up.

"You sound like shit, Carolina. Have you been crying?"

"Yes."

She was young and beautiful, still not much more than a child, lying on the floor, her hair scattered like a mane around her thin face.

"Want to join me?" Leyla said.

"I promised my parents I'd stay home. But it'd be great if you could come over. I don't want to be alone."

"I'll get a cab and be right there."

Carolina hung up and took from her pocket a plastic sachet containing a clear powder. Ketamine. She poured some into the bottom of the glass, diluted it with vodka, and swallowed it in one go.

It was not until the following morning, a Saturday, that Eden discovered the vodka bottle, three-quarters empty. He then searched through the garbage can in the kitchen and found the butts of two joints. He was ready to tip his daughter from her bed, but Cynthia begged him to wait until she got up.

As soon as Carolina emerged from her room, he demanded an explanation.

"You betrayed our trust again!" he cried, brandishing the bottle and the butts.

"Oh, don't be so hung up!" Carolina said. "It's like you were never young."

She went straight to her room and got back into bed. Her parents came into the room after her.

"Do you realize you got through almost a whole bottle of vodka and smoked marijuana in our house?" her father said, furious.

"Why are you destroying yourself like this?" Cynthia said, trying hard not to offend her.

"What do you care?" Carolina said. "You'll be pleased when I'm not here!"

"Carolina!" her mother protested. "How can you say such things?"

"There were two glasses in the sink," Eden said. "Who was here? Do you just invite people like that?"

"I invite friends, what's the problem?"

"The problem is that you're consuming marijuana!"

"Relax, it was just a joint."

"You think I'm some kind of idiot? I know the crap you take! Who was with you? That little bitch Neila?"

"It's *Leyla*, Daddy, not *Neila*! And she's not a bitch! Stop thinking you're superior to everybody just because you have money!"

"It's my money that keeps you going!" Eden shouted at her

"Sweetheart," Cynthia said, in an attempt to calm things down, "your father and I are worried. We think you should go and have your addiction problem treated."

"I'm already seeing Dr Lern."

"We were thinking of somewhere more specialized."

"A detox clinic? I'm not going back to a place like that! Get out of my room!"

She grabbed a fluffy toy that jarred with the rest of the room and threw it in the direction of the door.

"You'll do what we say," Eden said.

"I won't go, do you hear me? I won't go! I hate you, both of you!"

She got up from her bed and slammed the door on them. Then, in tears, she phoned Leyla.

"What's going on, Carolina?" Leyla said, hearing her sobs.

"My parents want to send me to a clinic."

"To detox, you mean? When?"

"I don't know. They'll probably talk to the shrink on Monday. But I won't go. Do you hear me, I won't go. I'm getting out of here tonight. I never want to see these dumbos again. As soon as they're asleep, I'm taking off."

That same morning, in Worcester, Betsy, who had spent the night in her parents' house, was bombarded with questions by her mother at the breakfast table.

"Mom," Betsy finally said, "I have a hangover. I'd like to drink my coffee in peace if that's at all possible."

"So that's it, you drank too much!" her mother said, exasperated. "So you're drinking now?"

"When everyone pisses me off, Mom, yes, I drink."

Her mother sighed. "If you were still with Mark, we'd be living next door to you now."

"It's a good thing we aren't together then," Betsy said.

"Is it really over between Mark and you?"

"Mom, we've been divorced for a year!"

"You know that doesn't mean anything these days. Couples live together first and get married later, and then divorce three times, and finally get together for good."

Betsy's only response was to sigh. She stood up from the table, taking her cup of coffee.

"Since that terrible day at Sabar's jewelry store," her mother said, "you haven't been the same. Being with the police has ruined your life, that's what I think."

"I took a man's life, Mom," Betsy said. "And there's nothing I can do to change that."

"So you'd rather punish yourself by going to live in a one-horse town?"

"I know I'm not the daughter you'd have liked, but in spite of what you may think, I'm happy in Orphea."

"I thought you were going to become police chief there. What happened?"

Betsy did not reply. She went out onto the porch, hoping for a brief moment of peace.

I remember that morning in the spring of 2014, a few weeks before the events surrounding Stephanie Mailer's disappearance. They were the first fine days. Although it was still early, it was already hot. I went out onto the porch of my house to pick up the daily edition of the *Chronicle*, and sat down in a comfortable armchair to read it over my coffee. Just then, Cody Springfield, my neighbor, passed on the street and waved to me.

"Congratulations, Betsy!"

"Congratulations for what?"

"For the article."

I unfolded the paper and was amazed to see a big photograph of me on the front page, under the headline:

WILL THIS WOMAN BE THE NEXT CHIEF OF POLICE?

With the current chief of police, Ron Gulliver, due to retire this fall, there is a rumor that his successor will not be his deputy, Jasper Montagne, but his second deputy, Betsy Kanner, who arrived in Orphea last September.

I was overcome with panic. Who had told the *Chronicle* this? And above all, how were Montagne and his colleagues going to react? I drove to the station. All the officers bombarded me. "Is it true, Betsy? Are you going to replace Chief Gulliver?" Without replying, I hurried to Gulliver's office, hoping to avert disaster. But it was too late, the door was already closed. Montagne was inside. I heard him yell:

"What's this all about, Chief? Have you read this? Is it true? Is Betsy going to be the next chief of police?"

Gulliver seemed as surprised as he was. "Stop believing everything you read in the paper, Montagne. It's bullshit! I never heard anything as ridiculous in my life. Betsy, the next chief? Don't make me laugh. She only just got here! And anyhow, the guys would never agree to be bossed around by a woman!"

"But you made her deputy."

"Second deputy. You know who the second deputy was before her? Nobody. And you know why? Because it's a ghost title, made up by Mayor Brown who wants to look modern by fast-tracking girls everywhere. Equality, my ass. You know as well as I do it's bullshit."

Montagne was still anxious. "But does that mean I have no choice but to appoint her my deputy when I'm chief?"

Gulliver did what he could to reassure him. "Jasper, when you're chief, you can appoint whoever you like. The post of second deputy is just for show. Mayor Brown forced me to hire Betsy and I'm tied hand and foot. But when I'm gone and you're chief, you can fire her if that's what you want. Don't worry, I'll straighten her out. I'll show her who's in charge."

In a little while, I was summoned to Gulliver's office. He motioned me to a chair opposite him and picked up the copy of the *Chronicle* that was on his desk.

"Betsy," he said in a flat voice, "let me give you some advice. As a friend. Keep a low profile, a very low profile. Make yourself as small as a mouse."

"I don't know anything about that article, sir, I—"

But Gulliver didn't let me finish my sentence. "Betsy, I'm going to be very frank with you. You were appointed second deputy only because you're a woman. So stop climbing on your high horse and believing you were hired for your supposed skills. The only reason you're here is because Mayor Brown, with his fucking revolutionary ideas, wanted to have a woman on his police force. He kept bugging me with all that bullshit about diversity and discrimination. He put a hell of a lot of pressure on me. You know how it works—I didn't want to start an undeclared war with him the year I was leaving, or for him to play dirty tricks with our budget. So anyhow, he wanted a woman at all costs and you were the only female candidate. So I took you. But don't start fucking around in my station. You're just a quota, Betsy. Nothing but a quota!"

When Gulliver had finished, and having no desire to endure any more attacks from my colleagues, I went out on patrol. I parked behind the big billboard at the side of Route 17 where, ever since I had arrived in Orphea, I had taken shelter every time I needed to think in peace.

All the while keeping an eye on the traffic, which was still sparse at that hour of the morning, I replied to a message from Lauren. She had found the perfect man for me and wanted to arrange a dinner so that she could introduce us. When I declined, she came out with her usual refrain: "If you go on like this, Betsy, you're going to end up alone." We exchanged a few more texts. I complained about Chief Gulliver, Lauren suggested I return to New York. But I had no desire to do that. Apart from the difficulties I was having fitting in at work, I liked living in the Hamptons. Orphea was a quiet town, a nice place to be, with the ocean on one side and all that nature around. The long sandy beaches, the deep forests, the ponds covered with water lilies, the sinuous arms of the sea with their abundant fauna—these were magical places, all within easy reach. Summers here were wonderfully warm, the winters harsh but filled with light.

I knew it was somewhere I could finally be happy.

JESSE ROSENBERG
Monday, July 7, 2014
Nineteen days to opening night

The front page of the *Orphea Chronicle*, edition of Monday, July 7, 2014:

THEATER FESTIVAL THREATENED

Could this be the last curtain for Orphea's theater festival? Having been the center of the town's summer season for twenty years, this year's festival seems more under threat than ever after the volunteers, uniquely in the history of this institution, voted to strike over fears for their safety. Now the question everyone is asking is: Without the volunteers, can the festival go ahead?

Betsy had spent her Sunday following up the Kirk Hayward lead. She had tracked down his father, Cornelius Hayward, in a senior citizens' home in Poughkeepsie, three hours' drive from Orphea. She had contacted the director, who was expecting us.

"You worked yesterday, Betsy?" I asked in surprise as the two of us set off for the home. "I thought you went to your parents' for the weekend."

She shrugged. "The festivities were cut short. I was pleased to have something to do to take my mind off things. Where's Derek?"

"At troop headquarters, looking through the 1994 case file. It's bugging him that we could have missed something."

"What happened between the two of you in 1994, Jesse? From what you say, I get the feeling you were the best of friends."

"We still are."

"But in 1994 something came between you . . ."

"Yes, but I'm not sure I'm ready to talk about it."

She nodded, then said, "What about you, Jesse? What did you do on the Fourth of July?"

"I stayed home."

"On your own?"

"On my own. I made myself hamburgers with Natasha's Sauce." I smiled—I didn't need to have said that.

"Who's Natasha?"

"My fiancée."

"You're engaged?"

"I was. Now I'm a confirmed bachelor."

She laughed. "Me, too. Since my divorce, my girlfriends all predict I'll end up alone."

"That hurts!"

"It does, a little. But I still hope I'll find someone. How come it didn't work out with Natasha?"

"Life sometimes plays strange tricks on us."

I could see from the look in her eyes that Betsy understood what I was trying to say.

The senior citizens' home, called The Oaks, occupied a small building with flower-filled balconies on the outskirts of Poughkeepsie. In the lobby, old people in wheelchairs watched out for anyone coming in.

"Visitors! Visitors!" an old man with a chessboard on his knees cried out when we appeared.

"Have you come to see us?" asked another old man, a toothless fellow who resembled a tortoise.

"We've come to see Cornelius Hayward," Betsy said politely.

"Why haven't you come to see me?" a little old lady as thin as a twig asked in a quivery voice.

"My children haven't been to see me in two months," the chess player said.

We presented ourselves at the reception desk, and a few moments later the director of the establishment appeared, a pudgy little man in a sweat-stained suit. He eyed up Betsy in her uniform and shook our hands vigorously. His own hand was sticky.

"What do you want with Cornelius Hayward?"

"We're looking for his son in connection with a case we're investigating."

"And what has this son of his done?"

"We'd just like to talk to Mr Hayward."

He led us along corridors to a large room in which the residents were sitting here and there. Some were playing cards, others reading, others simply staring into space.

"Cornelius," the director said, "you have a visitor, two visitors."

A tall, thin old man with disheveled white hair, dressed in a thick dressing gown, rose from his armchair.

"The police from Orphea?" he said, staring at Betsy's black uniform as he came toward us. "What's going on?"

"Mr Hayward," Betsy said, "we need to get in touch with your son Kirk."

"Kirky? What do you want with him?"

"Let's sit down, Mr Hayward."

We took our seats, all four of us, including the director, in a corner furnished with a couch and two armchairs. A horde of curious old people gathered around us.

"What do you want with my Kirky?" Mr Hayward said anxiously.

The way he spoke answered our first question. Kirk Hayward was alive and well.

"We're looking into one of his old cases," Betsy said. "In 1994, your son did a great job investigating a case of homocide in Orphea. We have reason to believe that the same person may be responsible for the death of a young woman a few days ago. We need to speak to Kirk in order to solve this new case. Are you in touch with him?"

"Yes, of course. We telephone each other often."

"Does he come here?"

"Oh no. He lives too far away!"

"Where does he live?"

"In California. He's a great director, you know. He's going to become very famous. Very famous! When he gets an Oscar, I'll put on a wonderful suit I have and cheer him to the rafters. You want to see my suit? It's in my room."

"Maybe not today, but tell me, Mr Hayward, how can we reach your son?"

"I have a telephone number. You have to leave him a message and he calls you back."

He took a notebook from his pocket and dictated the number to Betsy.

"How long has Kirk been living in California?" I said.

"I can't remember exactly. A long time. Maybe twenty years."

"So when he left Orphea, he went straight to California?"

"That's right, straight there."

"Why do you think he gave it all up so suddenly?"

"He knew everything. He found out who really committed those murders in 1994, so he had to leave."

"But then why didn't he arrest him?"

"You'd have to ask my Kirky. And please, if you see him, tell him his dad sends his regards."

When it was mid-morning in California, Betsy dialed the number that the old man had given us.

"Hello, Beluga Bar," a woman's voice answered.

"Hello," Betsy said, once she had gotten over her surprise. "I'd like to speak to Kirk Hayward."

"Leave me your message and he'll call you back."

Betsy left her name and cell phone number and added that it was about an extremely important manner. Once she had hung up, we did a quick search online. The Beluga Bar was an establishment located in the Meadowood neighborhood of Los Angeles. The name was not unfamiliar. And then I made the connection. I called Derek and asked him to dig out Stephanie's credit card statement.

"Your memory is correct," he confirmed after looking through the papers. "It seems Stephanie was at the Beluga Bar three times when she was in Los Angeles in June."

"That's why she was in Los Angeles!" I said. "She had tracked down Chief Hayward and she went to see him."

*   *   *

New York, the same day

In the Edens' apartment, Cynthia was beside herself. Carolina had been missing for two days. The police had been informed and had launched a search. Eden and his wife had crisscrossed the city, speaking with all her friends, but in vain. Right now, they were pacing up and down their living room, hoping for news that did not arrive. Their nerves were on edge.

"I'm sure she'll come back when she needs cash to buy her shit," Eden said, at the end of his tether.

"Jerry, I don't recognize you anymore! This is our daughter we're talking about! You used to be so close, remember? When she was little, I was even jealous of how close you were."

"I know, I know," Eden replied, anxious to calm his wife.

They had not realized that their daughter was gone until Sunday. They had thought she was sleeping and hadn't gone to her room until early in the afternoon.

"We should have looked in on her when we came home," Cynthia said.

"What difference would that have made? And anyway, we're supposed to be 'respecting her inner space'. That's what I was told in one of those family therapy sessions. All we've done is apply that fucking principle of trust recommended by your fucking Dr Lern!"

"Don't distort everything, Jerry! When we talked about that in the session, it was because Carolina was complaining that you kept searching her room for drugs. Dr Lern said we should make her room a space just for her, a space we would respect, and thereby establish a principle of trust. He never said we shouldn't go in there to see if our daughter was alright!"

"For all we knew, she was sleeping in. I wanted to give her the benefit of the doubt."

"Her cell phone is still off!" Cynthia said in a choked voice, having tried in the meantime to reach her daughter. "I'm going to call Dr Lern."

Just then, the landline rang. Eden rushed to pick up.

"Mr Eden? This is the N.Y.P.D. We have your daughter. Don't worry, she's fine. A patrol found her sleeping in an alley, apparently drunk. She's been taken to Mount Sinai for tests."

* * *

When we got back to Orphea, Betsy and I dropped by the Grand Theater. On the drive from Poughkeepsie, we had called Cody Springfield. We needed to find out anything more we could about the first festival. We were particularly curious to learn about the play Hayward had proposed, which Mayor Gordon had initially turned down.

Betsy led me through the building to the backstage area. Springfield was waiting for us in his office. From the archives he had prepared a cardboard box filled with assorted mementos.

"What are you looking for in particular?" he said.

"Any information about the first festival. The name of the company that performed the opening show, for example."

"The opening play was 'Uncle Vanya'. Look, here's the program."

He took out an old, yellowing brochure and held it out to me. "You can keep it," he said. "I have others." Then, rummaging some more in his box, he took out a booklet. "Oh, I'd forgotten this even existed. It was an idea of Mayor Gordon's at the time. You may find it useful."

I took the booklet and read the title.

HISTORY OF THE ORPHEA THEATER FESTIVAL
by Steven Bergdorf

"What is this?"

"Steven Bergdorf?" Betsy said, reading the author's name.

Springfield told us about an episode that had occurred two months before the Gordon murders.

*   *   *

Orphea, May 1994

Sitting in his little office in the bookstore, Springfield was busy processing orders when Meghan Padalin shyly opened the door.

"Sorry to bother you, Cody, but the mayor's here. He'd like to see you."

Springfield immediately stood up and walked from the back room into the store. He was curious. For some reason, Mayor Gordon had not been to the store for two months or so. Cody could not understand why. He had the impression the mayor was avoiding it. He had been seen buying books from the bookstore in East Hampton.

Gordon was waiting on the other side of the counter, nervously fingering a little booklet.

"Mayor Gordon!"

"Hello, Cody."

They shook hands cordially.

"We're very fortunate," Mayor Gordon said, gazing at the bookshelves, "to have such a wonderful bookstore here in Orphea."

"Is everything alright, Mr Mayor? I've had the impression you've been avoiding me recently."

"Avoiding you? What a strange idea! You know, I'm impressed by how much people here read. They always have a book in their hands. The other day, I was having dinner in the restaurant, and, believe it or not, at the next table was a young couple sitting face to face, each of them deep in a book! I told myself, people have gone crazy. Talk to each other, dammit, instead of being engrossed in your book! On top of that, sun-bathers go to the beach carrying piles of reading matter. It's their drug."

Springfield listened, amused, to the mayor's story. He found him affa-ble, sympathetic, good-natured. Maybe he'd been barking up the wrong tree. But there was an ulterior motive behind Gordon's visit.

"I wanted to ask you a question, Cody," the mayor said. "As you know, July 30 is the opening night of our very first theater festival."

"Yes, of course I know," Springfield said enthusiastically. "I've already ordered several different editions of 'Uncle Vanya' for my customers."

"What a good idea! Anyway, here's what I wanted to ask you. Steven Bergdorf, the editor of the *Chronicle*, as you know, has written a little book about the festival. Do you think you could put it on sale here? Look, I brought you a copy."

He handed Springfield the booklet. The cover had on it a photograph of the mayor posing outside the Grand Theater, with the title above it.

"*History of the Festival*," Springfield read out loud. "But this is only the first festival, isn't it? Don't you think it's a bit premature to have a book about it?"

"Well, there's already so much to say about the subject. You may be in for quite a surprise."

Springfield did not see what possible interest there might be in the book, but he wanted to show willing to the mayor, so he agreed for it to be sold in his store. Once Gordon had left, Meghan Padalin reappeared.

"What did he want?"

"To promote a booklet he's publishing."

She softened and leafed through the little book. "It doesn't look too bad. You know, there are quite a lot of people in the area who self-publish. We should put a little corner aside for them so they can put their works on sale here."

"A corner? We're short of space as it is. And besides, nobody will be interested. People don't want to read their neighbors' books."

"Let's use the storeroom in back," Meghan said. "A coat of paint and it'll be like new. We'll make it a room for local writers. You'll see—writers buy books. They'll come from all over the region to see their own books on the shelves and at the same time they'll make purchases."

Yes, Springfield thought, it might be a good idea. And besides, he wanted to please Mayor Gordon. He could sense that something was amiss and he did not like that.

"We can try it if you like, Meghan," he said. "We have nothing to lose. If nothing more comes of it, we'll have tidied the storeroom. Anyway, thanks to Mayor Gordon, I've discovered that Steven Bergdorf is a writer in his spare time."

*　　*　　*

"So Steven Bergdorf used to be the editor of the *Chronicle*?" Betsy said. "Did you know that, Jesse?"

I had had no idea. Had I met him in 1994? I couldn't remember.

"Do you know him?" Springfield asked, surprised by our reaction.

"He's the editor of the magazine Stephanie Mailer used to work for in New York," Betsy said.

How was it I didn't remember Steven Bergdorf? Going further into it, we discovered that Bergdorf had resigned from his post as editor of the *Chronicle* just after the Gordon killings and had been replaced by Michael Bird. A strange coincidence. What if Bergdorf had left with questions that still nagged at him today? What if he was the person who had commissioned the book Stephanie had been writing? She had hinted at someone who couldn't write it themselves. It was understandable if the one-time editor of the local paper was unwilling to come back twenty years later and declare an interest in the case. We absolutely had to go to New York and speak with Bergdorf. We decided to do so first thing the next day.

This was not our final surprise. The same day, late in the evening, Betsy received a call. "Deputy Kanner?" a man's voice said. "This is Kirk Hayward speaking."

DEREK SCOTT

Monday, August 22, 1994. Three weeks after the murders.

Jesse and I were on our way to Hicksville, a town on Long Island between New York and Orphea. The woman who had contacted us worked as a clerk in a branch of the Long Island Bank.

"She's agreed to meet us in a coffee shop downtown," I told Jesse in the car. "Her boss doesn't know she got in touch with us."

"But is this about Gordon?" Jesse said.

"It seems so."

It was early in the morning, nevertheless Jesse was eating a hot meat sandwich, the meat covered in a brown sauce that smelled wonderful.

"Want to try it?" Jesse said between mouthfuls, holding out his sandwich to me. "It's seriously good."

I bit into the bread. I had seldom tasted anything as delicious.

"It's the sauce that's incredible. I don't know how Natasha does it. I call it Natasha's Sauce."

"You mean Natasha made you this sandwich this morning before you left?"

"She got up at four to try out dishes for the restaurant. Darla will be dropping by later. I had an embarrassment of choice. Pancakes, waffles, Russian salad. There was enough for a regiment. I suggested she serve these sandwiches at Little Russia. People are going to fight over them."

"And with lots of fries," I said, already picturing myself there. "There can never be enough fries."

*

The clerk from the Long Island Bank was called Macy Warwick. She was waiting for us in an otherwise empty coffee shop, nervously stirring her cappuccino.

"I was in the Hamptons last weekend and I saw a photograph in a newspaper of that family that was murdered. I thought I recognized the man, and then I realized he was a customer of the bank."

She had with her a cardboard folder containing bank documents. She pushed it across the table in our direction.

"It took me a while to find his name. I didn't bring the newspaper back with me and I couldn't remember the surname. I had to go into the bank's computer system to find the transactions. These last few months he had been coming several times a week."

As we listened to her, Jesse and I consulted the copies of statements that Macy Warwick had brought. There were several deposits of $20,000 in cash into an account registered with her bank.

"Several times a week? Joseph Gordon came to your branch and deposited these sums?" Jesse said in surprise.

"Yes," Macy said. "$20,000 is the maximum a customer can deposit without needing to give an explanation."

Studying the statements, we discovered that these deposits had started the previous March.

"And besides, my boss doesn't like too many questions being asked. He says if the customers don't come here, they'll go somewhere else. Apparently the bank's directors are planning to close some branches."

"So the money is still in this account in your bank?"

"In our bank, if you like, but I took the liberty of checking which account the money was deposited in. It was a different account, still in Mr Gordon's name, but opened in our branch in Bozeman, Montana."

Jesse and I were astonished. In the bank statements we had found in Gordon's house, there were only personal accounts held in a bank in the Hamptons. What was this other account in the wilds of Montana?

We immediately contacted the Montana State Police to get more

information. And what they discovered was more than enough justifica-
tion for Jesse and me to fly to Yellowstone Bozeman Airport, by way
of Chicago. We took a few sandwiches with Natasha's Sauce to survive
the flight.

Mayor Gordon had been renting a house in Bozeman since April.
We were able to establish that because of the regular debits from his
account there. We tracked down the realtor, who took us to a sinister
little single-story shack built out of planks at the intersection of two
streets.

"Yes, that's him, Joseph Gordon," the realtor said when we showed
him a photograph of the mayor. "He came to Bozeman just once, in
April. He was alone. He'd driven all the way from New York State. His
car was full of cardboard boxes. He confirmed that he would take the
house even before he'd seen it. At a price like that, he said, how can
you refuse?"

"Are you certain this was the man you saw?" I said.

"Oh, yes. I didn't trust him, so when he wasn't looking I took a
photograph, so that I had at least his face and his license plate, just in
case."

The realtor took a photograph from his pocket. On it, Mayor
Gordon could be seen unloading boxes from a convertible.

"Did he tell you why he wanted to live here?"

"Not really, but in the end he did say something along the lines of
'It's not especially beautiful around here, but it's quiet and out of
the way.'"

"And when was he supposed to be moving in?"

"He rented the house from April, but he didn't know when exactly
he'd be coming for good. I didn't really care. As long as the rent is paid,
the rest is no concern of mine."

"Can I take this photograph for our file?" I said.

"Go ahead, Sergeant."

The bank account opened in March, the house rented in April. Mayor
Gordon had been planning his escape. The night he died, he really was

on the verge of leaving Orphea with his family. Could the killer have known that?

We also had to figure out where that money came from. Because now it was a near certainty that there was a link between his murder and those huge sums of cash he had transferred to Montana—a total of almost $500,000.

Our first idea was to check if that money might be the connection between Mayor Gordon and Tennenbaum. We had to use all our persuasive skills on Major McKenna for him to agree to send a request to the assistant D.A. for access to Tennenbaum's bank details.

"You know," the major warned us, "with a lawyer like Starr on the case, if you screw up one more time, you'll be dragged in front of the disciplinary board—or even in front of a judge—for harassment. And let me tell you this right now: if that happens, it's your careers down the toilet."

We knew that perfectly well, but we could not help but notice that the mayor had started to receive those mysterious sums of money just when the refurbishment work on the Café Athena building had started. What if Mayor Gordon had been screwing money out of Tennenbaum in return for agreeing not to block the work and letting it open in time for the festival?

After hearing our arguments, the assistant D.A. thought our theory was sufficiently persuasive to issue a warrant. And that was how we discovered that between February and July 1994 Tennenbaum had withdrawn $500,000 from an account inherited from his father in a Manhattan bank.

JESSE ROSENBERG

Tuesday, July 8, 2014
Eighteen days to opening night

That morning, as we drove to New York, Betsy told Derek and me about the call she had had from Kirk Hayward.

"He refused to tell me anything over the phone, but he agreed to meet tomorrow, Wednesday, at 5 p.m. in the Beluga Bar."

"In Los Angeles?" I said. "Is he joking?"

"He seemed serious to me. I've checked the schedules. You can take a flight tomorrow morning from J.F.K., Jesse."

"What do you mean, *Jesse*?" I protested.

"This is a job for a State Police Officer, and Derek has children."

We had not warned Bergdorf we were coming because we wanted to surprise him. We found him in the editorial offices of the *New York Literary Review*. He ushered us into his untidy office.

"I just heard about Stephanie," he said immediately. "Such a tragedy! Do you have any leads?"

"A possible one, which may have something to do with you," Derek said. It was clear that he had lost none of his flair—even after twenty years out of the field.

"Me?" Bergdorf said, turning pale.

"Stephanie got herself hired at the *Chronicle* so that she could discreetly carry out an investigation into the quadruple murder in 1994. She was writing a book about it."

"I had no idea. I'm amazed. But that does explain why she would choose to take such a step down in her career."

"We know the idea for the book was suggested to Stephanie by someone who was in Orphea on the night of the murders. More specifically, was in the Grand Theater. Where were you at the time of the murders, Mr Bergdorf? I'm sure you remember."

"It's true, yes, I was in the Grand Theater. Like everyone in Orphea that night! But I never talked about it with Stephanie, it didn't really matter that much to me."

"You were the editor of the *Chronicle* and you resigned in the days following the murders. There's also the book you wrote about the festival, a festival that Stephanie was especially interested in. That makes a lot of connections, don't you think? Mr Bergdorf, did you commission Stephanie Mailer to investigate the 1994 murders and write a book about them?"

"I swear I did not! Why would I have done something like that?"

"When was the last time you were in Orphea?"

"I went there for a weekend in May last year, at the invitation of the town council. I hadn't been back since 1994. Frankly, I have had no ties in Orphea since I left. I settled in New York, met my wife here, and continued my career as a journalist."

"Why did you leave Orphea just after the murders?"

"Actually, it was because of Mayor Gordon."

With these words, Bergdorf plunged us back twenty years into the past.

"Joseph Gordon was a fairly mediocre man, personally and professionally," he said. "He was a failed businessman. His companies had all collapsed and he only went into politics when the opportunity to become mayor presented itself. He was attracted to the post because of the salary that went with it."

"How did he manage to get elected?"

"He was a smooth talker, he could make a good surface impression. He would have sold snow to the Eskimos, but he wouldn't have been able to deliver the goods, if you see what I mean. By the time of the mayoral election in 1990, the town of Orphea was not doing well financially, in fact things were looking dire. Gordon told people what they wanted to hear and he was elected. But very soon, people saw what a second-rate politician he was and didn't think much of him."

"Second-rate, maybe," I said, "but Mayor Gordon did create the theater festival, and that's had a major impact on the town."

"It wasn't Mayor Gordon who created the festival, Captain Rosenberg. It was his deputy, Alan Brown. Very soon after he was elected, Mayor Gordon realized he needed help in running Orphea. At the time, Alan Brown, who was raised locally, had just gained his law degree. He agreed to become deputy mayor, which was a significant first position for someone who'd only recently graduated. It didn't take Brown long to show what an intelligent man he was. He did everything he could to relaunch the town's economy. And he succeeded. The good years that followed the election of President Clinton helped a lot, but Brown had laid the groundwork with all his ideas. He boosted tourism enormously, then there were the Fourth of July celebrations, the annual fireworks display, help with setting up new businesses, the refurbishment of Main Street."

"And he was promoted to mayor when Gordon died, is that right?" I said.

"Promoted, no, Captain. After Gordon's murder, Alan Brown deputized as mayor for barely a month. There was going to be an election in September 1994 anyway, and Brown had already planned to stand. He was elected with a big majority."

"Let's get back to Mayor Gordon," Derek said. "Did he have enemies?"

"He didn't follow a clear political line, so he put everybody's back up at one time or another."

"Including Ted Tennenbaum?"

"Not really. Sure, they quarreled about a building Ted wanted to turn into a restaurant, but that was no reason to kill a man and his family."

"Really?"

"Oh, yes. I never believed he could have done it for such a trivial reason!"

"Why didn't you say anything at the time?"

"To whom? To the police? Can you see me going to the station and calling an investigation into question? I imagine there must have been solid evidence. I mean, the poor guy did die. Not that I cared much, to be honest. I wasn't living in Orphea anymore. I followed the story from a distance. Anyway, to get back to what I was telling you. Alan Brown's desire to rebuild the town was a blessing to the small businessmen: the refurbishment of the town hall, the refurbishment of restaurants, the construction of a municipal library and various other new buildings. At least that was the official version. Because under cover of stating that he wanted to get the townspeople back to work, behind the scenes Mayor Gordon was asking them to overprice their services in return for obtaining the contract."

"Gordon was taking kickbacks?" Derek said.

"Oh, yes!"

"Why did nobody ever mention this when we were investigating?"

"What would you have wanted?" Bergdorf said. "For the contractors to own up? They were as guilty as the mayor. Why not confess to the Kennedy assassination while they were about it?"

"How did you find out?"

"The contracts were public. When the work was being done, you could look up the fees paid by the council to the various contractors. And the firms taking part in municipal construction projects also had to present their balance sheets to the council, which wanted to make sure that they wouldn't go bust while the work was being carried out. At the beginning of 1994, I arranged to get hold of the balance sheets of the chosen companies and compared them with the sums officially paid out by the council. In most cases, the sum paid by the council was lower than the one on the contract."

"How come nobody realized?" Derek said.

"I assumed there was one invoice for the council and one for accountants and the two sums did not correspond, but nobody, apart from me, thought to check."

"And you said nothing?"

"Well, I prepared an article for the *Chronicle* and I went to see Mayor Gordon to ask him for an explanation. And you know what he told me?"

* * *

Mayor Gordon read the article that Bergdorf had brought him. Gordon seemed calm while Bergdorf was the nervous one. At last, the mayor put the article down, looked up at Bergdorf, and said in an almost comical tone:

"What you've shown me here is very serious, my dear Steven. So there's corruption at the highest level in Orphea?"

"Yes, Mr Mayor."

"This is going to create quite a stir. Of course, you have copies of the contracts and the balance sheets to prove all this?"

"Yes, Mr Mayor."

"You've done a very thorough job. Congratulations. You know, my dear Steven, it's a remarkable coincidence that you should come to see me. I was planning to talk to you about a great project. I'm sure you're aware that in a few months' time we'll be celebrating the opening of our first theater festival?"

"Absolutely, Mr Mayor," Bergdorf replied, none too sure where Gordon was going with this.

"Well, I'd like you to write a book about the festival. A little book in which you go behind the scenes and talk about the creation of the festival, all of it illustrated with photographs. It would appear just as the festival opens. It would make a souvenir to be treasured. The audiences will lap it up. By the way, Steven, what kind of fee would you ask for a job like that?"

"I . . . I don't know, Mr Mayor. I've never done anything like it before."

"In my opinion, it should be about $100,000."

"You . . . you'd pay me $100,000 to write this book?"

"Yes, that strikes me as normal for a writer of your calibre. On the other hand, obviously, it wouldn't be possible if an article were to appear in the *Chronicle* about the handling of the municipal accounts. Because then the accounts would be subject to scrutiny and people wouldn't understand my paying you such a sum. You see what I mean . . ."

*   *   *

"And you wrote the book!" I said. The book that Betsy and I had found at Springfield's. "You took the bribe."

"Oh, no, Captain Rosenberg!" Bergdorf said. "No insults, please! I could hardly refuse an offer like that. How could I? It was an opportunity to make a little money. I could have bought myself a house with it. Unfortunately, I was never paid, because that idiot Gordon got himself murdered before I could get my hands on the money. To stop me turning against him once I had my $100,000, he told me he'd pay me after the book was published. Two days after Gordon died, I went to see Alan Brown, who was standing in as mayor. There was no written contract between Gordon and me, and I didn't want our agreement to end on the scrapheap. I supposed Brown was in on it, but I soon realized he knew nothing. He was so stunned that he asked me to resign with immediate effect. If I didn't, he would go to the police. He told me he wouldn't tolerate a corrupt journalist on the *Chronicle*. I had no choice but to leave, and that's how that cockroach Bird ended up as editor, even though he writes like an amateur!"

*　　*　　*

In Orphea, Charlotte Brown, the mayor's wife, had somehow managed to tear her husband away from his office and take him out to lunch at Café Athena. He struck her as terribly tense and nervous. He barely slept, ate hardly anything, and his features were drawn. She had thought that a lunch in the sun on the terrace would do him a lot of good. The initiative was a success: Brown, having assured her that he didn't have time for lunch, had finally let himself be persuaded. The break did seem to do him good. The respite was short-lived, though: his cell phone started vibrating on the table and when he saw the name of the person calling him, he looked worried. He moved away from the table to answer.

Charlotte Brown could not catch the gist of the conversation, but she heard a few outbursts and saw extreme agitation in her husband's gestures. She heard him suddenly say in an almost imploring voice,

"Don't do that, I'll find a solution," before hanging up and coming back, furious, just as a waiter was serving the desserts they had ordered.

"I have to go to the town hall," Brown said.

"Already? At least eat your dessert. It can wait a quarter of an hour, can't it?"

"I have a problem, Charlotte. That was the manager of the company that's due to perform the main play in the festival. He says he's heard about the strike and the actors are afraid for their safety. They've decided to withdraw. I don't have a play. It's a disaster."

He left the restaurant, not noticing the woman sitting at a table with her back to him since the beginning of his lunch, who had heard the whole conversation. She waited for Charlotte Brown to also leave, then picked up her phone.

"Is that Michael Bird? This is Sylvia Tennenbaum. I have some information about the mayor that should interest you. Can you drop by Café Athena?"

*   *   *

When I had asked Bergdorf where he was on the night Stephanie Mailer had gone missing, he had assumed an offended air and replied, "I was at a private view, and you can check that, Captain." Which we did, as soon as we got back to Betsy's office in the police station.

The gallery that had organized the event confirmed that Mr Bergdorf had been there, but pointed out that the private view had ended at 7.00 p.m.

"Leaving Manhattan at seven, he could have been in Orphea by ten," Betsy said.

"Do you think he could have killed Stephanie?" I said.

"Bergdorf is familiar with the editorial offices of the *Chronicle*. He would have known how to get in there to steal the computer. He also knew that Bird was the editor, which is why he sent him the text message from Stephanie's cell phone. Plus, he might have been afraid that someone in Orphea would recognize him. That's why he finally gave up on the idea of meeting with Stephanie at the Kodiak Grill and arranged to meet her on the beach. Remind me why we didn't book him earlier?"

"Because this is all speculation, Betsy," Derek said. "We don't have anything to go on. A lawyer would pull it apart in minutes. We don't really have anything against him. Even if he had been alone in his own home, it'd be impossible to prove it. And besides, his lousy alibi is an indication that he doesn't know what time Stephanie was murdered."

Derek was not wrong about that. Nevertheless I stuck a photograph of Bergdorf on the whiteboard.

"I still think Bergdorf was the person who commissioned Stephanie's book," Betsy said.

She took extracts from the text found in the computer, which we had stuck on the board, and said:

"When Stephanie asks the sponsor why he doesn't write the book himself, he replies: 'Me? Impossible! What would people say?' So it must have been someone who would have no credibility as author of the book and entrusted it to someone else."

I then read the following extract:

"*Just before seven, I went out onto the street to get a breath of fresh air and saw a van drive by. Sometime afterward, reading the newspapers, I realized it was Tennenbaum's vehicle. The problem is, it wasn't him at the wheel.* Well, Bergdorf did tell us he had doubts about Tennenbaum's guilt. And he was in the Grand Theater that night."

"We have to find out who was driving that van," Betsy said.

"What I wonder," Derek said, "is why Mayor Brown never told anyone that Mayor Gordon was corrupt. If we'd known at the time, it would have changed the course of the investigation. And if the money Gordon transferred to Montana came from the kickbacks he was getting from the contractors, then why the cash withdrawals made by Tennenbaum that he could never account for?"

There was a long silence. Seeing Derek and me at a loss, Betsy asked:

"How did Tennenbaum die?"

"He died while he was being arrested," I said bleakly.

Derek changed the subject. "Let's go get a bite to eat," he said. "We never had lunch. I'm paying."

*　　*　　*

Mayor Brown had come home unusually early. He needed peace and quiet to think through the various scenarios that would come into play if the festival were canceled. He paced up and down the living room, a concentrated look on his face. Charlotte, watching him from a distance, could sense how nervous he was. At last she went to him and tried to reason with him.

"Alan, darling," she said, tenderly running her hand through his hair, "maybe this is a sign you should give up on the festival? It's getting you in such a state . . ."

"How can you say that? You used to be an actress, you know what it means! I need your support."

"But I think it may be fate. The festival's been losing money for a long time."

"The festival has to take place, Charlotte! The town depends on it."

"But what are you going to do to replace the main play?"

He sighed. "I don't know. I'm going to be a laughingstock."

"It'll work out, Alan, you'll see."

"How?"

She had no idea. She had only said it to cheer him up. She applied herself to finding a solution. "I . . . I'm going to reach out to my contacts in the theater!"

"Your contacts? Darling, that's sweet of you, but you haven't set foot on a stage in twenty years. You don't have any contacts, not anymore."

He put an arm around his wife and she leaned her head on his shoulder.

"It's a disaster," he said. "Nobody wants to come to the festival. Not the actors, not the media, not the critics. We sent out dozens of invitations and nobody replied. I even wrote to Meta Ostrovski."

"Ostrovski of the *New York Times*?"

"Ex-*New York Times*. He works for the *New York Literary Review* now. It's better than nothing. But I didn't get an answer from him either. We're less than three weeks from opening night and the festival's on the verge of collapse. Maybe I should just set fire to the theater and—"

"Alan, don't say such things!"

Just then, the doorbell rang.

"Maybe that's him," Charlotte joked.

"Are you expecting someone?" Alan said, in no mood for humor.

"No."

He went to the door. It was Michael Bird.

"Hello, Michael."

"Hello, Mr Mayor. Sorry to bother you at home, I've been trying desperately to call you on your cell phone, but it's off."

"I needed a little peace and quiet. What's going on?"

"I wanted your comment on the rumor, Mr Mayor."

"What rumor?"

"That you don't have a main play for the theater festival."

"Who told you that?"

"I'm a journalist."

"Then you should know how worthless rumors are."

"I quite agree with you, Mr Mayor. That's why I took the trouble to call the company's manager, who confirmed that the show has been canceled. He told me the cast don't feel safe in Orphea anymore."

"That's ridiculous," Brown said, keeping his composure. "And if I were you, I wouldn't publish it."

"Oh? Why not?"

"Because . . . you'd be making a fool of yourself!"

"*I'd* be making a fool of myself?"

"That's right. I've already got around the problem of that first company pulling out."

"Really? Why haven't you announced it yet?"

"Because . . . because what I'm putting in its place is something

185

really major," Brown said without thinking. "Something unique! Something that'll be such a sensation, the audience will come running. I want to make a proper announcement, not just dash off a press release that nobody will notice."

"And when are you going to make this crucial announcement?"

"This Friday. Yes, that's right, this Friday, July 11, I'll hold a press conference at the town hall, and believe me, what I announce then will be a surprise to everyone!"

"Well, thank you for that information, Mr Mayor, I'll put it all in tomorrow's issue," Bird said, eager to see if the mayor was bluffing or not.

"Please do that," Brown said in a tone he was trying hard to keep confident.

Bird nodded and made to go. But Brown couldn't help adding:

"Don't forget it's the council that subsidizes your paper by not charging you rent, Michael."

"What are you trying to say, Mr Mayor?"

"That you shouldn't bite the hand that feeds you."

"Are you threatening me, Mr Mayor?"

"I'd never do that. I'm just giving you a piece of friendly advice."

Bird nodded goodbye and left. Brown closed the door and clenched his fist in anger. He felt a hand on his shoulder: Charlotte. She had heard everything and now looked at him fearfully.

"A big announcement?" she said. "But what are you going to announce, darling?"

"I have no idea. I have two days for a miracle to happen. Otherwise I'll be announcing my resignation."

-5

The Darkest Night

WEDNESDAY, JULY 9 – THURSDAY, JULY 10, 2014

From the front page of the *Orphea Chronicle*, Wednesday, July 9, 2014:

MYSTERY PLAY FOR THE OPENING OF THE THEATER FESTIVAL

In a change of program, the mayor will make an announcement on Friday about the play to be performed on opening night. He is promising a spectacular production that is expected to make this 21st festival one of the most memorable in its history.

I put down the newspaper as my plane landed in Los Angeles. It was Betsy who had given me her copy of the *Chronicle* when Derek and I had met with her in the morning to take stock of the situation.

"Here," she had said, handing me the paper, "it'll be something to read on the flight."

I had smiled on reading the front page before slipping it into my bag. "Either the mayor is a genius, or he's up to his neck in shit."

Betsy had laughed. "I'd put my money on the second option."

It was one in the afternoon in California. I had taken off from New York mid-morning, and, despite a six-and-a-half-hour flight, the magic of the time difference still left me a few hours before my meeting with Hayward. I wanted to put them to good use by trying to work out what Stephanie had come here to do. My return flight was booked for the following afternoon. I had only twenty-four hours.

Following procedure, I had informed the California Highway Patrol—the equivalent there of the State Police—of my visit. An officer answering to the name of Cruz had come to pick me up from the airport. He would be at my disposal for the duration of my stay. I asked Sergeant Cruz if he could drive me straight to the hotel where, according to her credit card bill, Stephanie had stayed. It was a stylish Best Western, no distance from the Beluga Bar. It was an expensive place. Money had clearly not been a problem on this journey. Someone had financed her trip. Who? Her mystery backer?

The hotel's receptionist immediately recognized Stephanie when I showed him her photograph.

"I remember her well," he said.

"Was there something in particular that struck you?"

"A pretty, nicely dressed young woman always strikes you. But I was especially impressed because she was the first writer I had ever met."

"Did she tell you she was a writer?"

"Yes, she said she was writing a mystery novel based on a true story, and that she'd come here to look for answers."

Sergeant Cruz drove me to the Beluga Bar. We arrived around half an hour early. Behind the counter, a young woman was wiping glasses. She asked if there was anything she could help us with. When I mentioned the name Kirk Hayward, she gave an amused smile.

"Kirk?" she said, polishing a glass that was already dazzling. "Take a seat. He usually comes by around this time. What can I get you? It's on the house."

I turned to Sergeant Cruz, who shrugged, then ordered two black coffees.

"I'll bring them over," the young woman said, gesturing towards a booth.

We sat down and Cruz spread out a newspaper on the table and buried his nose in the crossword puzzle. I started to flick through a copy of the *L.A. Times* I had picked up in the airport, but I was distracted by thoughts of Stephanie Mailer. If she had come all the way to L.A. to see Kirk Hayward, what was it she thought he knew about the 1994 murders?

Half an hour later, right on time, a man who was just about recognizable as Kirk Hayward came into the bar. He headed straight for a booth right across from where we were sitting and at once took a sheaf of paper out of a leather satchel, placing it carefully on the table.

I got up and went over to greet him.

"Hello, Kirk. I'm Jesse Rosenberg. Do you remember me?"

His eyes narrowed, then he shook his head.

"Captain Rosenberg," I went on, "New York State Police. We worked together twenty years ago, investigating a quadruple murder."

His face suddenly lit up. "Of course! You haven't changed, Rosenberg. What brings you here?"

"You spoke with Deputy Betsy Kanner of the Orphea police department. She's the one who sent me."

"Right," he said. "Deputy Kanner." He looked a little disappointed. "I thought she'd be flying out here herself."

"We're working together on a case," I said. "Could we sit down?"

He nodded, but with little enthusiasm. As he slid into the booth, he swept his papers off the table and placed them on the seat beside him, but not before I'd had a chance to glance at the words on the top page of the pile.

THE DARKEST NIGHT
A Play by Kirk Hayward

Wherever we went, these three words kept cropping up. I had already suspected that Hayward had something to hide. Now I was sure of it. But when I had settled in the booth, I didn't mention his play, but instead asked him about Stephanie Mailer.

"Stephanie Mailer?" Hayward said. "Yes, I met with her right here. She said she was writing a book about the 1994 murders in Orphea. Why do you want to talk to me?"

"She's dead. She was murdered."

"Hell!"

"I think she died because of what she discovered about those murders. What exactly did you tell her?"

"That I was sure you had gotten the wrong man."

"So it was you who put that idea in her head? But why didn't you tell us that during the investigation?"

"I didn't realize it until later."

"Was that when you left Orphea in such a hurry?"

"I can't tell you anything. Not yet."

"What do you mean, not yet?"

"You'll understand. When the time is right."

"Listen, Hayward, I've come two and a half thousand miles to see you."

"You needn't have come. I can't risk compromising my play."

"Your play? What does your 'Darkest Night' mean? Is it connected to what happened in 1994? I need to know exactly what happened on the evening of July 30. Who killed the mayor and his family? And I need to know why you ran away."

Just then I heard an embarrassed cough and turned to see Sergeant Cruz standing a little distance from the table, holding up the copy of the *Chronicle* Betsy had given me for the flight.

"Sorry, Captain," he said, coloring at the cheeks. "I finished my crossword. Mind if I make a start on this one?"

I raised my hand to wave him away, but Hayward was already half out of his seat.

"Is that the *Orphea Chronicle*?" he said, a look of childish excitement spreading across his face. "That brings back a few memories. Can I take a look?"

I scowled at Cruz, who looked crestfallen as he approached the table to hand the paper over.

Hayward unfolded it and glanced at the front page.

MYSTERY PLAY FOR THE OPENING OF THE THEATER FESTIVAL

"I don't believe it!" he cried.

"What's the matter?"

"What is this mystery play?"

"I don't know. To tell the truth, I don't think the mayor himself knows."

"What if this is the sign? The sign I've been waiting for for twenty years?"

"The sign of what?"

Hayward grabbed me by the shoulders. "I want to have 'The Darkest Night' put on at the festival in Orphea!"

"But the festival is in two weeks. How can you be ready to perform it in two weeks?"

"You don't understand."

"Understand what?"

"If I can put on 'The Darkest Night' you'll get the answers to your questions."

"About the murder of the mayor?"

"Yes, you'll know everything. On opening night, the whole truth about this business will be revealed!"

I telephoned Betsy. "Hayward says if he is allowed to put on this play of his, he'll tell us who killed Mayor Gordon."

"You mean he knows?"

"So he says."

"Is he bluffing?"

"Strangely enough, I don't think so. When he saw the front page of the *Chronicle* his reaction was immediate. He offered to tell me the truth if we let him perform his damn play."

"It's possible he's crazy. Maybe he killed the mayor and his family and he's at last going to own up to it."

"That never occurred to me."

"Tell Hayward it's a deal. I'll make sure he gets what he wants."

"Are you sure?"

"Yes. You need to bring him back here. If the worst comes to the worst we'll have him arrested, he'll be under our jurisdiction, and he'll have to talk."

"O.K.," I said. "Let me ask him."

I went back to Hayward.

"I'm on the line with the deputy police chief of Orphea. She says it's a deal."

"Do you take me for a fool?" Hayward said coldly. "Since when have the police decided on the program of the festival? I want a handwritten letter from the Mayor of Orphea."

*　　*　　*

With the time difference, it was after 8 p.m. on the east coast. Betsy had no choice but to go and see Mayor Brown at home, who at that moment was in his study, rereading the resignation speech he would make to his colleagues. He had not found anything to replace the opening play. The other companies he had considered were all amateur and too modest to attract an audience big enough to fill Orphea's Grand Theater. He could not bear the thought that three-quarters of the tickets might remain unsold, which would be disastrous for the town's finances. It was decided: tomorrow morning, Thursday, he would gather all the staff of the town hall and share with them the news of his standing down. On Friday, he would gather the press as planned and the news would be made public.

He was reading his speech out loud: "Ladies and gentlemen, it is with a heavy heart that I have gathered you all here to announce that the Orphea Theater Festival will not be taking place this year. You know how attached I was to this event, both personally and politically. I have not succeeded in making the festival the unmissable 'occasion' that would have restored the prestige of our town. I have failed in what should have been the major project of my mandate. It is therefore with a great deal of emotion that I must announce to you that I am resigning as mayor of the town of Orphea. I wanted you to be the first to know. I am counting on your total discretion. I do not want this news to be made public before Friday's press conference."

He felt almost relieved. He had been too ambitious, for himself, for Orphea, for this festival. When he had launched the project, he had been only the deputy mayor. He had imagined he would make it one of the major cultural events of the state, then of the country. The theatrical equivalent of the Sundance Festival. But it had been nothing but a magnificent failure.

Just then, the doorbell rang. He walked to the door. Charlotte was coming down the stairs. He looked through the peephole and saw that it was Betsy, in uniform.

"Alan," she said, "I'm really sorry to bother you at home. I wouldn't have come if it wasn't very important."

A few moments later, in the Browns' kitchen, Charlotte, who was making tea, couldn't get over the name she had just heard.

"Kirk Hayward?" she said.

"What does that lunatic want?" Brown said, visibly impatient.

"He's written a play and he'd like to put it on it at the festival. In return, he—"

Betsy did not have time to finish her sentence. Brown had already leaped out of his chair, the color suddenly back in his face.

"A play? Sure! Do you think he could fill the Grand Theater several nights in a row?"

"You know, I think he just might. In return for being able to perform his play, Hayward says he will give us crucial information about the 1994 murders, and very possibly about Stephanie Mailer's death, too. On opening night at the Theater itself."

"Darling," Charlotte Brown said softly, "don't you think—"

"I think it's a gift from heaven!" her husband said triumphantly.

"He has a few demands," Betsy said, unfolding the sheet of paper on which she had taken notes. "He's asking for a room in a good hotel, all his expenses to be paid, and he wants the Grand Theater to be placed at his disposal for the rehearsals. He also wants a written agreement signed by you. That's why I've come over here out of hours."

"Is he also asking for a fee?" Brown said.

"Apparently not."

"Amen! Then I'm fine with all of this. If we can put this in the form of an agreement, I'll sign it. Tell Hayward he'll be the main attraction of the festival! I need him to take the first flight to New York tomorrow. Can you give him that message? It's imperative that he's by my side on Friday morning for the press conference."

"I'll tell him."

Brown took a pen and paper and wrote out a brisk paragraph, followed by his signature.

"There you are, Betsy. That's my undertaking. It's up to you now."

Betsy left, but did not immediately walk down the front steps after Brown had closed the door behind her. She stayed there, eavesdropping on the conversation between the mayor and his wife.

"You're crazy to trust Hayward!" Charlotte said.

"Come on, darling, this is better than we could have hoped!"

"He's coming back here, to Orphea! Don't you realize what that means?"

"He's going to save my career, that's what it means."

*   *   *

My telephone rang at last.

"Jesse," Betsy said, "the mayor agrees. He's signed off on Hayward's conditions. He wants both of you to be in Orphea on Friday morning for a press conference."

I passed the message on to Hayward.

"Hell, yes!" he cried in excitement. "A press conference. Can I see the signed letter? I want to be certain you're not conning me."

"It's all in order," I said. "Betsy has the letter with her."

"Then get her to fax it to me!"

"Fax it to you? Hayward, who still uses fax these days? I'll get her to send a photograph of it."

*

One call and a couple of minutes later, Hayward read the letter on my cell.

"It's wonderful!" he said, handing it back. "'The Darkest Night' is going to be performed!"

Something about his delight at the prospect was rubbing me up the wrong way. I had come here to get the truth about Stephanie Mailer, not to give Hayward his shot at fame. "Hayward," I said nastily. "What have you been doing out here the last twenty years, anyway? Not writing this play the whole time, I suppose?"

If Hayward caught the note of sarcasm he didn't let on. He just smiled.

"Not at all. If you must know, I've made something of a name for myself in L.A. I left the force to write, and that's what I've been doing. Some scripts here and there, and a lot of editing. I'm the go-to guy for quite a few studios now. Beats police work, I can tell you that."

"Yeah? Anything I'd have heard of?"

"Oh, definitely," he said with another smile, but he did not elaborate.

"Look," I said with a sigh, "now that you have a guarantee your play will be performed in Orphea, can you tell me what you know about the Gordon killings?"

"On opening night, you'll find out everything!"

"Opening night is July 26. We can't wait that long. A whole police investigation depends on you."

"Nothing before opening night."

I said nothing to that, just shook my head before gathering my things and leaving the bar with Cruz. It was no surprise that Hayward had been left with so few friends on the force in Orphea. But I consoled myself that getting him to come back to the Hamptons was a step forward.

DEREK SCOTT

Late August 1994. A month had gone by since the murders. The vise was closing in on Tennenbaum. The suspicions Jesse and I already had were now supplemented by our knowledge of the pressure exerted by the mayor putting the timely completion of the work on Café Athena at serious risk.

Even though Tennenbaum's withdrawals and Mayor Gordon's deposits coincided, both in the amounts and as to the dates, they did not constitute full proof. We wanted to question Tennenbaum on the nature of his withdrawals, but above all we did not want to commit any blunders. So we summoned him officially, by mail, to troop headquarters. As we had anticipated, he came with his lawyer.

Tennenbaum laughed when he heard our story. "You think Mayor Gordon was putting the squeeze on me? This is getting more and more absurd, Sergeant Scott."

"Mr Tennenbaum," I said, "during the same period of time, an identical sum of money, give or take a few thousand dollars, left your account and went into Mayor Gordon's account."

"You know what, Sergeant?" Robin Starr said. "Every day millions of Americans unwittingly make similar transactions."

"Tell us what these withdrawals correspond to, Mr Tennenbaum." Jesse said. "Half a million isn't peanuts. And we know it wasn't for work on your restaurant; that's another account we've had access to."

"You've had access to it thanks to my client's goodwill," Starr said. "What Mr Tennenbaum does with his money is nobody else's business."

"Why don't you just tell us how you spent that money, Mr Tennenbaum, if you have nothing to hide?"

"I like going out," Tennenbaum said, "I like eating in restaurants, I like living. I don't have to justify myself."

"Do you have receipts to back up what you're telling us?"

"What if I spent the money on lots of girlfriends? The kind of girlfriends who don't give receipts? But enough of this mockery, gentlemen, that money's legal, I inherited it from my father. I can do what I like with it."

We had no choice but to accept that we would get nothing more from him.

Major McKenna told Jesse and me that we had a whole bunch of things that pointed to Tennenbaum, but no single solid thing that would nail him. "So far, Tennenbaum doesn't need to do anything to refute the weight of your evidence against him. You can't prove that his van was on the street, you can't prove the pressure from Mayor Gordon. Find something that'll force Tennenbaum to show his hand."

We went over our investigation from the beginning. There had to be something we had overlooked somewhere. In Natasha's living room, which had been entirely refurnished in the course of our investigation, we again pored over our notes, and still everything pointed to Tennenbaum.

Our focus was divided between two restaurants, Café Athena and Little Russia. Darla and Natasha's project was making great progress. They were cooking all day long, testing recipes that they then recorded in a big red book for possible inclusion on their menu. Jesse and I were the first beneficiaries. Every time we walked in, at any hour of the day or night, something was happening in the kitchen. There was even a brief diplomatic incident when I mentioned Natasha's sandwiches.

"Please tell me you're planning to include those incredible braised meat sandwiches on the menu."

"You tried them?" Darla said, aghast.

Natasha tried to limit the damage. "When they went to Montana last week, I gave Jesse some sandwiches for the flight."

"We agreed we'd let them taste everything together, the two of us, to see their reactions," Darla said.

"I felt bad about them taking a plane at dawn . . ."

I thought that was the end of it, but Darla mentioned it again a few days later, when we were alone.

"You know, Derek," she said, "I can't get over the fact that Natasha did something like that to me."

"Are you still talking about those damn sandwiches?"

"It may be nothing to you, but when you have a partner and your trust is broken, that makes it hard to work together."

"Don't you think you're exaggerating, Darla?"

"Whose side are you on, Derek? Mine or hers?"

I think Darla, wonderful as she was, was a little jealous of Natasha. But I imagine all the girls were jealous of Natasha at one time or another. She was smarter, prettier, and had more presence than anyone. When she entered a room, she was the only person anyone looked at.

As far as the investigation was concerned, Jesse and I concentrated on what we could prove. One thing in particular stood out: Tennenbaum's absence from the Grand Theater for a period of at least twenty minutes. According to him, he had not gone anywhere. So it was up to us to prove that he was lying. And on that point, we still had a margin for maneuver. We had questioned all the volunteers, but had not been able to speak with anyone from the company that had performed the opening play, since our suspicions had not turned to Tennenbaum until some time after the festival was over.

Unfortunately, the company, which was from the University of Albany, had disbanded in the meantime. Most of the students who had taken part had finished their courses and were scattered around the country. In order not to waste time, Jesse and I decided to concentrate on those who still lived in New York State, and we divided up the work.

It was Jesse who hit the jackpot when he questioned Buzz Lambert, the company's director, who was still teaching summer courses at the University of Albany.

When Jesse mentioned Ted Tennenbaum, Lambert immediately said:

"Did I notice any strange behavior in the fire officer on duty on opening night? The thing that I mainly noticed is that he wasn't doing his job. There was an incident in one of the dressing rooms, around seven. A hair dryer that caught fire. We couldn't find the guy, so I had to deal with it myself. Luckily, there was a fire extinguisher."

"The fire officer was nowhere to be found on the premises at seven o'clock?"

"That's right. When I saw the fire, I called for help and the actors who were in the next dressing room came running. They'll confirm that. As for that fire officer, I gave him a piece of my mind when he magically reappeared half an hour later."

"So the fire officer was away until 7.30?"

"That's correct."

JESSE ROSENBERG

Thursday, July 10, 2014
Sixteen days to opening night

While I was on my way back from California to Orphea, Betsy and Derek paid a visit to Buzz Lambert. He was living in New Jersey, where he was a drama teacher in a high school.

On the way there, Derek summed up the situation for Betsy.

"In 1994, there were two things that pointed to Tennenbaum: the parallel financial transactions, and his absence when there was a fire backstage at the Grand Theater. The possibility that he might have been absent looked crucial. One of the witnesses at the time, Lena Bellamy, who lived a few doors down from the Gordons, said she had seen Tennenbaum's van on the street when she heard the shots, whereas Tennenbaum claimed he had not left the theater where he was the duty fire officer. It was Ms Bellamy's word against his. But now Lambert, the director, had stated that just before the start of the performance, a hair dryer caught fire in one of the dressing rooms and they hadn't been able to find Tennenbaum."

"So if Tennenbaum wasn't in the Grand Theater," Betsy said, "it could have been because he had taken his van to drive to Mayor Gordon's house and kill the mayor and his family."

"Precisely."

In the living room where he received us, Lambert, now a balding man in his sixties, kept a framed poster of the 1994 show.

"A lot of people still remember 'Uncle Vanya' at the Orphea Festival. Don't forget, we were only a university drama group. The festival was in its infancy and the town council couldn't hope to attract a professional company. Nevertheless, our show was exceptional. For ten nights running, the Grand Theater was sold out, the critics were unanimous. It was a triumph. It was so successful that everyone thought the actors would go on to have professional careers."

It could be seen from the lively way the director talked about that period that for him it was a pleasant memory. As far as he was concerned, the Gordon killings had been nothing but a news item.

"And what happened?" Derek asked, curious. "Did the other members of the group make careers in the theater, like you?"

"No, nobody continued on that path. I can't blame them, it's such a difficult world. I know what I'm talking about—I wanted to be on Broadway and I ended up in a private high school in the suburbs. Just one person among them could have become a real star: Charlotte Carrell. She played Yelena, the wife of Professor Serebryakov. She was remarkable. When she was on stage she was magnetic. She had a kind of innocence and detachment that gave her a real presence. To be honest with you, we owed the success of the show to her. None of us could hold a candle to her."

"Why didn't she go on in the theater?"

"She didn't want to. She was in her final year in Albany, where she'd been studying to be a vet. The last I heard, she had opened a clinic for animals in Orphea."

"Wait," Betsy said, struck by a sudden realization. "The Charlotte you're talking about—could she be Charlotte Brown, now the wife of the mayor of Orphea?"

"Oh, yes. It was thanks to the play that they met. It was love at first sight. They were a wonderful couple. I was at their wedding, but over the years we've lost touch. Which is a pity."

"So Kirk Hayward's beautiful girlfriend in 1994," Derek said, "was Charlotte, the future wife of the mayor?"

"That's right. Didn't you know that, Sergeant?"

"No, I didn't."

"That Kirk Hayward was a cop with pretensions, an artist manqué. He had always wanted to be a playwright and a director."

"I was told his first play was quite a success."

"The real reason it was a success was because Charlotte was in it. Charlotte enhanced everything she was in. The play itself was not a masterpiece. But when Charlotte was onstage, she could read the telephone book and you'd be knocked out, it was so beautiful. I never could figure out what she was doing with a policeman like Hayward. It's one of the unexplained mysteries of life. We've all met stunning girls infatuated with guys as ugly as they were stupid. And this guy was so stupid, he couldn't even keep her."

"Were they together for long?"

Lambert took his time before replying. "A year, I think. Hayward was doing the rounds of the New York theaters and so was Charlotte. That's how they met. She acted in that famous first play of his, and its success went to his head. That was in the spring of 1993. I remember that because it was when we were starting to work on 'Uncle Vanya'. He got a big head, wrote another play. When the project of a theater festival in Orphea came up, he was convinced his play would be chosen as the main attraction. At the same time, I suggested 'Uncle Vanya' to the festival's artistic committee, and after several auditions our group was chosen."

"Hayward must have been mad at you."

"He said I'd betrayed him, that without him I wouldn't have thought to suggest our production to the festival. Which was true. But his play would never have been performed anyway. Even the mayor was against the idea."

"Mayor Gordon?"

"Yes. One day when he'd asked to see me in his office, I overheard a conversation between the two of them. It must have been mid-June. I'd arrived early and was waiting outside the door. Suddenly, Gordon threw the door open and said, 'Your play is not good enough, Kirk. You'll never put it on it in my town while I'm alive!' And right in front of everyone, he tore up the script of the play that Hayward had entrusted to him."

"The mayor said, 'While I'm alive'?"

"His exact words. In fact, when he was murdered, the whole company wondered if Hayward had been involved."

"Why did you never tell the police about that conversation between Mayor Gordon and Hayward?"

Lambert made a face. "What would have been the point? It would have been his word against mine. And besides, to be honest, I couldn't really see the guy murdering the whole family. On the phone, you said you wanted to talk about a particular incident."

"That's right, Mr Lambert," Derek said. "We're interested in a hair dryer that caught fire in one of the dressing rooms before the opening night of 'Uncle Vanya.'"

"Yes, that's right, I remember now. A detective asked me if the fire officer had behaved in any unusual way."

"That was my colleague at the time, Jesse Rosenberg."

"That's right, his name was Rosenberg. I told him the fire officer had seemed nervous. The main thing, though, was that when the hair dryer caught fire, he was nowhere to be seen. Fortunately, one of the actors found a fire extinguisher and got the fire under control before the whole dressing room could go up in smoke. It could easily have been a disaster."

"According to the report at the time, the fire officer didn't come back until 7.30."

"That's what I remember, but if you've read my testimony, why come see me now? It was twenty years ago. Are you hoping I can tell you anything more?"

"In the report, you say you were in the corridor, you saw smoke coming out from under the door of a dressing room, and you called the fire officer, but he wasn't to be found."

"I remember opening the door, saw the hair dryer smoking and about to catch fire. It all happened very quickly."

"That's understandable," Derek said. "But what struck me when I looked again at your testimony is why the person in the dressing room didn't do anything about the fire."

"Because the dressing room was empty," Lambert said, as if only just realizing this. "There was nobody there."

"But the hair dryer was on?"

"Yes," Lambert said, a troubled look on his face. "I don't know why that never struck me before. I was pretty much focused on the threat of a full-blown fire.

"Sometimes, we have something right in front of our eyes and we don't see it," Betsy said, half recalling those fateful words of Stephanie Mailer's.

"Tell me, Mr Lambert," Derek said, "whose dressing room was it?"

"Charlotte's," Lambert said immediately.

"How can you be so sure?"

"Because that faulty hair dryer was hers. She used to say that if she used it too much, it would overheat and start to smoke."

"Would she have left it to get too hot? And why?"

"Oh, no," Lambert said, summoning his memories. "There was a big power outage that night. There was a problem with the fuses, which couldn't support all the power necessary. It was around seven o'clock. I remember that because we were one hour from the beginning of the show and I was panicking because the technicians couldn't restore the power. It took quite a while, but finally they managed it, and, soon afterward, there was that little fire."

"That means Charlotte left her dressing room during the outage," Betsy said. "The hair dryer was plugged in, and started working again while she was absent."

"But if she wasn't in her dressing room, where was she?" Derek said. "Somewhere else in the theater?"

"If she'd been in the backstage area," Lambert said, "she would definitely have come running because of all the commotion. There was a lot of shouting, a lot of movement. But I do remember she came and complained to me at least half an hour later that her hair dryer had disappeared. I'm quite clear about that because by then I was terrified at the thought that we might not be ready in time for the start of the show. The official part of the evening had already started, and we couldn't afford to be late. Charlotte came into my dressing room and told me that someone had taken her hair dryer. I got angry and said to her, 'Your hair dryer got burned, it's in the garbage! Isn't your hair ready yet, and why are your shoes wet?' The shoes she was to wear on stage were soaked. As if she'd been walking through water. Thirty minutes before going on stage! You can imagine the state I was in."

"Her shoes were wet?" Derek said.

"Yes. I remember all these things because at the time I thought the show was going to be a disaster. What with the fuses blowing, that little fire, and my leading lady not yet ready and showing up with wet shoes, I could never have imagined the show would turn out to be such a huge success."

"And after that, everything went on smoothly?"

"Absolutely."

"When did you find out that Mayor Gordon and his family had been murdered?"

"There was some talk during the intermission, but we didn't really pay attention. I wanted my actors to concentrate on the play. When we started again, I noticed that some people in the audience had left, including Mayor Brown, which I particularly noticed because he'd been sitting in the front row."

"When exactly did he leave?"

"That I couldn't tell you. But if it might help in any way, I do have a videocassette of the play."

Lambert went and rummaged through a heap of relics on a bookcase and came back with an old V.H.S. cassette.

"We made a recording of the opening night as a souvenir. The quality isn't good, because of the technical limitations of the time, but it does capture some of the atmosphere. Just promise me I'll get it back. It means a lot to me."

"Of course," Derek said. "Thank you for your invaluable help, Mr Lambert."

Leaving Buzz Lambert's, Derek seemed preoccupied.

"What's the matter, Derek?" Betsy said as they got in the car.

"It's that thing about the shoes," he said. "On the night of the murders, the pipe in the Gordons' automatic sprinkler system was broken and the lawn in front of their house was soaked."

"Do you think Charlotte might have been involved?"

"We know now she wasn't in the theater around the time of the murders. If she was gone for half an hour, that would have given her plenty of time to get to Penfield and back while everybody thought she was in her dressing room. And I'm thinking again about those words of Stephanie Mailer's: something in front of our eyes that we didn't see. What if that night, when the Penfield neighborhood was cordoned off and roadblocks had been put up all around the region, the person who had committed those murders was actually on the stage of the Grand Theater in front of hundreds of people, using them as her alibi?"

"Do you think this video might help us get a better idea?"

"I dare hope so, Betsy. If it shows us the audience, we may be able to spot something that escaped us. I must admit that, at the time of our investigation, what happened during the show didn't seem all that interesting to us. The fact that we're looking at it now is down to Stephanie Mailer."

* * *

Meanwhile, in his office at the town hall, Alan Brown was listening less and less patiently to the doubts of his deputy, Peter Frogg.

"Kirk Hayward is your trump card for the festival? The former chief of police?"

"Peter, it seems his new play is really good."

"But what do you know about it? You haven't even read it! You're crazy to have promised 'a sensational play' in the press!"

"What else could I have done? Bird had me in a corner, I had to find a way out. Peter, we've been working together for twenty years. Have I ever given you occasion to doubt me?"

The door of the office opened, and a secretary shyly put her head inside.

"I asked not to be disturbed!" Mayor Brown said.

"I know that, Mr Mayor, but you have an unexpected visitor: a Mr Ostrovski."

"That's all we need!" Frogg said, aghast.

A few minutes later, Meta Ostrovski, all smiles, was sprawling in an armchair facing the mayor. He was pleased to have left New York to come to this charming town where he felt respected. But the mayor's first question upset him.

"Mr Ostrovski, would you mind telling me what you're doing here in Orphea?"

"Well, I was charmed by your invitation and I've come to witness your famous theater festival."

"But you know the festival doesn't start for another two weeks?"

Frogg, conscious of his boss' exasperation, took over. "The mayor would like to know if there's a reason for your coming—how shall I put it?—so prematurely."

"A reason for my coming? But you invited me yourselves. And now that I'm here, to show fraternal solidarity, you ask me what I'm doing here? If you'd prefer it, I'll go back to New York."

"Don't go anywhere, Mr Ostrovski! As it happens, I need you." Mayor Brown had suddenly had an idea.

"Ah, you see . . ."

"Tomorrow, Friday, I'm giving a press conference to announce the opening play of the festival. It's going to be a world premiere. I'd like you to be by my side and declare that it's the most extraordinary play you've ever been lucky enough to read in your career."

Ostrovski stared at the mayor, astonished by his request. "You want me to praise to the skies a play I've never seen?"

"Absolutely," Mayor Brown confirmed. "In return for which, I'll get you a suite at the Lake Palace, beginning tonight, and you can stay there until the end of the festival."

"Let's shake hands right now!" Ostrovski cried enthusiastically. "For a suite, I promise you the highest praise!"

When Ostrovski had left, Mayor Brown gave his deputy the task of arranging the critic's stay.

"A suite at the Palace for three weeks, Alan?" Frogg said. "That's going to cost us a fortune."

"Don't worry, Peter. We'll find a way to balance the books. If the festival is a success, my re-election will be assured and the citizens won't give a damn whether or not we went over the budget. We'll cut back on next year's festival if we have to."

*　　*　　*

In the Edens' apartment, Carolina was resting in her room. Lying on her bed, staring up at the ceiling, she was crying silently. She had finally been able to leave Mount Sinai Hospital and come home.

She could no longer remember what she had done after running away on Saturday. She vaguely recalled joining Leyla at a party, getting smashed on ketamine and alcohol, then wandering around various unfamiliar places, a club, an apartment, kissing a guy—a girl, too. She remembered finding herself emptying a bottle of vodka on the roof of a building, and approaching the edge to look down at the movement on the street below her. She had felt attracted by the void. She had wanted to jump, just to see what it was like. But she hadn't done it. Maybe that was the reason she had got smashed. To have the courage to do it one day. To disappear. To be at peace. Some police officers had woken her in an alley where she was sleeping soundly, in rags. According to the examinations the doctors had made her undergo, she had not been raped.

She was staring at the ceiling. A tear rolled over her cheek to the corner of her lips. How could she have gotten to this point? She had been a good pupil, gifted, ambitious, loved. She had had everything going for her. An easy life, with no problems, and parents who had been with her every step of the way. Everything she had wanted she had had. And then there had been Tara Scalini and the tragedy that had ensued. Since that episode, she had hated herself. She wanted to destroy herself.

She wanted to scratch her skin until it bled, to harm herself, so that all the world could see from her marks how much she hated herself and how much she was suffering.

Her father had his ear stuck to the outside of the door. He could not hear her breathing. He half opened the door. She immediately closed her eyes and pretended to be asleep. He walked to the bed, his steps muffled by the deep carpet, saw that her eyes were shut, and left the room. He crossed the vast apartment to the kitchen, where Cynthia was waiting for him, sitting on a high stool by the counter.

"Well?" she said.

"She's asleep." He poured himself a glass of water and leaned on the counter, facing his wife.

"What are we going to do?" Cynthia said desperately.

Eden sighed. "I don't know. Sometimes I tell myself there's nothing we *can* do. It's hopeless."

"Jerry, I don't recognize you anymore. She might have been raped! When I hear you talking like this, I get the feeling you've given up on your daughter."

"Cynthia, we've tried individual therapy, family therapy, gurus, hypnotists, every kind of doctor, everything! We've twice sent her to detox and both times it was a disaster. She doesn't seem like my daughter anymore. What do you want me to say?"

"You haven't tried, Jerry!"

"What do you mean?"

"Yes, you sent her to every possible doctor, you even went with her sometimes, but you yourself haven't tried to help her!"

"But what more could I do that the doctors couldn't?"

"What more could you do? Dammit, you're her father! You haven't always been like this with her. Have you forgotten how close you used to be?"

"You know perfectly well what's happened in the meantime, Cynthia!"

"Yes, I know, Jerry! That's why you have to mend it. You're the only one who can do that."

"And what about that girl who died?" Eden said, his voice choked. "Can we ever mend that?"

"Stop it, Jerry! We can't turn the clock back. Not me, not you, not anybody. Take Carolina away, I beg you, and save her. New York is killing her."

"Take her where?"

"Where we were happy. Take her to Orphea. Carolina needs a father, not a couple of parents who yell at each other all day long."

"We yell at each other because—"

Eden had raised his voice and his wife immediately placed her finger on his mouth to silence him.

"Save our daughter, Jerry. Only you can do that. She has to leave the city, get far away from her ghosts. Leave, Jerry, I beg you. Leave and come back to me. I want to see my husband again, I want to see my daughter again. I want to see my family again."

She burst into tears. Eden nodded, and she took her finger away from his lips. He left the kitchen and walked resolutely toward his daughter's room. He flung the door open and drew up the blinds.

"Hey, what are you doing?" Carolina protested, sitting up in bed.

"What I should have done a long time ago." He opened a drawer at random, then another, and searched them roughly.

Carolina leaped out of bed. "Stop! Stop, Daddy! Dr Lern said . . ."

She tried to get in between her father and the drawers, but Jerry pushed her aside with a vigorous gesture that surprised her.

"Dr Lern said you should stop getting high!" Eden roared, waving a sachet filled with whitish powder.

"Leave that!" she screamed.

"What is this? Fucking ketamine?"

Without waiting for an answer, he walked toward the en suite bathroom.

"Stop! Stop!" Carolina yelled at him, trying to recover the sachet from her father's hand, while he held her at a distance.

"What are you trying to do?" he said as he lifted the toilet lid. "To die? To end up in prison?"

"Don't do that!" she implored him, starting to cry—whether out of anger or sorrow was not clear.

He poured out the powder and flushed the toilet, while his daughter looked on, powerless.

"You're right!" she screamed. "I'm trying to die so that I don't have to put up with you anymore!"

Her father looked at her sadly and announced in a surprisingly calm voice:

"Pack your bags, we're leaving first thing tomorrow morning."

"What do you mean, *we're* leaving? I'm not going anywhere."

"I'm not asking for your opinion."

"Where the hell are we going?"

"Orphea."

"Orphea? What's gotten into you? I'm not going back there! And anyway I already made plans. Leyla has a friend who has a house in Montauk and—"

"Forget Montauk. Your plans just changed."

"What? No, you can't do this to me! I'm not a baby anymore, I can do what I want!"

"No, you cannot do what you want. I let you do what you wanted for far too long."

"Get out of my room at once and leave me alone!"

"You're my daughter, you're nineteen years old, and you're going to do what I tell you. And what I tell you is: pack your bags."

"What about Mom?"

"It'll be just you and me."

"Why should I go anywhere with you? I want to discuss it with Dr Lern first."

"No, there won't be any discussion with Lern, or with anybody. It's time we put limits on you."

"You can't do this to me! You can't force me to go away with you!"

"Yes, I can. Because I'm your father and I order you to do it."

"I hate you! I hate you, do you hear me?"

"I know you do, Carolina, you don't need to remind me. Pack your bags now. We're leaving first thing tomorrow morning." There was urgency in his tone.

He left the room resolutely, went and poured himself a Scotch, and drank it down in a few mouthfuls, gazing through the picture window at the spectacular night sky over New York.

PART TWO

Toward the Surface

-4

Secrets

JESSE ROSENBERG

Friday, July 11, 2014
Fifteen days to opening night

I was drinking a coffee with Derek while waiting for Betsy. We were at the marina in Orphea.

"So he wouldn't tell you anything?" Derek said. "Not even when you got him what he asked for?"

"Nothing. He told me that he's been thinking about this play for years and now that he has the chance to put it on he's not going to discuss it in any detail until the time is ripe. He said that all would be revealed on opening night, or some nonsense like that."

Betsy arrived a few minutes later, but she didn't sit down.

"Mayor Brown wants to see us," she said. "Before his press conference."

I downed the last of my coffee. "Let's go."

When we entered the mayor's office, he seemed in a good mood.

"I wanted to thank you, Captain Rosenberg," he said, motioning for us to sit, "for finding us a play for the festival. You've done this town a great service."

Derek and Betsy sat, but I remained standing.

"Thank you, Mr Mayor," I said, "but I can't pretend that I don't have concerns about Hayward. Betsy arranged for me fly out to L.A. because we had reason to believe he met with Stephanie Mailer before her death. But he refused to tell me what they discussed or what he knows until opening night. A woman has been murdered and Hayward wants us to wait two weeks! That's totally unsatisfactory in my view. Now that he's here, I think we should take him in for questioning."

Brown got to his feet, color rising to his cheeks. "Rosenberg. This man is all that's standing between us and canceling the festival. Don't you think he deserves the benefit of the doubt? That this town deserves it? We need him. Without a play we're sunk. All I'm asking is that you back off for two weeks. And, please . . . Be civil to Hayward."

Just then, over the intercom, Brown's secretary announced Kirk Hayward's arrival.

"Starting now, Rosenberg," Brown said, straightening his tie.

The office door opened and Hayward appeared.

"Chief Hayward," Brown said, shaking his hand. "Glad to see you back. You look well. I'm looking forward to hearing more about this play you're putting on for us." He gestured toward Betsy, Derek and me. "You know Captain Rosenberg, of course. And you may remember Sergeant Scott. But perhaps you haven't yet been introduced to Betsy Kanner, Deputy Police Chief here in Orphea."

"We spoke on the telephone," Betsy said, offering Hayward her hand.

"They were just leaving, as it happens," Brown said, shooting me a stern glance.

Moments later, Meta Ostrovski arrived at the mayor's office door. Entering the room, he looked Hayward up and down for a moment before introducing himself.

"Meta Ostrovski, the most famous and most feared critic in the country," Hayward said with a smile. "The play I'm putting on is going to have ramifications well beyond the festival, and, of course, I have every hope that it will please as distinguished a critic as you are, sir."

"Only a critic can decide what's good and what's bad. And my judgment will be unsparing!"

"Mr Ostrovski, you are going to say the play is terrific!" Mayor Brown advanced upon them. "We made a deal, and I require you to abide by it . . ."

Ostrovski scowled, but after a moment's pause murmured his assent.

Brown turned to Hayward. "Where's the cast?"

"I don't have one yet," Hayward said.

"What do you mean, you don't have a cast?"

"I'm going to cast the play here, in Orphea."

Brown opened his eyes wide in astonishment. "What do you mean, you're going to cast it here? The first night is in two weeks' time!"

"Don't worry, Alan. I'll prepare everything over the weekend. Auditions on Monday, first rehearsal on Thursday."

"Thursday?" Brown said in a choked voice. "But that'll leave you only nine days to rehearse a play that's going to be the centerpiece of the festival!"

"That's more than enough time. I've been thinking about the play for twenty years. Trust me: this play will cause such a stir, they'll be talking about your festival all over the country."

At that moment, one of the mayor's staff opened the inner door. "Mr Mayor, the press are all here and they're getting impatient."

Brown sighed. There was no way he could back down now. He had no alternative but to give Hayward all the support he could.

*　*　*

Bergdorf entered the town hall, announced himself at the reception desk, and asked directions to the press room. He had just arrived in Orphea. He had last been back for the festival the year before, when he had been inspired to write a rave article for the *Review*, titled "The Smallest of the Great Festivals", in which he urged readers to visit the town. No surprise then that he had been put on the council's mailing list. Yesterday he had been sent a reminder about the press conference that would be held the following day at eleven o'clock at the town hall, in the course of which the mayor was going to "*reveal the exceptional play which would be performed as a world premiere for the opening of the theater festival.*"

A municipal employee showed him the way, leading him to a room in which journalists were listening attentively as Mayor Brown finished his introduction:

". . . and that's why I'm very pleased to announce that 'The Darkest

Night', a brand-new creation by director Kirk Hayward, will be performed as a world premiere at our festival."

He was sitting at a long table, facing the auditorium. Bergdorf noticed, much to his astonishment, that Meta Ostrovski was on the mayor's left, and that on his right sat Kirk Hayward, who, the last time he had seen him, had been the town's chief of police. It was now Hayward's turn to speak.

"I've been working on 'The Darkest Night' on and off for many years alongside my Hollywood commitments, and I'm very proud that the public will at last get a chance to discover this gem, which is already arousing enormous enthusiasm among the country's most important critics, including the legendary Meta Ostrovski, who's right here and will be able to tell you how highly he rates this play."

Thinking about his vacation in the Lake Palace—paid for by the taxpayers of Orphea—Ostrovski smiled and nodded at the crowd of photographers snapping him.

"A great play, my friends, a very great play," he assured them. "A play of uncommon quality. You know that I don't hand out compliments lightly. But this is really something! A triumph of world theater!"

Bergdorf wondered what the hell Ostrovski was doing here.

Hayward, galvanized by the warm welcome he was getting, now resumed: "What makes this production so remarkable is that the play is going to be performed by a cast from the local population. I've always wanted to give a chance to the inhabitants of Orphea."

"An amateur cast and an unknown director!" Michael Bird raised his voice. "Mayor Brown is knocking it out the park!"

There was laughter, and a murmur ran around the room. Mayor Brown, determined to salvage what he could, declared:

"Kirk Hayward has come here, interrupting his work in L.A., to bring us a class act."

"What makes this play exceptional," Hayward said, "is that it's going to be the opportunity for some amazing revelations! There are things still to be said about the murders that took place here in 1994. By inviting me to put on my play, Mayor Brown will make it possible for the veil to be lifted, for the truth to be revealed."

The gathering was now spellbound.

"We have come to an understanding," Mayor Brown said—he would have preferred to remain silent about this detail, but he could see that it was a way to get the attention of the assembled press. "I have agreed with Mr Hayward, whom some of you will remember as Chief Hayward, that while we are proud to be putting on 'The Darkest Night', it is in addition our hope—indeed our expectation—that in the course of the play its author will reveal crucial information based on his own twenty-year study of the 1994 killings. It is my particular hope that the presentation of this play will lead the police to bring their investigation to a successful close.

"On opening night," Brown went on, "I hope there will be a very large audience to support a play that will allow the truth to be at last established."

At these words, there was a moment of stunned silence, at the end of which the journalists, sensing they had a priceless piece of news, burst into noisy movement.

Steven Bergdorf was deep in thought, a new gleam in his eyes. This whole idea of putting on a play in return for revelations about a criminal case was unique in the history of culture. His instinct told him to stay a while in Orphea.

Just as the conference was on the verge of breaking up, a journalist stood to address a question to Ostrovski. "Mr Ostrovski. You've read the play. If Mr Hayward won't share with us the sensational information it reveals, can you tell us who the killer was?"

Ostrovski smiled, ignoring the warning look from Brown. "My dear boy," he said to the journalist, "I would only be too happy to, but I'm afraid that certain passages were redacted."

Hayward cut in. "There's no point asking anyone else. Only I will have access to the secret the play will reveal. And I will not divulge anything until opening night."

*   *   *

In her office in the Orphea police station, Betsy had installed a T.V. and a V.H.S. player.

"We got a video of the 1994 play from the director Buzz Lambert," she told me. "We need to watch it. We hope it might show us something new."

"Was your visit to Lambert productive?" I asked.

"Very," Derek said enthusiastically. "First of all, Lambert described an altercation between Hayward and Mayor Gordon. Hayward wanted to perform his play during the festival and Gordon apparently said, 'You'll never perform that play while I'm alive.'"

"Do you think he could have killed the mayor?"

Derek was not convinced. "It seems beyond belief that he would kill the mayor and his family, and a woman out jogging, over a play."

"Hayward was chief of police," Betsy said. "Meghan would have recognized him coming out of the Gordon house and he would have had no choice but to kill her, too. It stands up."

"So on July 26," Derek said, "before his play opens, Hayward is going to take the mike and say: 'Ladies and gentlemen, I was the man who slaughtered everyone.'"

I laughed, imagining this scene. "Surely he isn't lunatic enough to pull a stunt like that."

Derek studied the whiteboard. "We know now that the mayor's money roughly corresponded to the many kickbacks paid by local businessmen, i.e., not by Ted Tennenbaum. But if his withdrawals were not intended for the mayor, I'd really like to know what Tennenbaum used that $500,000 for."

"There's also the question of his van being out on the street around the time of the murders," I said. "Our witness was in no doubt it was his van. Was Lambert able to confirm to you that Tennenbaum was absent from the Grand Theater at the time of the murders?"

"Yes, Jesse, he did confirm it. But Tennenbaum was not the only one to have disappeared for half an hour. Believe it or not, Charlotte, who was one of the actors in the company, and who was also Hayward's girlfriend—"

"The beautiful girlfriend who left him?"

"The very one. Well, according to Lambert she was gone from the theater from just before 7.00 until 7.30. And she came back with wet shoes."

"Wet like Mayor Gordon's lawn?" I said.

"Precisely," Derek said with a smile, amused that I remembered that detail. "Wait, that's not all. The same Charlotte left Hayward for Alan Brown. It was love at first sight and they ended up getting married. They still are."

"Damn!"

I stared at the papers we had found in the self-storage facility. There was an airline ticket for Los Angeles and the words *Find Kirk Hayward*. Well, we'd done that. But had Hayward told her more than he told me? My gaze next came to rest on the clipping from the *Chronicle*, including the front-page photograph, circled in red, showing Derek and me staring down at the sheet covering Meghan Padalin, outside Mayor Gordon's house, and, just behind us, Kirk Hayward and Alan Brown. They were looking at each other, maybe talking. I looked closer and noticed Brown's hand. It seemed to be forming the number 3. Was it a sign for someone? For Hayward? Beneath the photograph, Stephanie's words, in red pen: *What nobody saw.*

"What is it?" Derek said.

"What's the link between Hayward and Brown?" I said.

"Charlotte Carrell Brown."

"Charlotte Brown. I know at the time the experts said it must have been a man, but could they have been wrong? Could a woman have been the killer? Is that what we didn't see in 1994?"

Next we watched the video of the play. The image quality was not good, and the camera kept to the stage throughout, so the audience was not visible at all. But the recording started with the official part of the evening. We saw Deputy Mayor Alan Brown get up onstage, looking embarrassed, and approach the microphone. There's a moment of hesitation. Brown seems to be hot. After a pause, he unfolds a sheet of paper that he has taken from his inside jacket pocket, which presumably contains hastily made notes. "Ladies and gentlemen," he says, "I'm speaking to you in the place of Mayor Gordon, who's absent this evening. I admit I thought he would be among us, so unfortunately I haven't had time to prepare a real speech. So I'll limit myself to wishing a hearty welcome to . . ."

"Stop!" Betsy shouted at Derek. He paused the cassette, and the image froze. "Look!" We could see Alan Brown, alone on the stage, his sheet of paper in his hands. Betsy stood up from her chair and went and took one of the images from the board, something else found in the self-storage facility. It was exactly the same scene: Brown, at the microphone, the sheet of paper in his hands, which Stephanie had circled in red felt-tip.

"That image is from the video," Betsy said.

"Which means Stephanie saw this video," I said. "Who got it for her?"

Derek said, "Stephanie's dead, but she's still one step ahead of us. Why did she put a circle round that sheet of paper?"

We listened to the speech, but it was of no interest. Had Stephanie circled the sheet of paper in Brown's hand because of the speech or because of what was written on the paper?

*   *   *

Ostrovski was walking along Bendham Road. He could not reach Stephanie—her phone was still off. Had she changed numbers? Why wasn't she answering?

He decided to visit her at home. He counted the numbers of the houses, again checked the address, which he had written in a leather-bound notebook he always kept with him. He finally reached the building and stopped, aghast. It had been burned down and access was barred by police tape.

At that moment, he spotted a police patrol car coming slowly up the street and he signaled to the officer at the wheel.

Deputy Chief Montagne pulled up and lowered his window. "How can I help you, sir?"

"What happened here?"

"There was a fire. Why do you ask?"

"I'm looking for someone who lives here. Her name's Stephanie Mailer."

"Stephanie Mailer? She was murdered and her apartment was burned."

Ostrovski was struck dumb. Montagne got a radio call about an argument between a couple in the parking lot of the marina. He told the switchboard operator he would go straight there and switched on his flashing lights. A minute later, he got to the parking lot. In the middle of it, a black Porsche was parked, with both doors open, and a young girl was running toward the jetty, sluggishly pursued by a tall man old enough to be her father. Montagne sounded his siren. A flock of seagulls flew up and the couple froze. The girl looked amused.

"Oh, terrific, Carolina!" Eden cried. "Now the police are here! This has got off to a good start!"

"Orphea Police, don't move," Montagne said. "We got a call about a couple having an argument."

"A couple?" the man repeated as if astonished. "That's just terrific! This is my daughter!"

"Is this your father?" Montagne asked the girl.

"Unfortunately, yes."

"Where have you come from?"

"Manhattan."

Montagne checked their identities, then asked Carolina, "And why were you running like that?"

"I was trying to run away."

"Run away from what?"

"Life."

"Did your father assault you?"

"Me, assault her?" Eden cried.

"Please be quiet, sir," Montagne said curtly. "I am talking to the young lady."

He took Carolina aside and asked her the question again. She started crying.

"No, of course not. My father didn't touch me," she said between sobs.

"Then why are you in this state?"

"I've been in this state for a year."

"Why?"

"Oh, it'd take too long to explain."

Montagne did not insist and let them go.

"Stop messing around!" Eden yelled as he slammed the door of his car. A few minutes later, they were at the Lake Palace, where Eden had booked a suite, and a procession of porters installed them in room 308.

In the next suite, 310, Ostrovski sat on his bed, holding a picture frame in his hands. It was a photograph of a radiant young woman: Meghan Padalin. He gazed for a long time at the image, then whispered, "I'm going to discover who did that to you. I promise." He kissed the glass.

Meanwhile, in his hotel, Steven Bergdorf was deep in thought, a new gleam in his eyes. His instinct told him to stay a while in Orphea. He went out onto the balcony to telephone Skip Nalan, his deputy at the *Review*.

"I'll be away a day or so longer," he told him, and went on to describe what he had just witnessed. A former police chief who had become a theater director putting on his play in return for revelations about a twenty-year-old criminal case that everyone had assumed was over and done with. "I'm going to write an article from inside, everyone will be talking about it, I think we may even boost our sales."

"You think it's for real?" Nalan said. "Take all the time you need."

"For real? It's huge."

Bergdorf next called his wife and told her he would be away for a few more days for the reasons he had just given Nalan. After a moment's silence, Tracy asked, in a worried voice:

"Steven, what's going on?"

"This weird play, darling. I think we might just give the subscriptions a shot in the arm. God knows we need one."

"But a woman was murdered, Steven. I don't want you getting mixed up in anything dangerous."

"I promise I'll be careful. But I can't let this opportunity pass by."

She sighed. "Do what you have to do. But keep in touch. I need to know you're safe."

JESSE ROSENBERG

Saturday, July 12, 2014
Fourteen days to opening night

We had decided to give ourselves a break for the weekend. We needed to step back and take a breather. For the second week in succession, I spent Saturday in my kitchen, working on my sauce and my hamburgers.

Derek took the opportunity to spend time with his family.

As for Betsy, she could not get our case out of her mind. I think she was particularly troubled by Lambert's revelations about Charlotte Brown. Where had Charlotte gone on opening night in 1994? And why? What was she hiding? Alan and Charlotte Brown had both been very friendly to Betsy when she had moved to Orphea. She had lost count of the number of times they had invited her to dinner, asked her out for long walks or boat rides. She had regularly had dinner with Charlotte, mostly at Café Athena, where they had spent hours chatting. Betsy had let her in on her problems with Chief Gulliver, and Charlotte had told her about her move to Orphea. At the time, she had just finished her studies. She had found a job with a grumpy vet who confined her to secretarial tasks and would put his hands on her buttocks and laugh.

Betsy could absolutely not imagine Charlotte breaking into a house and shooting anyone dead.

The previous day, after viewing the video, we had telephoned Lambert and asked him two questions: Did the members of the theater company have cars? And who else owned a copy of the video recording of the play?

On the matter of cars, he was categorical: the whole company had come on the bus. Nobody had a car. As for the video, six hundred copies had been sold to the town's inhabitants, from various outlets. "There were some in the stores on Main Street, groceries, gas stations. People thought it was a nice souvenir. Between the fall of 1994 and the following summer, they sold out."

So, Stephanie could easily have come by a secondhand copy—there was even a copy in the town's public library. And the fact that Charlotte did not have a car meant that in the time she was absent on the night of the murders—approximately half an hour—she could not have gone far, only somewhere that was a thirty-minute round trip on foot from the Grand Theater. Derek, Betsy and I had concluded that if she had taken one of the town's few taxis, or if she had asked someone to drive her to Penfield, the driver would surely have come forward after the tragic events.

That morning, Betsy decided to take the opportunity of going for her usual jog to see how long it took her to get from the theater to Mayor Gordon's house and back on foot. It turned out to be nearly forty-five minutes at normal walking pace. Charlotte had been absent for approximately half an hour. What was the margin of interpretation of the word *approximately*? Running, it took just twenty-five minutes. A fit runner could do it in twenty. For someone with unsuitable footwear, it would have to have been closer to thirty, thirty-five. So it was feasible. Charlotte would theoretically have had time to run to the Gordons', kill them, and get back to the Grand Theater.

As Betsy was thinking, sitting on a bench in the little park facing what had been Mayor Gordon's house, she received a call from Michael Bird.

"Betsy," he said in a worried voice, "could you come over to the office right away? Something very strange has happened."

In his office, Bird told Betsy about the visit he had just had.

"Meta Ostrovski, the literary critic, came here. He wanted to know what had happened to Stephanie. When I told him about the murder, he got into a terrible state. 'Why didn't anybody tell me?' he shouted at me."

"What's his connection with Stephanie?" Betsy said.

"I don't know. That's why I called you. He started asking me all kinds of questions. He wanted to know everything. How she had died, why, what leads the police were following."

"What did you tell him?"

"Just what everyone knows, what he can find in the papers."

"And then?"

"Then he asked me for old issues of the *Chronicle* that mentioned Stephanie's disappearance. I gave him what copies we still had. He insisted on paying for them. Then he left."

"Do you know where he went?"

"He said he was going back to his hotel to study them. He's staying at the Lake Palace."

After quickly going home and taking a shower, Betsy set off for the Lake Palace. She put a call through to Ostrovski's room and he agreed to join her in the hotel bar.

"I knew Stephanie from the *New York Literary Review*," Ostrovski said. "She was a brilliant young woman, with an immense talent. Potentially a great writer."

"How did you know she'd moved to Orphea?"

"After she left the paper, we kept in touch. A few exchanges."

"Weren't you surprised that she had taken a job in a small town in the Hamptons?"

"Now that I'm back here, I'd say it was an excellent choice. She said she wanted to write and this town was perfect for that, being so quiet."

"Quiet," Betsy said. "Well, it's hardly that right now. Tell me, this isn't the first time you've been here, is it, Mr Ostrovski?"

"You're well informed, officer. I came here twenty years ago for the very first festival. There was an exceptional production of 'Uncle Vanya' and I liked the town."

"And you haven't been back to the festival since 1994?"

"No, never."

"Why come back now after twenty years?"

"Mayor Brown was kind enough to invite me, and I thought: why not?"

"Was this the first time you've been invited back since 1994?"

"No. But this year I really felt like coming."

Betsy sensed that Ostrovski was not telling her the whole truth.

"Mr Ostrovski, how about you stop treating me like a simpleton? I know you went to the offices of the *Chronicle* today and asked questions about Stephanie. The editor told me that you did not seem in a calm, normal state. What's going on?"

Ostrovski took offense at this. "What's going on? I'll tell you what's going on, dammit. A young woman I had a great deal of respect for has been murdered! Forgive me if I find it hard to conceal my emotions when hearing of this tragedy."

His voice cracked. It was obvious he was at the end of his tether.

"How come you didn't know what had happened to Stephanie? Did no-one mention it at the *Review*? Surely that's the kind of thing people talk about at the coffee machine?"

"Maybe," Ostrovski said, his voice almost breaking. "But I didn't know, because I was fired from the *Review*. Thrown out! Humiliated! Treated like a nobody! Overnight that scoundrel Bergdorf fires me, chases me out with my things in cardboard boxes, I'm not allowed back into the office, my phone calls go unanswered. Me, the great Ostrovski, treated as if I were nothing. Just imagine, officer, there was only one person in this country who still treated me with kindness, and that woman was Stephanie Mailer. Being on the verge of depression in New York, and unable to reach her, I decided to come see her in Orphea, thinking the mayor's invitation was a blessed coincidence, maybe even a sign from fate. But once I got here and still couldn't reach my friend, I decided to go to her apartment, and there a policeman informed me she had been murdered. Drowned in a muddy lake, it turns out, her body left to the insects, the worms, the birds, the leeches. That's why I'm so upset and angry, officer."

There was a moment's silence. He blew his nose, wiped away a tear, and breathed deeply to regain his composure.

"I'm truly sorry for the death of your friend, Mr Ostrovski," Betsy said.

"Thank you, officer, for sharing my grief."

After her conversation with Ostrovski, Betsy went to Café Athena to have lunch. As she was about to sit down at a table, a voice hailed her:

"You look good in plain clothes, Betsy."

Betsy turned. It was Sylvia Tennenbaum, who was smiling at her, apparently well disposed.

"I didn't know about your brother," Betsy said. "I didn't know what had happened to him."

"What difference does that make now?" Sylvia said. "Are you going to look at me any differently?"

"I meant, I'm sorry. It must have been terrible for you. I like you and I feel sorry for you. That's all."

Sylvia smiled sadly. "That's kind of you. Will you allow me to join you for lunch, Betsy? It's on me."

They sat at a table in the outside dining area, some distance from the other customers.

"For a long time, I was the monster's sister," Sylvia said. "People here would have liked to see the back of me. They just wanted me to sell his restaurant and get out."

"Tell me about your brother."

"He was kind and generous, with a heart of gold. But too impulsive, too quarrelsome. That was his undoing. All his life, he spoiled things by being too quick with his fists. Even at school. As soon as there was a problem with another kid, he couldn't avoid getting into a fight. He was forever getting expelled. Our father's business was doing well, and he'd put us down for the best private schools in Manhattan, where we lived. My brother went through one school after another, and in the end had to have a tutor at home. Then he was accepted at Stanford. And he was expelled from there after a year because he got into a fight with a professor. A professor, can you imagine? When he got back to New York, he found a job. It lasted eight months, then he had a fight with one of his colleagues and was fired. We had a vacation home in Ridgesport, not very far from here, and my brother moved there. He found a job managing a restaurant. He really liked it, the restaurant was coming along well, but he got into bad company. After work, he'd hang around a disreputable bar. He was arrested for being drunk, for possessing marijuana. And then there was a really violent fight in a parking lot. Ted was sent to prison for six months. When he got out, he wanted to go back to the Hamptons, but not to Ridgesport. He said he wanted to draw a line under his past and start over again. That's how he ended up in Orphea. Because he'd done time—even though it was a short sentence—he had a lot of trouble finding a job. Finally, the owner of the Lake Palace hired him as a bellboy. He was a model employee, he quickly climbed the ladder. He became concierge, then assistant manager. He played a part in local activities. He became a volunteer firefighter. Everything was going fine."

Sylvia broke off. Betsy sensed she didn't want to say more, but she urged her on.

"Ted had great business savvy," Sylvia resumed. "In the hotel, he had noticed that many of the guests complained that they couldn't find a really good restaurant in Orphea. That gave him the idea of starting his own. Our father had died in the meantime and left us a large bequest, and Ted was able to buy up a dilapidated building downtown, ideally located. He had the idea of renovating it and turning it into this place, Café Athena. Unfortunately, things soon degenerated."

"You mean the fire?"

"You know about that?"

"Yes. I heard there was a lot of tension between your brother and Mayor Gordon, who refused to allow a change of use for the building. They say Ted set fire to it to be granted authorization to start work. But the tension with the mayor continued after that."

"You know, Betsy, I heard all that. I can assure you that my brother did not set fire to the building. He was easily angered, yes. But he wasn't some small-time crook. He was a smart man, a man who had values. It's true that after the fire tension persisted between my brother and Mayor Gordon. I know they were seen by quite a few people having a violent dispute in the street. But if I tell you the real reason for the bad blood between them, I don't think you'll believe me."

Main Street, Orphea
February 21, 1994, two weeks after the fire

When Tennenbaum arrived at the site of the future Café Athena, he found Mayor Gordon waiting for him outside, pacing up and down to warm himself.

"Ted," Mayor Gordon said by way of greeting, "I see how stubborn you are."

Tennenbaum didn't understand at first. "I'm not sure I follow you, Mr Mayor. What's going on?"

Gordon took a sheet of paper from his coat pocket. "I gave you the names of these companies, and you haven't used any of them."

"That's right," Tennenbaum said. "I asked for estimates and I chose the ones that gave me the best prices. What's wrong with that?"

Mayor Gordon raised his voice. "Ted, stop splitting hairs. If you want to start your renovations, I advise you to contact these companies. They're much more qualified than the ones you chose."

"I chose perfectly competent local businesses. I'm free to do as I see fit, aren't I?"

Mayor Gordon lost patience. "I won't permit you to work with these businesses!"

"You won't permit me?"

"No. I'll block the work as long as I have to, by every means at my disposal."

A few passers-by, intrigued by the raised voices, stopped to watch. Tennenbaum, who had moved closer to the mayor, shouted:

"What difference does it make to you, Gordon?"

"*Mr Mayor*, please," Gordon said, placing a finger on his chest as if to emphasize his words.

Tennenbaum saw red and grabbed him roughly by the collar, then let go.

"Think you can frighten me, Tennenbaum?" Gordon said defiantly. "Try to behave with some decency instead of making a spectacle of yourself!"

Just then a police car drove up and Deputy Gulliver sprang out.

"Is everything O.K., Mr Mayor?" he said, his hand on his nightstick.

"Everything's fine, Deputy. Thank you."

*　　*　　*

"That's the reason for their quarrel," Sylvia said to Betsy. "The choice of companies for the construction work."

"I believe you," Betsy said.

Sylvia seemed surprised. "Really?"

"Yes, I know that Mayor Gordon was getting kickbacks from the businesses he awarded contracts to. I assume the construction work on Café Athena would have accounted for relatively large sums and the mayor wanted his slice of the cake. What happened next?"

"Ted agreed. He knew the mayor would be able to block the work and make life very difficult for him. Things worked out and Café Athena was able to open a week before the opening of the festival. Everything was going fine. Until Mayor Gordon was murdered. But my brother didn't kill Mayor Gordon, I'm certain of that."

"Sylvia, do the words 'The Darkest Night' mean anything to you?"

"'The Darkest Night,'" Sylvia said, taking time to think. "I've seen that somewhere."

She spotted a copy of that day's *Chronicle* that had been left on a nearby table and picked it up.

"In fact, here it is," she said, reading the front page of the newspaper. "It's the title of the play that's being performed for the opening of the festival."

"Were former police chief Hayward and your brother connected in any way?" Betsy asked.

"Not as far as I know. Why?"

"Because the words 'The Darkest Night' were used in some strange graffiti that appeared around town in the year leading up to the first festival. The same words were found written in the ruins after the fire in February 1994. Were you aware of that?"

"No, I wasn't. But don't forget I only moved here later. At the time, I was living in Manhattan, I was married and I'd taken over my father's business. When my brother died, I inherited Café Athena and chose not to sell it. It had meant so much to him. I hired a manager. And then I divorced, and I decided to sell my father's company. I wanted to start over. I moved here in 1998. So I missed all that part of the story, including the 'Darkest Night' graffiti. I had no idea about the connection with the fire, but on the other hand I do know who started the fire."

"Who?" Betsy said, her heart suddenly pounding.

"I mentioned that Ted got into bad company in Ridgesport. There was a small-time crook named Jeremiah Fold, who extorted money, and who had some kind of quarrel with him. Jeremiah was a dubious character, a lousy guy. He'd sometimes show up at the Palace with a bunch of girls and his pockets bulging with banknotes. He'd drive up on a huge motorcycle, making a lot of noise. He was loud, vulgar, often stoned. He'd flash his money around, treat whole tables full of people to an orgy of eating and drinking, and throw hundred-dollar bills at the waiters. The owner of the hotel didn't like it, but he didn't dare stop Jeremiah from coming because he didn't want trouble from him. One day, Ted, who was still working there, decided to step in. Out of loyalty to the owner, who had given him his chance. After Jeremiah had left the hotel, Ted set off after him in his car. He eventually forced him to stop at the side of the road. He told him he wasn't welcome at the Palace anymore. But Jeremiah had a girl on the back of his bike. Probably to impress her he tried to punch Ted, and Ted smashed his face. Jeremiah was humiliated. Sometime later, he came to see Ted at home, with two of his toughs, and got them to beat him up. Then, when Jeremiah found out Ted was planning to open a restaurant, he came to him and demanded to be made a partner. He wanted a commission to let the work continue, then a percentage of the profits once the restaurant was open. He had sensed the potential."

"And what did Ted do?"

"At first he refused. And one night in February, the building went up in smoke."

"And that was this Fold's doing?"

"Yes. On the night of the fire, Ted came to see me at three in the morning, and told me the whole story."

*   *   *

Sylvia Tennenbaum's apartment in Manhattan
Night of February 11, 1994

The telephone woke Sylvia. It was 2.45. It was the doorman. Her brother was downstairs. He was saying it was urgent.

She had him sent up and when the elevator doors opened, there was Ted, ashen-faced, barely able to stand. She settled him in the living room and made him tea.

"Café Athena has burned down," Ted said. "I had everything in my constrction cabin there, the plans, my files, months of work gone up in smoke."

"Surely the architects have copies?" Sylvia said, anxious to calm her brother.

"No, you don't understand!" Ted said. "This is really serious."

He took a crumpled sheet of paper from his pocket. It was the typed note he had found behind the windshield wiper of his car when he had rushed out of his house after being called about the fire.

```
Next time it'll be your house that burns down.
```

"It was arson?" Sylvia said, horrified.

Ted nodded.

"Who did it?"

"A man called Jeremiah Fold."

"Who is he?"

Her brother told her how he had forbidden Fold to come back to the Palace, the fight they had, and what had happened subsequently.

"Jeremiah wants money," Ted said. "He wants a lot of money."

"You have to go to the police."

"That's impossible right now. Knowing Fold, he will have paid a guy to do this. The police will never be able to pin it on him. At least not now. The only thing it'll get me is more reprisals. He's a psycho, and it'll only get worse. Best-case scenario, he'll burn down everything I own. Worst-case, someone will end up killed."

"And you think that if you pay, he'll leave you alone?"

"I'm sure of it. He loves money."

"Then pay him for now. We have enough money. Pay him, wait for things to calm down, and then go to the police."

*　*　*

"So my brother decided to pay, at least for the time being, to resolve the situation," Sylvia told Betsy. "His restaurant meant so much to him. It was his pride and joy, the mark of his success. He hired the companies Mayor Gordon told him to, and regularly transferred large sums of money to Fold to stop him sabotaging the work. That way, Café Athena was able to open on time."

Betsy was more than intrigued.

"Did you tell all this to the police at the time?"

Sylvia sighed. "No."

"Why not?"

"My brother came under suspicion for the Gordon family murders. Then one day he disappeared, and eventually he was killed in a car chase with the police. I didn't want to blacken his name any more than it was blackened already."

*　*　*

While Betsy and Sylvia Tennenbaum were at Café Athena, Kirk Hayward was making his slow way down Main Street. Seeing a suitable patch of bare wall, he stopped and from a shoulder bag he took a pot of glue and a brush and stuck up one of the posters he had just had printed.

CASTING CALL

In preparation for the performance of
THE ORPHEA FESTIVAL PLAY

"The Darkest Night"
THE DIRECTOR SEEKS ACTORS –
WITH OR WITHOUT EXPERIENCE
Auditions Monday, July 14, 10 a.m. at the Grand Theater

A few hundred yards away, Jerry and Carolina Eden came across one of these posters as they strolled on Main Street.

"An audition for a play," Eden read. "How about going along? When you were little, you had ambitions to be an actress."

"But not in some small-town play," Carolina said.

"Let's try our luck," Eden said, making an effort to stay enthusiastic. "You never know."

"It says here the auditions are on Monday. How long are we staying?"

"I don't know, Carolina. As long as we have to. Please don't start, we only just got here. Do you have other plans? Going to college, maybe? Oh no, I forgot, you're not enrolled anywhere."

Carolina pouted and resumed walking ahead of her father. They came to Cody Springfield's bookstore. Carolina went in, and stared fascinated at the shelves. On a table, she spotted a dictionary. She picked it up and leafed through it. One word led to another, she let the definitions parade in front of her eyes. She felt her father's presence behind her.

"It's been so long since I last saw a dictionary," she said.

She put the dictionary under her arm and started searching in fiction.

Springfield came up to her. "Are you looking for anything in particular?"

"A good novel," she said. "I haven't read anything in a while."

He noticed the dictionary under her arm. "That's not a novel," he said with a smile.

"It's much better. I'll take it. I can't remember the last time I looked through a paper dictionary. I usually use spellcheck when I write on my laptop."

He sighed. "A strange century we live in."

Carolina nodded. "When I was little, I went in for spelling competitions. My father trained me. We'd spend all our time spelling words. It drove my mother crazy. There was a time when I could be hours reading the dictionary, memorizing the spelling of the most complicated words. Go on, choose a word."

She handed the dictionary to an amused Springfield, who took it and opened it at random. He looked down the page and said:

"Holosystolic."

"Easy: h-o-l-o-s-y-s-t-o-l-i-c."

He gave a mischievous smile. "Did you really use to read the dictionary?"

"Oh, yes, all day long."

She laughed and her eyes gleamed.

"Where are you from?" Springfield said.

"Manhattan. My name's Carolina."

"I'm Cody."

"I love your bookstore, Cody. I would have liked to be a writer." Her face clouded over.

"Would have? What's stopping you? I'm sure you're not even twenty yet."

"I can't write anymore."

"Anymore? What does that mean?"

"Not since I did something very serious."

"What did you do?"

"It's too serious to talk about."

"You could write about it."

"I know, that's what my shrink says. But it won't come. Nothing comes. I'm all empty inside."

That evening, Eden and Carolina had dinner at Café Athena. Eden knew that Carolina had previously liked the place and had hoped to please her by taking her there. But she sulked all the way through the meal.

"Why did you drag us here?" she said, putting aside her seafood pasta.

"I thought you liked it," her father said.

"I mean Orphea. Why did you drag me here?"

"I thought it would do you good."

"You thought it would do me good? Or did you want to show me how much I disappoint you and to remind me that it was because of me you lost your house here?"

"How can you say such a horrible thing?"

"I ruined your life, I know!"

"Carolina, you have to stop blaming yourself. You have to move on, start over."

"Don't you understand? I'll never be able to make up for what I did, Daddy! I hate this town, I hate life!"

Unable to hold back her tears, she took refuge in the toilets so that nobody should see her crying. When at last she came out, after twenty long minutes, she asked her father if they could go back to the Lake Palace.

Eden had not noticed that there was a minibar in each of the two bedrooms that made up the suite. Carolina noiselessly opened the door of the cabinet, and removed a miniature vodka bottle from the little fridge. She poured out the whole bottle and took a few sips. Then, rummaging in the drawer where her underwear was, she took out a vial of ketamine. Leyla said it was practical and more discreet like this than in powder form.

Carolina broke off the end of the tube, emptied the contents into a glass, stirred it with her fingertip and swallowed it all.

After a few minutes, she felt a sense of calm rise within her. She was lighter, happier. She lay full length on the bed and gazed up at the ceiling. The white paint seemed to crack open slowly to reveal a wonderful fresco. She recognized the house in Orphea and longed to walk around inside it.

*   *   *

Orphea, ten years earlier
July 2004

There was a great deal of excitement at the breakfast table in the Eden family's luxurious summer home on Ocean Road.

"*Acupuncture*," Jerry Eden announced.

Carolina, who was nine, lifted the end of her nose and made a mischievous pout, which gave rise to an enchanted smile from her mother. With the spoon in her bowl, the girl moved the cereal letters around and steadily spelled out the word:

"A-c-u-p-u-n-c-t-u-r-e."

As she uttered each of the letters, she placed the corresponding piece of cereal on a plate next to her. She gazed at the final result, satisfied.

"Congratulations, sweetheart!" her father said, impressed.

Her mother laughed and clapped. "How do you do that?"

"I don't know, Mommy. It's like I see a photograph of the word in my head and it's usually right."

"Let's try another one," Eden said. "*Rhododendron*."

Carolina rolled her eyes, making her parents laugh, then spelled the word. The only letter missing was the "h".

"Almost!" her father said.

"At least I learned a new word," Carolina said philosophically. "I won't make that mistake again. Can I go to the swimming pool?"

"Yes, put your bathing suit on," her mother said.

Carolina let out a cry of joy and ran from the table. Tenderly, Eden watched her disappear into the hall and Cynthia took advantage of that moment of calm to go and sit on her husband's knees.

"Thank you, darling, for being such a wonderful husband and father."

"Thank *you* for being such an amazing woman."

"I never imagined I could be so happy," Cynthia said, eyes shining with love.

"Me neither. We're so lucky."

JESSE ROSENBERG

Sunday, July 13, 2014

Thirteen days to opening night

On that sweltering Sunday, Derek and Darla had invited Betsy and me to come and take advantage of their little swimming pool. It was the first time we had all gotten together like this outside the investigation. In fact, for me, it was the first time I had spent an afternoon at Derek's house in a very long while.

The main purpose of the invitation was so that we could relax over a few beers. But when Darla had to go off for a moment and the children were happily playing in the water, we could not resist the temptation to talk about the case.

Betsy told us about her conversation with Sylvia, detailing how Ted Tennenbaum had come under pressure both from Mayor Gordon, trying to impose his choice of businesses, and from the local gangster Jeremiah Fold, who had decided to extort money from him.

"'The Darkest Night,'" Betsy said, "may be connected with this man Fold. He was the one who set fire to Café Athena in February 1994, to put the squeeze on Tennenbaum."

"Could 'The Darkest Night' be the name of a gang?" I said.

"It's worth checking out, Jesse. I didn't have time to get back to the station to find out more about this Fold. But from what I gather, it was the fire that finally persuaded Tennenbaum to pay up."

"So the money transfers we saw in Tennenbaum's bank statements were for Fold?" Derek said.

"Yes. Tennenbaum wanted to make sure that Fold would let him continue with his work in peace and that Café Athena would open in time for the festival. And since we now know that Gordon was getting kickbacks from companies working on the project, it's clear why he would have received transfers during the same period. He's bound to have demanded commissions from the companies that were chosen, telling them it was thanks to him that they had the contracts."

"What if there was some connection between Mayor Gordon and Fold?" Derek said. "Do you think the mayor may have had links with the local underworld?"

"Was that a lead you followed back then?" Betsy said.

"No, it wasn't. We thought the mayor was just a run-of-the-mill politician, not that he was taking kickbacks at all levels."

"Let's suppose 'The Darkest Night' was the name of a criminal organization," Betsy went on. "What if it was the murder of Mayor Gordon that was being predicted in the graffiti on the walls of Orphea? That would mean the murder was already signed off, in full view of everyone, but nobody saw it."

"What nobody saw!" Derek said. "What was in front of our eyes and we didn't see! What do you think, Jesse?"

"It would imply that Chief Hayward was investigating this organization at the time," I said after a moment's thought. "And that he knew the whole story. That might be the reason why he took his file with him."

"That's what we'll have to look into tomorrow. As a matter of priority," Betsy said.

"What I can't figure out," Derek said, "is why, in 1994, Tennenbaum never told us he was under pressure from this Fold when we questioned him about the bank transfers."

"Fear of reprisals?" Betsy said.

Derek looked dubious. "Maybe. But if we missed this business with Fold, we may have missed something else. I'd also like to take another look at the context of the case and see what the local papers were saying about it at the time."

"I can ask Bird to let us see all he has on the murders in the archives."

"Good idea," Derek said.

When evening came, we stayed for dinner. As they did every Sunday, Derek and Darla ordered pizzas. When we were sitting in the kitchen,

Betsy noticed a photograph pinned to the wall. It showed Darla, Derek, Natasha, and me, standing outside Little Russia while it was under construction.

"What's Little Russia?" Betsy said innocently.

"The restaurant I never opened," Darla said.

"You wanted to be a professional chef?"

"There was a time when it was my whole life."

"And who's the girl with you, Jesse?" Betsy asked me, pointing to Natasha.

"Natasha," I said.

"Natasha, your fiancée at the time?"

"Yes."

"You never told me what happened between you."

Shaking her head, Darla said:

"My God, Jesse, haven't you told her?"

*   *   *

After the press conference on Friday, Bergdorf had booked himself into a hotel just off Main Street. He had considered taking a room in the Lake Palace, but with a sigh he had decided that the *New York Literary Review*'s expense account could not stretch that far. On Saturday, he had followed Kirk Hayward from a distance as he pasted up posters for his auditions around town. On Sunday, on his way back to his hotel, he bumped into Ostrovski.

"Bergdorf!" the critic said, unable to hide his dismay. "What are you doing here? I leave the city to get a bit of peace and quiet, and who do I run into?"

"I came to find out more about this mysterious play that's going to be performed."

"I was here first, Steven, so why don't you just go back to New York?"

"Look, Meta." Bergdorf said. "I've been meaning to write to you to tell you again just how sorry I am for what happened. The fact is that the *Review* has been really struggling and you were on the highest wage."

Ostrovski had the impression that Bergdorf was sincere and he was moved by his apology. "Thank you, Steven," he said.

"I really mean it, Meta. Is it the *New York Times* that sent you here?"

"Far from it. I'm unemployed. Who would want to hire an obsolete critic?"

"You're a great critic, Meta. Any newspaper would hire you."

Ostrovski sighed. "Maybe that's the problem."

"What do you mean?"

"Since yesterday, I've been obsessed with one idea: I'd like to audition for 'The Darkest Night.'"

"Why don't you?"

"It's out of the question. I'm a critic of literature and drama. That means I can't write books and I can't act in plays."

"Meta, I'm not sure I follow you."

"Come on, Steven, make a little effort, for heaven's sake! Explain to me by what miracle a theater critic could act in a play? Can you imagine if literary critics started writing books or writers became literary critics? Can you imagine Don DeLillo reviewing David Mamet's new play for the *New Yorker*? Can you imagine Jackson Pollock having reviewed the latest exhibition by Mark Rothko in the *Times*? Could you see Jeff Koons tearing Damien Hirst's new offering to shreds in the *Washington Post*? Could you imagine Spielberg reviewing the latest Coppola in the *L.A. Times*, saying, 'Don't go to see this shit, it's terrible'? Everyone would cry foul and accuse them of bias, and with good reason. You can't criticize an art you practice."

"Technically, Meta, you're not a critic anymore," Bergdorf said.

Ostrovski's face lit up: Bergdorf was right. The former critic went straight back to his room. Once there, he laid out the copies of the *Chronicle* with reports of the disappearance of Stephanie Mailer.

What if it was written somewhere that I had to go over to the other side? Ostrovski thought. And what if Bergdorf had actually given him back his freedom? What if, in all this time, he had been a creative artist without realizing it?

He cut out the articles and spread them on the bed. On the night table, the photograph of Meghan Padalin was watching.

*　*　*

After dinner, at Derek and Darla's

Night had fallen. Betsy and Derek cleared the table. Darla was outside, smoking by the pool. I joined her there. It was still very warm. The crickets were singing.

"Look at me, Jesse," Darla said in a sarcastic tone. "I wanted to open a restaurant and here I am ordering pizzas every Sunday."

I felt her dismay and tried to comfort her. "Pizza is a tradition."

"No, Jesse, it isn't. And you know it. I'm tired. Tired of this life, tired of a job I hate. Every time I pass a restaurant, you know what I say to myself? 'That could have been mine.' Instead of which, I work myself to the bone as a medical assistant. Derek hates his job, too. He's hated it for twenty years. And in the last week, since he got back together with you and went back out into the field, he's been happy as a lark."

"His place is out in the field, Darla. Derek is an incredible policeman."

"He can't be out in the field, Jesse. Not after what happened."

"Then let him quit. Let him do something else. He's entitled to his pension."

"The house isn't paid off."

"Then sell it! In two years' time, your kids will have gone off to college anyway. Go find yourselves a quiet spot, far away from it all."

"And do what?" Darla said in a desperate tone.

"Live," I said.

She stared into the distance. I could only see her face by the light from the pool.

"Come," I said. "I'd like to show you something."

"What?"

"The project I'm working on."

"What project?"

"The project I'm quitting the police for. I didn't want to tell you about it because I wasn't ready yet. Come."

We left Derek and Betsy and set off in the car. We drove to Queens, then to Rego Park. When I parked in that side street, Darla understood. She got out of the car and looked at the single-story building.

"Did you rent it?" she said

"Yes. It was a dry goods store and wasn't doing well. I got it for a good price. I'm about to start work."

She looked up at the sign, which was covered with a sheet. "Don't tell me . . ."

"Yes," I said. "Wait here a minute."

I went inside to light the sign and find a ladder, then came back out, climbed up, and lifted off the sheet. The letters shone in the dark.

LITTLE RUSSIA

Darla didn't say anything. I felt ill at ease.

"Look, I still have the red book with all your recipes," I said, showing her the treasured collection, which I had brought out with the ladder.

Darla still said not a word. Trying to get a reaction, I continued:

"True, I'm a lousy cook. I'll make hamburgers. That's all I can do. Hamburgers in Natasha's Sauce. Unless you want to help me, Darla. Set this thing up with me. I know it's a little bit crazy, but—"

"A little bit crazy!" she cried out at last. "Totally insane, you mean! You've lost your mind, Jesse! Why did you do something like this?"

"For redemption," I said quietly.

"But Jesse," she shouted, "none of it is redeemable! Do you hear me? What happened can never be redeemed!"

She burst into tears and ran off into the darkness.

-3

Auditions

MONDAY, JULY 14 – WEDNESDAY, JULY 16, 2014

JESSE ROSENBERG

Monday, July 14, 2014
Twelve days to opening night

That morning the three of us began looking into the records to see what we could learn about Jeremiah Fold. It turned out that he had died in a road accident on July 16, 1994, in other words, two weeks before the death of Mayor Gordon.

Much to our surprise, Fold did not have a criminal record. The only thing in his file was an investigation opened by the A.T.F.—the Federal Bureau of Alcohol, Tobacco, Firearms and Explosives—that had apparently led nowhere. We contacted the police in Ridgesport to try to learn more, but the officer we spoke with was no help. "There's nothing on Jeremiah Fold here," he assured us. That meant that Fold's death had not been considered worth recording or suspicious.

"If Fold died before the Gordon murders," Derek said, "it rules out his involvement in them."

"I checked the F.B.I. files," I said. "There's no criminal organization called 'The Darkest Night'. It wasn't some kind of premature claiming of responsibility on the part of organized crime."

So we could rule out Fold. But we had another lead we needed to look into. Who had commissioned Stephanie's book?

Derek had brought cardboard boxes filled with newspapers. "The small ad that attracted Stephanie Mailer's attention must have appeared in a newspaper," he said. "In the conversation she reports, the man says he's been advertising for twenty years."

He read from Stephanie's first chapter again:

The ad was in between one for a shoe repairer and another for a Chinese restaurant offering an all-you-can-eat buffet for less than $20.

DO YOU WANT TO WRITE A BESTSELLER?
MAN OF LETTERS SEEKS AMBITIOUS WRITER
FOR SERIOUS WORK. REFERENCES ESSENTIAL.

"It must be a regular publication. Apparently, Stephanie only had one subscription, and that was for the magazine of the literature faculty of Notre Dame, where she studied. So we got hold of all the issues from the past year."

"She could have read the ad in any magazine she came across," Betsy said. "In a coffee shop, on a subway seat, in a doctor's waiting room."

"Maybe," Derek said, "maybe not. If we find the ad, it might lead us to the man who commissioned the book and we'll finally find out who was at the wheel of Tennenbaum's van on the evening of the murders."

*　　*　　*

At the Lake Palace, in the sitting room of Suite 308, Carolina sprawled on the couch while her father opened his laptop on the desk.

"We should go to this audition," he said. "It'll give us something to do together."

"The theater's a drag!" Carolina said.

"How can you say such a thing? What about that wonderful play you wrote that was supposed to be performed in your school?"

"But it never was. I don't give a damn about the theater anymore."

"When I think how curious you were about this when you were younger!" Eden said. "What a curse it is, this generation's obsession with cell phones and social networks! You don't read anymore, any of you, you're not interested in anything except taking photographs of your lunch. What a time we live in!"

"Where do you get off lecturing me?" Carolina complained. "It's your lousy T.V. shows that turn people into dickheads!"

"Don't be vulgar, Carolina, please."

"I'm just saying, forget about those auditions. If they take us, we'll be stuck here till August."

"What do you want to do, then?"

Carolina pouted. "Nothing."

"Shall we go to the beach?"

"No. When are we going back to the city?"

"I don't know, Carolina," Eden said wearily. "I'm prepared to be patient, but can you at least make a small effort? I have other things to do than be here. Channel 14 doesn't have a flagship show for the fall and—"

"Then let's get out of here, and you can do what you have to do."

"No. I made arrangements to run everything from here. In fact, I have a video conference call starting now."

"Obviously, there's always a call, always work! That's the only thing that interests you."

"Carolina, it'll only take ten minutes! I'm giving you all the time I can, you could at least acknowledge that. Just give me ten minutes and then we'll do whatever you want."

"I don't want to do anything," Carolina muttered, and went and locked herself in her room.

Eden sighed and switched on the camera of his laptop to start the conference call with his team. Ten minutes in, eyes fixed to the screen, he did not notice that Carolina had left her room. She looked at him, saw he was engrossed in his call, and left the suite. She walked up and down the corridor, not knowing what to do with herself. She passed Room 310, in which Ostrovski was preparing to go to the audition by reciting classics of the theater. She made up her mind to leave the Palace. She asked the parking valet for her father's Porsche, and set off for Orphea. When she got to Ocean Road, she drove past the beachfront houses. She was nervous. She soon came to what had been their vacation home, the house where they had been so happy together. She parked by the gate and sat there gazing at the wrought-iron inscription: THE GARDEN OF EDEN.

She could not hold back for much longer. Clutching the wheel, she burst into tears.

*   *   *

"Jesse," Bird said to me with a smile when he saw me put my head around the door of his office, "to what do I owe the pleasure?"

Back at the station Betsy and Derek were still looking through the issues of the Notre Dame college magazine, and I had gone to the offices of the *Chronicle* to collect the articles about the Gordon murders that the editor had put together for us.

"I need access to the newspaper's archives," I told him. "Would you be able to help me with that without it appearing in tomorrow's issue?"

"Of course, Jesse. I still feel bad about betraying your trust. It wasn't professional of me. You know, I can't stop playing it in my head—could I have protected Stephanie?"

I saw him stare at Stephanie's desk, which faced his and had stayed as it was. He looked sad.

"There's nothing you could have done," I said, hoping to comfort him.

He shrugged and took me down to the basement, where the archives were kept.

Bird was proving to be a valuable support. He helped me to sort through the issues of the *Orphea Chronicle*, find the articles that seemed pertinent, and photocopy them. I also took advantage of the immense knowledge that he had of the community to question him about Jeremiah Fold.

"Never heard of him. Who is he?"

"A gangster from Ridgesport. He was extorting money from Ted Tennenbaum by threatening to prevent the opening of Café Athena."

Bird was astonished. "Tennenbaum had pressure put on him by a gangster?"

"Yes. We missed that in 1994."

Thanks to Bird, I was also able to do some more checking about "The Darkest Night". He called other newspapers in the area, in particular the *Ridgesport Evening Star*, and asked if they had in their archives any article containing the keywords "Darkest" with "Night". But there was nothing. The only reference to it was the graffiti that had appeared in Orphea between the fall of 1993 and the summer of 1994.

I took all the photocopies back to the station and plunged in. I started reading, cutting out, underlining, discarding, classifying, while Betsy and Derek continued their search in the copies of the Notre Dame magazine. Betsy's desk was starting to resemble a newspaper distribution center. Suddenly, Derek cried, "Bingo!" He had found the ad. On page 21 of the Fall 2013 issue, there it was:

DO YOU WANT TO WRITE A BESTSELLER?
MAN OF LETTERS SEEKS AMBITIOUS WRITER
FOR SERIOUS WORK. REFERENCES ESSENTIAL.

All we had to do now was contact the person at the magazine who dealt with classified ads.

*   *   *

Carolina was still outside the gate of The Garden of Eden. Her father had not called her. He must hate her, she thought, like everyone else. Because of what had happened in the house. Because of what she had done to Tara Scalini. And she would never forgive herself.

She burst into tears again. Things would never get better, she thought. She no longer wanted to live. Through misty eyes, she searched in her bag for a vial of ketamine. She needed to feel better. As she searched, she found the little plastic box she had been given by her friend Leyla. It was heroin, to be snorted. Carolina had not tried it yet. She laid a line of white powder on the dashboard and twisted to move her nose closer.

Inside the house, Gerald Scalini, who had been told by his wife that a car had been parked outside the gate for quite a while now, decided to call the police.

Several police cars were outside The Garden of Eden. In the back of Montagne's car, Carolina, her hands cuffed behind her back, was crying. Montagne was questioning her through the open door.

"What were you doing here? Waiting for a customer? Do you sell this shit here?"

"No, I swear," Carolina said, weeping, half-conscious.

"You're too high to answer, you idiot! And don't go throwing up on my seats, got that? Fucking junkie!"

"I'd like to talk to my father."

"Sure, what else? With what we found in the car, you'll be hauled up in front of a judge. The next stop for you, girl, is a prison cell."

The afternoon was coming to its end, and in the quiet residential neighborhood where the Browns lived, Charlotte, who had just gotten back from her day at the clinic, was daydreaming on the porch. Her husband, returning from the Grand Theater, sat down next to her. He seemed exhausted.

She lit a cigarette. "Alan . . ."

"Yes?"

"I'd like to take part in the play."

He smiled. "You should," he said encouragingly.

"I don't know . . . I haven't been on a stage in twenty years."

"You'll be a hit."

By way of reply, Charlotte gave a long sigh.

"What's going on?" Alan said, seeing that something wasn't right.

"I've been telling myself it may be better to keep a low profile, and stay away from Hayward."

"What are you afraid of?"

"You know perfectly well, Alan."

A few miles away, at the Lake Palace, Eden was in a state. Carolina had disappeared. He had looked for her all over the hotel, in the bar, around the pool, in the fitness room. She wasn't answering her phone and had not left a message. He had finally informed hotel security. Camera footage showed Carolina leaving her room, wandering for a while in the corridor, then going down to reception, asking for his car and driving away. The head of security, unable to suggest a solution, suggested contacting the police. Then Eden's cell phone rang.

"Carolina?"

"Mr Eden?" said a solemn voice. "Deputy Jasper Montagne of the Orphea police department."

"Police? What's going on?"

"Your daughter Carolina is currently being held at the station. She was arrested for possession of drugs and will appear before a judge tomorrow morning. She'll be spending the night in a cell."

JERRY EDEN

In the summer of 1994, I was the director of a radio station in New York City. I was earning a modest living and had just married Cynthia, my high school sweetheart, the only girl who had ever believed in me.

You should have seen us at the time. We were in love, we were just thirty, we were free as air. My most precious possession was a second-hand Corvette. We spent the weekends traveling around the country, driving from one town to another, staying in motels or boarding houses.

Cynthia was working for the administration of a small theater. She had all the best tips and we saw lots of plays on Broadway without spending a single dollar. We weren't rich, but what we had was more than enough. We were happy.

1994 was the year we married. Our wedding was in January, and we decided to postpone our honeymoon till the weather improved. We had a limited budget, so could only choose destinations we could get to in the Corvette. It was Cynthia who heard about the new theater festival in Orphea. There was quite a buzz about it in artistic circles and famous journalists were expected to attend, which suggested the quality of it. I found us a delightful family-run boarding house, not far from the ocean, in a log house surrounded by hydrangeas. We were sure that the ten or so days we would spend there would be memorable. And they were, from every point of view. When we got back to New York, Cynthia discovered she was pregnant. In April 1995, our only child, our beloved daughter Carolina, was born.

*

I don't want to take anything away from our happiness at the arrival of Carolina in our lives, but we hadn't planned to have a child so soon. The months that followed were like those of all young parents whose life is turned upside down by the presence of a little creature. We had to sell the two-seater and buy a bigger car, change apartments to have an extra room, and carry the cost of diapers, baby clothes, a crib, a stroller, and so on. In short, we had to make do.

To make matters worse, Cynthia was fired by the theater when she got back from her maternity leave. As for me, the radio station was bought by a large group, and after hearing all kinds of rumors about restructuring and fearing for my position, I was obliged to accept less airtime and more administrative work and responsibilities for the same salary. Our weeks became a true race against the clock: work, family, Cynthia looking for a job and not knowing what to do with Carolina, me coming back in the evening exhausted. It was quite a trial for both of us. So when summer arrived, I suggested we spend a few days at the end of July in our little boarding house in Orphea, to recharge our batteries. And once again the Orphea miracle worked.

It was the same in the following years. Whatever happened in the bustle of the city, whatever daily life threw at us, Orphea made everything better.

Cynthia had found a job in New Jersey, an hour's train ride away. She had three hours traveling to do each day, and had to juggle diaries and calendars, taking the little one to nursery, then to school, doing shopping, going to meetings, doing the best we could at work and at home, from morning to evening and all the days that God gave us. Our nerves were at full stretch, some days we barely saw each other. But once a year, all the stress and misunderstandings and rush were wiped out as soon as we arrived in Orphea. The town was cathartic for us. The air seemed purer, the sky more beautiful, life quieter. The owner of the boarding house, who had grown-up children, took wonderful care of Carolina and was happy to look after her whenever we decided we'd like to see a show at the festival. At the end of our stay, we would set off back to the city happy, rested, calmer. Ready to resume our lives.

*

I have never been especially ambitious. I don't think I would have risen as far as I have in my career if it hadn't been for Cynthia and Carolina. Because, as the years went by, having gone back to Orphea so often and feeling so good there, I wanted to give them more. I started wanting more than the little family boarding house, wanting to spend more than a week a year in the Hamptons. I wanted Cynthia not to have to do three hours' traveling a day and barely be able to make ends meet, I wanted Carolina to go to a private school and benefit from the best possible education. It was for their sakes that I began to work even harder, aiming for promotion, demanding better pay. It was for them that I agreed to give up my airtime and take on more responsibilities, in positions that interested me less but were better paid. I began climbing the ladder, seizing all the opportunities that presented themselves, being first in the office and last to leave. In three years, I went from being the director of a radio station to the head of T.V. series development for the whole group.

My salary doubled, trebled, and our quality of life went up with it. Cynthia was able to stop working and enjoy Carolina, who was still quite young. She devoted part of her time to working for free for a theater company. Our vacations in Orphea grew longer: they lasted three weeks, then a whole month, then the whole summer, in rented houses that were ever larger and more luxurious, with a cleaning woman once a week, then twice a week, then every day, who took care of the house, made the beds, cooked for us, and picked up whatever we left lying around.

It was a good life, rather different from what I had imagined in the days when we spent our week's vacation in the boarding house. I was completely disconnected from work. With my new responsibilities, I couldn't take more than a few days at a time. While Cynthia and Carolina enjoyed two months by the pool without having to worry about a thing,

I would go back to Manhattan at regular intervals to deal with business. Cynthia was upset that I could not stay longer, but everything was going well. What did we have to complain about?

My rise continued. Maybe even despite myself, I don't know. My salary, which I thought was already astronomical, continued to increase, as did the amount of work. Media groups were buying one another to form all-powerful conglomerates. I found myself in a big office in a glass skyscraper. I could measure my professional ascent by the size and height of the offices I moved to. My remuneration followed my progress up the floors. My bonus grew tenfold, a hundredfold. Ten years after being director of a small radio station, I found myself the C.E.O. of Channel 14, the most watched and most lucrative T.V. channel in the country, which I ran from the 53rd and final floor of the glass tower, for a salary, including bonuses, of $9 million a year. In other words, $750,000 a month. I earned more money than I could ever spend.

Everything I wanted to give Cynthia and Carolina, I was able to. Luxury clothes, sports cars, a fabulous apartment, a private school, dream vacations. If the New York winter depressed us, we would leave in a private plane for a revitalizing week in St Barts. As for Orphea, I built the house of our dreams there, for a vast amount of money, a house by the ocean. I called it The Garden of Eden and put the name in wrought-iron letters on the gate.

Everything had become so simple, so easy. So extraordinary. But it had a cost, not only a financial one. I had to devote myself even more to my work. The more I wanted to give to my two lovely women, the more I had to give to Channel 14, in time, energy, and concentration.

Cynthia and Carolina spent the summers and every weekend when the weather was good in our house in the Hamptons. I would join them as soon as I could. I had set up an office there, from which I could deal with business and hold telephone conferences.

But the easier our existence appeared to be, the more complicated it actually became. Cynthia wanted me to spend more time with her and Carolina, without my being constantly concerned with my work, but without my work there could not be a house. It was like a snake biting its own tail. Our vacations were a succession of reproaches and quarrels: "What's the point in your coming here if all you do is shut yourself up in your office?" "But we're together!" "No, Jerry, you're here, but you're not with us." And this would continue on the beach or at a restaurant. Sometimes, during my walks, I would go as far as the old family boarding house, which had closed when its owner had died. I would look at the pretty plank house and dream of what our vacations had been, so modest, so short, so wonderful. I wished I could turn the clock back. But I didn't know how.

If you ask me, I'll tell you that I did all this for my wife and daughter.

If you ask Cynthia or Carolina the same question, they'll tell you that I did it for myself, for my ego, my workaholic nature.

But it doesn't really matter whose fault it was. Over the course of time, the magic of Orphea stopped working. Our marriage, our family, no longer mended itself or came back together during our stays there. On the contrary, those stays helped to tear us farther apart.

And then everything changed dramatically.

Things happened in the spring of 2013 that forced us to sell the house in Orphea.

JESSE ROSENBERG

Tuesday, July 15, 2014
Eleven days to opening night

Finding the ad in the Notre Dame student magazine did not help us to trace the person who had placed it. At the editorial offices, the person in charge of advertising had no information. The ad had apparently been placed in reception and paid for in cash. A dead-end mystery. On the other hand, the student was able to find the same ad in the archive, published exactly a year earlier. And the year before that. The ad had appeared every year in the fall issue.

"What's special about the fall issue?" I said.

"It's the most widely read. It's when people come back to college or come for their first year."

The return to college, Derek pointed out, marked the arrival of new students and therefore of potential candidates to write this book. "If I was the person wanting that book to be written," he said, "I wouldn't limit myself to one magazine, I'd place the ad more widely."

We called the editorial offices of the magazines of literature faculties in several colleges in New York to check out this hypothesis. A similar ad had indeed appeared in a number of other fall issues for years. But whoever had placed them had left no trace.

We knew that it was a man, that he had been in Orphea in 1994, that he had information suggesting that Tennenbaum was not the murderer, that he considered the matter serious enough to be the subject of a book, and that he could not write this book himself. That was the strangest part of it.

"Who would like to write but can't?" Derek wondered out loud. "To the point of looking desperately for someone to do it by placing ads year after year in student magazines?"

Betsy wrote on the whiteboard what looked like a mystery worthy of the Sphinx of Thebes:

I WANT TO WRITE BUT CAN'T. WHO AM I?

For want of anything better, all we could do was continue looking through the articles from the *Chronicle*. We had skimmed through them without success. Suddenly Derek became excited and circled a paragraph in red.

"Listen to this," he said, staring incredulously at the photocopy he had in his hand. "This is an article that appeared in the *Chronicle* on August 2, 1994. It says: *According to police sources, a third witness has come forward. This testimony may prove crucial for the police, who have almost no leads at the moment.*"

"What is all this?" I said. "A third witness? There were only two witnesses, the two people who lived in the neighborhood."

"I know that, Jesse," Derek said, as surprised as I was.

Betsy immediately contacted Michael Bird. He had no memory of this witness, but recalled that in the days after the murders the town had been awash with rumors. Unfortunately, it was impossible to question the author of the article, who had died ten years earlier, but Bird told us with certainty that the police source was Chief Gulliver, who had always been a gossip.

Chief Gulliver was not in the station. When he returned, he came to see us in Betsy's office. When I told him we had discovered a reference to a third witness, he immediately said:

"That was Marty Connors. He worked in a gas station near Penfield Crescent."

"Why were we never told about him?"

"Because we checked him out, and his testimony was worthless."

"We'd have liked to judge that for ourselves," I said.

"You know, at the time, there were dozens like that. We checked them all out carefully before we passed them on to you. People were contacting us about all kinds of things. They'd felt a presence, heard a strange noise, seen a flying saucer. We had to filter them, or you would have been snowed under. We did everything by the book."

"I don't doubt that. Was it you who questioned him?"

"No. I can't remember who did."

As he was leaving the room, Gulliver stopped in the doorway and said:

"A one-armed man."

The three of us stared at him.

"What are you talking about, Chief?" I said.

"That thing on the board: *I want to write, but I can't. Who am I?* Answer: a one-armed man."

"Thanks, Chief."

The gas station Gulliver had mentioned was still there. And by a stroke of luck, twenty years later, so was Marty Connors.

"Marty works nights," the clerk told me over the phone. "He starts his shift at eleven."

"Is he working tonight?"

"Yes. You want me to leave him a message?"

"No, that's kind of you. I'll come over to see him."

＊　＊　＊

Those who have no time to waste getting to the Hamptons from Manhattan travel by air. From the heliport at the southern tip of the island, twenty minutes by helicopter are enough to connect the city with any town on Long Island.

In the parking lot of the airfield in Orphea, Jerry Eden was sitting at the wheel of his car, waiting. A loud engine noise tore him from his thoughts. He looked up and saw the helicopter arriving. He got out of the car and watched the machine come down onto the asphalt a few dozen yards away. Once the engine had been turned off and the propellers stopped, the side door of the helicopter opened and Cynthia

Eden got out, followed by their lawyer, Benjamin Graff. They came through the gate separating the landing pad from the parking lot and Cynthia rushed into her husband's arms, sobbing.

Eden, still embracing his wife, exchanged a friendly handshake with his lawyer.

"Benjamin," he said, "tell me there is no chance Carolina can go to prison."

"What quantity of drugs did she have on her?"

"I have no idea."

"Let's go straight to the police station. We have to prepare for the hearing. In normal circumstances, I wouldn't be worried, but there is the background of the Scalini case. If the judge prepares his case properly, he's bound to find out about that and may be tempted to take it into account. That could be a problem for Carolina."

Eden was shaking. His legs could barely support him. He asked Benjamin to take the wheel. A quarter of an hour later, they presented themselves at the police station in Orphea. They were admitted to an interrogation room, and a short while later Carolina was led in by two police officers. She was in handcuffs. When she saw her parents, she burst into tears. One of the officers removed her handcuffs and she immediately rushed into their arms. "My baby!" Cynthia cried, hugging her daughter to her as hard as she could.

The officers left them alone in the room and they sat down around the plastic table. The lawyer took out a file and a notepad from his briefcase and immediately got to work.

"Carolina," he said, "I need to know exactly what you told the police. I particularly need to know if you told them anything about Tara."

*

At the Grand Theater, Hayward's auditions were in full flow. Mayor Brown was sitting onstage next to the director, growing more and more anxious as the hours passed. Nobody seemed suitable.

"Don't worry," Hayward kept saying. "There's talent in this town, I know it. It's just a matter of time."

"Time is the one thing we don't have," the mayor said glumly.

Hayward called the next two aspiring actors up onstage. Two men stood and made their way to the stage. Meta Ostrovski and Steven Bergdorf.

"What are you two doing here?" Hayward asked.

"I'm here to audition," Ostrovski said.

"So am I," Bergdorf said.

Hayward got up to hand both men their lines. Then he sat again and read out the stage directions that were their cue.

It is a gloomy morning. Rain is falling. On a country road, the traffic is paralyzed. A vast bottleneck has formed. The motorists, at the ends of their tethers, blow their horns angrily. A man is jogging along the side of the road, past the line of motionless cars. He approaches the officer on duty.

Ostrovski jogged towards Bergdorf, making a convincing show of being out of breath. Mayor Brown sat up a little in his seat.

OSTROVSKI: What's going on?

STEVEN BERGDORF: There's been an accident.

OSTROVSKI: How? What happened?

STEVEN BERGDORF: It was a motorcycle. The man went straight into a tree. It's a mess back there. If I were you, I'd keep on going.

As the scene unfolded, against all his expectations the mayor found himself being drawn into their performances. The difference from what had come before was night and day.

"Kirk," he hissed. "Are you thinking what I'm thinking?"

Thirty seconds later, Hayward had made his decision.

"O.K.," he said, getting to his feet. "I think I've seen enough."

"No, wait, Kirk!" Ostrovski said, putting his hands together as if in prayer. "You've got to give us more time."

"Relax, Meta," Hayward said with a sly smile. "You're in the play."

He then turned to face the auditorium and the other waiting aspirants, as Ostrovski went over to clap Bergdorf on the back.

"We have our first two cast members!" the director announced.

*　　*　　*

The afternoon was coming to an end when, in the main room of the courthouse in Orphea, after an interminable wait, Carolina Eden finally appeared before Judge Abe Cooperstein.

Escorted by a police officer, she advanced unsteadily toward the judge, her body exhausted by a night in the cells and her eyes red with tears.

"So, what do we have here?" Judge Cooperstein said, skimming through the report he had been passed. "Case number 23450, municipality of Orphea against Miss Carolina Eden. Miss Eden, I read here that you were arrested yesterday afternoon at the wheel of a car, while stuffing heroin up your nose. Is that correct?"

Carolina threw a terrified glance at Benjamin Graff, who encouraged her with a nod of the head to answer as they had agreed.

"Yes, your honor," she replied.

"May I know, miss, why a nice girl like you is taking drugs?"

"I made a big mistake, your honor. I'm in a weird place in my life right now. But I'm doing everything I can to get out of it. I'm seeing a psychiatrist in New York."

"So this isn't the first time you've taken drugs?"

"No, your honor."

"Are you a regular consumer?"

"No, your honor. I wouldn't say that."

"But the police did find a large quantity among your effects."

Carolina lowered her head. Jerry and Cynthia Eden felt their stomachs knotting. If the judge knew anything about Tara Scalini, their daughter was in big trouble.

"What are you doing with your life?" Cooperstein said.

"Not much right now," Carolina said.

"Why's that?"

Carolina started crying. She wanted to tell him the whole story, to tell him about Tara. She deserved to go to prison. Since she couldn't get a grip on herself, she couldn't answer the question, and Cooperstein went on:

"I admit, Miss Eden, that there's a point in the police report that troubles me."

There was a moment's silence. Jerry and Cynthia felt their hearts explode in their chests. The judge knew the whole story. Prison was guaranteed. But Cooperstein asked:

"Why did you park outside that house to take the drugs? I mean, anyone else would have gone to the woods, the beach, a private place, right? But you parked by the gate of a house. Just like that, in full view. It's hardly surprising the occupants called the police. You must admit that's strange."

The tension for the Edens was too great.

"It's our old vacation home," Carolina said. "My parents had to sell it because of me."

The judge was intrigued. "Because of you?"

Eden wanted to stand up, or cry out, or do anything to stop the hearing. But Graff got in first. He took advantage of Carolina's hesitation to reply in her place:

"Your honor, all my client asks is to make amends and come to terms with life. It's obvious that what she did yesterday was a cry for help. She parked outside the house because she knew she would be found. She knew her father would think to look for her there. Carolina and her father came to Orphea to find themselves and get their lives back on the right footing."

Judge Cooperstein looked away from Carolina, gazed at the lawyer for a moment, then returned to the defendant.

"Is that true, young lady?"

"Yes," she said in a low voice.

The judge seemed satisfied with the answer. Graff's stratagem had worked.

"I think you deserve a second chance," Cooperstein decreed. "But remember: this is an opportunity you have to seize. Is your father here?"

Eden stood up immediately.

"I'm here, your honor. Jerry Eden, Carolina's father."

"Mr Eden, this concerns you, too, since I understand you came here with your daughter to rebuild your relationship."

"That's correct, your honor."

"And what were you planning to do with your daughter here in Orphea?"

The question caught Eden off guard. The judge, noticing his hesitation, added:

"Don't tell me, Mr Eden, that you came here just to let your daughter see out her angst by a hotel swimming pool?"

"No, your honor. We wanted to audition together for the play. When Carolina was little, she said she wanted to be an actress. She even wrote a play three years ago."

The judge allowed himself a moment's thought. He looked at Eden, then at Carolina, and declared, "Very well. Miss Eden, I suspend the sentence provided you participate with your father in this play."

"Thank you, your honor," Carolina said with a smile. "I won't disappoint you."

"I hope not, Miss Eden. Let's be quite clear about this: if you fall down again, or if you are again arrested in possession of drugs, you won't be treated with such leniency. Your case will be dealt with in a state court. That means that if you offend again, you'll go straight to prison for several years."

Carolina promised and threw herself into her parents' arms. They went back to the Lake Palace. Carolina was exhausted and fell asleep as soon as she sat down on the couch in their suite. Eden drew Cynthia out onto the balcony to talk in peace.

274

"How about you stay with us? We could spend the time together, as a family."

"You heard the judge, Jerry, it's you and Carolina."

"There's nothing to stop you staying with us."

Cynthia shook her head. "No, you don't understand. We can't spend the time together as a family. Right now I don't have the feeling we are a family anymore. I . . . I don't have the strength. I don't have the energy. For years now, you let me handle everything. Oh, sure, you pay for it all, Jerry, and I'm truly grateful, don't think I'm not. But when was the last time you did anything for this family, apart from the financial aspect? All these years you've left me alone to handle everything and make sure the family functions properly. All you did was go to work. And not once, Jerry, not once did you ask me how I was. How I was getting along. Not once, Jerry, did you ask me if I was happy. You assumed happiness, you assumed that in St Barts or in an apartment with a view of Central Park we must be happy. Not once, Jerry, did you ask me that fucking question."

"Did you ever ask me if I was happy?" Jerry said. "This fucking work of mine, which you and Carolina hate so much—did you ever ask me if I hated it, too?"

"What stopped you from resigning?"

"The only reason I did all that, Cynthia, was to offer you a dream life. Which the two of you don't seem to want, when it comes down to it."

"Oh, really, Jerry? Are you going to tell me you preferred that little boarding house to our house by the ocean?"

"Maybe," Eden said.

"I don't believe you!"

Cynthia contemplated her husband in silence for a moment. Then she said in a choked voice:

"I need you to repair our family, Jerry. You heard the judge. Next time it'll be prison for Carolina. How are you going to make sure there isn't a next time, Jerry? How are you going to protect our daughter from herself and stop her ending up in jail?"

"Cynthia, I—"

She would not let him speak. "I'm going back to the city, Jerry. I'm leaving you here with the mission of repairing our daughter's life. This is an ultimatum. Save Carolina. Save her, or I'm leaving you. I can't live like this anymore."

*　　*　　*

"Here it is, Jesse," Derek said, pointing to the run-down gas station right at the end of Penfield Road.

I turned off, drove across the concrete forecourt and pulled up outside the lighted store. It was 11.15. There was nobody at the pumps, and the place seemed deserted.

Outside, the air was stifling in spite of the late hour. Inside, the air-conditioning made the atmosphere icy. We advanced along the aisles of magazines, drinks, and potato chips until we came to the counter, behind which, hidden by a display rack of chocolate bars, a white-haired man sat watching T.V. He greeted me without taking his eyes off the screen.

"Which pump?" he said.

"I'm not here for gas," I said, showing him my badge.

He immediately switched off the T.V. and got to his feet. "What's this about?"

"Are you Marty Connors?"

"Yes, that's me. Why are you here?"

"We're investigating the death of Mayor Gordon, Mr Connors."

"Mayor Gordon? But that was years ago."

"According to my information, you witnessed something that evening."

"Yes, that's right. I told the police about it at the time, and they told me it was nothing."

"I need to know what you saw."

"A black vehicle driving at high speed from Penfield Road and going straight ahead in the direction of Sutton Street. It drove right past here. I was at the pump, I just had time to see it go past."

"Did you recognize the model?"

"Of course. A Ford E-150 van, with a strange design at the back."

Derek and I looked at each other. Tennenbaum drove a Ford E-150 van.

"Did you see who was driving?" I asked.

"No, I didn't. At the time I thought it was just kids playing around."

"And what time was this exactly?"

"Around 7.00, but I can't tell you the exact time. It might have been 7.00, it might have been 7.10. You know, it happened in a fraction of a second, and I didn't really pay attention. It was only later, when I found out what had happened to the mayor and his family, that I thought there might be a connection. That's when I contacted the police."

"Who did you talk to? Do you remember the name of the officer?"

"Yes, of course, it was the chief himself who came to question me. Chief Hayward."

"And what did you tell him?"

"The same thing I just told you. He said it was nothing to do with the case."

Lena Bellamy had seen Tennenbaum's van outside Mayor Gordon's house in 1994. Now Marty Connors, who had spotted the same vehicle coming from Penfield Road, had confirmed that. Why had Hayward hidden it from us?

Leaving the store, we sat in the car for a while. Derek unfolded a map of the town and we studied the route the van had taken, according to Marty Connors.

"The van went down Sutton Street," Derek said, moving his finger across the map, "and Sutton Street leads to the top of Main Street."

"If you remember, on the opening night of the festival, Main Street was blocked off apart from a section at the top to allow vehicles with permission to get to the Grand Theater."

"You mean like the kind of permission the volunteer fire officer on duty might have had?"

Even back in 1994, we had already wondered if anyone had seen Tennenbaum drive past the barrier on Main Street in order to get to the Grand Theater. But the only thing that emerged from questioning the volunteers and the police officers who had been on duty was that there had been such chaos that nobody had seen anything. The festival had been a victim of its own success: Main Street was crowded, the parking lots were overwhelmed. The teams had been unable to cope. The instructions to channel the crowds and the traffic had not been followed for long. People had started parking anywhere they could and walking where there was space, treading on the flowered borders. It was quite impossible to know who had gone through the barrier and at what time.

"So Tennenbaum came along Sutton Street to get back to the theater, just as we thought," Derek said.

"But why did Hayward never tell us that? If we'd known of that testimony, we'd have been able to pin it on Tennenbaum much earlier. Did Hayward want him to get away with it?"

Connors suddenly appeared at the door of the store and came over to us.

"It's lucky you're still here," he said. "I just remembered something. Back then, I mentioned the van to the other guy."

"What other guy?" Derek said.

"I don't remember his name. But I know he wasn't from around here. The year after the murders, he came back to Orphea regularly. He said he was conducting his own investigation."

Wednesday, July 16, 2014
Ten days to opening night

The front page of the *Orphea Chronicle*:

THE DARKEST NIGHT:
FIRST ROLES CAST

Today is scheduled to be the last day of the auditions that have attracted an extraordinary number of aspiring actors from all over the region, much to the delight of the town's storekeepers. The first to have been cast in a role is none other than the famous critic Meta Ostrovski (photograph opposite). He has spoken of the play as a chrysalis from which "those who thought they were caterpillars emerge as beautiful butterflies".

Betsy, Derek and I got to the Grand Theater just before the start of the third day of auditions. The auditorium was deserted. Hayward was alone onstage. Seeing us arrive, he cried:

"You have no right to be here!"

I did not bother to reply. I took hold of him by the collar. "What have you been hiding from us, Hayward?"

I dragged him into the wings, where nobody could see us.

"You knew at the time that it was Tennenbaum's van parked outside the Gordons' house. And you covered up the gas station attendant's testimony. What do you know about this case?"

"I'm not saying anything!" Hayward blustered. "How dare you bully me like this?"

I took out my pistol and stuck it in his belly.

"Jesse, what are you doing?" Betsy said.

"Let's calm down," Hayward said in a wheedling voice. "What is it you want to know? I'll allow you one question."

"I want to know what 'The Darkest Night' is," I said.

"'The Darkest Night' is my play," Hayward said. "Are you dumb or something?"

"I'm talking about 1994. What did 'The Darkest Night' mean then?"

"In 1994 it was also my play. Well, not the same play. I had to rewrite everything because of that idiot Gordon. But I kept the same title because I thought it was a good one."

"Don't bullshit us," I said, losing it. "There are a whole bunch of things connected with 'The Darkest Night', which you know full well because you were police chief at the time. There was the graffiti that appeared all across town, then the fire at what was going to be Café Athena. It was like a countdown to Gordon's death."

"You're crazy!" Hayward cried in exasperation. "That was all me! It was a way of drawing attention to my play! When all those things started, I was sure I'd be able to put on 'The Darkest Night' as the opening event of the festival. I thought that when people made a connection between the graffiti and the announcement of my play, it would generate interest."

"So you set fire to the Café Athena site?" Derek said.

"Of course not! I was called to the fire scene and I stayed there until the middle of the night, until the firefighters managed to put out the fire. I took advantage of a time when people were busy elsewhere to go into the ruins and write 'The Darkest Night' on the walls. It was a heaven-sent opportunity. When morning came and the firefighters saw it, it made quite an impression. It wasn't a countdown to Gordon's death, it was a countdown to the opening night of the festival. I was absolutely sure I'd be chosen as the opening night attraction and that July 30 would mark the coming of 'The Darkest Night', the sensational play by the dramatist Kirk Hayward."

Just then, we heard a noise coming from the auditorium. The latest batch of auditioners was arriving. I let him go.

"You never saw us here, Kirk," Derek said. "Is that clear? It had better be."

Hayward did not reply. He straightened his shirt and went back onstage, and we went out through the emergency exit.

In the auditorium the first person to come forward was none other than Samuel Padalin, who had come to exorcise his ghosts and pay tribute to his dead wife. Hayward chose him immediately, because he felt sorry for him.

"Oh, my poor friend, if only you knew. I picked your poor wife from the sidewalk, all smashed up. A little piece here, a little piece there!"

"I know," Padalin said. "I was there, too."

Then, to Hayward's amazement, Charlotte Brown walked up onstage. He was really touched to see her. He had long dreamed of this moment. He would have liked to act hard, to put her down in front of everyone as she had humiliated him by dumping him for Brown, but he could not. It took just one glance to see the magnetism that emanated from her. She was a born actress.

"You haven't changed," he said.

She smiled. "Thank you, Kirk. Neither have you."

He shrugged. "Oh, I've turned into a crazy old man. You really want to go back on the stage?"

"I think I do."

"Then you're hired."

He added her name to his list.

*   *   *

The fact that Hayward was behind the whole "Darkest Night" business made him in our eyes even more of a fanatic. But it was Brown who intrigued us. Why had Stephanie stuck up on the wall of her cubicle at the self-storage facility an image of him making his speech on the opening night of the 1994 festival?

In Betsy's office, we looked at the video extract again. What Brown had to say was quite banal. What else could there be? Derek suggested sending the cassette to the police experts to have the sequence analyzed. Then he stood up and looked at the whiteboard. He erased the words *The Darkest Night*. That mystery had been solved.

"I still can't believe it was just the title of the play that Hayward wanted to drum up publicity for," Betsy sighed. "When I think of all the theories we concocted!"

"Sometimes the solution is right there in front of our eyes," Derek said, smiling.

Just then, my phone rang. It was Connors, from the gas station.

"I know who he is," he said.

"Who do you mean?"

"The guy who was doing his own investigation the year after the murders. I just saw his photograph in today's *Chronicle*. He's going to act in the play. His name's Ostrovski."

* * *

At the Grand Theater, Jerry and Carolina Eden got up onstage to audition.

Hayward looked Eden up and down.

"What's your name and where are you from?" he asked sternly.

"My name is Jerry Eden, and I'm from New York. It was Judge Cooperstein who—"

Hayward interrupted him. "You came from New York to be in my play?"

"I need to spend time with my daughter Carolina, to experience something new with her."

"Why?"

"Because I feel I'm losing her, and I'd like to find her again, since you ask."

There was a silence. Hayward considered Eden for a moment and decreed, "I like that. The father's hired. Let's see how good the daughter is. Come into the light, please."

Carolina stepped into the spotlight. Hayward gave a start. There was an extraordinary strength emanating from her. She threw him an intense look, almost too strong to be sustained. Hayward grabbed the script of the scene from the table and stood up to take it to Carolina, but she said:

"No need, I've been listening to this scene for the last three hours, I know it by heart."

She closed her eyes and stayed like that for a moment. All the other auditionees could not take their eyes off her, struck by her magnetism. Hayward was speechless.

Carolina opened her eyes and declaimed:

It is a gloomy morning. Rain is falling. On a country road, the traffic is paralyzed. A vast bottleneck has formed. The motorists, at the ends of their tethers, blow their horns angrily. A young woman walks along the side of the road, past the line of motionless cars. She approaches the police cordon and questions the officer on duty.

Then she lifted the collar of the coat she wasn't wearing, jumped to avoid an imaginary puddle, and ran toward Hayward as if to avoid the drops of rain falling on her.

"*What's going on?*" she said.

Hayward gazed at her spellbound and said nothing. She repeated, "*Well, officer, what's going on here?*"

Hayward, getting a grip on himself, gave her the next line:

"*A man is dead. There's been a terrible motorcycle accident.*"

He stared for a moment at Carolina, then, with a triumphant look on his face, cried:

"We have all the actors we need! Tomorrow, first thing, rehearsals can begin."

The audience applauded. Mayor Brown heaved a deep sigh of relief.

"You're amazing," Hayward said to Carolina. "Have you ever had acting classes?"

"No, never, Mr Hayward."

"You're going to play the main role!"

They looked at each other again with fierce intensity.

"Have you ever killed anyone, child?" Hayward said.

She turned pale and started shaking. "How . . . How did you know?" she stammered.

"It's written in your eyes. I've never seen such a dark soul. It's fascinating."

Carolina was unable to hold back the tears.

"It's alright, my dear," Hayward said gently. "You're going to be a great star."

*　　*　　*

It was almost 10.30. Sitting in her car outside Café Athena, Betsy was watching the interior of the restaurant. Ostrovski had just paid his check. As he stood up, she said into her radio:

"Ostrovski's on his way out."

Derek and I, waiting in the outdoor seating area, intercepted the critic as he was leaving the establishment.

"Mr Ostrovski," I said, pointing to the police car parked below, "if you wouldn't mind coming with us, we have some questions to ask you."

Ten minutes later, Ostrovski was sitting in Betsy's office in the station, drinking coffee.

"It's true," he admitted, "I was fascinated by the case. I'd covered theater festivals before, but never had a series of murders take place on opening night. Like any slightly curious human being, I was eager to get to the bottom of the story."

"According to the gas station attendant," Derek said, "you returned to Orphea several times the following year. But by then, the case was over and done with."

"From what I gathered, the murderer had died before he could confess, although the police were persuaded of his guilt. I admit at the

284

time it excited me. And without a confession, I felt there was something missing."

Derek gave me a circumspect look.

"So," Ostrovski went on, "taking advantage of the fact that I regularly come to this wonderful region of the Hamptons to relax, I passed through Orphea from time to time and asked one or two questions here and there."

"How did you know the gas station attendant had seen something?"

"Pure chance. I stopped for gas one day. We had a chat. He told me what he had seen and that he had informed the police, but that his testimony had apparently not been considered relevant. As for me, over time, my curiosity faded."

"Is that all?" I said.

"That's all, Captain Rosenberg. I'm really sorry I can't help you more than that."

I thanked Ostrovski for his cooperation and offered to drive him somewhere.

"That's kind of you, Captain, but I feel like walking a little and enjoying this wonderful night."

He stood up and said goodbye. But as he was going through the door, he turned and said:

"A critic."

"I beg your pardon?"

"Your little riddle up there on the board," Ostrovski said proudly. "I've been looking at it for a while. And I've just understood. *Who would like to write, but can't?* Your answer is: a critic."

He gave us a farewell nod of the head and left the room.

"It's him!" I cried to Betsy and Derek, who didn't catch on immediately. "The one who would like to write but can't, and who was in the Grand Theater on the evening of the murders. It's Ostrovski! He's the man behind Stephanie's book!"

A few moments later, Ostrovski was in the interrogation room, for a much less pleasant conversation than the previous one.

"We know everything, Ostrovski," Derek said angrily. "For the last twenty years, you've been putting an ad in the fall issues of college magazines in the New York area, trying to find someone to write a book investigating the Gordon murders."

"Why that ad?" I said.

Ostrovski looked at me as if it was blindingly obvious. "Come on now, Captain. Can you imagine a great literary critic lowering himself to write a mystery novel? Can you imagine what people would say?"

"Where's the problem?"

"In the order of respect granted to literary genres, at the top there is the incomprehensible novel, then the intellectual novel, then the historical novel, then the straight novel, and only after that, almost at the bottom of the list, just above the romantic novel, there's the mystery novel."

"Is this a joke?" Derek said.

"No, of course not! No, that's just the problem. Ever since those murders, I've been held captive by a brilliant mystery plot, but I can't write it."

*   *   *

Orphea, July 30, 1994
The night of the murders

When the performance of "Uncle Vanya" was over, Ostrovski left the auditorium. A decent production, good acting. Since the intermission, he had heard people in his row getting agitated. Some of the audience had not returned for the second act. He only discovered the reason for that when he walked through the lobby, which was in a state of feverish excitement. Everyone was talking about a murder that had been committed in the town.

From the steps of the building, looking down at the street, he observed the crowd heading in a continuous stream in the same direction: toward the Penfield neighborhood. Everyone wanted to see what had happened there. The atmosphere was electric, with a hint of frenzy. The human torrent reminded him of the tide of rats in "The Pied Piper of Hamelin". As a critic, when everyone rushed somewhere, that was precisely where he did not go. He did not like what was fashionable, jeered at what was popular, loathed anything that aroused general enthusiasm. And yet, fascinated by the atmosphere, he felt a desire to let himself be carried along with it. He realized it was morbid curiosity. He threw himself into the human river plunging down Main Street and converging from the adjacent streets into a quiet residential neighborhood. Ostrovski, walking at a good pace, soon came to Penfield Crescent. There were many police cars there. The walls of the houses were illumined by the revolving blue and red lights. Ostrovski made his way through the crowd massed against the police barriers. The air on this tropical summer night was stifling. People were excited, nervous, anxious. They were saying it was the mayor's house. They said the mayor had been murdered. Along with his wife and son.

Ostrovski stayed in Penfield Crescent for a long time, fascinated by what he was seeing. The real spectacle of the evening had not after all taken place at the Grand Theater, but here. Who had killed the mayor, and why? He was devoured by curiosity. He started constructing theories.

Once back at his hotel, he went to the bar. Late as it was, he was too exhilarated to sleep. What was going on? Why was he so fascinated by an everyday news item? Suddenly, he understood. He asked for paper and a pen. For the first time in his life, he had the plot of a book in his head. The idea was a special one: while the whole town is busy with the opening of a theater festival, a killing occurs. It was like a magic trick: the public looks to the left while everything is happening on the right. Ostrovski even wrote in capital letters the words THE CONJURING TRICK. That was the title! First thing tomorrow, he would make haste to the bookstore and buy all the mystery novels they had in stock. That was when he suddenly stopped, grasping the terrible reality. If he published that book, everyone would say it was a work of an inferior genre: a mystery novel. His reputation would never recover.

* * *

"So I could never write the book," Ostrovski was saying in the interrogation room of the police station. "I dreamed about it, thought about it incessantly. I wanted to read that story, but I could not write it. Not a crime story, a mystery novel. It was too risky."

"So you decided to hire someone else?"

"Yes. I couldn't ask an established author. Just imagine, he could have blackmailed me by threatening to reveal my secret fascination with a mystery plot. It seemed to me that hiring a student would be less risky. And that was how I came across Stephanie Mailer. I knew her from the *Review*. Stephanie was an exceptional writer, a pure talent. She agreed to write the book. She said she had been looking for a good subject for years. It was the happiest meeting of minds."

"Did you keep in contact with Stephanie?"

"At first, yes. She came regularly to the city. We'd meet in the coffee shop near the *Review*. She'd keep me up to date with her progress and sometimes read me passages. But when she was busy with her research, she would not get in touch for a while. That's why I wasn't worried last week when I couldn't reach her. I had given her free rein, and $30,000 in cash for her expenses. I was glad to let her have the money and the fame, I only wanted to know how the story worked out."

"Because you had reason to think Tennenbaum did not commit the murders?"

"I followed the developments in the case closely. I knew a witness had stated that Tennenbaum's van had been outside the mayor's house. From the description I was given of it, I knew I had seen that same van pass the Grand Theater just before seven on the evening of the murders. I had arrived at the theater much too early, and it was boiling hot inside. I went outside for a smoke. To avoid the crowd, I went into the street at the side of the theater, which is a dead-end street leading to the stage door. That was when I saw that black vehicle drive by. It attracted my attention because there was a strange drawing on the rear window. It was Tennenbaum's van, the one everybody talked about afterward."

"But that night you saw who the driver was, and it wasn't Tennenbaum?"

"Yes," Ostrovski said.

"Who was it, Mr Ostrovski?" Derek said.

"It was Charlotte Brown, the mayor's wife. She was the one driving Tennenbaum's van."

-2

Rehearsals

THURSDAY, JULY 17 – SATURDAY, JULY 19, 2014

JESSE ROSENBERG

Thursday, July 17, 2014
Nine days to opening night

Charlotte Brown's veterinary clinic was located in the industrial quarter of Orphea, close to two large shopping malls. As she did every morning, she got to the almost deserted parking lot at 7.30 and parked in the place reserved for her in front of the clinic. She got out of the car, a coffee in her hand. She seemed to be in a good mood. She was so lost in thought that, even though I was only a few paces from her, she did not notice me until I said:

"Good morning, Mrs Brown. I'm Captain Rosenberg, State Police."

She gave a start and rolled her eyes. "You scared me," she said with a smile. "But yes, I know who you are."

Then she saw Betsy, who was standing behind me, leaning against her patrol car.

"Betsy?" Charlotte said in surprise, and suddenly panicked. "Oh, my God, has Alan . . ."

"Don't worry, Mrs Brown," I said, "your husband's fine. But we need to ask you a few questions."

Betsy opened the rear door of her car.

"I don't understand," Charlotte Brown said.

"You will soon," I said.

We drove her to the police station, where we allowed her to telephone her clinic to cancel her appointments for the morning, then a lawyer as she was allowed by right. Rather than a lawyer, she preferred to call her husband, who came in a great hurry. But even though he was mayor of the town, Alan Brown could not sit in on his wife's interrogation. He caused a scene until Chief Gulliver said, "Alan, they're doing you a favor by questioning Charlotte here, quickly and discreetly, rather than dragging her to the troop headquarters of the State Police."

Sitting in the interrogation room, her cup of coffee in front of her, she seemed in a feverish state.

"Mrs Brown," I said, "a witness has formally identified you as leaving the Grand Theater just before seven o'clock on the evening of Saturday, July 30, 1994, on board a vehicle belonging to Ted Tennenbaum. That same vehicle was seen a few minutes later outside Mayor Gordon's house, around the time he and his family were murdered."

Charlotte Brown lowered her eyes. "I didn't kill the Gordons," she said.

"Tell us what did happen that evening."

There was a moment's silence. She sat there impassively, then said, "I knew this day would come. I knew I couldn't keep the secret to the end of my life."

"What secret is that, Mrs Brown?" I said. "What have you been hiding for twenty years?"

After a hesitation, she said in a low voice:

"Yes, I did take Ted Tennenbaum's van on opening night. I'd seen it parked outside the stage door. You couldn't miss it, with that owl on the rear window. I knew it was his because some of the other actors and I had spent the previous few evenings at Café Athena and Ted had driven us back to the hotel. So that day, when I needed to be absent for a while, just before seven, I immediately thought to borrow it from him. To save time. Nobody in the company had a car in Orphea. Obviously, I'd planned to ask his permission. I went to look for him in the little room he had as fire officer, next to our dressing rooms. But he wasn't there. I had a quick look around the backstage area, but I couldn't find him. There'd been a problem with the fuses, so I assumed he was busy with that. I saw the keys in his room, lying there on the table in full view. I didn't have much time. The official part of the evening was going to begin in half an hour and Buzz, the director, obviously didn't want us to leave the theater. So I took the keys. I didn't think anyone would notice. And besides, Tennenbaum was on duty for the show, so he wouldn't be going anywhere. I snuck out of the theater by the stage door and got in his van."

"But what did you have to do that was so urgent you needed to be away just half an hour before the opening?"

"I absolutely had to speak to Mayor Gordon. A few minutes, as it turned out, before he and his family were murdered, I dropped by his house."

*   *   *

Orphea, July 30, 1994, 6.50 p.m.
The evening of the murders

Charlotte Brown started Tennenbaum's van and drove out of the dead-end lane onto Main Street. She was astonished by the indescribable bustle there. The street was full of people and closed to traffic. When she had arrived with the cast that morning, the place had been deserted. Now a dense crowd filled the street.

At the intersection, a volunteer in charge of traffic was busy giving directions to families who were clearly lost. He pushed open the police barrier to allow Charlotte through, signaling to her that she could only go up the street along a corridor left free to allow access to emergency vehicles. She obeyed—she had no choice. She did not know Orphea, and all she had to orientate herself was a rough map on the back of a booklet published by the tourist office for the festival. Penfield Crescent wasn't on it, although she could see the Penfield neighborhood. She decided to head there and then ask a passer-by for directions. So she drove as far as Sutton Street, then followed the street until she came to Penfield Road, which marked the entrance to the residential neighborhood of the same name. But the place was like a maze, with streets going off in all directions. Charlotte wandered, making U-turns, and even got lost for a brief while. The streets were deserted, almost ghostly: there wasn't anyone out of doors. Time was passing, she had to hurry. Finally, she got back onto Penfield Road, the main thoroughfare, and drove quickly along it. She had to come across someone in the end. It was then that she spotted a young woman doing exercises in a park. Charlotte immediately pulled up at the side of the road, got out of the van, and walked across the grass.

"Excuse me," she said to the young woman. "I'm lost. I need to get to Penfield Crescent."

"You've reached it," the woman said, smiling. "It's that semicircle on the edge of the park. What number are you looking for?"

"I don't even know the number," Charlotte admitted. "I'm looking for Mayor Gordon's house."

"Oh, it's right there," the young woman said, pointing to a cozy-looking house on the other side of the park.

Charlotte thanked her and got back in the van. She turned onto Penfield Crescent and pulled up outside the mayor's house, leaving the vehicle on the street, with the engine on. According to the dashboard it was 7.04. She had to be quick. She ran to the door of the house and rang the bell. No response. She rang again and stuck her ear to the door. She thought she could make out some sounds inside. She banged on the door with her fist. "Is there anybody there?" she shouted. But there was no response. As she walked back down the porch steps, she noticed that the drawn curtains at one of the windows in the house were moving slightly. She saw a boy looking at her. He immediately pulled back the curtain. She called out: "Hey, you, wait!" and made to run across the lawn to the window. But the lawn was flooded, and Charlotte found herself up to her ankles in water. When she got to the window, she called the boy again, but to no avail. She didn't have time to keep on with this. She had to get back to the theater. She tiptoed back across the lawn to the sidewalk. What rotten luck! Her stage shoes were soaked. She got back in the van and set off at high speed. According to the dashboard it was 7.09.

*　　*　　*

"So you left Penfield Crescent just before the murderer got there?" I said.

"Yes, Captain Rosenberg," Charlotte said. "If I'd stayed a minute longer, I'd have been killed, too."

296

"Maybe he was already there somewhere," Derek suggested, "waiting for you to leave."

"Maybe."

"Did you notice anything?" I said.

"No, nothing. I got back to the theater as rapidly as I could. There were so many people on Main Street, everything was blocked, I didn't think I'd get back in time for the play. I'd have been quicker on foot, but I couldn't abandon Tennenbaum's van. I finally got to the theater at 7.30. The official part had already begun. I put back the keys to the van and ran to my dressing room."

"And Tennenbaum didn't see you?"

"No, and I didn't say anything to him later either. But in any case, my little escape had been a total fiasco. I hadn't seen Gordon. And Buzz, the director, had discovered my absence because of my hair dryer catching fire. But he didn't hold it against me. We were about to start, and he was mainly relieved to see me backstage. And the play was a success. We never spoke about it again."

"Charlotte," I said, finally coming to what mattered most to us, "why did you have to speak with Mayor Gordon?"

"I had to recover Kirk Hayward's play, 'The Darkest Night'. He'd been pestering me about it for days. He said the mayor had his play and would not give it back. The day the festival was due to start he came to see me in my dressing room."

"By this point you had broken up with Hayward, is that right?" I said.

"I was already seeing Alan and had split up with Kirk, but he wouldn't let go. He was making my life a misery."

*   *   *

Orphea, July 30, 1994, 10.10 a.m.
Nine hours before the murders

Walking into her dressing room, Charlotte Brown was startled to see Hayward, in his uniform, sprawled on the couch.

"What are you doing here?"

"If you leave me, Charlotte, I'll kill myself."

"Oh, for God's sake, Kirk, grow up!"

"Grow up, you say?" Leaping off the couch, he pulled out his gun and stuck it in his mouth.

"Kirk, stop this, for heaven's sake!" Charlotte was in a state of panic.

He put his gun back in his belt. "You see," he said, "I'm not joking."

"I know, Kirk. But you have to accept that it's over between us."

"What does Alan Brown have that I don't?"

"Everything."

He sat down again.

"Kirk, it's the opening of the festival, shouldn't you be at the station? You must be snowed under with work."

"I didn't dare say anything, Charlotte, but things are going badly at work. Very badly, in fact. It's now that I need moral support. You can't leave me now."

"It's over, Kirk. Once and for all."

"Charlotte, nothing's going right in my life anymore. I need your help."

"Help with what?"

"Mayor Gordon has what is literally the only script of my play and he's refusing to let me have it back. Please help me get it back."

"What do you mean, he has your play? Why on earth don't you have a copy?"

"Well, about two weeks ago there was a little misunderstanding with the guys at the station. In someone's idea of a prank they turned my office upside down and destroyed all my scripts. I had everything there, Charlotte. Everything I had of 'The Darkest Night' has disappeared. The only copy left is the one that's in Gordon's possession. If he doesn't give it back, well, I can't answer for my actions!"

Charlotte looked at the man standing before her, this unhappy man she had once loved. She knew how hard he had worked on the play.

"Kirk," she said, "if I get the script back from Gordon, do you promise you'll leave Alan and me alone?"

"Oh, Charlotte, you have my word!"

"Where does Mayor Gordon live? I'll go there tomorrow."

"On Penfield Crescent. But you have to go today."

"Kirk, that's just not possible, we're rehearsing until at least 6.30."

"Charlotte, I beg you. I'm having a drink with a Broadway producer this evening. With a little luck I can persuade him to read my play. But not if you don't get that copy! I'll come to see you during intermission to collect it. Promise me you'll go to see Gordon today."

Charlotte sighed. She felt genuinely sorry for him.

"I promise, Kirk. Come backstage during intermission. I'll have your play."

*   *   *

In the interrogation room, Derek interrupted Charlotte's account. "Why didn't you tell us at the time that it was you in the van?"

"Because you only latched on to Tennenbaum after the festival, and I didn't hear about it immediately. I'd gone back to Albany, then did an internship for several months with a vet in Pittsburgh. I didn't get back to Orphea until six months later, to settle down with Alan, and it was only then that I heard about what had happened. In any case, you had tracked down Tennenbaum. He was the murderer, wasn't he?"

No-one answered.

"What about Hayward?" I said. "Didn't he talk to you about it?"

"No. After the festival, I didn't hear from him. When I moved to Orphea in January 1995, I was told he had left very abruptly and nobody ever found out why."

"I think he left because he thought you were guilty of the murders, Charlotte."

"What?" she said. "He thought I'd seen the mayor, the mayor had refused to give me the play, and I'd killed all those people out of revenge? That would be insane."

"I can't be as certain as that," I said, "but what do I know is that you were seen leaving the theater driving Tennenbaum's van, just before the murders. The same witness has told us that he learned that Tennenbaum had been the chief suspect because of that very van. He went to see Chief Hayward to talk to him about it. That was in October 1994. My belief is that Hayward was so upset that he preferred to resign and leave Orphea."

So Charlotte Brown was out of the frame. After leaving the station, she went with Mayor Brown immediately to the Grand Theater. We found that out thanks to Michael Bird, who was there and reported the scene to us.

As soon as Charlotte entered the auditorium, Hayward cried out cheerfully:

"Charlotte is here early! This day can't get any better."

Charlotte advanced down the aisle in silence.

"Is everything alright, Charlotte?" Hayward said. "You look strange."

She looked him up and down for a long time, then said, "Did you run away from Orphea because of me, Kirk?"

He did not reply. She went on:

"You found out it was me driving Tennenbaum's van. Did you think I'd killed four people?"

"It doesn't matter what I think, Charlotte, the only thing that matters is what I know. As I promised your husband, on opening night, you'll discover everything."

"Kirk, a woman is dead. And the person who killed her is probably the same person who killed the Gordon family. We can't wait for July 26, you have to tell us everything now."

"On opening night, you'll discover," Hayward repeated.

"But that's insane, Kirk! Why are you behaving like this? People have died, don't you understand?"

There was a long silence. All eyes were on Hayward and Charlotte.

"So next Saturday," Charlotte said, exasperated and on the verge of tears, "the police will have to wait quietly for the end of the show before you deign to reveal what you know?"

Hayward looked at her in surprise. "The end of the show? No. It will be more toward the middle."

"The middle? Kirk, what are you talking about?" She seemed lost. Hayward, grim-faced, declared:

"I said you'll discover everything on opening night, Charlotte. That means the answer is in the play. 'The Darkest Night' contains the solution to the case."

Early September 1994. It was one month since the Gordon murders, and Jesse and I were in no doubt about Tennenbaum's guilt. The case was almost wrapped up.

Tennenbaum had killed Mayor Gordon because the mayor had been putting pressure on him because of his urgent need to get on with the work on Café Athena. The sums of money exchanged corresponded to the withdrawals and payments in their several accounts, a witness stated he had deserted his post at the Grand Theater at the very time the murders had taken place, and his van had been seen outside the mayor's house. In addition, we had established that he was a good shot.

Other officers would have already put Tennenbaum in preventive detention and let the law finish the job. There was enough evidence to charge him with homicide in the first degree and to get the legal process going, but that was the problem. Knowing Tennenbaum and his fiend of a lawyer, they might well manage to convince a jury that there was reasonable doubt, and Tennenbaum would be acquitted.

So we did not want to rush in and make an arrest. Our progress had impressed the major, and we had decided to wait a little. Time was on our side. Tennenbaum was bound to lower his guard eventually and make a mistake. Our reputations, Jesse's and mine, depended on our being patient. Our colleagues and our superiors were watching us closely and we knew it. We wanted to be the tireless young detectives who had sent a quadruple murderer to prison, not a couple of amateurs crushed by Tennenbaum getting acquitted and being awarded damages, his legal costs paid by the State.

Furthermore, there was one element of the investigation that remained unexplored: the murder weapon. A Beretta with a filed-off serial number. A professional criminal's weapon. That was what intrigued us: how had a man from a respectable Manhattan family procured that kind of gun?

The question led us to crisscross the Hamptons, discreetly. We ended up focusing on a disreputable bar in Ridgesport, where Tennenbaum had been arrested for a violent brawl a few years earlier. We staked the place out for four days, hoping Tennenbaum would show up. It was because of that stakeout that we were called to Major McKenna's office early one morning. There was another man there, who immediately started bawling us out.

"I'm Special Agent Grace, A.T.F. So you're the two assholes who are sabotaging a federal investigation."

"Good morning to you, too," I said. "I'm Sergeant Derek Scott and this is—"

"I know who you two clowns are!" Grace cut in.

The major explained the situation more diplomatically. "The A.T.F. spotted the two of you outside a bar in Ridgesport that they already have under surveillance."

"We rented a house opposite the bar. We've been there for months," Grace added.

"Special Agent Grace, are we allowed to know why you're interested in that bar?" Jesse said.

"Because of a guy who was arrested holding up a bank on Long Island in February, and who started talking in return for a reduced sentence. He told us he'd bought his gun in that bar. When we looked into it, we found it was a place where stolen army weapons are being resold. And these thefts are inside jobs, if you see what I mean. In other words, military personnel are involved. So you won't be upset if I don't tell you more. It's sensitive."

"Could you at least tell us what kind of weapons we're talking about?" Jesse said.

"Berettas, with the serial numbers filed off."

Jesse threw me a startled look. Maybe we were on the verge of playing our match ball. It was in that bar that the murderer had acquired the murder weapon.

JESSE ROSENBERG

Friday, July 18, 2014

Eight days to opening night

The announcement made by Kirk Hayward the day before at the Grand Theater, that the name of the killer from 1994 would be revealed in the course of his play, had caused a great stir. Orphea was seething with excitement. In my opinion, Hayward was bluffing.

One point bothered us, however: "The Darkest Night". How could Mayor Gordon, having, as we knew, torn up his copy, still have been in possession of a copy of the script? To try to answer this question, Betsy, Derek and I were on board the ferry that ran from Port Jefferson in the Hamptons to Bridgeport, Connecticut. We were on our way to New Haven to question Mayor Gordon's brother Ernest, who was a professor of biology at Yale. With his brother's family all dead, he had inherited everything. It was he who had sorted through his brother's affairs at the time, so maybe he had come across that playscript. He was our last hope.

Ernest Gordon was now seventy. He was Joseph's elder brother. He received us in his kitchen, where he had cookies and coffee ready. His wife was also present. She seemed nervous.

"On the telephone you said you had new information about the murder of my brother and his family," Gordon said.

His wife could not stay seated.

"That's right, Mr Gordon," I said. "To be honest with you, there are a number of things we've discovered recently that lead us to think we may have been mistaken twenty years ago about the guilt of the man called Ted Tennenbaum."

"You mean he wasn't the killer?"

"Yes, that is what I mean. What we came today to discover, Mr

Gordon, was whether you can remember seeing among your brother's effects a playscript entitled 'The Darkest Night'."

Gordon sighed. "My brother had an incredible amount of paperwork at home. I tried to sort through it a little, but there was too much. In the end, I threw most of it away."

"We have the impression this play was quite important. Apparently he had resisted giving it back to its author. This suggests that he might have kept it somewhere secure. Somewhere unusual, too, a place where nobody would think to look for it."

Gordon stared at us. There was a heavy silence. It was his wife who finally broke it.

"Ernie," she said, "we have to tell them everything. It may be important to these officers."

Gordon sighed again. "After my brother's death, I was contacted by a notary public. Joseph had drawn up a will, which surprised me because he didn't have any other property apart from his house. But this will mentioned a safe deposit box in a bank."

"We were never told about this safe deposit box back then," Derek said.

"I didn't inform the police about it," Gordon admitted.

"Why?"

"Because there was cash in that box. A lot of cash. Enough to send our three children to college. So I decided not to tell anyone about it."

"These were the kickbacks that Gordon had not managed to transfer to Montana," Derek said.

"What else was in the box?" I said.

"Assorted papers, Captain Rosenberg. But I confess I didn't go through them carefully."

"Shit," Derek said. "I suppose you threw it all away!"

Gordon said, "I didn't tell the bank my brother had died, and I gave the notary public enough money to pay the rental of the box until I die. I suspected the money in it wasn't entirely clean and I thought the best way to keep the existence of the box secret was to stay well away. I told myself that if I approached the bank about canceling it—"

Derek didn't let him finish. "What bank was this, Professor Gordon?"

"I promise I'll give it all back," Gordon said.

"We don't care about the money, we have no intention of chasing you for it. But we do need to see what other papers your brother was hiding in the box."

*

A few hours later, Betsy, Derek and I entered the safe deposit area of a private bank in Manhattan. A clerk opened the safe for us and took out a box, which we hastened to open.

Inside, we discovered a heap of bound pages. On the cover was:

THE DARKEST NIGHT
by
Kirk Hayward

"Well, well," Betsy said. "Why did Mayor Gordon put the script in a safe deposit box?"

"And what's the connection between the play and the murders?" Derek said.

The box also contained bank documents. Derek leafed through them and seemed intrigued.

"What have you found, Derek?"

"Bank statements, with details of large amounts paid in. Presumably kickbacks. There are withdrawals, too. I think they correspond to the sums that Gordon was sending to Montana prior to running away."

"We already knew that Gordon was corrupt," I said, not sure why he sounded so astonished.

"The account is in the names of Joseph Gordon and Alan Brown."

So Brown was involved, too. And this wasn't the last of our surprises. After the bank, we went to troop headquarters to get the results of the analysis of the video of Brown's speech on the opening night of the first festival.

The imaging experts had identified a split second in the video sequence where the backlighting from the theater's spotlights on the sheet of paper Alan Brown was holding revealed, through the paper, the text that was on it. Their report indicated summarily: "Of the few words that can be made out, the text spoken by the speaker seems to correspond to what is written on the paper."

I looked at the enlargement, speechless.

"What is it, Jesse?" Derek said. "You just told us that the text on the paper was indeed Brown's speech, didn't you?"

I showed him the image. "The text on the paper is typewritten. On the evening of the murders, contrary to what he stated, Brown did not ad-lib his speech. He had typed it out in advance. He knew Mayor Gordon would not be coming. He had prepared everything."

JESSE ROSENBERG

Saturday, July 19, 2014

Seven days to opening night

The bank documents discovered in Gordon's safe deposit box were genuine. The account through which the dirty money had passed had been opened by Gordon and Brown together. Brown had himself signed the documents opening it.

In the early hours of the morning, with the greatest discretion, we rang the doorbell of Alan and Charlotte Brown's house and drove them both to headquarters for questioning. Charlotte must have known about her husband's involvement in the corruption that had blighted Orphea in 1994.

Despite our best efforts not to be noticed as we were taking the Browns away, a female neighbor, an early riser, glued to the window of her kitchen, had seen them climb into two State Police cars. The information passed from house to house, at the exponential speed of a text message. Some, incredulous, were so curious that they went and rang the Browns' bell. Among them was the *Chronicle* editor, no doubt eager to check the veracity of the rumor. The shock wave soon spread among the local media: the mayor of Orphea and his wife had been arrested by the police. Peter Frogg, the deputy mayor, bombarded by telephone calls, shut himself up in his house. Chief Gulliver, on the other hand, was happy to answer all inquiries, even though he knew nothing. A scandal was brewing.

When Hayward got to the Grand Theater, just before rehearsals were scheduled to begin, he found reporters pacing up and down outside. They were waiting for him.

"Mr Hayward, is there a link between your play and the arrest of Charlotte Brown?"

Hayward hesitated for a moment before replying. "You'll have to come and see the play. Everything's in it."

The reporters grew even more excited and Hayward smiled. Everyone was starting to talk about "The Darkest Night".

*

We questioned Alan and Charlotte Brown in separate rooms. It was Charlotte who cracked first. When I showed her the bank statements found in Mayor Gordon's safe deposit box, she turned pale.

"Taking kickbacks?" she said. "No, Alan would never have done anything like that. He's the most honest man I know."

"The evidence is here, Charlotte," Betsy said. "You recognize his signature, don't you?"

"Yes, I agree, that is his signature, but I'm sure there's a sensible explanation. What has he said?"

"So far, he's denied everything. If he doesn't help us, we won't be able to help him in return. He'll be referred to the D.A. and put in provisional detention."

Charlotte burst into tears. "Oh, Betsy, I swear I don't know about any of this!"

Betsy placed a sympathetic hand on hers. "Charlotte, did you tell us everything the other day?"

"There is one thing I left out." Charlotte was finding it difficult to get her breath back. "Alan knew the Gordons were planning to run away. He knew that on the opening night of the festival they were going to sneak out of town."

*   *   *

Orphea, July 30, 1994, 11.30 a.m.
Eight hours before the murders

On the stage of the Grand Theater, Buzz Lambert was putting his cast through their paces for the very last time. He had a few details he wanted to polish. Charlotte took advantage of a scene she wasn't in to go to the bathroom. In the lobby, she ran into Alan and happily threw herself into his arms. He drew her away from prying eyes and they kissed.

"Did you come to see me?" she said. Her eyes were sparkling wickedly. But he seemed troubled.

"Is everything going well?" he said.

"Very well, Alan."

"No news about that nut Hayward?"

"Yes, actually there is. Good news, in fact. He says he's prepared to leave me alone. No more suicide threats, no more scenes. He's going to behave himself from now on. All he wants is for me to help him recover the script of his play."

"What kind of blackmail is that?"

"No, Alan, I'm happy to help him. He worked so hard on his play. It seems there's only one copy left and Mayor Gordon has it. Can you ask him to give it back? Or to give it to you and then we'll get it to Kirk?"

Brown immediately dug in his heels. "Forget about the play, Charlotte."

"Why?"

"Because I'm asking you. Hayward can get lost."

"Alan, why are you reacting like this? It isn't like you. Hayward's weird, O.K. But he deserves to get his script back. You know what a huge amount of work it was for him."

"Listen, Charlotte, I respect Hayward as a police officer, but, please, forget his play. And forget Gordon."

"Oh, Alan, surely you can do this for me. You don't know what it's like having Kirk endlessly threatening to blow his brains out."

"Let him do it!" Brown said, exasperated.

"I didn't know you were so stupid, Alan. I guess I was wrong about you."

She turned away from him and made to head back to the auditorium. He caught her by the arm.

"Wait, Charlotte. Please forgive me, I'm really sorry. I'd like to help Kirk, but it's impossible."

"Why impossible?"

Brown hesitated for a moment, then said, "Because Gordon is about to leave Orphea. Forever."

"What? *Tonight*?"

"Yes, Charlotte. Gordon and his family are getting ready to disappear."

*   *   *

"Why do you think the Gordons had to leave?" Betsy asked Charlotte.

"I have no idea," Charlotte said. "I didn't even want to know. I did think there was something strange about Mayor Gordon. All I wanted was to retrieve the script of Hayward's play. But I couldn't leave the theater all day. Lambert insisted on rehearsing some scenes, then he asked for a read-through, and then had private conversations with each of us in turn. There was a lot at stake and he was nervous. It was only at the end of the day that I finally had a free moment to go to the mayor's house, and I went straight there. Without even knowing if they were still there, or had already left. I knew it was the last chance I had to get the script back."

"And later?" Betsy said.

"When I heard that the Gordons had been killed, I wanted to talk to the police, but Alan persuaded me not to. He said it might get him into serious trouble. And me, too, because I'd been there just before they were killed. When I told him that a woman exercising in the park had seen me he looked terrified. 'She's dead, too,' he said. 'Everyone who saw anything is dead. I think it's best not to talk about this to anyone.'"

Betsy next went to see Brown in the adjoining room.

"Alan, you knew that Gordon would not be coming to the opening ceremony. Your supposedly improvised speech had been typed."

He lowered his eyes. "I can assure you I had nothing to do with the deaths of the Gordon family."

Betsy put the bank statements down on the table. " In 1992 you opened a joint account with Joseph Gordon into which half a million dollars was transferred over two years, deriving from kickbacks linked' to work on buildings in Orphea."

"Where did you find these?"

"In a safe deposit box belonging to Joseph Gordon."

"Betsy, I swear to you I'm not corrupt."

"Then explain all this to me! Because right now all you're doing is denying everything, and that doesn't help your case."

After one last hesitation, Brown finally plunged in. "At the beginning of 1994, I discovered that Gordon was corrupt."

"How?"

"From an anonymous phone call, around the end of February. It was a woman's voice. She told me to examine the books of companies chosen by the council for public works and compare the internal billing of the companies and the billing received by the council for the same contracts. There was a sizeable difference. All the companies were systematically overbilling. Someone in the council was making a packet. Someone in a position to take the final decisions in awarding contracts. In other words, either Gordon or me. I knew it wasn't me."

"What did you do?"

"I went straight to Gordon and asked him to explain. I admit I was still giving him the benefit of the doubt. What I wasn't expecting was the way he counter-attacked."

*　　*　　*

Orphea, February 25, 1994
Mayor Gordon's office

Mayor Gordon looked rapidly through the documents that Alan Brown had brought in. Brown sat facing him, uncomfortable at Gordon's lack of reaction.

"Joseph," he said, "tell me you're not mixed up in corruption. Tell me you didn't ask for money in return for awarding contracts."

Mayor Gordon opened a drawer and took out some papers, which he handed across the desk to Alan.

"Alan," he said, almost apologetically, "we're just a couple of small-time crooks."

"What are these?" Alan said, looking through the papers. "And why is my name on this statement?"

"Because we opened that account together, two years ago, don't you remember?"

"We opened an account for the council, Joseph! You said it would make accounting easier, especially for expenses. What I see here is a personal account, nothing to do with the council."

"You should have read it carefully before you signed."

"But I trusted you, Joseph! Are you telling me you tricked me? Oh, my God . . . I even gave you my passport to show to the bank."

"Yes, and I'm grateful for your cooperation. That means if I go down, you go down with me, Alan. This money is ours, the two of us. Don't try taking the law into your own hands, don't go to the police, don't go rummaging about in this account. Everything is in both our names. So unless you want us to share a cell in a federal prison for corruption, it's best you forget the whole story."

"But this is bound to come out, Joseph! If only because every contractor in town knows you're corrupt!"

"Stop moaning, Alan. The contractors are all in the same boat as you. They won't say anything because they're as guilty as I am. You can rest easy. And besides, this has been going on for a while now and everyone's happy. The contractors are assured of work, so they're not going to risk taking the moral high ground now."

"Joseph, you don't understand. Somebody knows about your schemes and is ready to talk. I received an anonymous call. That's how I discovered everything."

For the first time, Mayor Gordon showed signs of unease. "What? Who?"

"As I said, it was an anonymous call."

In the interrogation room, Brown looked at Betsy in silence.

"I was in a corner," he said. "I knew I'd never be able to prove I wasn't involved in the general corruption. The account was in my name, too. Gordon was clever, he had planned it all. He may have seemed a little soft sometimes, a little indecisive, but he knew exactly what he was doing. I was at his mercy."

"What happened next?"

"Gordon was still in a panic over the anonymous phone call. He was so sure that everyone would keep their mouth shut that he had never imagined anything like that happening. This made me think that the corruption involved even more people than I knew of, and that he was in real danger. The months that followed were very difficult. Our relations were strained, but we had to save face. Gordon wasn't the kind of man to do nothing and I suspected he was looking for a way out. And, in fact, in April, he asked me to meet him one evening in the marina parking lot. 'I'm going to leave town soon,' he told me. 'Where are you going, Joseph?' 'That doesn't matter.' 'When?' 'As soon as I've finished cleaning up this mess.' Another two months went by. To me, they were an eternity. At the end of June 1994 he summoned me again to the marina parking lot and told me he would be leaving at the end of the summer. 'I'll announce after the festival that I won't be standing for re-election in September. Right after that, I'll move out.' 'Why don't you leave before? Why wait another two months?' 'I've been gradually emptying the bank account since March. I can only make transfers up to a certain level in order not to arouse suspicion. At this rate, it'll be cleared by the end of the summer. The timing's ideal. We'll close the account. It'll cease to exist, and you'll never be implicated. The town will be yours. That's what you always dreamed of, isn't it?' 'And in the meantime, this business can blow up in our faces at any moment. And even if you do close the account, there must still be traces of the transactions somewhere. You can't just wipe everything out, Joseph!' 'Don't panic, Alan. I've thought of everything, as usual.'

"Mayor Gordon actually said: 'I've thought of everything'?"

"Yes, those were his very words. I'll never forget his face when he said them. It was ice-cold, terrifying. After all that time rubbing shoulders with him, I'd never realized that Joseph Gordon was the kind of man who let nothing stand in his way."

Betsy nodded as she took notes. She looked up at Brown.

"But if Gordon had planned to leave after the festival, why did he change his mind and decide to leave on opening night?"

Alan made a face. "It was Charlotte who told you that, wasn't it? It could only have been her, she was the only person who knew. As the festival approached, I found it hard to live with the fact that Gordon was getting all the credit even though he didn't have anything to do with creating or organizing it. All he'd done was put more money in his pocket, giving accreditation to vendors setting up stands on Main Street. I couldn't bear it any longer. He'd even published a little book in praise of his work. Everyone was congratulating him. What a sham! The day before the festival, I went to see him in his office and demanded that he leave the following morning. I didn't want him to be taking all the credit, I didn't want him to make the opening speech. He was planning to leave, sneaking out quietly after getting all the prestige, leaving the memory of an outstanding politician, even though I was the one who'd done everything. It was intolerable to me. I wanted Gordon to run away like a dog, with his tail between his legs. I demanded that he take off on the night of July 29. But he refused. On the morning of July 30, there he still was, provoking me, parading up and down Main Street, pretending to check that everything was going well. I told him I was going straight to his house to talk to his wife. I jumped in my car and drove to Penfield Crescent. Just as his wife, Leslie, was opening the door of the house and greeting me in a friendly fashion, I heard Gordon drive up behind me at high speed. Leslie Gordon already knew everything. In the kitchen, I said to them: 'If you haven't left Orphea by tonight, I'll tell everyone, on the stage of the Grand Theater, that Joseph Gordon is corrupt. I'll let it all out! I don't care about the consequences for myself.

315

Today is your one chance to escape.' Joseph and Leslie Gordon realized I wasn't bluffing. I was about to explode. They promised me they'd get out that evening at the latest. I left their house and I went to the theater. It was late morning by now. I saw Charlotte, who'd gotten it into her head to recover something that Gordon had in his possession, some fucking play that Hayward had written. She was so insistent that I had to tell her Gordon was planning to take off in a few hours."

"So you knew and Charlotte knew that the Gordons were going to leave that day?" Betsy said.

"Yes, we were the only people who knew. I can assure you of that. Knowing Gordon, I'm sure he didn't tell anyone else. He didn't like the unexpected. His method was to control everything. That's why I can't figure out how come he was killed at home. Who could have known he was there? By then, he was supposed to be at the Grand Theater, with me, shaking hands with the invited guests. It was in the program: *7.00 – 7.30, Official reception in the lobby of the Grand Theater with Mayor Joseph Gordon.*"

"And what happened to the bank account?"

"It stayed open, I suppose. It had never been declared to the I.R.S., so far as I knew. It was as if it didn't exist. I never touched it. That seemed the best way to bury the whole story. I guess there must still be quite a lot of money in it."

"How about the anonymous phone call? Did you ever find out who made it?"

"No, I never did."

*   *   *

That evening, Betsy invited Derek and me to dinner at her house.

The meal was excellent and so was her claret. As we were sipping liqueurs in her living room, she said:

"The two of you can sleep here if you want. The bed in the guest room is very comfortable. I have a new toothbrush for each of you, and a whole bunch of my ex-husband's T-shirts that I kept, God knows why. They would fit you perfectly."

"Now there's a good idea," Derek said. "We could take the opportunity to tell each other our life stories. Betsy will tell us about her ex-husband, I can talk about my terrible life sitting behind a desk, and Jesse can talk about the restaurant he's planning to open."

"You're planning to open a restaurant, Jesse?" Betsy said.

"Don't listen to him, Betsy, the poor guy's had far too much to drink."

Derek noticed the copy of "The Darkest Night" on the low table. Betsy had brought it home to read. He picked it up.

"You really never stop, do you?" he said.

The atmosphere suddenly turned serious again.

"I don't understand why this play was so precious to Gordon that he put it in a safe deposit box," Betsy said.

"Along with the bank statements incriminating Mayor Brown," I said. "Could it be he was keeping the play as a guarantee to protect himself from someone?"

"Do you mean from Kirk Hayward, Jesse?" Betsy said.

"I don't know. The script doesn't seem particularly interesting in itself. And Mayor Brown says he never heard Gordon talk about the play."

"Can we believe Alan Brown after everything he hid from us?" Derek said.

"He'd have no reason to lie about that," I said. "And besides, we've known from the start that at the time of the murders he was in the lobby of the Grand Theater, shaking hands with dozens of people."

Derek and I had both read Hayward's play, but, perhaps because we were tired, we had not seen what Betsy had picked up on.

"What if there was a connection with the underlined words?" she now said. "There are about ten words underlined in pencil."

"I supposed they were notes made by Hayward," Derek said. "Changes he might want to make in the play."

"No," Betsy said, "I think they're something else."

We sat down around the table. Derek picked up the script and Betsy noted down the underlined words as he read them out. The result was the following piece of gibberish:

jammed enough return event my interest
arrogant horizontal funny outside lake destiny

"What the hell does that mean?" I said.

"Maybe it's a code," Derek said.

Bent low over the sheet of paper, Betsy wrote the sentence out again, this time beginning each word with a capital letter:

Jammed Enough Return Event My Interest
Arrogant Horizontal Funny Outside Lake Destiny

JEREMIAHFOLD

DEREK SCOTT

Mid-September 1994. Six weeks since the murders.

If what Special Agent Grace of the A.T.F. had told us was correct, then we had located the source of the murder weapon: the bar in Ridgesport, where you could acquire an army Beretta with its serial number filed off.

At the request of the A.T.F. (we characterized it as a sign of goodwill) Jesse and I suspended our stakeout. We only had to wait until the A.T.F. made up their minds to carry out a raid. In the meantime, we would occupy ourselves with other cases. Our patience and our diplomacy paid off. Late one afternoon in mid-September, Special Agent Grace invited Jesse and me to join the raid. They seized arms and ammunition, among them the latest Berettas from the stolen consignment, and arrested an infantry corporal who went by the name of Ziggy. This Ziggy wasn't an especially bright spark, presumably more cog than mastermind in the arms trafficking operation.

Neither the A.T.F. nor the military police, who had joined in, thought Ziggy had obtained the weapons alone. As for us, we needed to know who he had sold his Berettas to. We ended up coming to an arrangement. The A.T.F. let us question Ziggy, and we made a deal with him: he would give the A.T.F. the names of his associates, and in return would receive a reduced sentence. Everyone was happy.

We showed Ziggy a whole bunch of photographs, including one of Ted Tennenbaum.

"I don't remember any faces, I swear."

Jesse showed Ziggy a photograph of an electric chair.

"This, Ziggy," he said in a calm voice, "is what you can expect if you don't talk."

"What do you mean?" Ziggy whispered.

"One of those guns of yours was used to kill four people. You're going to be charged with their murders."

"But I didn't do anything!" Ziggy yelled.

"You can tell that to the judge."

"Unless your memory comes back, you little prick," Jesse said.

"Show me those pictures again," Ziggy said. "Maybe I didn't look at them closely enough."

"Do you want to stand by the window so you get more light?" Jesse suggested.

"Yeah, maybe I didn't have enough light."

We went over to the window and he looked carefully at each of the photographs we had brought.

"I sold this guy a gun," he said.

The photograph he held out to us was the one of Tennenbaum.

"Are you sure?" I said.

"I'm certain."

"And when did you sell him that gun?"

"In February. I'd seen him in the bar before, but that was years ago. He needed a gun. He had cash on him. I sold him a Beretta and some ammunition. I never saw him again."

Tennenbaum was well and truly caught.

-1

Dies Irae: Day of Wrath

MONDAY, JULY 21 – FRIDAY, JULY 25, 2014

JESSE ROSENBERG

Monday, July 21, 2014
Five days to opening night

Orphea was in a state of high tension. The news that the play was going to reveal the identity of a murderer who had gone unpunished had spread like wildfire. In the space of a weekend, the media had arrived en masse, as well as a horde of tourists in search of sensation. The townspeople, too, were agog. Main Street was almost overrun with vendors from out of town who were seizing the opportunity to sell drinks, food, and even T-shirts with the slogan I WAS IN ORPHEA, I KNOW WHAT HAPPENED IN 1994. The crush was at its greatest around the Grand Theater. Access had been blocked by the police, and dozens of T.V. reporters were lined up outside, broadcasting regular updates.

"Who killed the Gordon family, a jogger, and a reporter who was about to publish the answer? We'll know in five days' time, here in Orphea, New York State . . ."

". . . In five days' time, one of the most remarkable plays in a long while will reveal the secrets of . . ."

". . . A killer is on the prowl in a quiet town in the Hamptons, and a play will reveal his name . . ."

". . . Truth is stranger than fiction here in Orphea, where the authorities have announced that the town will be cordoned off on opening night. Reinforcements are expected from the region, while the Grand Theater, where the play is currently being rehearsed, is under twenty-four-hour surveillance . . ."

To add to this unreal atmosphere, the excitement was also political. Following the latest revelations, Sylvia Tennenbaum was demanding that her brother be formally exonerated. She had gathered a support committee that paraded in front of the T.V. cameras with banners saying

JUSTICE FOR TED. Sylvia Tennenbaum was also demanding the resignation of Mayor Brown and for the municipal elections to be brought forward: "Mayor Brown has been questioned by police in relation to the 1994 murders. He has lost all credibility."

But Mayor Brown, being the experienced political animal he was, had no intention of abandoning his job. This turmoil served his cause. Now more than ever, Orphea needed someone in charge. In spite of the doubts raised by his being taken in for questioning by the police, Brown was still widely trusted, and those townspeople worried about the situation certainly did not want to lose their mayor at a time of crisis. As for the town's merchants, they could hardly have been happier. Restaurants and hotels were packed, souvenir shops were running out of stocks, and advance ticket sales for the festival looked likely to break records.

We knew more than most about what was going on in the Grand Theater, thanks to Michael Bird, who had become an indispensable ally in our investigation. Because he was trusted by Hayward, Bird was the only person outside the company able to get inside the Grand Theater. In return for Bird's promise to reveal nothing of the content of his play before opening night, Hayward had granted him special access. "It's essential that one day a journalist can bear witness to what happened in Orphea," Hayward had said. So we had appointed Bird to be our eyes inside the theater and, if possible, to occasionally film the rehearsals for us. That morning, he invited us to his house to show us what he had recorded the day before.

He and his family lived in a very pretty house outside Orphea, on the road to Bridgehampton.

"He can afford this on his salary as the editor of a local paper?" Derek said as we pulled up outside the house.

"His wife's father has money," Betsy said. "Clive Davis, you may know him. He ran for mayor of New York a few years ago."

And it was Michael's wife who greeted us: a very beautiful blonde, who must have been under forty, in other words a lot younger than her husband. She offered us coffee and led us into the living room, where we found Bird connecting his T.V. to a computer.

"Thanks for coming," he said.

We watched his video scenes for a short while, but there was predictably nothing in them of interest to our investigation. That left Jeremiah Fold as our only lead. We mentioned the name to Bird, but it meant nothing to him.

I asked Betsy, "Do you think it could be something other than *Jeremiah Fold*?"

"I doubt it, Jesse. I spent the whole day yesterday rereading 'The Darkest Night'. I tried every possible combination and, from what I could see, nothing else makes sense."

Why had a code been hidden in the script of "The Darkest Night"? And by whom? Hayward himself? What did Hayward really know? What kind of game was he playing with us and the whole town of Orphea?

Just then, Betsy's cell phone rang. It was Montagne.

"Betsy, we've been looking for you everywhere. We need you at the station right now. Your office was burglarized during the night."

When we got to the station, some of Betsy's colleagues were gathered in the doorway of her office, looking at the fragments of glass on the floor and the smashed-in shutter, and trying to figure out what had happened. The answer, though, was simple. The station was all on one story. The offices were all at the rear of the building and looked out on a patch of lawn surrounded by a picket fence. The only security cameras were in the parking lot and at the main entrance. The intruder would have had no difficulty in climbing over the fence, crossing the lawn, and getting to the window of the office. He had then forced up the roll-down shutters, broken the window, and climbed into the room. The officer who had delivered her mail had been the one to discover the break-in.

Another officer had been in there the previous afternoon, when everything had been intact. So this had happened during the night.

"How come nobody realized what was going on?" I said.

"If all the officers are on patrol at the same time, there's nobody in the station," Betsy said. "It sometimes happens."

"What about the noise?" Derek said. "It must make a lot of noise lifting those shutters. Didn't anybody hear?"

All the buildings in the immediate vicinity of the station were offices or municipal warehouses. The only likely witnesses might have been the firefighters in the next-door fire station. But when a police officer informed us that during the night, around one in the morning, a major traffic accident had necessitated the intervention of all patrol cars and firefighters from the fire station, we realized that the intruder had had free rein.

"He was hiding somewhere," Betsy said, "waiting for the right moment to do what he did. He might even have been waiting for several nights in a row."

A viewing of the footage from security cameras inside the station allowed us to confirm that there had in fact been no break-in at the front of the office. There was one camera in the hallway, aimed straight at the door of Betsy's office. The door had remained closed. It was clearly her room that had been the target.

"I don't understand," Betsy said. "There's really nothing to steal. In fact, so far as I can see, nothing's missing."

"There's nothing to steal, but there is something to see," I said, pointing to the whiteboard and the walls covered with papers connected with the case. "Whoever got in here wanted to know what stage the investigation had reached. And he had access to Stephanie's work and ours."

"Our killer is taking risks," Derek said. "He's starting to panic, exposing himself. Who knows your office is here, Betsy?"

Betsy shrugged. "Everyone. I mean, it's no secret. Even people who come to the station to lodge a complaint have to come along this corridor and they see my office. My name's on the door."

Derek drew us aside and whispered in a grave tone:

"Whoever broke in here knew what he was doing when he took

that risk. He knew perfectly well what was in that office. It's someone on the inside."

"Oh, my God," Betsy said, "you mean it's one of our colleagues?"

"If it was anyone on the force," I objected, "all he'd have to do would be to go into the office when you weren't there, Betsy."

Derek said, "He'd have been caught by the camera in the corridor. If he thinks he's under surveillance, he's definitely not going to make that mistake. But by breaking in, he puts us off the scent. There may be a rotten element inside the station."

That meant we were no longer safe there. But where could we go? I no longer had an office at troop headquarters and Derek's office was open-plan. We needed somewhere where nobody would come looking for us. That was when I thought of the archive room of the *Chronicle,* which we could access by going through the back door of the offices.

Bird was pleased to welcome us.

"Nobody will know you're here," he assured us. "The reporters never come to the basement. I'll leave you a key, along with a duplicate, so you'll be the only ones to have access. And the key to the back door, too, so you can come and go at any hour of the day or night."

Within a few hours, in the greatest secrecy, we had set up a recon-struction of our investigation wall.

*

That evening, Betsy was due to have dinner with Lauren and Paul. They were back in Southampton for the week and had planned to meet her at Café Athena to make up for the disastrous previous dinner.

At home to change, Betsy suddenly remembered her conversation with Springfield concerning Bergdorf's book about the theater festival. Springfield had told her that in the spring of 1994 he had decided to set aside a space in the bookstore to local authors. What if Hayward had put his play on sale there? Before leaving for supper, she dropped by Springfield's house. She found him on the porch with a glass of whiskey, enjoying the mildness of the early evening.

"Yes, Betsy," he said, "we did devote a room in the rear of the store to local authors. A gloomy little cubbyhole, which we turned into an annex called the 'Local Writers' Room'. It was an immediate success. More so than I could have imagined: tourists love local stories. Actually, that section still exists and it's in the same place. But I've knocked down a wall since then, so it's part of the main store. Why are you interested?"

"Just curious," Betsy said. "I was wondering if you remember which writers gave you their books back then."

Springfield was amused at the question. "There were so many! I think you overestimate my memory. But I remember there was an article about it in the *Chronicle* early in the summer of 1994. I must have a copy in the store, would you like me to get it for you? You may find some useful information in it."

"No, Cody. Thank you, though. I'll drop by the store tomorrow."

"Are you sure?"

"I am. Thanks."

Betsy set off to join her friends. But when she got to Main Street, she decided to stop off at the *Chronicle*. Supper could easily take a short delay. She walked around the outside of the building and went in through the back door to the archive room. She sat down at the computer they were using. She typed in the keywords "Cody Springfield", "bookstore", and "local writers" and soon found an article from the end of June 1994.

IN THE ORPHEA BOOKSTORE,
WRITERS FROM THE HAMPTONS HONORED

For the past two weeks, the bookstore in Orphea has been bigger than before. There is now a room devoted to local writers. This initiative has been a great success, with many authors coming along to the store and leaving their works in the hope of becoming more widely read. The owner of the store, Cody Springfield, has even had to enforce a strict one-copy-per-writer policy in order to have enough space for everyone.

The article was illustrated with a photograph of Springfield, posing proudly in the doorway of that former cubbyhole, over the entrance to which was now a wooden plaque with the words LOCAL WRITERS' ROOM. The interior of the room could be made out, with walls filled with shelves of books and bound scripts. Betsy zoomed in and peered at each title. Right there, in the middle of the image, was a bound booklet, its cover displaying in capital letters the words THE DARKEST NIGHT BY KIRK HAYWARD. Now she knew where Mayor Gordon had acquired the script of the play. It was from Springfield's bookstore.

*   *   *

Ostrovski had just come back from a late stroll in the grounds. It was a mild night. Seeing the critic walk across the lobby of the hotel, one of the Lake Palace receptionists came over to him.

"Mr Ostrovski, there's been a DO NOT DISTURB sign on your door for the last few days. I just wanted to make sure everything is alright."

"It's deliberate," Ostrovski assured him. "I'm in the midst of a period of artistic creativity. I mustn't be disturbed for any reason."

"Of course, sir. Would you like us to bring you some bath towels? Do you need any cosmetic products?"

"Nothing at all, my friend. Thank you for your concern."

Ostrovski went up to his room. He liked being an artist. He at last felt at home. It was as if he had grown his true skin. He switched the light on. He had papered one whole wall with articles about Stephanie's disappearance. He studied them for a long time and pasted up some more. Then he sat down at the desk, which was covered in sheets of notes, and looked at the framed photograph of Meghan that he had propped up there. He kissed the glass and muttered aloud, "My darling." He took up his pen and started to write.

At that very same moment, a Porsche sped past the sinister parking lot of Motel 17, headed for the ocean. At the wheel was Carolina, who had told her father she was going to the hotel gym but was now fleeing in her car. She did not know if she had knowingly lied, or if her legs had refused to obey her. She turned onto Ocean Road, then continued her pilgrimage until she reached the house that had belonged to her parents, The Garden of Eden. She looked at the doorbell on the gate. Where the words EDEN FAMILY had once stood, it now read SCALINI FAMILY. She got out and walked alongside the hedge, observing the premises through the foliage. She could see light. She finally found a way through. She climbed over the fence and through the hedge. Her hands and cheeks were scratched. There was nobody there. She walked stealthily across the lawn, as far as the swimming pool. She wept in silence.

From her bag, she took a plastic bottle in which she had mixed ketamine with vodka. She swallowed the liquid in one go, then sat on a sun recliner beside the pool. She listened to the gentle lapping of the water and closed her eyes. She thought about Tara Scalini.

CAROLINA EDEN

The first time I met Tara, in March 2004, I was nine years old. We had both ended up in the finals of the spelling competition in New York. We became immediate friends. That day, neither of us wanted to beat the other. It got to a point where we were drawn. One after the other, we deliberately gave the wrong answer in spelling the word the competition judge submitted to us. He kept saying to each of us, "If you spell the next word correctly, you win the competition!"

But it did not end. Finally, after an hour going around in circles, the judge declared us both winners, first equal.

That was the start of a wonderful friendship. We became inseparable. We were besotted with each other.

Tara's father, Gerald Scalini, worked in an investment bank. The family lived in a huge apartment overlooking Central Park. Their lifestyle was amazing: a driver, a cook, a house in the Hamptons.

At that time, my father was not yet the boss of Channel 14 and we weren't as rich as they were. We lived comfortably, but we were nowhere close to matching the Scalinis' lifestyle. At the age of nine, I thought Gerald Scalini was very kind to us. He loved having us around to his apartment, he would send his driver to fetch me so I could come and play with Tara. In the summer, when we were in Orphea, he would invite us to lunch at their house in East Hampton.

But young as I was, it didn't take me long to realize that, in inviting us, Tara's father was not being so much generous as condescending. He wanted to impress.

He loved to invite us to his 6,000-square-foot duplex, so that he could then come to our place and say: "You've done a really nice job on your apartment." He relished it when we came for lunch at his incredible property in East Hampton, after which he would come for a coffee in the modest house my parents rented in Orphea and say, "Nice little place you have here."

I think my parents spent time with the Scalinis mainly to please me. Tara and I loved each other. We were much alike: very good pupils, particularly gifted in literature, we devoured books and we both dreamed of becoming writers. We spent our days concocting stories together, and writing them down, sometimes on paper, sometimes on the family computer.

Four years later, in the spring of 2008, Tara and I were nearly thirteen. My father's career had taken a major leap forward. He had been promoted several times, was talked about in the specialist journals, and had finally been appointed head of Channel 14. Our life had changed rapidly. We, too, now lived in an apartment overlooking Central Park, my parents were having a holiday home built in Orphea, and, much to my delight, I had started at Hayfair, the prestigious school that Tara already attended.

I think Mr Scalini started to feel a little threatened by my father. I don't know what was said in the Scalinis' kitchen, but I had the feeling Tara's behavior toward me had changed.

For a long time, I had been telling Tara that I dreamed of having a laptop. I wanted a computer of my own, so that I could write my stories in the privacy of my own room. But my parents refused. They said there was a computer in the little sitting room—we now had a big and a little sitting room—which I could use as much as I liked.

"I'd rather write in my room."

"The sitting room is fine," my mother would reply, unwilling to compromise.

That spring, Tara was given a laptop. Exactly the model I wanted. I didn't recall her ever mentioning that she wanted one. And now there she was, parading her new toy at school.

I made an effort not to pay any attention. Especially as there was something more important occupying my mind. The school was organizing a writing competition and I intended to enter something. So did Tara, and we worked together in the school library, she on her laptop, and I obliged to write in an exercise book, before having to transcribe it all in the evening onto the computer in the little sitting room.

Tara said her parents found her piece extraordinary. They had even asked one of their friends, apparently a well-known writer in New York, to read it and help her a little. When my piece was ready, I gave it to her to read before submitting it for the competition. She told me it "wasn't bad". From the tone she used, I had the impression I was hearing her father. And when her piece was finished, she refused to show it to me. "I wouldn't like you to copy me," she said.

At the beginning of June 2008, at a ceremony held in the auditorium of the school, the name of the winner was announced with great fanfare. Much to my surprise, I was awarded first prize.

A week later, Tara complained in class that her computer had been stolen. We all had individual lockers in the corridor, closed with padlocks that could only be opened with a code. The school principal declared that the bags and lockers of every pupil in the class would be inspected. To my horror, when it was my turn to open my locker, in front of the principal and the deputy principal, I discovered Tara's computer inside it.

It was an enormous scandal. I was summoned to the principal's office with my parents. However much I swore that I had had nothing to do with it, the evidence was impossible to ignore. There was a second meeting with the Scalinis, who said they were horrified. Once again I protested and proclaimed my innocence, but I had to appear in front of the disciplinary board. I was excluded from school for a week.

The worst of it was that my friends turned their backs on me. They did not trust me anymore. They called me a thief. Tara, though, would tell anyone prepared to listen that she forgave me. If I had asked her she would have lent me her computer. I knew she was lying. Only one other person had the code to my locker: Tara.

I was very alone and very upset. But this episode, rather than weakening me, drove me to write more. Words became my refuge. I would often isolate myself in the school library to write.

For the Scalinis, things were about to change. In October 2008, the terrible financial crash directly affected Gerald Scalini. He lost a large part of his fortune.

Tuesday, July 22, 2014
Four days to opening night

That morning, when Derek and I joined Betsy in the archive room at the *Chronicle*, she was wearing a triumphant smile. I looked at her, amused, and held out the coffee I had brought her.

"You apparently have a lead," I said.

Betsy showed us an article on Springfield's bookstore, dated June 15, 1994.

"Look at the photograph. In the background, on the right, you can see a copy of 'The Darkest Night' on a shelf. So it's quite possible that it was from the bookstore that Gordon got the script."

"At the beginning of June," Derek said, "Mayor Gordon tears up Hayward's play. Then he goes and gets another copy from the bookstore. Why?"

"That I don't know," Betsy said. "On the other hand, I have found a connection between the play Hayward is rehearsing right now and Jeremiah Fold. Coming back from dinner last night, I dropped by the station and spent part of the night looking through the database. Jeremiah Fold had a son who was born just before his father died. I managed to find the name of the mother. It's Virginia Parker."

"And . . . ?" Derek said. "Should that name mean anything to us?"

"No, but I spoke with her. And she told me how Jeremiah died."

"A traffic accident," Derek said, not sure where Betsy was going with this. "We already know that much."

"A motorcycle accident, to be precise," Betsy said. "He smashed his motorcycle into a tree."

"Let's try to do things by the book. And let's start by figuring out why the police in Ridgesport—when we got in touch with them—didn't even have a file on the accident."

"Because it's the New York State Highway Patrol that deals with fatal accidents," Betsy said.

"Then let's contact the Highway Patrol right away and get a copy of the report."

Betsy handed us a bundle of papers. "Already done, gentlemen. Here it is."

The accident occurred on the night of July 15, 1994. The police report was succinct. *Mr Fold lost control of his motorcycle. He was not wearing a helmet. Witnesses saw him leave Ridge's Club at about midnight. He was found by a motorist at about 0700, unconscious but still alive. He died in the hospital.* The file contained photographs of the motorcycle. All that remained of it was a heap of metal and scattered debris in a shallow trough by the tree. It was recorded that a copy of the report had been sent to Special Agent Grace of the A.T.F. at his request.

"It was thanks to Special Agent Grace," Derek told Betsy, "that we made the connection with Tennenbaum, because he arrested the man who provided Tennenbaum with the murder weapon."

"We need to get in touch with him," I said. "He must have retired by now, he was all of fifty back then."

"In the meantime, we should talk to Fold's former partner, this Virginia Parker," Derek said. "She may be able to tell us more."

"She's waiting for us at her place," Betsy announced, clearly one step ahead of us. "Let's go."

Virginia Parker lived in a run-down little house at the entrance to Ridgesport. She was a woman of fifty, who must have been beautiful once.

"Jeremiah was a scumbag," she told us when we had sat down in her living room. "The only good thing he ever made was his kid. Our son is a good boy. He works for a gardening company, and he's well liked."

"How did you meet Jeremiah?" I said.

Before replying, she lit a cigarette and inhaled deeply. She had long, thin fingers that ended in blood-red nails. It was only when she had blown out a cloud of white smoke that she said:

336

"I was a singer at Ridge's Club. It was a fashionable place back then, it's pretty tacky today. Miss Parker. That was my stage name. I still sing there from time to time. Back then I was kind of a local star. I had all the men at my feet. Jeremiah was one of the owners. What a handsome guy! I liked his whole tough-guy shtick at first. He had a dangerous side that attracted me. It wasn't until he'd knocked me up that I realized what he was really like."

*   *   *

Ridgesport, June 1993, 6 p.m.

Laid low with nauseous spells all day, Virginia was lying on the couch when there was a knocking at the door of her house. She thought it was Jeremiah, worried about her condition. She had left a message at the club twenty minutes earlier to tell him she wasn't in a fit state to sing that evening.

"Come in," she called out. "The door's open."

The visitor came in. It wasn't Jeremiah but Costico, his henchman. The size of a wardrobe, with hands like battering rams. She hated him as much as she feared him.

"What the hell are you doing here, Costico?" she said. "Jeremiah isn't here."

"I know that, he sent me. You have to come to the club."

"I can't, I've been throwing up all day."

"Hurry up, Virginia. I didn't ask you for a medical report."

"Costico, look at me, I'm in no state to sing."

"Get a move on, Virginia. The customers come to the club to hear you sing. Just because Jeremiah fucks you up the ass doesn't mean you get any special favors."

"As you can see from my belly," Virginia retorted, "that's not how he likes it."

"Shut your mouth and get moving," Costico said. "I'll wait for you in the car."

*   *   *

"And did you go?" Betsy asked.

"Of course. I didn't have any choice. My pregnancy was hell. I was forced to sing at the club until just before I went into labor."

"Did Jeremiah beat you?"

"No, it was worse than that. He was weird that way. He didn't think of himself as a criminal, but as a 'businessman'. He referred to Costico as his 'associate'. The back room where he did his wheeling and dealing was the 'office'. Jeremiah thought he was cleverer than anyone else. He'd say that if you want to keep one step ahead of the law, you mustn't leave a trail. He never used account books, the only gun he owned he had a license for, and he never gave written orders. The money he squeezed out of people, the arms dealing and drug dealing, he took care of that through his 'after-sales service'. That was his name for a group of guys he had at his mercy. He called them his 'slaves'. They were mainly family men he had compromising evidence on that could ruin their lives: photographs with prostitutes in embarrassing positions, that kind of thing. In return for his silence, the slaves had to do him favors. He'd send them out to collect money from people he was putting the squeeze on, deliver drugs to dealers, collect his share. All this was done by these respectable guys that nobody would suspect. Jeremiah was never on the front line. His slaves would come to the club, as if they were customers, and leave an envelope with the barman, to be handed on to Jeremiah. There were never any direct interactions. The club was also used by Jeremiah as a way of laundering money. There, too, he played according to the rules: he'd put it all back into the club. Everything was covered up in the accounts, and, since the club was doing well, it was impossible to detect anything. Jeremiah paid a lot of tax. He was untouchable. He could show off as much as he liked: everything was declared to the I.R.S.

"I know the police tried to investigate him, but they never found anything. The only people who could have brought him down were his

338

slaves, but they knew what they'd be letting themselves in for if they turned him in: at best, their social and professional lives would be wrecked. Not to mention that they also risked jail time for their involvement in his criminal activities. And besides, those who refused were punished to get them back on the right path. Again, without leaving a trail."

*   *   *

Ridgesport, 1993
Back room of the club

Jeremiah had just filled a big bowl with water when the door of the office opened. He looked up as Costico pushed a frail-looking man in a suit and tie into the room.

"Hello there, Everett!" Jeremiah said cheerfully. "Nice to see you."

"Hello, Jeremiah," the man said, shaking like a leaf.

Everett was a model family man who had been filmed by Costico with an underage prostitute.

"So, Everett," Jeremiah said in a soft voice, "I hear you don't want to be part of my business anymore?"

"Listen, Jeremiah, I can't afford to take these kinds of risks. It's madness. If I get caught, I'll go to jail for several years."

"Not much more than you might get for banging a fifteen-year-old girl," Jeremiah said.

"I was sure she was older," Everett said feebly.

"Listen, Everett, you're a little shit who bangs underage girls. As long as I decide, you'll work for me, unless you prefer to end up in jail with guys who'll cut your dick off with a razor."

Before Everett could reply, Costico grabbed him forcefully, bent him double and plunged his head in the bowl of ice-cold water. After keeping it there for about twenty seconds, he pulled it up again. Everett took a huge gulp of air.

"You're working for me, Everett," Jeremiah said. "Got that?"

Costico plunged the unfortunate man's head back into the water. The torture continued until Everett promised to be loyal.

*   *   *

"Fold drowned people?" I said, immediately making the parallel with the way Stephanie had died.

"Well, pretended to, Captain Rosenberg," Virginia said. "He and Costico made it their specialty. They only tried it on ordinary guys who were easy to impress and easy to manipulate. But at the club, whenever I saw a poor guy come out of the office with wet hair and tears streaming down his face, I knew what had happened. Jeremiah destroyed people, without ever leaving any traces that anyone could see."

"Did Fold ever kill people that way?"

"Probably. He was capable of it. I know people disappeared without trace. Were they drowned? Burned? Buried? Given to pigs to eat? I don't know. Jeremiah wasn't scared of anything, except going to prison. That's why he was so cautious."

"And then what happened?"

"I had my baby in January 1994. It didn't change anything between Jeremiah and me. We never talked about marriage, or even living together. But he did give me money for the baby. No cash, though. He'd write me a check or put money in my bank account. All official. It lasted until July. Until he died."

"What happened the night he died?"

"I think Jeremiah was scared of prison because he was claustrophobic. He said the idea of being locked up was something he couldn't contemplate. As much as he could, he went around on a huge motorbike instead of in a car and never wore a helmet. Every night, he'd take the same ride. He'd leave the club around midnight, sometimes later, and go home along Route 34, which is pretty direct. He always rode like a madman. He thought he was free, invincible. Most of the time, he was drunk. I always thought he'd end up killing himself on that bike. I never would have imagined he'd just crash, and lie there like a dog by the side of the road, taking hours to die. In the hospital, the doctors said that if he'd been found earlier, he might have survived. I never felt so relieved in my life as when they told me he was dead."

"Does the name Joseph Gordon mean anything to you?" I said. "He was the mayor of Orphea until July 1994."

"Joseph Gordon? Never heard of him, Captain. Why?"

"He was a corrupt mayor, and it may be that he was in league with Fold."

"I was never involved in Jeremiah's business affairs. The less I knew, the better."

"And what did you do after Fold died?"

"The only thing I could: I kept singing at Ridge's Club. It was well paid. That idiot Costico is still there."

"He took over the business?"

"He took over the club. Jeremiah's other business stopped when he died. Costico is strictly small-time and not very bright. All the employees steal from the till, he's the only one not to know. He even did time for a few small deals."

We left Virginia Parker and went to Ridge's Club. The establishment did not open until the evening, but inside employees were cleaning the place in a desultory manner. It was an old-fashioned basement club. The decor of the place might have been considered cool in 1994. By 2014 standards, it was tired. Beside the counter, we saw a well-built man, the kind who'd been strong once but hadn't aged well, receiving crates of alcohol.

"Who let you in here?" he said when he saw us. "We don't open until six."

"Special opening hours for police officers," Derek said, showing him his badge. "Are you Costico?"

We realized it was him from the way he immediately took off. He dashed across the room and into a passageway that led to an emergency exit. He was running fast. Betsy and I set off after him, while Derek opted for the main stairs. Costico, after climbing a narrow flight, went through a door that led outside and disappeared in the blinding daylight.

By the time Betsy and I got outside, Derek had already pinned Costico down in the parking lot and was handcuffing him.

"Well, Derek," I said, "looks like you still have what it takes!"

He smiled. He seemed suddenly radiant. "It's good to be back in the field, Jesse."

Costico's real name was Costa Suarez. He had done time for drug dealing, and the reason for his fleeing now was the big packet of cocaine he had in his jacket. Judging by the amount, he was clearly still selling it. But that wasn't what interested us. We wanted to take advantage of the element of surprise to question him, and we did so in his club. There was a back room, the door of which bore a plate with the word OFFICE. The room was just as Virginia had described: cold and windowless. In a corner, a washbasin and, beneath it, an old copper bowl.

It was Derek who led the interrogation.

"We don't give a damn what you get up to in your club, Costico. We have questions to ask you about Jeremiah Fold."

Costico looked surprised. "Nobody's talked to me about him in a great many years."

"I'm sure you remember him, though," Derek said. "And this is where you got up to your dirty business?"

"It was Jeremiah who liked that kind of thing. If it had been up to me, I'd have just used my fists."

Costico showed us his thick knuckles laden with heavy, sharp-edged chrome-plated rings. As we had been told, he wasn't someone who oozed intelligence. But he had enough common sense to tell us what we wanted to know rather than get himself arrested for possession of drugs. It emerged that Costico had never heard of Joseph Gordon.

"Mayor Gordon? Can't say the name rings a bell."

Costico went on to tell us that he didn't have a good memory for names, so we showed him a photograph of Gordon. It didn't change his mind. "I swear to you this guy never set foot in here. I never forget a face. Believe me, if I'd seen this guy, I'd have remembered him."

"So he had no connection with Jeremiah Fold?"

"Definitely not. At the time, I knew everything. Jeremiah never did anything by himself. I know people laugh behind my back and say I'm dumb, but back then Jeremiah trusted me."

"If Joseph Gordon never did business with you, could he have been one of your 'slaves'?"

"No, that's impossible. I'd remember the face. I have the memory of an elephant, I tell you. That's why Jeremiah liked me. He never wanted anything written down. Anything at all. But I remembered everything: the instructions, the faces, the figures. And anyhow, Orphea really wasn't our territory."

"And yet you were squeezing money out of Ted Tennenbaum, the owner of Café Athena in Orphea."

Costico seemed surprised to hear the name. He nodded. "Ted Tennenbaum was tough. Not the kind of guy Jeremiah usually went up against. Jeremiah never took risks. He only targeted guys who'd piss their pants when they saw me show up. But Tennenbaum was something else. That was a personal matter. The guy had hit him in front of a girl, and Jeremiah wanted his revenge. We beat up Tennenbaum in his house, but that wasn't enough for Jeremiah. He decided to put the squeeze on him, although that was an exception, Jeremiah generally stayed in his territory. He had control of Ridgesport, he knew everybody here."

"Do you remember who set fire to Ted Tennenbaum's future restaurant?"

"Now you're asking a lot. It must have been one of our slaves. They did everything, those guys. We never got our hands dirty. Unless we had a problem to solve. Otherwise, all the minor tasks, that was them. They received the drugs, took them to the dealers, brought the money back to Jeremiah. We just gave the orders."

"And where did you find these men?"

"They all liked hookers. There was a sleazy motel on Route 16. Half the rooms were rented by hookers for their tricks. Everyone in the area knew about it. I knew the owner and the hookers, and we had an agreement. We'd leave them alone, and in return we could use a room on the quiet. Whenever Jeremiah needed slaves, he'd get an underage girl to go on the game. I found a very beautiful girl. She knew exactly which kind of customers to choose. Family men, impressionable. She'd take them to the room, tell the client, 'I'm underage, I'm still at school, does that turn you on?' The guy would answer yes, and the girl would ask him to do really filthy stuff. I'd be hidden somewhere, usually behind a curtain, with a movie camera. At the right moment, I'd come out, shout, 'Surprise!' and point my camera at the guy. The guy would make a face like you can't imagine! I loved that. It'd crease me up. I'd tell the girl to go, then I'd look at the guy, all naked, all ugly, shaking. I'd start by threatening to beat him up, then I'd tell him that we could come to an arrangement. I'd pick up his pants and take out his wallet. I'd look through his credit cards, his driving license, the photographs of his wife . . ."

"So you had a list of all these guys who were in your power?"

"No. I'd make them think I was keeping everything, but I'd quickly get rid of their wallets. Just as there was never any film in the camera, in order not to risk incriminating ourselves. Jeremiah said there mustn't be any evidence. I had my little network of guys, and I would call on them alternately in order not to arouse suspicion. One thing's for sure, though: your guy Gordon never did business of any kind with Jeremiah."

* * *

Bird brought us up to date on the progress of the rehearsals when Betsy, Derek and I got back from Ridgesport and joined him in the archive room of the *Chronicle*.

He played us a recording of another scene he had covertly filmed, in which Charlotte Brown played a singer in a bar with whom all the

344

customers are in love. A makeshift set had been erected: a few chairs, a red curtain at the back. Eden was playing a customer, sitting at the front of the stage sipping a cocktail. Padalin this time played the owner of the bar. He was looking at his singer, who stood some way farther back.

Piano bar music was playing.

"This can't be a coincidence," Derek cried, noticing a sign that was part of the set. "That's Ridge's Club!"

"Ridge's Club?" Bird said.

"The club that Jeremiah Fold owned."

The traffic accident, then the club. This was neither invention, nor chance. In addition, from what we could see, the same actor was playing the dead body in Scene 1 and the bar owner in Scene 2.

"Scene 2 is a flashback," Derek said. "This character is Jeremiah Fold."

"So the solution to the mystery really is in this play?" Bird said.

"Michael," I said, "I don't know what's going on here, but whatever you do, don't let Hayward out of your sight."

We wanted to speak to Springfield about the script of "The Darkest Night" that had been on sale in his bookstore in 1994. Betsy tried to reach him on his cell phone, but he wasn't picking up, so we went to the store. The assistant told us she hadn't seen her boss all day.

It was very strange. Betsy suggested we drop by his house. When we got to there, she immediately noticed his car parked outside. Springfield must be at home. But despite our insistent ringing, he did not come to the door. Betsy pressed down on the handle: it was open. At that moment, I felt a sense of déjà vu.

We went in. An icy silence reigned. The lights were all on, even though it was broad daylight.

It was in the living room that we discovered him.

Slumped against a low table in a pool of blood.

Springfield had been murdered.

DEREK SCOTT

Late November 1994. Four months after the Gordon killings.

Jesse didn't want to see anybody.

I dropped by his house every day, rang his bell for a long time, begged him to open the door, in vain. Sometimes I waited for hours. But there was nothing I could do.

He let me in at last when I threatened to break the lock and started kicking at the door. What I saw in front of me was a ghost: unwashed, hair disheveled, cheeks overgrown with beard, a grim look in his eyes. His apartment was a mess.

"What do you want?" he said in a gruff tone.

"To make sure you're O.K., Jesse."

He gave a cynical laugh. "I'm fine, Derek, really fine! I've never felt so well."

In the end he threw me out.

Two days later, Major McKenna came to see me in my office.

"Derek, I need you to go to the 54th precinct in Queens. Your pal Jesse has been acting up, he was arrested by the N.Y.P.D. last night."

"Arrested? Where? He hasn't been out of his apartment in weeks."

"Well, he must have wanted to let off steam because he trashed a restaurant under construction. A place called Little Russia. Mean anything to you? Anyway, find the owner and sort this shit out for me. And reason with him, Derek. Or he'll never be allowed back in the force."

"I'll handle it," I said.

Major McKenna looked me up and down. "You're not looking too good yourself, Derek."

"Things haven't been going so well."

"Did you see the shrink?"

I shrugged. "I come here every morning, sir, but it's like I'm on automatic pilot. I don't think my place is here anymore. Not after what happened."

"But Derek, goddammit, you're a hero. You saved his life. Never forget that. Without you, Jesse would be dead today. You saved his life!"

JESSE ROSENBERG

Wednesday, July 23, 2014
Three days to opening night

Orphea was in a state of shock. Cody Springfield, the town's mild, good-natured bookseller, had been murdered.

It had been a short night, both for the police and the inhabitants of the town. The news of a second murder had attracted reporters and onlookers to Springfield's house. People were fascinated and frightened at the same time. First Stephanie Mailer, now Cody Springfield. They were starting to talk about a serial killer. Citizens' patrols were being organized. In this atmosphere of general anxiety, the most important thing was to avoid panic. The State Police and all the local police forces had put themselves at Mayor Brown's disposal to ensure the safety of the town.

Betsy, Derek and I had been up half the night, trying to figure out what might have happened. We had been there when Dr Ranjit Singh delivered his initial observations. Springfield had died from blows to the back of the skull from a big metal lamp, which had been found beside the body, covered in blood. In addition, the body was in a strange position, as if Springfield had been on his knees, his hands over his face, either rubbing his eyes or trying to hide them.

"Was he begging his murderer?" Betsy wondered.

"I don't think so," Dr Singh replied. "If he had, he'd have been struck from the front, not from the back. And besides, from what I see, for the skull to be cracked in that way, the murderer was much taller than him."

"Much taller?" Derek said. "What do you mean?"

Dr Singh improvised a little reconstruction. "Springfield opens the door to his killer. He may know him. In any case, he trusts him, because there's no trace of a struggle. I believe he says hello and leads him into the living room. It seems like a visit. But Springfield turns and is blinded.

He lifts his hands to his eyes and falls to his knees. The killer grabs this lamp from the table and brings it down with all his strength on his victim's head. Springfield is killed immediately, but is still struck several times, as if the murderer wanted to be certain that he was dead."

"Hold on a minute, doc," Derek cut in. "What did you mean when you said he was blinded?"

"I think the victim was neutralized with tear gas. Which would explain the traces of tears and mucus on his face."

"Tear gas?" Betsy said. "Like the attack on Jesse in Stephanie Mailer's apartment?"

"Yes," Dr Singh said.

I said to him: "You're saying the killer wants to be certain he kills his victim, but at the same time he comes here unarmed and uses a lamp? What kind of murderer works like that?"

"Someone who doesn't want to kill, but who has no choice," Singh replied.

"Is he wiping out traces of the past, is that it?" Derek said.

"I think so. Someone in this town is willing to go to any lengths to protect his secret and prevent you from seeing your investigation through to the end."

What had Springfield known? What connection was there between him and this whole case? We searched his house, thoroughly scoured his bookstore, but in vain. We found nothing.

That morning, Orphea, the state of New York, and soon the whole country woke to the news bulletins reporting the murder of Cody Springfield. More than the death of a bookseller, it was the succession of events that gripped people. The national media were talking about it now. There was bound to be an unprecedented influx of people into the town.

In response to the situation, an emergency meeting was held at the town hall with Mayor Brown, Major McKenna of the State Police, representatives of the neighboring towns, Chief Gulliver, Montagne, Betsy, Derek and me.

The first question was whether the festival should go ahead. During the night, it had been decided to put all the members of the cast under police protection.

"My advice would be to cancel the show," I said. "It can only make matters worse."

"Your opinion doesn't count, Captain Rosenberg," Brown said curtly. "For some reason I'm unaware of, you have something against my good friend Kirk Hayward."

"Your good friend Kirk Hayward?" I said ironically. "Did you call him that twenty years ago when you stole his girlfriend?"

"Captain," the mayor cried, "your tone and your insolence are unacceptable!"

"Jesse," Major McKenna said, "I suggest you keep that sort of observation to yourself. What's important is: do you believe Kirk Hayward really knows something about the Gordon killings?"

"We think there may be a connection between his play and the case."

"You *think*? There *may* be?" The major sighed. "Jesse, do you have any indisputable evidence?"

"No, only suppositions, but well-informed ones."

"Captain Rosenberg," Mayor Brown cut in, "everyone says you're a great detective and I respect that. But it seems to me that, since you arrived in this town, you've been causing nothing but chaos, without actually making any progress in your case."

"It's because we're closing in on the killer that he's getting nervous."

"Oh, I'm pleased to have an explanation for the mess we're in right now," the mayor said. "Anyway, I'm continuing with the play."

"Mr Mayor," Derek said, "I believe Hayward is just making fun of you and won't actually reveal the name of the killer."

"*He* may not, but his play will!"

"Don't play with words, Mr Mayor. I'm convinced that Hayward has no idea of the killer's identity. We shouldn't take the risk of letting this play go on. I don't know how the killer will react if he thinks his name is going to be revealed."

350

"Precisely," Mayor Brown said. "This is something we've never seen before. Look at the T.V. cameras, the crowds outside: Orphea is the center of attention. The whole country has forgotten video games and stupid T.V. shows and is holding its breath for a play! It's remarkable! What's going on, here and now, is simply unique!"

Major McKenna turned to Gulliver.

"What's your opinion, Chief Gulliver? Should the play go ahead?"

"I've made my feelings on this matter abundantly clear over the last few days, but I'll say it again. I believe very strongly that the festival should be canceled and the play with it." He turned to Mayor Brown. "Alan, if you are hell-bent on going ahead, you leave me no choice but to bring forward my retirement and resign with immediate effect. It's been an honor to work with you, but I won't let this happen on my watch."

"Very well," Mayor Brown said in a flat voice. He turned to Montagne. "Deputy Montagne, I appoint you interim police chief."

Montagne's smile was ill-concealed. Betsy forced herself to remain impassive. The mayor turned to Major McKenna.

"What about you, Major, what do you think?"

"It's your town, Mayor Brown. It's your decision. I think that even if you cancel everything, that won't solve the problem of security. The town will still be overrun with media and onlookers. But if you continue with the play, you will have to take drastic measures."

The mayor thought this over for a moment or two, then declared in a firm voice:

"We provide the town with exceptional security and we continue with the play."

McKenna listed the security measures that would have to be taken. All access to the town would be controlled, and Main Street closed to traffic. The cast of the play would be lodged at the Lake Palace, which would be placed under police surveillance. A bus with a police escort would bring them to and from the Grand Theater.

When the meeting was finally closed, Betsy cornered Mayor Brown in a corridor.

"Shit, Alan," she exploded, "how could you appoint Montagne to take Gulliver's place? You brought me to Orphea to take over, didn't you?"

"It's temporary, Betsy. I need you to concentrate on the investigation."

"You resent me because you were questioned as part of the investigation, is that it?"

"You could have warned me, Betsy, instead of hauling me in like a criminal."

"If you had told us all you knew, you would never have been a suspect."

Brown, in no mood to discuss matters further, said, "If this business costs me my job, Betsy, you can pack your bags anyway. So now prove to me what you're capable of. Lay your hands on whoever is terrorizing this town."

*   *   *

The Lake Palace had been transformed into a barracks. The cast of the play had been led into a reception room guarded by the police.

Media representatives and onlookers crowded the front forecourt, boiling in the midday sun, hoping to see Hayward and the cast. Excitement doubled when first a minibus and then some police cars arrived. The cast was about to move to the Grand Theater to begin rehearsals. After a long wait, the actors finally appeared, surrounded by police officers. Behind the security barriers, they were cheered, and their names were called out. The onlookers demanded photographs and autographs, the reporters wanted a statement.

Ostrovski was the first to respond to these requests and he was quickly followed by others. Carried away by the enthusiasm of the crowd, those still worried about the risk of performing in "The Darkest Night" were now relieved of their anxiety. They were on the verge of becoming famous. Live on T.V. screens, the whole of America was discovering the faces of this amateur cast caught in a sensation.

"I told you you'd be stars," Hayward said.

*

A few miles away, in their house by the ocean, Gerald Scalini and his wife were astonished to see Carolina Eden's face on their T.V. screen.

In New York, Bergdorf's wife Tracy, alerted by her colleagues, discovered, to her amazement, her husband playing at being an actor.

In Los Angeles, at the Beluga Bar, Hayward's drinking companions stared spellbound at their friend appearing on all the news channels. The whole country was talking about his play, "The Darkest Night".

*   *   *

The only lead that Betsy, Derek and I could envisage at this stage was that Springfield had been connected to Jeremiah Fold and his small-time criminal activities. So we decided to go back to Ridge's Club. But when we showed Costico a photograph of Springfield, he told us he had never set eyes on him.

"Who is this guy?"

"A man who was murdered last night," I said.

"Oh, hell, I hope you guys aren't planning to come see me every time you find a stiff?"

"You never saw this man at the club? Or hanging around with Jeremiah?"

"No, never. What makes you think there's a connection?"

"Everything points to the fact that Mayor Gordon, who you don't know, bought the script of a play called 'The Darkest Night' from this man in his bookstore. In that script, Jeremiah Fold's name appeared in code."

"Do I look like a man involved with plays?" Costico said.

Costico was too stupid to be a good liar, so we could believe him when he said he had never heard of either Gordon or Springfield.

Was Gordon involved in Fold's criminal activities? Could Springfield's bookstore have served as a cover? What if this whole thing about local writers had been a decoy to cover a criminal enterprise? The hypotheses jostled each other in our minds. Once again, we had no evidence.

We decided to go to the motel where Costico had told us he trapped his "slaves". When we got there, we realized that the establishment had hardly changed with the years. And when we got out of our car, Betsy's uniform and the police badges on our belts unleashed a stirring of panic among the fauna in the parking lot.

We rounded up the prostitutes, who were all around fifty or older. Among them was one who looked like the madam—her name was Regina—who told us that she'd been in charge here since the mid-'80s.

She admitted us to the room that served as her office, so that we could be quiet, and, above all, so that we did not scare away the clients.

"What's going on?" she said, motioning the three of us to an imitation leather coach. "You don't look like Vice to me, I've never seen you before."

"Homicide," I said. "We're not looking to get you in any trouble. We have some questions about Jeremiah Fold."

"Jeremiah Fold?" Regina repeated the name as if we were talking about a ghost.

I nodded. "If I mention Fold's slaves, does that mean anything to you?"

"Sure it does, sweetheart."

"Do you know these two men?" I said, showing her the photographs of Gordon and Springfield.

"Never seen them before."

"I need to know if they were connected with Jeremiah Fold."

"Connected with Fold? Now, that I really don't know."

"Could they have been his slaves?"

"It's possible. But, honestly, I have no idea. Jeremiah got his slaves from the occasional clients. The regulars generally frequented the same girls and knew they mustn't touch Mylla."

"Who's Mylla?" Derek said. "The girl who was used as bait?"

"Yes. She wasn't the only one, but she's the one who lasted longest. Two years. Until Jeremiah died. The others didn't last three months."

"Why not?"

"They all did drugs. In the end they weren't presentable anymore and Jeremiah would get rid of them."

"Get rid of them how?"

"Overdose. The police didn't suspect anything. He'd dump the body somewhere and the cops reckoned only that that was one junkie less."

"But this Mylla didn't do drugs?"

"No. Never touched any of the stuff. She was a smart girl, very well brought up, who somehow found herself in Jeremiah's clutches. He kept her because he must have been a little bit in love with her. She was really beautiful. I mean, the girls outside, they're hookers. She had something more. Like a princess."

"And how did she trap the slaves?"

"She'd work the side of the road, bring them back to the room, and there they'd be caught by Costico. You know Costico?"

"Yes," Betsy said, "we spoke with him. But I don't understand why none of these men rebelled."

"Oh, you should have seen Costico twenty years ago. He was all muscle. And seriously violent. You couldn't control him. I saw him break people's arms and knees to get his way. One day he broke into a slave's house, woke him in his bed with his wife and beat him up in front of her. What could the guy have done afterward? Complain to the police when he was acting as a mule for drug traffickers? He'd have ended up in a federal penitentiary."

"So you let him get on with it?"

"It isn't my parking lot, lady, and it isn't my motel. And besides, Jeremiah left us in peace. Nobody wanted any trouble with him. I only once saw a guy put Costico in his place. That was a sight for sore eyes."

"What happened?"

"It was in January 1994, I remember that because it was snowing really hard. The guy comes out of Mylla's room, stark naked. All he has on him are his car keys. Costico runs after him. The guy opens his car door and takes out a canister of tear gas. He sprays it over Costico, who starts shrieking like a little girl. It was hysterical. The guy gets in his car and takes off. Stark naked! In the snow! What a scene that was!"

Regina laughed at the memory.

"You say a tear gas canister?" I said, intrigued.

"Yes, why?"

"We are looking for a man, maybe connected with Jeremiah Fold, who uses tear gas."

"I don't know about that, sweetheart. All I saw was his ass, and that was many years ago. Maybe Costico remembers something. The guy left his pants with his wallet in the room, so I assume Costico didn't miss the opportunity."

I didn't insist, but asked instead:

"What became of Mylla?"

"When Jeremiah died, she vanished. Good for her. I hope she has a new life somewhere."

"Do you have any idea of her real name?"

"No idea at all."

Betsy, who sensed that Regina wasn't telling the whole story, said, "We need to talk with this woman. It's very important. There's a guy who's killing innocent people and causing a whole lot of panic. This guy may be connected with Jeremiah Fold. What was Mylla's real name? If you know, you have to tell us."

Regina looked us up and down, then stood up and went and rummaged in a box of souvenirs. She took out a press clipping.

"I found this in Mylla's room after she left."

She handed us the piece of paper. It was a missing persons notice from the *New York Times*, from 1992. The daughter of a politician and businessman in Manhattan had run away and was nowhere to be found. Her name was Miranda Davis. Along with the notice was a photograph of a girl, then aged seventeen. I recognized her immediately. It was Miranda, the wife of Michael Bird.

CAROLINA EDEN

When I was little, my parents would always tell me you shouldn't judge people too quickly and should always give them a second chance. I made an effort to forgive Tara and did everything I could to rebuild our friendship.

Following the crisis of 2008, her father had had to give up his apartment, his house in the Hamptons, and cut back his whole lifestyle. Compared with the majority of Americans, the Scalinis did O.K. for themselves. They moved to a nice apartment on the Upper East Side, and Gerald made sure that Tara could stay in the same school, which was something. But it wasn't quite the same as before. No more chauffeur, no more cook, no more weekends in the country.

Mr Scalini put on a good show, but Tara's mother would say to anyone prepared to listen, "We've lost everything. I'm a slave now, I have to rush to the dry cleaners, then pick up my daughter from school and make food for everyone."

In the summer of 2009, we moved into The Garden of Eden, our amazing house in Orphea. I say amazing without exaggeration: there was a wonderful spirit given off by the place. Everything had been built and decorated with taste. Every morning that summer, I had breakfast facing the ocean. I would spend my days reading, and above all writing. This house was a writer's house, I thought, like the ones I'd read about in books.

Toward the end of the summer, my mother persuaded me to invite Tara to spend a few days in Orphea. I really didn't want to.

"The poor girl's stuck in the city all summer," my mother said.

"That's no reason to feel sorry for her, Mom."

"Darling, you must learn to share. And to be patient with your friends."

"She annoys me," I said. "She acts like she knows it all."

"Maybe because she feels threatened. You must cultivate your friendships."

"She isn't my friend anymore."

"You know the proverb: a friend is someone we know well and love anyway. And you were happy when she invited you to her place in East Hampton."

In the end, I did invite Tara. My mother was right: our reunion did us good. We recovered the energy we'd had at the beginning of our friendship. We spent whole evenings lying on the lawn, talking. One evening, in tears, she confessed she had arranged for her computer to be stolen so that I should take the blame. She admitted she had been jealous of my story, but said it would never happen again, she loved me more than anything. She begged me to forgive her and I did. All those things were in the past.

Now that we had resumed our friendship, relations between our parents, which had become strained along with ours, grew strong again. The Scalinis were even invited to The Garden of Eden for a weekend, during which Mr Scalini, as unbearable as ever, constantly criticized my parents' choices: "Oh, what a pity you chose this material!" Or, "I'd never have done it this way!" But Tara and I became again inseparable, spending our time in each other's houses. We also started writing together again. This period coincided with my discovery of the theater. I loved it. I would read plays avidly, even thought to write one. Tara said we could try writing it together. Because of his work on Channel 14, my father was invited to all the previews, so we went regularly to see new plays.

In the spring of 2010, my parents finally bought me the laptop I'd been dreaming about. I couldn't have been happier. I spent all summer writing, on the porch of our house in Orphea. My parents grew worried.

"Don't you want to go to the beach, Carolina? Or into town?" they would ask me.

"I'm writing," I would say. "I'm very busy."

For the first time, I was writing a play, which I had called "Mr Constantine". It was about an old man called Mr Constantine who lives alone in a huge house in the Hamptons. His children never come to see him. One day, tired of feeling abandoned, he tells them he's dying. The children, each hoping to inherit the house, rush to his bedside and give in to all his whims.

It was a comedy. I was passionate about it. I spent a whole year writing it. Whenever my parents looked for me, they'd find me at my computer.

"You're working too hard!" they would say.

"I'm not working, I'm enjoying myself."

"Then you're enjoying yourself too much!"

I took advantage of the summer of 2011 to finish "Mr Constantine", and when school restarted I showed it to my English teacher, whom I admired a lot. Her first reaction, when she had finished reading it, was to send for me along with my parents.

"Have you read your daughter's play?" she asked my parents.

"No," they replied. "She wanted you to read it first. Is there a problem?"

"A problem? Are you kidding? It's wonderful! What an amazing play! I think your daughter has a real gift. That's why I wanted to see you. As you may know, I'm involved with the school drama club. Every year, in June, we put on a play, and I'd like this year's play to be Carolina's."

I couldn't believe it: my play was going to be performed. Soon that was the only thing anyone talked about in the school. I'd always kept a low profile, but now my reputation went through the roof.

Rehearsals were due to start in January. I still had a few months to refine the script. That was all I did, including during the winter vacation. I really wanted it to be perfect. Tara would come over every day, and we'd shut ourselves in my room. Sitting at my desk, eyes glued to the screen, I would read the lines out loud. Tara, lying on my bed, would listen thoughtfully and give me her opinion.

Everything changed on the last Sunday of the vacation. The day before I was due to hand in my script. Tara was with me, as she had been on all the previous days. It was late afternoon. She told me she was thirsty, and I went to the kitchen to fetch her some water. When I got back to my room, she was getting ready to leave.

"Are you going already?" I said.

"Yes, I didn't notice what time it was. I have to get home."

She seemed strange all of a sudden.

"Is everything O.K., Tara?"

"Yes, everything's fine. See you at school tomorrow."

I walked her to the door. When I got back to my computer, my play was no longer on the screen. I thought there was a technical glitch, but when I tried to reopen the file I realized it had vanished. Then it occurred to me I was looking in the wrong folder. But I soon discovered that my play was nowhere to be found. When I tried looking in the computer's trash and saw that it had been emptied, I finally understood: Tara had deleted my play, and there was no way to get it back.

I burst into tears, which became hysterics. My parents came running to my room.

"Don't worry," my father said. "You have a copy somewhere, don't you?"

"No!" I screamed. "Everything was there! I've lost everything."

"Carolina," he said, starting to lecture me, "I did tell you—"

"Jerry," my mother cut in, having understood the gravity of the situation, "I think now's not the time."

I told my parents what had happened: Tara asking me for water, me going out of the room for a moment, then her hurried departure and the play gone. My play could not have simply flown away. It could only have been Tara.

"But why would she have done something like that?" my mother said, trying to take it in.

She telephoned the Scalinis and told them what had happened. They defended their daughter, swore she would never have done anything like that, and rebuked my mother for making such accusations.

"Gerald," my mother said on the telephone, "this play didn't get deleted by itself. May I talk with Tara, please?"

But Tara did not want to talk with anyone.

My last hope was the printed copy of the play I had given my English teacher in September. But she couldn't find it. My father took my computer to one of Channel 14's I.T. specialists, but the man confessed himself powerless to do anything. "When the trash is emptied, it's emptied," he told my father. "Didn't you make a copy of the file?"

My play had ceased to exist. A year's work trashed. A year's work gone up in smoke. It was an indescribable feeling. As if a light had gone out inside me.

My parents and my English teacher could only make stupid suggestions. "Try to rewrite your piece from memory. You knew it by heart." It was obvious they had never written anything. It was impossible to bring a year's work back to life in a few days. They suggested I should write another play for the following year. But I didn't want to write anything more. I was too depressed.

Of the months that followed, all I remember is a feeling of bitterness. A pain deep in my soul. A sense of profound injustice. Tara must pay the consequences. I didn't even want to know *why* she had done it, I just wanted reparation. I wanted her to suffer as I was suffering.

My parents went to see the principal of the school, but he would accept no responsibility.

"From what I understand," he said, "this took place outside the school environment so there is nothing I can do. This little difference of opinion must be settled directly with Tara Scalini and her parents."

"A little difference of opinion?" my mother said. "Tara ruined a year's work by my daughter! They're both pupils here, you have to do something."

"Listen, Mrs Eden, maybe the two girls need to put some distance between them. They never stop playing dirty tricks on each other. First Carolina steals Tara's computer—"

"She didn't steal that computer!" my mother said, getting carried away. "Tara plotted the whole thing!"

The principal sighed. "Mrs Eden, it would be better if you settled this directly with Tara's parents."

Tara's parents didn't want to know. They defended their daughter tooth and nail and called me a compulsive liar.

Months went by, and everyone forgot the incident, except me. I carried this wound in my heart, a deep gash that would not heal. I talked about it endlessly. Even my parents ended up telling me that I had to stop going over it, that I had to move on.

In June, the school drama club finally performed a Jack London adaptation. I refused to attend the first night. I locked myself in my room and cried the whole evening. My mother, instead of comforting me, said, "Carolina, it's been six months now, you have to live your life."

But I could not. I sat there in front of my computer screen, not knowing what to write. I felt drained. Drained of all desire and all inspiration.

I was bored to death. I demanded attention from my parents, but my father was busy with his work and my mother was never there. I had never before realized how busy they were.

At The Garden of Eden that summer, I spent my time on the Internet. I devoted my days to surfing, especially on Facebook. It was that or boredom. I became aware that, apart from Tara, I hadn't made many friends lately. I guess I'd been too busy writing. Now I was trying to make up for lost time, virtually.

Several times a day, I'd take a look at Tara's Facebook page. I wanted to know what she was doing, who she was seeing. Since that Sunday in January when she had come over for the last time, we hadn't spoken. But I spied on her through her Facebook account, and I hated everything she put on it. It might have been my way of exorcizing all the hurt she had caused me. Or was I just feeding my resentment?

By November 2012, we had not spoken in ten months. One evening, as I was shut up in my room chatting on Facebook, I received a message from Tara. It was a long letter.

I soon understood that it was a love letter.

Tara told me how much she had suffered, how it had gone on for years. She told me that she could not forgive herself for what she had done to me. That since the spring she had been seeing a psychiatrist who was helping her to get a clearer picture of the matter. She said it was time for her to accept herself as she was. She told me she was gay and that she loved me. That she had said it to me many times, but I had never understood. She explained that she had ended up by being jealous of the play I was writing, because she was on my bed, offering herself to me, while I had eyes only for my script. She told me how difficult it was for her to express her true identity and asked me to forgive her for her behavior. She said she wanted to make amends, and she hoped that this confession of her feelings would allow me to understand that senseless act, for which, she said, she hated herself every day. She was sorry that her love for me, which was so strong, such a burden, so hard to confess, had made her lose her head.

I reread the letter several times. I was troubled, ill at ease. I did not want to forgive her. I think I had carried this anger inside me too long for it to vanish all at once. So, after a brief hesitation, I passed Tara's letter on to all my classmates via Facebook Messenger.

By the following morning, the whole school had read the letter. Tara was now Tara the lesbian, with all the pejorative derivatives of the term that could be imagined. I don't think it was what I originally intended, but I realized that it did me good to see Tara pilloried like this. After all, she had admitted that she had destroyed my play. At last the truth was coming out. The culprit had been exposed and the victim justified. But what everyone remembered about the letter was Tara's sexual orientation.

That very evening, Tara messaged me: *Why did you do that?* Straight-away I replied: *Because I hate you.* I think at that moment I really did feel hate. And that hate consumed me. Tara was soon the object of every-one's mockery, and passing her in the corridors of the school I told myself it served her right.

It was at this time that I became friendly with Leyla. She wasn't in my class, but she was in the same grade. She was the center of attention, charismatic, always well dressed. She sat at my table one day in the cafeteria. She told me she thought it was great that I had passed on Tara's letter. She had always found Tara pretentious, she said. "What are you doing on Saturday night? Want to hang out at my place?"

Saturdays at Leyla's became a ritual. Several girls from the school would be there, we'd shut ourselves in her room, drink alcohol she stole from her father, smoke cigarettes in the bathroom, and send Tara insulting messages on Facebook. *Bitch, whore, muff diver.* Everything got thrown in. We told her we hated her and called her every name under the sun. We reveled in it. *We're going to kill you, you bitch. You slut. You whore.*

That was the kind of girl I had become. A year earlier, my parents had been urging me to go out and make friends, but I preferred to spend my weekends writing. Now I was spending my evenings in Leyla's room, insulting Tara. The more I attacked her, the smaller she became in my eyes. I had once admired her so much, now I enjoyed dominating her. In the corridors at school, I started jostling her. One day, Leyla and I dragged her into the toilets and beat her up. I had never hit anyone before. When I landed the first blow, I was afraid of her reaction, afraid she would defend herself and overcome me. But she let herself be beaten. I felt strong, seeing her cry, seeing her begging me to stop hitting her. I liked that. That feeling of power. Seeing her reduced to nothing. The punishments resumed every time we had the opportunity. One day, while I was hitting her, she pissed herself. And that evening on Facebook, I bombarded her with more insults. *The best thing you can do is die, you bitch. That's the best thing that could happen to you.*

This lasted three months.

One morning in mid-February, there were police cars outside the school. Tara had hanged herself in her room.

*

It didn't take long for the police to get to me.

A few days after the tragedy, as I was getting ready for school, some detectives came looking for me at home. They showed me dozens of pages containing the messages I had sent to Tara. Daddy contacted his lawyer, Benjamin Graff. When the police officers left, he said we could rest easy: the police wouldn't be able to prove a direct causal link between my messages on Facebook and Tara's suicide. I remember he said something like:

"It's a good thing the Scalini girl didn't leave a farewell note explaining why she was doing what she did, or Carolina would be in real trouble."

"*A good thing?*" my mother screamed. "Do you realize what you're saying, Benjamin? You all make me want to throw up!"

"I'm just trying to do my job," Graff said, "and stop Carolina from ending up in jail."

But she *had* left a letter. Her parents found it a few days later in her room. In it, Tara explained at length that she preferred to die rather than continue to be humiliated by me every day.

The Scalinis lodged a complaint.

The police came again. It was then that I really became aware of what I had done. I had killed Tara. The handcuffs. The police station. The interrogation.

Graff, when he arrived, was not as arrogant as the first time. He was even worried. He said the D.A. wanted to make an example of me and send a strong signal to those who harassed their friends on the Internet. Depending on how it was done, incitement to suicide could even be considered a kind of homicide.

"You could be tried like an adult," Graff told me. "If that happens, you face seven to fifteen years in prison. Unless we can come to some arrangement with Tara's family and get them to withdraw their complaint."

"An arrangement?" my mother said.

"Money," Graff said. "In return for which they would give up on the idea of taking Carolina to court. There'd be no trial."

My father instructed Graff to approach the Scalinis' lawyer. Graff returned with their demand.

"They want your house in Orphea," he told my parents.

"Our house?" my father repeated, incredulous.

"Yes," Graff confirmed.

"Then it's theirs," my father said. "Call their lawyer immediately and assure him that, if the Scalinis drop their charges, I'll see to the paperwork."

JESSE ROSENBERG

Thursday, July 24, 2014
Two days to opening night

Former Special Agent Grace of the A.T.F., now seventy-two, was retired and living in Portland, Maine. When I had contacted him by telephone, he had expressed interest in our case. "Could we meet?" he had asked. "I need to show you something."

To avoid my having to drive all the way to Maine, we agreed to meet halfway, in Worcester, Massachusetts. Grace gave us the address of a little restaurant he liked a lot, where we would be left in peace. When we got there, he was already at a table with a pile of pancakes. He was thinner than before, his face was lined.

"Rosenberg and Scott, the two terrors of 1994," he said with a smile when he saw us. "I always thought our paths would cross again."

We sat down facing him. On seeing him again, I had the impression I had taken a leap into the past. He had aged, but he had not changed much.

"So you're interested in Jeremiah Fold?" he said.

I gave him a detailed update.

"Fold was like an eel, Captain Rosenberg," Grace said. "Slippery, untouchable, quick, electric. Everything a detective could hate."

"Why was the A.T.F. interested in him then?"

"To be honest, we were only indirectly interested in him. For us, the real big deal was the stolen army weapons being sold in the Ridgesport area. Before we cottoned on that it was all happening in that bar where our paths crossed in 1994, it took us months of investigation. One of the leads we followed was Fold. We knew from our informers that he had his fingers in all kinds of pies. I soon grasped that he wasn't our man, but the few weeks of observation we did on him really knocked me back. The guy was a maniac, incredibly organized. In the end, we lost interest in him. And then, one morning in July 1994, his name suddenly cropped up again.

*   *   *

It was seven in the morning when Agent Riggs arrived at the A.T.F. stakeout to relieve Grace, who had spent the night there.

"I came by Route 16," Riggs said. "There's been a bad accident. A biker got killed. You'll never guess who it was."

"The biker? No idea," Grace said. He was in no mood for riddles.

"Jeremiah Fold."

Agent Grace was stunned. "Fold is dead?"

"Almost. According to the officers I spoke to, he'll be checking out soon. He's in a terrible state. Apparently, he was riding without a helmet."

Grace was intrigued. Fold was a cautious, meticulous man. Not the kind to get himself killed stupidly. Something wasn't quite right. Leaving the stakeout, Grace decided to go over to Route 16. Two highway patrol vehicles and a breakdown truck were still there.

"The guy lost control of his bike," one of the officers told Grace. "He veered off the road and went straight into a tree. He lay there for hours. The ambulance guys say he was pretty smashed up."

"And you think he lost control of his bike all alone?" Grace said.

"There's no trace of brakes anywhere on the road. Why's the A.T.F. interested?"

"The guy was a local mobster. A very careful man. I can't see him killing himself."

"But not careful enough to wear a helmet," the officer said. "You think this was a gangland killing?"

"I have no idea," Grace said. "But there's something that bugs me, I don't know what."

368

"If they had wanted to kill this guy, they'd have done it. I mean, they'd have knocked him down and shot him. But this guy was left to die in a ditch. If he'd been found earlier, he might have been saved. Not the perfect murder."

Grace agreed. He handed the officer a business card. "Please send me a copy of your report."

"O.K., Special Agent Grace. You can count on me."

Grace spent a while longer inspecting the side of the road. The officers of the Highway Patrol had left by the time his attention was drawn to a piece of matt plastic and a few transparent shards buried in the grass. He picked them up. It was a flake of a bumper and some fragments of headlights.

*   *   *

"There were just those very few pieces," Grace said between two mouthfuls of pancake. "Nothing else. Which meant that either they had been there for a while, or that someone had cleaned up during the night."

"Someone who rammed Fold's bike?" Derek said.

"Yes. Which would explain why there were no traces of brakes. It must have been quite a crash. Whoever was at the wheel would have been able to collect most of the pieces so as not to leave any trace. His own hood must have been smashed in, but the car was still drivable. After that, this person must have told his garage mechanic that he'd hit a stag to explain the state of the car. He won't have been asked any more questions."

"Did you follow up on this?"

"No, Captain Rosenberg. I found out later that Fold never wore a helmet because, it was said, he was claustrophobic. So he wasn't always as careful as his reputation suggested. And anyhow, it had nothing to do with the A.T.F. I already had enough work, I didn't need to look into traffic accidents. But I always had that doubt in me."

"But you went no further?" Derek said.

"No. Although some months later, toward the end of October 1994, I was contacted by the chief of police in Orphea, who'd been asking himself much the same questions as me."

"Chief Hayward got in touch with you?" I said.

"Yes, that was his name, Hayward. We talked briefly about the case. He told me he'd contact me again, but he never did. I assumed he dropped it. Time passed, and I dropped it, too."

"So you never had the pieces of headlight analyzed?" Derek said.

"No, but you can. I kept them."

Grace had a wicked gleam in his eye. He wiped his mouth with a paper napkin and handed us a plastic bag. Inside, there was a piece of a black bumper and fragments of glass. He smiled and said:

"It's your turn now, gentlemen."

The day it took us to drive to Massachusetts and back was going to be worth it. If Fold had been murdered, we might have our connection with the death of Mayor Gordon.

*   *   *

In the secrecy of the Grand Theater, surrounded by crowds and defended like a fortress, rehearsals continued. In the middle of the morning, when she was not involved, Carolina Eden slipped out of the auditorium, eager for a smoke. She got to the stage door, which looked out on a dead-end alley, access forbidden to press and onlookers. She would be undisturbed there.

She lit her cigarette, sitting on the top of the steps in the sun. It was then that she saw a man appear, a press card hanging around his neck.

"Frank Vannan, *New York Times*," he said.

"How did you get this far?" Carolina said.

"The art of journalism is getting to where you're not wanted. Are you in this play?"

"Yes, I'm one of the actresses. Carolina Eden."

"What part are you playing?"

"I'm sorry, I'm not allowed to say. The director is very strict about leaks. None of us has even read the full script."

Vannan took out a notepad and scribbled a few notes.

"Write what you want," Carolina said, "but please don't quote me."

"No problem. So you don't know yourself what this play is going to reveal?"

"You know, Frank, it's a play about a secret. And a secret, when it comes down to it, is more important for what it hides than what it reveals."

"What do you mean?"

"Take a look at the cast, Frank. Every one of the actors is hiding something. If you want my opinion, the question isn't what this play is going to reveal but what it's hiding."

Carolina turned to go back in through the stage door, which she had propped open with a brick.

"Come in if you want," she said. "It's worth a look. But don't tell anyone I let you in."

*   *   *

While Derek and I were in Massachusetts, Betsy went to see Michael Bird's wife Miranda, formerly Miranda Davis.

Miranda ran a clothes store on Main Street in Bridgehampton called Keith & Danee, next door to the Golden Pear coffee shop. She was alone in the store when Betsy came in. She recognized her immediately and smiled, although she was puzzled by her visit.

"Hello, Betsy. Are you looking for Michael?"

Betsy smiled back, gently. "It's you I'm looking for, Miranda."

She showed her a xerox of the missing persons notice she was holding. Miranda's face crumpled.

"It's nothing to worry about," Betsy said. "I just need to talk."

Miranda was immediately ashen. "Let's get out of here and go for a drive. I don't want my customers to see me like this."

They closed the store and took Betsy's car. They drove for a while in the direction of East Hampton, then turned onto a dirt track until they came to the edge of the forest, beside a field of wild flowers. Miranda got out of the car as if she were nauseous, knelt in the grass, and burst into tears. Betsy crouched beside her and tried to calm her. It was only after a long quarter of an hour that Miranda was able to speak, and even then with difficulty.

"My husband and kids don't know. Don't destroy me, Betsy. I beg you, don't destroy me."

As she voiced the thought that her secret might be discovered by her family, Miranda was once more shaken by uncontrollable sobs.

"Don't worry, Miranda, no-one will know. But I do need you to tell me about Jeremiah Fold."

"Jeremiah Fold? Oh, my God, I hoped I would never hear that name again. Why him?"

"Because he may have been involved in some way in the killings of 1994."

"Jeremiah?"

"It may seem strange because he died before the killings, but his name keeps recurring in our investigation."

"What do you think I can tell you?"

"First of all, how you ended up at the mercy of Jeremiah Fold."

Miranda looked sadly at Betsy. After a long silence, she said:

"I was born in 1975. But I only started to live on July 16, 1994, the day I learned Jeremiah Fold was dead. Jeremiah was the most charismatic and also the cruelest person I have ever met. He was perverted. He was nothing like any idea people might have of a cold, brutal criminal, he was much, much worse than that. He was a true force of evil. I met him in 1992, after I ran away from home. I was seventeen, and I resented the whole world for reasons I can't figure out anymore. I was at war with my parents, and one night I just took off. It was summer, it was great to be outdoors. I spent a few nights in the open air, then I let myself be persuaded by some guys I met by chance to join a squat. An abandoned

372

old house that had become a kind of hippie community. I liked that kind of carefree life. And besides, I had a little money with me, so I could eat and live. Until the night some guys in the squat saw that I had money. They tried to rob me, they started hitting me. I ran away and got as far as the road, and there I was almost knocked down by a guy on a motorbike. He wasn't wearing a helmet. He was quite young, very handsome, dressed in a well-cut suit and nice shoes. He saw how scared I was and asked me what was going on. Then he saw the three guys coming after me, and he punched all three of them. As far as I was concerned, I had just met my guardian angel. He took me to his place on the back of his bike. He rode slowly, because I didn't have a helmet and it was dangerous, he said. He was a very, very cautious man."

*   *   *

August 1992

"Where shall I take you?" Fold asked Miranda.

"I don't have anywhere to go," she said. "Could I crash with you for a few days?"

Fold took Miranda to his place and installed her in his guest room. She hadn't slept in a bed in weeks. The following day they had a long talk.

"Miranda," Fold said, "you're only seventeen. I have to take you back to your parents."

"Please let me stay for a while. I won't be any trouble, I promise."

In the end, Fold agreed. He gave her two days, which were then extended indefinitely. He let Miranda go with him to the club he ran, but wouldn't let her be served alcohol. Then, since she was asking to work, he hired her for the club as a welcome hostess. Miranda would have preferred to be in the room, serving, but Fold did not want it. "You're not legally of an age to serve alcohol, Miranda." The man fascinated her. One night she tried to kiss him, but he cut her off mid-move. He said, "Miranda, you're seventeen. I could get into trouble."

Then, strangely, he started calling her Mylla. She had no idea why, but she quite liked the fact that he had given her a pet name. She had the feeling she had a special connection with him. Then he asked her to do favors for him. She had to take packages to strangers, go to restaurants where they would give her thick envelopes she had to take back to Fold. One day, she woke up to what Fold was doing: she was transporting drugs, money, and God knows what for him. She went to see him.

"I thought you were a good guy, Jeremiah."

"I am a good guy!"

"People say you're a drug dealer. I opened one of those packages."

"You shouldn't have done that, Mylla."

"My name isn't Mylla!"

He told her she wouldn't have to do it again. But the very next day, he summoned her like a dog. "Mylla! Mylla, go take this package to X!" She got scared. She decided to run away. She took the package, as he had asked, but didn't go where she was supposed to go. She threw the package in a garbage can, then took the train. She wanted to go back to her parents in New York. She wanted to be back in the warm feeling of home. With the money she still had, she finished her journey by taxi. When the taxi dropped her outside her parents' building, she felt a deep happiness come over her. It was midnight on a fine autumn night. The street was deserted, asleep. Suddenly, she saw him, sitting on the front steps of the building. Fold. He glared at her. She wanted to scream, to run away, but Costico, his henchman, came up behind her. Fold made a sign to Miranda to be quiet. They drove her back to Ridge's Club. For the first time, they took her to the room they called "the office". Fold asked her where the package was. Miranda was crying. She immediately admitted that she had thrown it away. She was sorry, she promised not to do it again. Fold kept saying, "You're not going to leave me, Mylla, do you understand that? You belong to me!" Still crying and terrified, she got down on her knees. Fold finally said, "I'm going to punish you, but I'm not going to mess you up." Miranda didn't understand at first. Then Jeremiah grabbed her by the hair and dragged her over to a large

374

bowl of water. He plunged her head into it, for several seconds. She thought she was going to die. When he had finished, as she was lying on the ground, crying and shaking, Costico threw photographs of her parents in her face. "If you disobey," he said, "if you do anything stupid, I'll kill both of them."

*　*　*

Miranda interrupted her account for a long while.

"I'm really sorry I'm making you relive all this," Betsy said gently, placing her hand on hers. "What happened after that?"

"It was the start of a new life. I was at Fold's beck and call. He set me up in a room in a motel by the side of Route 16, mainly used by hookers."

*　*　*

September 1992

"This is your new home," Jeremiah told Miranda as they walked into the motel room. "It'll be better for you here, you can come and go as you like."

Miranda sat down on the bed. "I want to go home, Jeremiah," she said.

"Don't you like it here?"

He had spoken in a gentle voice. That was how perverse he was: one day he would mistreat her, the next day he would take her shopping and be as nice to her as he had been at the beginning.

"I'd like to leave," Miranda said.

"You can go if you like. The door is wide open. But I wouldn't want anything to happen to your parents."

With these words, Fold left. For a long time Miranda looked at the door of the room. She just had to walk through it and take a bus to New York. But that was impossible. She was Fold's prisoner.

Fold forced her to resume her deliveries. Then he tightened his grip on her by involving her in the recruiting of his "slaves". One day, he summoned her to his office. She entered it shaking, thinking she was going again to the bowl. But Fold seemed in a good mood.

"I need a new director of human resources," he said. "The last one just took an overdose."

Miranda felt her heart pounding. What did Fold want of her?

"We're going to trap a few perverts who are looking for an underage girl to fuck. And the underage girl is going to be you. Don't worry, nobody will do anything to you."

The plan was simple: Miranda was to hustle in the parking lot of the motel, and when a client approached her she would lead him to her room. There she would ask him to undress, she would do the same, and only then admit to the man that she was underage. The man would probably say that that wasn't a problem, on the contrary, and at that moment Costico would come out of his hiding place and handle the rest.

And that was what happened. Miranda agreed to it, not only because she had no choice, but because Fold promised her that once she had helped him trap three "slaves" for him she would be free to leave.

Having fulfilled her side of the contract, Miranda went to see him and demanded that he let her leave. She ended up with her head in the bowl of water. "You're a criminal, Mylla," he said as she tried to catch her breath. "You're trapping guys and blackmailing them. They've all seen you and they even know your real name. You're not going anywhere, Mylla, you're staying with me."

Miranda's life became hell. When she wasn't delivering packages, she was being used as bait in the parking lot, and every night she was at the reception in the club, where she was much appreciated by the customers.

*   *   *

"How many guys did you trap like that?" Betsy said.

"I don't know. In the two years it lasted, maybe dozens. Fold would

376

often renew his stock of slaves. He didn't want to use them for too long, for fear they might be identified by the police. He liked to cover his tracks. I was scared, depressed, unhappy. I didn't know what was going to happen to me. The girls in the parking lot said that those who had been the bait before me had ended up either killing themselves or dying of an overdose."

"A girl in the motel told us about an argument between Costico and a guy who wouldn't let them get one over on him."

"Yes, I remember something like that," Miranda said.

"We'd like to track this man down."

Miranda opened her eyes wide. "It was twenty years ago, I don't remember it very well. What's the connection with your investigation?"

"The man sprayed Costico with tear gas. And the man we're looking for now has the habit of using tear gas. I have a feeling it's no coincidence. I need to find that man."

"Unfortunately, he never told me his name, and I doubt I'd be able to remember his face. Twenty years is a long time."

"According to my information, the man ran off naked. Could you have noticed any distinguishing marks on his body? Anything that struck you?"

Miranda closed her eyes, as if searching in her memories. Suddenly, something occurred to her.

"He had a tattoo across his shoulder blades. An eagle in flight."

Betsy noted this down. "Thank you, Miranda. That could be very useful information. I have one last question."

She showed Miranda photographs of Mayor Gordon, Ted Tennenbaum, and Cody Springfield, and said:

"Was one of these men a slave of Fold's?"

"No," Miranda said. "Especially not Cody Springfield! What a lovely man he was."

"Tell me, what did you do after Fold died?"

"I was able to get back to my parents in New York. I finished school and went to college. I gradually got myself back on track. A few years later, I met Michael. It's thanks to him that I really recovered the strength to live. He's an exceptional man."

"That's true," Betsy said. "I like him a lot."

The two women drove back to Bridgehampton. As Miranda was getting out of the car, Betsy said, "Are you sure you're going to be alright?"

"I'm certain, thanks."

"Miranda, you'll have to tell your husband about all this one day. Secrets are always found out in the end."

"I know," Miranda said sadly.

JESSE ROSENBERG

Friday, July 25, 2014
One day to opening night

We were twenty-four hours from opening night. We were making progress, but were a long way from getting to the end of our investigation. During the last twenty-four hours, we had discovered that Fold might not have died accidentally, that he could have been murdered. The pieces of the bumper and the headlights picked up at the time by Special Agent Grace were now in the hands of the forensics team.

Thanks to Miranda Bird, whose secret we had promised to keep, we also had a description of a man with an eagle tattoo on his shoulder blades. According to our information, neither Tennenbaum nor Mayor Gordon had a tattoo like that. And nor had Cody Springfield.

Costico, who was the only person who could lead us to the man with the tear gas canister, had vanished into thin air since the day before. He wasn't at the club, and he wasn't at his home. His car was parked outside his building, his door wasn't locked, and when we went inside we found the T.V. on. As if Costico had left home in a big hurry. Or as if something had happened to him.

And as if that was not enough, we also had to lend our support to Michael Bird. He had been accused by Mayor Brown of divulging information about the play to the *New York Times*, which had published an article that morning that everyone was talking about.

Brown had summoned a meeting in his office. By the time we arrived, Montagne, Major McKenna, and Bird were already there.

"Can you explain this mess to me?" Mayor Brown shouted at poor Bird, waving a copy of the *New York Times*.

I intervened. "I thought you'd be glad of the publicity, Mr Mayor."

"I'm worried that just anybody can gain access to the Grand Theater,

Captain!" he roared. "It's amazing, isn't it? We have dozens of police guarding the building. How did this guy get in?"

"It's Montagne who's in charge of security now," Betsy said.

"We have a very strong presence," Montagne said.

"Strong, my ass!" Brown cried.

"Someone obviously let that reporter in," Montagne said, turning to Bird. "Maybe a colleague of yours?"

"It was nothing to do with me!" Bird said. "I don't even understand what I'm doing here. Can you imagine me letting in someone from the *New York Times*? Why would I sabotage my own exclusive? I promised not to publish anything before opening night and I'm a man of my word! If anyone let that idiot in, it was a member of the cast!"

Major McKenna did his authoritative best to establish a truce. "Listen, there's no point attacking each other. We just have to make sure it doesn't happen again. From tonight, the Grand Theater needs to be sealed off. All routes in and out will be guarded. Tomorrow morning, we'll search the auditorium with sniffer dogs. When the audience enter the building tomorrow night, they'll be searched and have to pass through metal detectors. Even accredited people, and that includes members of the cast. Get the word out: apart from small handheld items, all will be strictly forbidden. Rest assured, Mayor Brown, nothing will happen in the Grand Theater tomorrow night."

*

After the session at the town hall, we went back to our office at the *Chronicle*. We looked again at all the things we had collected and stuck on the walls. Derek took down the article on which Stephanie had written in red marker pen: *What nobody saw.*

He said out loud, "What was in front of our eyes that we didn't see?" He looked at the photograph illustrating the article. Then he said, "Let's go over there."

Ten minutes later, we were at Penfield Crescent, where everything had started on the evening of July 30, 1994. We parked on the quiet street and for a while sat looking out at the house that had been the Gordons'. We compared it with the photograph in the article. Nothing seemed to have changed since then, except that the houses on the street looked to have been repainted.

The new owners of the Gordons' house were a pleasant couple, now retired, who had bought it in 1997.

"Obviously, we knew what had happened here," the husband told us. "I won't deny we hesitated for quite a while, but the price was attractive. We'd never have been able to afford a house this size if we'd had to pay top dollar."

"Is the layout of the house the same as it was then?" I asked.

"Yes, Captain. We refurbished the kitchen, but the layout of the rooms was exactly as you see it now."

"Do you mind if we take a look around?"

"Go ahead."

We began with the front door, following the reconstruction in the police file. Betsy read out the report.

"The killer kicks the door down," she said. "He comes across Leslie Gordon in the hallway and shoots, then turns to his right and sees the Gordons' son in the living room, and shoots him. Then he heads for the kitchen, where he kills the mayor before going back out through the front door."

We walked the route from the living room to the kitchen, then from the kitchen to the front steps.

"As he comes out," Betsy continues, "he sees Meghan Padalin, who's trying to run away. He shoots her twice in the back, then finishes her off with a bullet in the head."

We now knew that the killer had not come in Tennenbaum's van as we had thought, but either in another vehicle or on foot. Betsy looked again at the garden and said suddenly:

"You know, there's something that doesn't make sense."

"What doesn't?" I said.

"The killer is trying to take advantage of the fact that everyone's at the festival. He wants to be invisible, silent, furtive. Logically, he should prowl around the house, slip into the garden, look into the house through a window."

"Maybe he did," Derek said.

Betsy frowned. "You told me there was a leak in the sprinkler system that day. Everyone who set foot on the lawn had wet shoes. If the killer had come through the garden before kicking down the door, he would have brought water into the house. But the report doesn't mention damp footprints. There should have been some, shouldn't there?"

"That's a good point," Derek said.

"Another thing," Betsy went on. "Why did the killer come in through the front door and not the kitchen door, at the back of the house? He'd only have had to break the glass. Why didn't he get in that way? Probably because he didn't know there was a glass door there. His M.O. is quick, brutal. He kicked down the door and shot everyone."

"Agreed," I said, "but what are you getting at, Betsy?"

"I don't think the mayor was the target, Jesse. If the killer had wanted to kill the mayor, why rush in through the front door, when he had better options?"

"What are you thinking? A burglary? But nothing was stolen."

"I know," Betsy said, "but there's a detail that doesn't ring true."

Derek thought about it in his turn and looked at the park near the house. He walked over to it, sat down on the grass, and said:

"Charlotte Brown stated that when she arrived Meghan Padalin was in this park doing exercises. We know from the timeline that the killer got here a minute after she left. So Meghan was still in the park. If the killer leaves his vehicle and goes to the house and kicks the Gordons' door down and shoots them, why does Meghan run in the direction of the house? It makes no sense. She should have run in the other direction."

"Oh, my God!" I cried.

It had just hit me. It wasn't the Gordon family that was targeted in 1994. It was Meghan Padalin.

The killer knew her habits, he had come to kill *her*. Maybe he had already attacked her in the park and she had tried to run away. He had then taken up position on the street and shot her. As far as he knew, the Gordons were away that day. The whole town was in the Grand Theater. But suddenly he had seen the Gordons' son in the window— Charlotte had also seen him a few minutes earlier. He had then kicked in the door of the house and killed all the witnesses.

That was what had been in front of the investigators' eyes from the beginning, but nobody had seen it: the body of Meghan Padalin in front of the house. She was the one who had been targeted. The Gordons had been collateral damage.

DEREK SCOTT

Mid-September 1994. A month and a half after the Gordon killings and a month before the tragedy that would strike Jesse and me.

We had Tennenbaum in a corner.

The very afternoon on which we had questioned Corporal Ziggy and he had admitted selling Tennenbaum a Beretta, we went to Orphea to proceed with the arrest. To make sure we didn't miss him, we had two teams from the State Police with us: one, led by Jesse, to break into his house, and the other, led by myself, to go to Café Athena. But we drew a blank: Tennenbaum was not at home, and the manager of his restaurant had not seen him since the day before.

"He's taken a break," the manager told us.

"A break?" I said in surprise. "Where to?"

"I don't know. Only a few days off. He should be back on Monday."

A search of Tennenbaum's house yielded nothing. Nor did a search of his office at Café Athena. We could not wait quietly until he deigned to return to Orphea. According to our information, he had not taken a plane, at least not under his own name. His immediate associates had not seen him. And his van wasn't there. We launched a search. His description was sent to the airports and the borders, his license number sent to all the police forces in the country. His photograph was distributed to all businesses in the Orphea area and to a large number of gas stations in New York State.

Jesse and I moved between our office at troop headquarters, which was the heart of the operation, and Orphea, where we mounted a stakeout in front of the Tennenbaum house, sleeping in our car. We were pretty sure that he was hiding in the area. He knew the place like the back of his hand, and had a lot of support. We even obtained permission to tap the phone of his sister, Sylvia Tennenbaum, who lived in Manhattan, as well as that of the restaurant. But to no avail. After three weeks, the taps were discontinued for reasons of cost. The officers the major had allocated to us were reassigned to cases that were higher priority.

"Higher priority than the arrest of a quadruple murderer?" I protested to Major McKenna.

"Derek," the major said, "I gave you unlimited resources for three weeks. This thing could go on months. We just have to be patient. We'll get him in the end."

Tennenbaum had given us the slip and was getting away. Jesse and I were sleepless. We wanted to find him, to arrest him, to bring this investigation to a close.

While our search was treading water, work on Little Russia was going well. Darla and Natasha were sure they could open the restaurant by the end of the year.

But lately, tension had emerged between them. The origin of these was an article published in a newspaper in Queens. The locals were all intrigued by the restaurant sign, and those passers-by who had come to ask questions had been charmed by the two owners. Soon, everyone was talking about Little Russia. It had aroused the interest of a reporter, who had asked if he could write an article. He had come with a photographer, who had taken a series of photographs, including one of Natasha and Darla together under the sign. But when the article appeared, a few days later, they discovered, to their dismay, that the only photograph was one of Natasha, alone, in an apron with the restaurant's logo, and with the following caption: "Natasha Darrinski, owner of Little Russia".

It was hardly Natasha's fault, but Darla was terribly hurt by this episode. It was also a good illustration of the fascination Natasha held for people.

Everything had gone so well until that point, but this was the beginning of some terrible disagreements. Every time their opinions diverged, Darla could not avoid saying:

"Well, Natasha, we'll do what you want anyway. You're the one who decides everything!"

"Darla, do I have to keep apologizing for that fucking article? It was nothing to do with me. I didn't want to do it, I said it was best to wait till the restaurant opened. That then it would be good publicity."

"Oh, so it's my fault?"

"I didn't say that, Darla."

When we all met up in the evenings, they were demoralized and subdued. Jesse and I sensed that Little Russia was starting to take on water.

Darla did not want anything to do with a project in which she would be overshadowed by Natasha.

As for Natasha, she was suffering from being Natasha, the girl who, despite herself, attracted all the attention.

It was such a pity. They had everything going for them, there was every prospect of success with a project they'd been dreaming about for ten years and had worked so hard for. Those hours spent toiling away at the Blue Lagoon, putting aside every dollar they earned for the restaurant they planned together, those years spent conceiving a place that would reflect their personalities—all this was crumbling.

Jesse and I didn't want to get involved. The last time all four of us had been together had been a disaster. Meeting in Natasha's kitchen to taste the dishes finally chosen for Little Russia's menu, I had made the worst possible blunder. After tasting that famous beef sandwich flavored with that very distinctive sauce, I had gone into ecstasies over it and made the error of referring to "Natasha's Sauce". Darla had made a scene.

"*Natasha's Sauce*? Is that what it's called? Why don't we just call the place Natasha's Restaurant?"

"It isn't Natasha's Sauce," Natasha had said, trying to calm Darla down. "It's our restaurant, both of ours, and you know that."

386

"No, I don't know that, Natasha! I feel I'm just an employee following orders, you decide everything."

She had left, slamming the door.

So, when a few days later the two of them suggested we join them at the printer's to decide on the design of the menus, Jesse and I declined. I don't know if they really wanted our opinions, or just wanted us to act as peacemakers, but neither Jesse nor I had any wish to get involved.

That day was Thursday, October 13, 1994. The day everything changed.

It was early afternoon. Jesse and I were in the office, eating sandwiches, when Jesse's phone rang. It was Natasha. She was in tears. She was calling from a hunting and fishing supplies store on Long Island.

"Darla and I quarreled in the car on the way to the printer's," she said. "She suddenly stopped and threw me out of the car. I left my purse inside. I'm lost, without money."

Jesse told her not to move, he would fetch her. I decided to go with him. We found poor Natasha still in tears. We tried to comfort her, promised her that everything would work out in the end, but she kept saying that as far as she was concerned the restaurant was over, she didn't want to hear about it anymore.

We only just missed Darla, who had done a U-turn and come back for her friend. She hated herself for what she had done, and was ready to do anything to be forgiven. Not finding Natasha, she stopped outside the hunting and fishing supplies store, there at the side of this deserted road. The owner told her that he had indeed seen a young woman in tears, that she had used his telephone, and that two men had come to pick her up. "They only just left," he said. "Not a minute ago."

I think that if she had only gotten there a few moments earlier, Darla would have seen us in front of the store. And everything would have been different.

We were driving Natasha home when our radio suddenly started crackling. Tennenbaum had been seen in a gas station. I took the microphone and announced myself to the switchboard. Jesse put the emergency light on the roof, then started the siren.

0

Opening Night

JESSE ROSENBERG
Saturday, July 26, 2014
Opening night

It was the night everything changed.

It was 5.30. The doors of the Grand Theater would soon be thrown open. Main Street, cordoned off by the police, was packed with people. The excitement was wild. Amid the reporters, the onlookers and the itinerant souvenir sellers, the ticket holders were crowded up against security barriers that still blocked access to the theater. People who had been unable to obtain tickets for opening night were walking up and down the crowd with homemade banners offering absurd sums.

A little earlier, the T.V. news channels had broadcast live the arrival of the cast, under stringent protection. Before being allowed through the stage door, each cast member had been searched and then had passed through a metal detector to ensure they weren't carrying a weapon.

At the main entrance to the theater, security people were finishing putting in metal detector gates. The public could not keep still. In just over two hours the performance of "The Darkest Night" would begin. The identity of the 1994 killer was at last to be revealed.

In the archive room of the *Chronicle*, Derek, Betsy and I were getting ready to set off for the theater. We were condemned to witness Kirk Hayward's ludicrous triumph. The previous day, Major McKenna had said to us, "Instead of doubting Hayward, just take whatever may come from the performance. We can all hope and pray that it helps you complete your investigation and discover the truth." That was provocative. Our obsession now, however, was: why had Meghan Padalin been killed? Who could have had a reason to eliminate this unremarkable, much-liked woman?

Bird had been of great help, spending most of one sleepless night working beside us. He had gathered everything he could on Meghan, allowing us to reconstruct her life story. She was born in Pittsburgh, and had studied literature at a small college in New York State. She had briefly lived in New York City before settling in Orphea in 1990 with her husband Samuel, who worked as an engineer in a local factory. Not long afterward, she had been hired by Cody Springfield.

And what was there to say about her husband, Samuel, who had suddenly reappeared in Orphea to take part in the play? After his wife's murder, he had moved to Southampton and had remarried.

Padalin, too, seemed to be unremarkable. He had joined a number of organizations as a volunteer. His new wife, Kelly, was a doctor. They had two children, aged ten and twelve.

Could there be a connection between Meghan Padalin and Fold? Or between Samuel Padalin and Fold?

We had telephoned former Special Agent Grace of the A.T.F., but the name Padalin meant nothing to him. For the time being, there was no questioning Costico, who was still nowhere to be found. We did talk again to Virginia Parker, the singer from the club, but she assured us she had never heard of either Samuel or Meghan Padalin.

Nobody had a connection with anybody. It was incredible. Now, as the doors of the theater were about to open, we had even started wondering if these were two distinct investigations.

"Meghan's murder on one side, and Gordon's involvement with Fold on the other," Derek said.

"Except that Gordon seems to have had no connection with Fold either," I said.

"But Hayward's play does appear to refer to Fold," Betsy pointed out, "and one of the characters is called Meghan. I do think everything's connected."

"If I understand correctly," Bird said, summing up, "everything's connected, but nothing's connected. It's a bit of a Chinese puzzle, this case of yours."

392

"You're telling us," Betsy said with a sigh. "Plus, there's Stephanie's killer. Could it be the same person?"

Derek made an effort to get us out of this confusion. "Let's try to put ourselves in the killer's shoes. If I were him, what would I be doing today?"

"I would either be a long way away by now," I said, "in Venezuela or some other country that doesn't extradite. Or else I would try to stop the show."

"Stop the show?" Derek said. "But the theater's been searched with dogs, and anyone wanting to get in will be searched and have to go through a metal detector."

"I think he'll be there," I said. "I think the killer will be in the theater, among us."

We decided to go and observe the audience as they entered the theater. Some unusual behavior might alert us. But we also wanted to know more about what Kirk Hayward was cooking up. If he knew the killer's identity, it would be better not to have to wait until opening night to find out.

The only way to read Hayward's mind was to be able to access the material in his possession. Especially the case file, which he was hiding somewhere. We sent Bird to search his hotel room when he was not there.

"Whatever I discover will have no value as evidence," Bird said.

"We don't need evidence. We need a name."

"But how do I get upstairs? There'll be police all over the hotel."

"Show them your accreditation for the theater and say that Hayward sent you to fetch his things. I'll call to let them know you're coming."

Although the officers were prepared to allow Bird upstairs, the hotel manager was unwilling to give him a duplicate of the room key.

"Mr Hayward gave specific instructions," he said to Bird. "Nobody is allowed in his room."

But Bird insisted, saying that it was Hayward himself who had sent him to look for a notebook. The manager decided to go with him to the suite.

The room was in perfect order. Looking around, watched suspiciously by the manager, Bird did not see any papers, any books, any notebooks. He checked the desk, the drawers, even the night table. But there was nothing. He glanced into the bathroom.

"I don't think Mr Hayward puts his notebooks away in the bathroom," the manager said.

"There's nothing in Hayward's room," Bird said, joining us in the lobby of the Grand Theater after passing through the endless security checks.

It was 7.30. The play would begin in half an hour. We had not managed to get one step ahead of Hayward. We were going to have to learn the name of the killer, like the rest of the audience, from his play. And we were about to find out how the killer, if he were in the auditorium, would react. We were going to be among the audience, watching like hawks.

*

7.58. In the wings, a few minutes from going onstage, Hayward had gathered his cast in the corridor that led to the stage. Facing him were Charlotte Brown, Carolina and Jerry Eden, Samuel Padalin, Meta Ostrovski, and Steven Bergdorf.

"My friends," he said, "I hope you are ready to discover the thrill of fame and success. Your performance will be unique in the history of the theater and will resonate throughout the nation."

*

8.00. The auditorium was plunged into darkness. The murmur of the audience subsided unevenly. The tension was palpable. Derek, Betsy and I were standing behind the last row of seats, each at one of the doors into the auditorium.

Mayor Brown appeared on stage for his speech of welcome. I thought again of the frozen image from the video of that same sequence, twenty years earlier, which Stephanie Mailer had circled with her felt-tip.

394

After a fairly conventional address, the mayor concluded with the words: "This is a festival that will be long remembered. Let the show begin." He walked down off the stage and took his seat in the front row. The curtain rose. A tremor went through the audience.

The play opened with one of the scenes we had watched in Bird's clandestine videos. The curtain was raised to reveal Padalin, playing the dead man, and, beside him, Eden as a police officer. From where I was standing, I could see Hayward watching from the wings. He looked nervous. There was something about him that struck me as odd, but I couldn't put my finger on it.

By the time we reached the scene in Fold's bar in Ridgesport, with Charlotte playing Virginia Parker, I had studied the face of every person in the auditorium, looking for any sign of tension or nerves that might betray the killer. I glanced at Hayward again, as Charlotte broke into song. It was at this point that I noticed that Hayward did not have anything in his hand. That was it. That was what was bothering me. He wasn't holding a script and he wasn't wearing his shoulder bag. I walked over to where Derek was standing.

"Hayward doesn't have his script with him. If he's left it in the dressing room, this could be our chance."

"What do you mean?" he whispered.

"I can't watch this anymore. I'm going to find out exactly what Hayward has in store for us. Are you coming?"

Derek and I made our way as silently and as swiftly as we could from the auditorium to the backstage area. We found Hayward's dressing room. It was locked. We forced the door. On a table, we immediately saw the police file, and also his famous sheaf of papers. We looked rapidly through the pages. There were the first scenes, which had just been played, but then, after the scene in the bar, came an appearance by Meghan Padalin, played by Carolina, on her own, declaring:

"The moment of truth has come. The name of the killer is . . ."

The sentence ended with an ellipsis. There was nothing more.

Nothing but blank pages. After a moment's astonishment, Derek cried:

"My God, Jesse, you were right! Hayward has no idea of the killer's identity. He's waiting for the killer to reveal himself by interrupting the show."

At that very moment, Carolina was moving downstage, alone, announcing, in a prophetic tone, "*The moment of truth has come.*"

Derek and I ran out of the dressing room. But we were too late. The auditorium was plunged into darkness. The darkest night. Only the stage was still lit. As we reached the stage, Carolina was beginning her sentence: "*The name of the killer is . . .*"

A shot rang out. And then a second. Carolina slumped to the floor.

The crowd started screaming. Derek and I took out our pistols and jumped up onto the stage, yelling into our radios, "Gunshots! One person down!" The auditorium lights went up and a general panic burst out. The terrified audience tried as best they could to get away, out of the theater. It was total chaos. We had not seen the shooter. Neither had Betsy. And we could not stop this human stream pouring out through the emergency exits. The shooter had mingled with the crowd. He might already be outside and gone.

Carolina was lying on the floor of the stage, convulsing. There was blood everywhere. Eden, Charlotte Brown, and Bird had rushed to help her. Eden was screaming. I pressed on her wounds to stop the bleeding, while Derek yelled into his radio, "We have one person down! Send first aid to the stage!"

The stream of spectators spilled out onto Main Street, unleashing a great wave of panic the police could not contain. People were screaming. They were talking about an attack. From Main Street, yells and sirens could be heard. Emergency vehicles were coming in from all sides.

It was chaos.

It was the Darkest Night.

Friday, September 21, 2012. The day everything changed.

Up until then, everything had been going well. In my professional life and in my life with Mark. I was a detective in the 55th precinct. Mark, working as a lawyer in my father's firm, had built up a portfolio of clients that generated substantial income. We loved each other. We were a happy couple. At work and at home. A happily married couple. I even had the impression that we were happier and more fulfilled than most of the other couples we knew, with whom I often compared myself.

I think the first sign of trouble in our relationship came with my change of assignment in the police. Having quickly proved myself in the field, it was proposed by my superiors that I join a unit dealing with hostage situations, as a negotiator. I took tests for this new post and passed with flying colors.

Mark did not at first fully understand what my new assignment entailed. Not until, unknown to myself, I appeared on T.V. during a hostage situation in a supermarket in Queens early in 2012. I was shown in my black uniform and bulletproof vest, holding my ballistic helmet in front of me. The images were seen by my family and all my friends.

"I thought you were a negotiator," Mark said in a shocked tone, after looking at the sequence on a loop.

"That's right," I assured him.

"Judging by what you were wearing, you seem to be more involved in the action than in calming things down."

"Mark, it's a unit that deals with hostage situations. You can't handle that kind of thing by doing yoga."

He was silent for a time. He poured himself a drink, smoked a cigarette, then came and told me:

"I don't know if I can bear you doing that job."

"You knew the risks of my profession when you married me," I pointed out.

"No, when I met you, you were a detective, you weren't up to that kind of nonsense."

"Nonsense? Mark, I'm saving lives."

The tension got worse after a madwoman shot dead two police officers parked on a street in Brooklyn with their patrol car windows open, drinking coffee.

Mark was worried. When I left in the morning, he would say to me, "I hope I see you again tonight." Months went by. Gradually, hints were not enough: Mark became more insistent and even proposed that I ask for a chance to retrain.

"Why don't you come and work with me in the firm, Betsy? You could help me with major cases."

"Help you? You want me to be your assistant? You think I'm not capable of handling my own cases? Do I need to remind you that I'm a qualified lawyer, no more or less than you?"

"Don't put words in my mouth. I just think you should think a bit farther than your immediate future and envisage a part-time job."

"Part-time? Why part-time?"

"Betsy, when we have kids, you're not going to spend your days away from them, are you?"

Mark had career-minded parents who had not bothered with him very much when he was a child. It had stayed with him, an open wound, and he made up for it by working flat out with the thought of being the sole breadwinner and allowing his wife to stay at home.

"I'm never going to be a housewife, Mark. That's something else you knew before you married me."

"But you don't need to keep working, Betsy, I earn enough money!"

"I love my job, Mark. I'm sorry you hate it so much."

"At least promise you'll think about it."

"The answer is no, Mark! But don't worry, we won't be like your parents."

"Don't bring my parents into this, Betsy!"

But he himself brought my father into it, by confiding in him. And my father talked to me about it one day when we were together. It was the famous Friday, September 21. I remember it as a wonderful day, a real Indian summer day. The sun was bright in New York, and the temperature was at least 70°F. I wasn't working that day, and I met my father for lunch in the outside seating area of an Italian restaurant that we were both fond of. It wasn't far from my father's office, and I thought that if he was arranging to meet with me there on a weekday, it was because he wanted to talk to me about something important.

And indeed, no sooner were we sitting at the table than he said:

"Betsy, darling, I know you're having problems in your marriage."

I almost spat out the water I was drinking. "Who told you that, Daddy?"

"Your husband. He's afraid for you, you know."

"I was already doing this job when he met me, Daddy."

"So you're going to sacrifice everything to be a police officer?"

"I love my work. Why can't anybody respect that?"

"You risk your life every day!"

"Daddy, I could just as easily be knocked down by a bus leaving this restaurant."

"Don't play with words, Betsy. Mark is a wonderful boy, don't make a fool of yourself with him."

That evening, Mark and I had a violent argument.

"I can't believe you went whining to my father!" I said angrily. "What happens between us as a couple is no-one's business but ours!"

"I was hoping your father could talk some sense into you. He's the only person who has any influence over you, it seems. But I guess when it comes down to it all you think about is your own personal happiness. You're so selfish, Betsy."

"I love my job, Mark! I'm good at what I do! Is that so hard to understand?"

"And can't you understand that I've had enough of feeling scared for

399

you? Of shaking when your cell phone rings in the middle of the night and you rush off to an emergency?"

"Don't be such a drama queen. That doesn't happen so often."

"But it does happen. Frankly, Betsy, it's too dangerous. It's not a job for you anymore!"

"And how do you know what's a job for me?"

"I know, that's all."

"I wonder how you can be so stupid."

"Your father agrees with me!"

"I'm not married to my father, Mark! I don't give a fuck what he thinks!"

Just then my cell phone rang. I saw on the screen that it was my chief. At such an hour, it could only be an emergency and Mark realized that immediately.

"Betsy, please don't pick up."

"Mark, it's my chief."

"You're on leave."

"That's just it, Mark. If he's calling me now, it must be important."

"Dammit, you're not the only police officer in this town, are you?"

I hesitated for a moment, then took the call.

"Betsy," my chief said, "we have a hostage crisis in a jewelry store on the corner of Madison and 57th. The area has been cordoned off. We need a negotiator."

"O.K.," I said, writing the address on a piece of paper. "What's the name of the store?"

"Sabar's."

I hung up and collected my bag with my things, always kept ready beside the door. I tried to kiss Mark, but he had disappeared into the kitchen. I sighed and ran out. As I left our building, I saw our neighbors, through their dining room window, just finishing dinner. They looked happy. For the first time, it occurred to me that other couples' marriages were probably more fulfilled than ours.

I got in my unmarked car, put on the emergency lights, and set off into the night.

DEREK SCOTT

Thursday, October 13, 1994. The day everything changed.

We drove at high speed. We didn't want Tennenbaum to get away this time.

We were so engrossed in our pursuit that I had forgotten Natasha, who was still in the back seat, holding on tight. Jesse, following the directions given on the radio, guided me.

We took Route 101, then 107. Tennenbaum was being pursued by two patrol cars, which he was trying to lose however he could.

"Keep straight on, then take Route 94," Jesse said. "We'll head him off and set up a roadblock."

I accelerated to gain ground and turned onto Route 94. But as we were approaching 107, Tennenbaum's black van, with his logo painted on the rear window, cut us off. I just had time to glimpse him at the wheel.

I set off in pursuit of him. He had managed to get a head start on the patrol cars. I was determined not to lose him. We soon saw the bridge crossing the Snake River ahead of us. We were almost bumper-to-bumper. I managed to accelerate some more and get almost level with him. There was nobody coming toward us.

"I'm going to try to pin him against the railing of the bridge."

"Good," Jesse said. "Do it."

As we drove onto the bridge, I gave a twist to the wheel and knocked into the back of Tennenbaum's van. He lost control and hit the railing. But instead of stopping him dead in his tracks, the railing gave way and he went off the road. I didn't have time to brake.

Tennenbaum's van plunged into the river, and so did our car.

PART THREE

Rising

1

Natasha

THURSDAY, OCTOBER 13, 1994

JESSE ROSENBERG
Thursday, October 13, 1994

That day we're chasing Tennenbaum and Derek loses control of the car and the railing of the bridge smashes to pieces, I see us plunging into the river in slow motion. As if suddenly time has stood still. I see the water moving closer to the windshield. The fall seems to go on for ten, twenty minutes. Obviously, it lasts only a few seconds.

As the car hits the water, I realize I haven't got my seat belt on. My head hits the glove compartment. Blackness swallows me. My life passes in front of my eyes.

I see myself at the end of the '70s, when I was nine and my mother and I had moved to Rego Park after my father's death, to be closer to my grandparents. My mother had had to increase her working hours in order to make ends meet and, since she didn't want me to be alone for too long after school, I would go to my grandparents, who lived one street away from my elementary school, and stay there until my mother came to pick me up.

Objectively, my grandparents were terrible people, but for sentimental reasons I felt deep affection for them. They were neither pleasant nor kind, and they were hardly capable of behaving properly in any situation. My grandfather's favorite phrase was "Bunch of jerks!" My grandmother's was "That's shit!" They would repeat this drivel all day long, like two stunted parrots.

On the street, they would scold children and insult passers-by. First would come "Bunch of jerks!" Then Grandma's "That's shit!"

In stores, they would abuse the staff. "Bunch of jerks!" Grandpa would proclaim, and Grandma would add her refrain.

At the supermarket checkout, they would brazenly push past

everybody else. If the other customers protested, Grandpa would say, "Bunch of jerks!" But if they said nothing, out of respect for their elders, Grandpa would still come out with "Bunch of jerks!" Then when the cashier, having scanned the barcodes, announced the total, Grandma would say, "That's shit!"

At Halloween, children who were misguided enough to ring their doorbell to ask for candies would be greeted by Grandpa yelling, "Bunch of jerks!" He would leave the door open and Grandma would appear and throw a bucket of ice-cold water over them to chase them away, screaming, "That's shit!" You would see their little disguised bodies running away, crying, soaked to the skin, through the freezing streets of a New York winter, condemned to a bout of flu.

My grandparents had the instincts of people who had known hunger. At the restaurant, Grandma would systematically empty the bread basket into her purse. Grandpa would immediately ask the waiter to refill it, and Grandma would continue her stocking up. Did you ever have grandparents to whom, in a restaurant, the waiter would say, "From now on we're going to have to charge you for bread, if you keep asking for more"? Well, I did. And the scene which would ensue was even more embarrassing. "That's shit!" Grandma would fling at him from her toothless mouth. To which Grandpa would add, "Bunch of jerks!" and throw pieces of bread at the waiter's chest.

The conversations my mother had with her parents consisted mainly of the words "Stop that now!" Or "Behave yourselves!" Or "Please don't show me up!" Or "At least make an effort in front of Jesse!"

Often, when we got back from their place, Mom would tell me she was ashamed of her parents. But I accepted them as they were.

Our move to Rego Park had involved a change of school. A few weeks after I started in the new school, one of my classmates decreed, "Your name's Jesse . . . short for Jessica!" It took less than fifteen minutes for my new nickname to spread. And all day long I had to endure taunts like "Jesse the girl!" or "Jessica the chick!"

That day, I came home from school crying.

"Why are you crying?" Grandpa asked curtly. "Men who cry are girls."

"My classmates call me Jessica," I said.

"Well, you see, they're right."

Grandpa led me to the kitchen where Grandma was making my after-school snack.

"Why's he sniveling like that?" Grandma asked Grandpa.

"Because his friends are calling him a girl," Grandpa said.

"Huh! Men who cry are girls," Grandma decreed.

"You see!" Grandpa said to me. "At least everyone agrees."

Since I had not overcome my distress, my grandparents made some useful suggestions.

"Don't just do nothing, hit them!" Grandma advised me.

"Yeah, hit them!" Grandpa said approvingly, searching in the refrigerator.

"Mom doesn't want me to get into fights," I said, hoping that would make them come up with a more dignified response. "Maybe you could go talk to my teacher?"

"Talking is shit!" Grandma said definitively.

"Bunch of jerks!" Grandpa added, taking some smoked meat out of the fridge.

"Hit your grandpa in the belly," Grandma said.

"Yeah, that's right, come here and hit me in the belly!" Grandpa said enthusiastically, spitting out pieces of the cold meat he was greedily chewing.

I refused categorically.

"If you don't do it, that means you're a little girl!" Grandpa said.

"Which do you prefer, to hit Grandpa or be a little girl?" Grandma said.

Faced with such a choice, I said I preferred to be a little girl rather than hurt Grandpa, and my grandparents called me "little girl" for the rest of the afternoon.

The next day, when I got to their house, a gift was waiting for me on the kitchen table. The words *For Jessica* were written on a pink

Post-it note. I undid the wrapping and found a little girl's blonde wig.

"From now on, you will wear this wig and we'll call you Jessica," Grandma said merrily.

"I don't want to be a girl," I protested, as Grandpa put it on my head.

"Then prove it," Grandma said. "If you aren't a girl, you'll be capable of getting the shopping from the trunk of the car and putting it away in the fridge."

I hastened to do as I was told. But once it was done, and I had demanded to be allowed to take off my wig and recover my dignity, Grandma said it wasn't enough. She needed more proof. I immediately asked for another challenge, which I again met successfully, but, once more, Grandma was not convinced. It was only after two days spent tidying the garage, rearranging Grandpa's chest of drawers, fetching the clothes from the dry cleaner's—which I had to pay for with my pocket money—washing the dishes, and polishing all the shoes in the house that I realized that Jessica was no more than a prisoner, my Grandma's serf.

Deliverance came with an episode that occurred in the parking lot of a supermarket where we went in my grandparents' car. As we drove in, Grandpa, who was a terrible driver, hit the bumper of a car that was backing out, although not hard. He and Grandma got out to check on the damage, while I remained in the back seat.

"Bunch of jerks!" Grandpa screamed at the other driver, a woman, and at her husband, who was inspecting the bodywork.

"Mind your language," the driver said, "or I'll call the police."

"That's shit!" Grandma said with her habitual good timing.

Becoming more agitated, the woman now scolded her husband, who was saying nothing, merely passing a finger sluggishly over the scratch to see if the bumper was damaged or if it was just a surface scrape.

"Say something, Robert, dammit!"

Onlookers were stopping with their shopping carts to observe the scene. The Robert in question looked at his wife without uttering a word.

"Lady," Grandpa said to the driver, "I suggest you look in the glove compartment, maybe that's where your husband keeps his balls."

Robert rose to his full height and lifted a threatening fist. "Are you saying I have no balls?"

Thinking he was about to hit Grandpa, I quickly got out of the car, still with my wig on my head. "Don't touch my grandpa!"

In the excitement, presumably misled by my blonde locks, Robert said:

"What does this girl want?"

That was too much. When would people finally understand that I wasn't a girl?

"This is where your balls are!" I cried in my childish voice, landing a well-placed punch that made him slump to the ground.

Grandma grabbed me, threw me in the back seat of our car, and climbed in after me. Grandpa, already back in the driver's seat, set off at speed. Both "Bunch of jerks!" and "That's shit!" were again heard by the witnesses, who took the license number of Grandpa's car and did indeed call the police.

Several good things came from this incident. One of them was the arrival of Ephraim and Becky Jenson in my life. They were my grandparents' neighbors and I had seen them occasionally. I knew that Becky sometimes went shopping for Grandma and that Ephraim did little favors for Grandpa—when, for example, the changing of a light bulb involved the skills of a tightrope walker. I also knew that they had no children, because one day Grandma had asked them:

"Don't you have any children?"

"No," Becky had replied.

"That's shit!" Grandma had said, sympathetically.

"I quite agree with you."

But it was soon after the incident in the parking lot of the mall in Rego and our hasty return from the supermarket that my relationship with them blossomed in earnest, when the police knocked at my grandparents' door.

"Has someone died?" Grandpa asked the two officers as they stood outside on the landing.

"No, sir. It seems you and a little girl were involved in an incident in the parking lot of the mall in Rego."

"The parking lot of the mall?" Grandpa repeated in an outraged tone. "Never been there in my life!"

"Sir, a vehicle registered in your name and corresponding to the one parked outside your house has been formally identified by a number of witnesses after a man was attacked by a little blonde girl."

"There's no little blonde girl here," Grandpa assured him.

Unaware of what was going on, I came to the door to see who Grandpa was talking to. I had my wig on my head.

"That's the little girl!" the other officer cried.

"I'm not a little girl!" I said, assuming a deep voice.

"Don't touch my Jessica!" Grandpa yelled, placing his body full in the doorway.

It was at this point that my grandparents' neighbor, Ephraim Jenson, made his entrance. Alerted by the rumpus, he came out and brandished a police officer's badge. I didn't grasp what he told the other two officers, but I realized that Ephraim was an important policeman. It only took a few words from him, and his colleagues apologized to Grandpa and left.

From that day on, Grandma, who had a certain awe of authority and uniforms from her days in Odessa, elevated Ephraim to the ranks of the just. And to thank him, every Friday afternoon she made a delicious cheesecake, such as only she knew how, filling the kitchen with delicious smells when I returned from school. I knew I wouldn't get even the smallest portion. When the cake was ready and wrapped, Grandma would say to me. "Take this to them, Jesse. That man is our Raoul Wallenberg!" I would present myself at the Jensons' and, in handing over the cake, had to say these words to them: "My grandparents thank you for saving our lives."

Going to the Jensons' every week as I did, I began to be invited to come in and stay for a while. Becky would say that the cake was enormous and there were only two of them, and, despite my protests, she would cut off a piece which I would eat in their kitchen with a glass of milk. I liked them a lot. Ephraim fascinated me and in Becky I found the mother's love that I missed, since I didn't see enough of my own mother. Before long, Becky and Ephraim were suggesting I go with them to Manhattan at weekends, to walk about or visit exhibits. They were getting me away from my grandparents. Whenever they rang the bell and asked my grandma if I could go with them, I had an immense feeling of joy.

As for the little blonde girl who punched people in the balls, she was never tracked down. Jessica disappeared forever and I never again had to wear that hideous wig. Sometimes, in moments of distraction, Grandma would remember Jessica. In the middle of a family meal, with twenty people around the table, she would suddenly declare:

"Jessica died in a supermarket parking lot."

A long silence would follow. Then a cousin would venture to ask: "Jessica who?"

"It must have been something that happened in the war," someone else would say.

And the whole company would assume a grave expression and lapse again into silence, because nobody ever talked about Odessa.

After that business with Robert's balls, Grandpa decided that I was now well and truly a boy, and even a brave boy. As a reward, he took me one afternoon to the back room of a kosher butcher, where an old man, originally from Bratislava, gave boxing lessons. The old man was the former butcher—the store was now run by his sons—and he spent his days giving the grandchildren of his friends free lessons in boxing, which consisted basically of making us punch stale carcasses while, in a voice with a hint of a faraway accent, he told us about the finals of the 1931 Czechoslovakian boxing championship.

So it was that I learned how every afternoon, in Rego Park, a coterie of old gentlemen, on the spurious pretext of wanting to spend time with their grandchildren, escaped from the family home and came to the butcher's. They would sit on plastic chairs, wrapped in their coats, and drink black coffee and smoke, while a whole lot of street boys banged away at quarters of meat suspended from the ceiling. And when we were

413

tired, we would sit on the floor and listen to the stories of the old man from Bratislava.

For months, I spent all my late afternoons boxing in the butcher's, in the greatest secrecy. It was thought I might have a gift for boxing and the rumor attracted lots of old men, with a thousand different smells, who packed into that cold room to watch me, sharing cans of produce from Eastern Europe that they spread on black bread. I would hear them encouraging me: "Go on, boy!", "Harder! Much harder!" And Grandpa, overflowing with pride, would say to anyone who would listen, "He's my grandson."

Grandpa had strongly advised me to say nothing to my mother about our new activity, and I was sure he was right. He had replaced the wig with a brand-new sports outfit that I kept in his house and that Grandma washed for me every evening so that it would be clean the next day.

For months, my mother suspected nothing. Until one April afternoon when the local hygiene service, accompanied by the police, raided that insalubrious butcher's shop after a wave of food poisoning. I remember the incredulous looks of the inspectors when they came into the back room, to be stared at by a bunch of boys in boxing kit and a whole lot of old men, smoking and coughing, amid an acrid smell that was a mixture of sweat and cigarettes.

"You sell meat that kids have been hitting?" one of the officers asked, unable to believe his eyes.

"Oh, yes," the old man from Bratislava replied, quite matter-of-factly. "It's good for the meat, makes it tender. And anyway, they wash their hands before the class."

"That's not true," one of the children whined. "We never wash our hands!"

"You're out of the club!" the old man from Bratislava fired back.

"Is this a boxing club or a butcher's shop?" another of the officers said, scratching his head uncomprehendingly.

"A bit of both," the old man said.

"The room isn't even refrigerated," one of the inspectors said in a shocked tone as he took notes.

"It's cold outside and we keep the windows open."

The police had informed my mother. But being stuck at work, she had called my grandparents' neighbor Ephraim, who came as quickly as he could and took me back to the house.

"I'm staying with you until your mother gets back," he said.

"What kind of policeman are you?" I asked him.

"I work in homicide."

"Are you important?"

"Yes, I'm a captain."

I was very impressed. I told him what worried me.

"I hope Grandpa won't be in trouble with the police."

"With the police, no," he said, with a reassuring smile. "But with your mother . . ."

As Ephraim had predicted, my mother spent days on end screaming at Grandpa over the telephone. "Daddy, have you gone crazy?" She told him I could have hurt myself, or gotten punch-drunk, or I don't know what. But I was enchanted: Grandpa, of blessed memory, had taken me on the road of life. And he wasn't going to stop there, since, after initiating me into boxing, it was he who, like a magician, brought Natasha into my life.

That happened a few years later, when I had just turned seventeen. I had recently transformed the big room in my grandparents' basement into a gym where I had my weights and my punching bag. I trained there every day. One day, in the middle of the summer vacation, Grandma announced: "Clear your shitty basement. We need the room." When I asked the reason for my eviction, she explained that they were generously welcoming a distant female cousin from Canada. Generously, my ass! I was sure they were asking her for rent. By way of compensation, they suggested I move to the garage, where I could continue my exercises amid the smells of motor oil and dust. During the days that followed, I cursed this fat, old, stinking cousin who was stealing my space. I could already picture her with her hairy chin, thick eyebrows, yellowing teeth, and foul breath, dressed in clothes from the Soviet era. Worse still, the day she arrived, I had to fetch her from the station in Jamaica, Queens, where she was arriving by train from Toronto.

Grandpa forced me to take along a placard with her name on it in Cyrillic.

"I'm not her driver!" I said angrily. "Want me to put on a cap while you're at it?"

"Without the sign, you'll never find her."

I left, furious, carrying the sign despite my protests, but swearing I wouldn't use it.

When I got to the concourse of the station in Jamaica, I wandered through the crowd of travelers, quite lost, and after approaching a few panicked old women who said they were not the disgusting cousin, I was obliged to resort to my ridiculous piece of cardboard.

I remember the moment I saw her. That girl in her twenties, with the laughing eyes, the fine, gorgeous curls, and the sparkling teeth, who came and stood in front of me and read my sign.

"You're holding your sign upside down," she said.

I shrugged. "What the hell business is it of yours? What are you, the sign police?"

"Don't you speak Russian?"

"No," I said, turning the sign the right way up.

"*Krasavchik*," the girl said, laughing.

"Who are you anyhow?" I asked irritably.

"I'm Natasha," she said with a smile. "That's my name on your sign."

Natasha had entered my life.

*

From the day Natasha arrived at my grandparents', all our lives were turned upside down. The cousin I had imagined to be old and horrible turned out to be a wonderful, fascinating young woman who had come to New York to study cookery.

She upset our habits. She took over the sitting room, where nobody ever went, settling there after her classes to read or go over her lessons.

She would curl up on the couch with a cup of tea after lighting scented candles which gave the room a delightful smell. Previously so gloomy, it became the room where everybody wanted to be. When I got back from school, I would find Natasha there, her nose in her papers, and, settled in armchairs facing her, Grandma and Grandpa drinking tea and gazing at her in admiration.

Whenever she wasn't in the sitting room, she'd be cooking. At all hours of the day or night. The house filled up with smells I had never known. Dishes were constantly being prepared, the fridge was always full. And when Natasha cooked, my grandparents, sitting at their little table, would watch her with fascination and relish the dishes she set in front of them.

The basement room that became her bedroom she turned into a comfortable little palace, papered in warm colors, where incense was permanently burning. She would spend her weekends there, devouring piles of books. I often went down as far as her door, intrigued by what was going on inside the room, but without ever daring to knock. In the end Grandma, seeing me hanging around the house, prodded me into action. "Don't just stand there doing nothing," she would say, giving me a tray loaded with a steaming samovar and freshly baked cookies. "Take that and be welcoming to our guest, will you?"

I would hasten down with my precious load and Grandma would watch me, smiling, touched. The first time I didn't even notice that she had put two cups on the tray.

I would knock at the door of Natasha's room, and, when I heard her tell me to come in, my heart would beat twice as fast.

"Grandma has made you some tea," I would say shyly, half opening her door.

"Thank you, *Krasavchik*," she would say with a smile.

She was most often on her bed, eating up books. After meekly placing the tray on the coffee table in front of a little couch, I would remain standing there awkwardly.

"Are you coming or going?" she would ask me.

In my chest, my heart was pounding.

"I'm coming."

I would sit down next to her. She would serve us tea, then roll a joint. I would watch in fascination as her fingers with the polished nails rolled the cigarette paper and she then licked the edge with the tip of her tongue.

Her beauty blinded me, her gentleness made me melt, her intelligence overwhelmed me. There was not a subject she could not talk about, or a book she had not read. She knew everything about everything. And above all, much to my delight and contrary to what my grandparents asserted, she wasn't really a cousin, or rather, we would have had to go back a good century to find a common ancestor.

Over the weeks, then the months, Natasha's presence gave rise to a new-found animation in my grandparents' house. She would play chess with Grandpa and have interminable conversations with him about politics. She became the mascot of the gang of old men from the butcher's shop, now exiled to a coffee shop on Queens Boulevard. She would converse with them in Russian. She would go with Grandma on shopping expeditions, and help her in the house. They cooked together, and Natasha turned out to be an amazing cook. I found myself spending more and more time at my grandparents' house and less and less at my mother's.

The house was often enlivened by the telephone conversations that Natasha had with her cousins—real ones—scattered throughout the world. She would sometimes say to me, "We're like the petals of a wonderful dandelion, and the wind has blown each of us to different corners of the earth." She would be on the telephone, whether the one in her room, the one in the hall, or the one in the kitchen with its extendable cord, and babble into the receiver for hours on end, in all kinds of languages and at all hours of the day or night, depending on the time difference. There was the cousin in Paris, the one in Zurich, the one in Tel Aviv, the one in Buenos Aires. Sometimes she would speak English, sometimes French, sometimes Hebrew, sometimes German, but most of the time it was Russian.

The calls must have cost astronomical sums, but Grandpa didn't say anything. On the contrary. Often, without her knowing it, he would pick up the receiver in another room and listen fascinated to the conversation. I would sit next to him and he would translate in a low voice. That was how I learned that she often talked to her cousins about me, she would say that I was handsome and wonderful and that my eyes shone. "*Krasavchik*," Grandpa explained one day after hearing her call me that, "means 'handsome boy'".

Then came Halloween.

That evening, when the first group of children rang the doorbell to ask for candies and Grandma rushed to open it with a bucket of cold water, Natasha cried:

"What are you doing, Grandma?"

"Nothing," Grandma said shamefacedly, stopping in her tracks, and taking the bucket back to the kitchen.

Natasha, who had prepared salad bowls filled with multicolored candies, gave one to each of my grandparents and sent them to open the door. The children, yelling excitedly, grabbed handfuls of them before disappearing into the night. And my grandparents, watching them run off, cried in a kindly manner: "Happy Halloween, kids!"

In Rego Park, Natasha was like a whirlwind of positive vibes and creativity. When she wasn't in class or cooking, she would take photographs in the neighborhood, or go to the municipal library. She would constantly leave notes behind to let my grandparents know what she was doing. She sometimes left a note for no reason, just to say hello.

One day when I got back from school, my grandma, seeing me walk in, pointed a threatening finger at me and said:

"Where were you, Jessica?"

When she was very angry with me, Grandma still sometimes called me Jessica.

"At school, Grandma," I said. "Just like every day."

"You didn't leave a note!"

"Why should I have left a note?"

"Natasha always leaves a note."

"But you know I'm at school every weekday! Where else would I be?"

"Bunch of jerks!" Grandpa declared, passing the kitchen door with a jar of pickled cucumbers.

"That's shit," Grandma said.

One of the great upheavals occasioned by the presence of Natasha was that Grandpa and Grandma had stopped swearing, at least in her presence. Grandpa had also stopped smoking his awful rolled cigarettes at mealtimes. I discovered that my grandparents could actually behave properly at the table and have interesting conversations. For the first time, I saw Grandpa wearing new shirts. ("Natasha bought them, she said my old ones had holes in them.") And I even saw Grandma with barrettes in her hair. ("Natasha did my hair. She told me I looked pretty.")

As for me, Natasha initiated me in what I had never known: literature and art. She opened my eyes to the world. When we went out, it was to go to bookstores, museums, galleries. Often, on Sundays, we would take the subway to Manhattan and visit a museum, the Met, MoMA, the Natural History Museum, the Whitney. Or else we would go to deserted, decrepit cinemas and see films in languages I couldn't understand. But I didn't care: I wasn't looking at the screen, I was looking at her. I was devouring her with my eyes, profoundly disturbed by this totally eccentric, totally extraordinary, totally erotic young woman. She would live the films: she would get angry with the actors, she would cry, get upset, cry some more. And when the show was over, she would say to me, "Beautiful, wasn't it?" And I would reply that I hadn't understood any of it. She would laugh and tell me she would explain everything. And she would then take me to the nearest coffee shop, thinking that I couldn't stand not understanding, and tell me the story of the film from beginning to end. Generally, I didn't listen to her, just gazed in admiration at her lips. I worshiped her.

When we would go to bookstores—those were the days when

bookstores still flourished in New York—Natasha would buy piles of books. When we got back to her room in my grandparents' house, she would force me to read, lying down next to me, rolling a joint and smoking peacefully.

One evening in December, when she had rested her head on my chest while I was supposed to be reading a history book about Russia—I had dared to ask her a question on the way the old Soviet republics were divided up—she touched my abdominals.

"How come your body's so hard?" she said, sitting up.

"I don't know," I said. "I like doing sports."

She took a long drag on her joint and put it down in an ashtray.

"Take off your T-shirt!" she said abruptly. "I'd like to see you for real."

I obeyed without thinking. I could feel my heart echoing through my body. I stood there bare-chested in front of her, and she peered through the half-light at my sculpted body, placed a hand on my pectorals, and slid it over my torso, touching me lightly with her fingertips.

"I don't think I've ever seen anyone so good-looking," she said.

"Good-looking? Me?"

She laughed. "Obviously you, you idiot!"

"I don't think I'm very good-looking," I said.

She gave me a wonderful smile, and said these words, which even today remain ingrained in my memory:

"Good-looking people never think they are, Jesse."

She gazed at me. I was fascinated by her and at the same time frozen with indecision. Finally, at the peak of nervousness and feeling obliged to break the silence, I stammered:

"Don't you have a boyfriend?"

She frowned wickedly and said:

"I thought you were my boyfriend . . ."

She moved her face close to mine and briefly touched my lips with hers, then kissed me as I had never been kissed. Her tongue mingled with mine with such an erotic charge that the sensation of it ran through me with an emotion I had never previously experienced.

421

That was the beginning of our love affair. From that evening on, and during the years that would follow, I would never leave Natasha.

She would be the center of my life, the center of my thoughts, the center of my attention, the center of my concerns, the center of my total love. And I would be the same for her. I was going to love and be loved as few people have been loved. At the movies, in the subway, at the theater, in the library, at my grandparents' dinner table, my place by her side was paradise. And nights became our kingdom.

Alongside her studies, to make a little money, Natasha had found a job as a waitress at Katz's, the restaurant where my grandparents liked to go. It was there that she made the acquaintance of a girl her age who also worked there, whose name was Darla.

For my part, once I had finished school, thanks to my very good scores, I was accepted by New York University. I loved studying, for a long time I had thought about becoming a teacher or a lawyer. But sitting in the lecture halls of the university, I finally understood the meaning of a phrase so often uttered by my grandparents: "Become someone important." What did it mean to be important? The only image that came to my mind was that of our neighbor Ephraim Jenson, the proud police captain. The righter of wrongs. The protector of the weak. Nobody had been treated with more respect and deference by my grandparents. I wanted to be a police officer. Like him.

Graduating from university after four years, I was accepted by the State Police Academy, finished top of my year, proved myself in the field, was quickly promoted to inspector and began working at troop head-quarters, where I would remain for the rest of my career. I remember my first day there, finding myself in Major McKenna's office, sitting beside a young man a little older than me.

"Inspector Jesse Rosenberg, top of your year," McKenna said. "Do you think you impress me with your qualifications?"

"No, sir," I said.

He turned to the other young man. "And you, Derek Scott, the youngest sergeant in the history of the State Police, do you think I'm blown away by that?"

"No, sir."

McKenna looked closely at both of us. "You know what they're saying at general headquarters? They're saying you're both champions. So we're going to put the two of you together and see if you make sparks."

We nodded in unison.

"O.K.," McKenna said. "We'll find two offices facing each other and give you all the cases of old ladies who've lost their cats. Let's see how you get on with that."

Natasha and Darla, who had been close since meeting at Katz's, had made some progress in their careers. After a few not very rewarding experiences, they had just been hired at the Blue Lagoon, supposedly as commis chefs, but the boss had eventually made them wait on tables, claiming that he lacked the staff.

"You ought to quit," I said to Natasha one evening. "He has no right to do that to you."

"I don't care," she said. "The money's good, it pays the bills, and I can even put a little aside. In fact, Darla and I have had an idea. We're going to open our own restaurant."

"That's wonderful!" I said. "You'll be wildly successful! What kind of restaurant? Have you already found premises?"

Natasha burst out laughing. "Don't get carried away, Jesse. There's a long way to go yet. We have to start by putting money aside and thinking about the concept. But it's a good idea, isn't it?"

"It's a fantastic idea."

"It's my dream," she said with a smile. "Jesse, promise me we'll have a restaurant one day."

"I promise."

"Promise properly. Tell me that one day we'll have a restaurant in a quiet spot. No more cops, no more New York, nothing but peace and quiet."

"I promise."

2

Desolation

SUNDAY, JULY 27 – WEDNESDAY, JULY 30, 2014

JESSE ROSENBERG

Sunday, July 27, 2014
The day after opening night

Seven in the morning. Day was breaking over Orphea. Nobody had slept during the night.

The center of town looked unusually bleak. Main Street was still cordoned off, still filled with police officers and emergency vehicles, and strewn with objects of all kinds abandoned by the audience in the wave of panic that had followed the shots being fired in the Grand Theater.

There had been a lot of action at first. Until late at night, the police intervention teams had closed off the area in search of the shooter, with no success. It had also been necessary to secure the town in order to avoid stores being looted in the turmoil. First aid tents had been set up outside the security barrier to treat those lightly wounded, most of them victims of being knocked down and badly bruised, some in shock. As for Carolina Eden, she was not in a good way. She had been flown in a desperate state by helicopter to a hospital in Manhattan.

Now, with a new day breaking, peace and quiet had returned. What had happened at the Grand Theater needed to be figured out. Who was the shooter? And how had he been able to bring a weapon into the theater despite all the security measures?

At the police station, which was still in a state of great agitation, Betsy, Derek and I were getting ready to question the cast, who had been the most direct witnesses of the events. Caught up in the panic, they had scattered across town, and finding them and bringing them in had been no easy matter. They were now all in a conference room, some sleeping on the floor, others slumped on the table in the middle, waiting to be interrogated in turn. The only one missing was Jerry Eden, who had left with his daughter in the helicopter.

The first to be questioned was Hayward, and our conversation would take a turn we were a long way from anticipating. Hayward no longer had anybody to protect him, and we didn't pull our punches.

"What the hell do you know!" Derek shouted at him, shaking Hayward like a plum tree. "I want a name now, or I'll smash your teeth in. I want a name! Right now!"

"I have no idea," Hayward said, "I swear."

Derek flung him angrily against the wall. Hayward slumped to the floor. I picked him up and sat him on a chair.

"You have to talk now, Kirk," I said. "You have to tell us everything you know. This has gone far enough."

Hayward was on the verge of tears. "How's Carolina?" he said in a choked voice.

"She isn't doing well!" Derek said. "And you alone are responsible for that!"

Hayward plunged his head into his hands.

"What is it you know?" I said in a firm but not aggressive tone.

He said in a low voice, "I never had the slightest idea who committed those murders."

"But you knew Meghan Padalin, not Mayor Gordon, was the target back in 1994?"

He nodded. "In October 1994, when the State Police announced that Tennenbaum was the killer, I did indeed have my doubts. Because Ostrovski had told me he had seen Charlotte driving Tennenbaum's van, which I couldn't figure out. But I would never have dug any farther if the Gordons' next-door neighbors hadn't called me a few days later. They had just discovered two bullet holes in their garage door. The marks weren't obvious, they'd only noticed them because they had quite by chance decided to repaint the door. I went there, extracted the two bullets, then asked the forensics department of the State Police to make a comparison with the bullets found in the victims. They came from the same weapon. Judging by the depth and angle at which the bullets were embedded, it was clear that they had been fired from the park.

That was when I understood that it was Meghan who had been the target. Her killer had missed her in the park, she had run in the direction of the mayor's house, presumably in search of help, but had been overtaken and killed. Then the Gordons were killed because they had witnessed the murder."

"Why were we never told this?" Derek said.

"I tried my damnedest to get in touch with you at the time," Hayward said. "I called you at troop headquarters, you and Rosenberg. I was told you'd had an accident and were both on indefinite leave. When I said it was about the Gordon killings, I was told very firmly that the case was closed. So I went to your houses. At your house, Derek, I was turned away by a young woman who told me not to come back and to leave you alone, especially if it was to talk about that case. Then I went to your place, Jesse, several times. I rang the bell but nobody ever came to the door!"

Derek and I looked at each other, realizing how disastrously wrong we had been about the case back then.

"What did you do?" Derek said.

"It was a mess!" Hayward said. "But in brief: Charlotte Brown had been seen at the wheel of Tennenbaum's van at the time of the murders, but Tennenbaum was the culprit according to the State Police, and I was convinced that there had been a mistake about the primary target. To make matters worse, I couldn't tell anybody. My colleagues in the Orphea police department had given me the cold shoulder, and the State Police officers in charge of the investigation—you two—had dropped out of sight. A real mess. So I decided to solve the case myself. I looked to see if there had been any other murders recently in the area. There weren't any. The only suspicious death was a guy who had been killed in a supposed motorcycle accident on a road near Ridgesport. It looked worth investigating. I got in touch with the Highway Patrol, and when I spoke with the officer dealing with the incident, I learned that an A.T.F. agent had been asking him questions. So I contacted this A.T.F. agent, who told me that the biker who had died was a gangster who had always evaded arrest and that his own belief was that his death was no accident. At this point, I was afraid of poking my nose into some dirty business with underworld connections. I tried to talk to one of my colleagues, Lewis Erban. But Lewis never came to the meeting I thought we'd fixed. More than ever, I was alone, dealing with a case that was beyond me. So I decided to disappear."

"Because you were afraid of what you were discovering?"

"No, because I was all alone! I couldn't stand it anymore. I told myself people would worry when they didn't see me around. Or they'd wonder why I suddenly quit the force. You know where I was, the first two weeks I was missing? At home! In my own house. Waiting for some-one to ring the bell and ask how I was. But nobody came. Not even a neighbor. Nobody at all. I stayed in, didn't go shopping, didn't leave the house. I didn't get one single telephone call. The only visitor was my father, who brought me some shopping. He sat with me on the couch in the living room for hours. In silence. Then he asked me, 'What are we waiting for?' I replied, 'Someone, but I don't know who.' In the end I decided to move to the other side of the country and start a new life. I told myself it was an opportunity to devote myself fully to writing, to movies, to a play. And what better subject than this criminal case that as far as I was concerned was still unsolved? One night, I snuck into the station—I still had the keys—and recovered the case file on the Gordon killings."

"But why leave that note in the box: 'Here begins The Darkest Night'?" Betsy said.

"Because I was already thinking that once I'd solved the case I'd come back to Orphea and reveal the truth. Tell the whole story in the form of a successful play. I was leaving Orphea a failure. I was deter-mined to come back a hero and put on 'The Darkest Night.'"

"Why use that title again?"

"It was my way of thumbing my nose at all the people who had turned their backs on me. 'The Darkest Night' in its original form didn't exist anymore. My colleagues, as payback for me not giving 120 percent of my days and nights to police work, had destroyed all the drafts and manuscripts I had kept in the station, and the only copy, which I had given to the bookstore, was in the hands of Mayor Gordon."

"How did you know?" I asked.

"Meghan Padalin told me. She worked in the bookstore. She was the one who had suggested I leave a copy of the play in the section for local writers. Sometimes Hollywood celebrities visited, and, who knows, it might have been read and liked by someone important. But now in mid-July 1994, after the dirty trick my colleagues had played on me, I went to get my script back from the bookstore, and Meghan told me Mayor Gordon had just bought it. So I went to him and asked for it back, and he told me he didn't have it anymore. I was convinced he was trying to screw me. After all, he had read the play and disliked it! He'd even torn it up in front of me! Why buy another copy from the bookstore except to do me some sort of harm? So, when I left Orphea, I wanted to prove that nothing can prevent the fulfilment of a work of art. You can burn it, jeer at it, ban it, censor it, but everything can be reborn. You thought you could destroy me? Well, here I am again, as strong as ever. That's what I imagined. So I entrusted my father with the task of selling my house and I moved to California. With the money from the sale, I had enough to get by for a while. I plunged back into the case file. But I found myself completely stuck, I was going round in circles. The less I advanced, the more the case obsessed me."

"And you've been going over and over it for the past twenty years?" Derek said.

"Yes, but I was also working day and night on scripts for movies. I made myself a living and something of a reputation. I had put the Orphea murders to one side until Stephanie Mailer turned up out of the blue."

"And what did you manage to come up with?"

"Not much. On one side, the motorcycle accident and, on the other, Meghan Padalin. That's all I had."

"Do you think Meghan Padalin was investigating Fold's motorcycle accident and that's why she was killed?"

"I really have no idea. I made that up for the play. I thought it made a good opening scene. But you tell me: is there really, in your view, a connection between Meghan and the accident?"

"We're as sure as you are that there's a link between the two deaths," I said, "but we haven't been able to find anything which connects them."

"It's been eating at me for twenty years," Hayward said. "I told myself I would never find the solution to this case. But when Stephanie Mailer came to see me in L.A. in June, it gave me hope of a breakthrough. I told her everything I knew, thinking she would do the same."

"So Stephanie knew that Meghan Padalin was the target?"

"That was something I told her."

"And what did *she* know?"

"I have no idea. When I told her I didn't know who had committed the murders, she immediately got up to go. She said, 'I have no time to waste.' I demanded that at least she share whatever new information she had, but she refused. We had a little argument in the Beluga Bar. When I tried to hold her back, her bag fell, and it emptied on the floor. The papers from her investigation, her cigarette lighter, her key ring with a ridiculous big yellow ball. As I helped her to pick up her things, I tried to take the opportunity to read her notes. But obviously I couldn't. And then you showed up, my dear Rosenberg. At first I thought I wouldn't tell you anything. Not after Stephanie Mailer refused to share what she knew with me. But then I told myself it could be my last chance to get back to Orphea and, who knows, for my play to be performed at the opening of the festival."

"But you had no real play."

"I had something better, don't you see that? I had a story, rooted in the history of a small town. I knew I could find a talented cast among the people coming for the festival, many of whom had some link to the the first festival and the murders. Charlotte Brown, who could have been a star if she hadn't left me for that idiot Brown. Ostrovski, who has seen every play from Broadway to State Street. Bergdorf, a respected literary editor. Eden, head of a T.V. network, and his daughter, practically a prodigy. And to top it off, Samuel Padalin, whose wife was one of the victims. All I needed was the name of the killer. I'd briefed that cast on every possible suspect. Once we had the name, I knew they could play it by ear."

"So that explains why you only wrote a handful of scenes."

"Exactly. I was counting on my promise to reveal the killer on opening night to sell tickets. But I was counting on you two to find the killer."

"But we didn't find him."

"That was why I added Carolina's line about his identity. I knew you would be in the auditorium, watching the audience. I was hoping to flush him out, force him to make a mistake."

"But we were in your dressing room," Derek said, glancing my way. "Trying to find out what you knew."

"Why didn't you just tell us, Hayward?" I said. "We could have worked together, like we did back in '94."

"And how far did that get us?" Hayward said. He sighed. "I thought I had it all figured out. I had once-in-a-lifetime publicity for my play and as talented a cast as I could possibly have hoped for. But now, because of me, that wonderful young woman is hovering between life and death."

There was a moment's silence.

"You were on the right track with your original investigation," I said at last. "It's not the ideal moment to mention this, but we did find your play. Mayor Gordon was keeping it in a safe deposit box. In it, in the form of a code, was the name Jeremiah Fold, the man who died in a motorcycle accident. So there is a connection between Fold, Gordon, and Meghan Padalin. You understood everything, Kirk. You had all the pieces of the puzzle in your hand. Now we simply have to put them together."

"Let me help you. It'll be my way of making amends."

*

Before anything else, we needed to figure out what had happened the previous night in the Grand Theater.

"I was in the wings, watching Carolina," Hayward said. "Jerry Eden was standing next to me. Then there were the shots. Carolina collapsed. Jerry and I rushed to her, soon joined by Charlotte."

"Could you tell from what direction the shots came?" Derek said. "From the front row? From the edge of the stage?"

"I had no idea. The auditorium was in darkness and we had the spotlights pointing at us. The shooter was on the audience side, I'm sure of that. Carolina was facing the auditorium and was hit in the chest. What I find incredible is how a weapon could have gotten into the theater. The security was so tight."

In an attempt to answer this question, and before questioning the other members of the cast, we joined Major McKenna, Acting Chief Montagne and Mayor Brown in a conference room for a first review of the situation.

At this point, we had absolutely no clue as to the identity of the shooter. There were no cameras in the Grand Theater and those members of the audience who had been questioned had seen nothing. They had all repeated the same litany: the auditorium had been in total darkness at the time of the shooting, the spotlights, from behind the audience, directed onto the stage. "It really was 'The Darkest Night' in there," they had said. "There were two gunshots, the girl collapsed, then there was panic. How is the poor girl?"

McKenna informed us that the weapon had not been found, either in the theater or on the surrounding streets. "The shooter has to have taken advantage of the panic to run away from the theater and dispose of the weapon."

"It was impossible for us to stop people from leaving," Montagne said, as if hoping to get himself off the hook. "They would have trampled each other, people could have died. Nobody ever thought the danger would come from inside. We had secured the theater from the outside."

This was the point on which, despite the absence of clues, we were going to advance in the investigation.

"How could an armed person have gotten into the theater?" I said.

"I can't figure that out," McKenna said. "The guys who were in charge of the access routes are used to difficult situations. They secure international conferences, parades, the President's visits to New York. The procedure was very strict. The theater was first searched by sniffer dogs, then placed under total surveillance. Nobody could have broken in during the night. And the audience and the cast all went through metal detectors on their way in."

Something had escaped us. We had to figure out how a weapon had gotten into the theater. In order for us to get a better idea, McKenna sent for the officer of the State Police responsible for securing the building. This man repeated for us in detail the procedure as the major had outlined it.

"After the search, the building was secured and remained so," the officer said. "I wouldn't have let the President himself get in there."

"Every single person was checked as they went in?" Derek said.

"Without exception."

"We weren't checked," Betsy said.

"Police officers weren't checked as long as they showed their badges," the officer conceded.

"Did many officers enter the auditorium?" I said.

"No, sir. A handful of plainclothes officers, a few of our men. Mainly movement between the auditorium and the outside of the theater to make sure everything was going well."

"Jesse," Major McKenna said anxiously, "don't tell me you suspect a police officer now."

"I'm just trying to get a crystal-clear picture," I said, and asked the officer to describe exactly how the search had been carried out.

In order to answer as precisely as possible, the officer fetched in the chief dog handler, who explained to us their *modus operandi*.

"We had three areas: the lobby, the auditorium, and the backstage area, including the dressing rooms. We always proceed through one area at a time, so as not to confuse the dogs. The cast was rehearsing onstage, so we started with the backstage area and the dressing rooms. That was the largest part, because there's quite a large basement. Once that was done, we asked the cast to interrupt their rehearsal while we searched the auditorium, so as not to distract the dogs."

"And where did the cast go while you were doing that?" I asked.

"To the backstage area. When they came back into the auditorium, they had to go through the metal detectors to guarantee that the area remained secure. That way they could go from one area to other without any problem."

Derek tapped his forehead. "Were the actors searched when they arrived that day at the theater?"

"No. But all their bags were sniffed by the dogs in the dressing rooms, and then they went through the metal detectors."

"But if an actor had arrived at the theater with the weapon on him the day before, and had kept it on him during the rehearsals, while you were searching the dressing rooms, he could then have gone back to his dressing room while you searched the auditorium and left the weapon there, as that was now considered a secured area. On opening night, he would have passed through the metal detector without any problem because the weapon was already in the theater. It was all done the day before. The security measures had been announced in the press, so the shooter had time to plan ahead. He had only to recover it from his dressing room yesterday, before the start of the show."

"So the shooter was one of the cast?" Mayor Brown said, horrified.

The shooter was there, in the next room.

We first made each cast member take a powder test, but none had any trace of it on their hands or clothes. We also tested their stage costumes, sent teams to search each person's dressing room, hotel room, and home if they were local. Of course, they could have been wearing gloves or even a coat at the time of the shooting. And besides, the shooter had by now had time to get rid of the weapon, to change, to take a shower.

Hayward had said he had been with Jerry Eden when the shots rang out. We were able to reach Eden by phone: Carolina had been in the operating room for hours, he said, but he had no news. He confirmed that Hayward had been next to him when his daughter had been shot. We trusted Eden: he had no known connection with the events of 1994 and it was scarcely conceivable that he would want to kill his own daughter. Thus we could eliminate Hayward from our list of suspects.

We spent all day questioning the other members of the cast, but without success. Nobody had seen anything. As for knowing where everyone was at the time of the shooting, they had all been in the back-stage area, close to Hayward, they stated. But nobody would swear to every one of the cast having been there.

By late afternoon, we had made no progress.

"What do you mean, you don't have anything?" Major McKenna said sharply when we informed him of the situation.

"There were no powder traces on any member of the cast," I said. "Nobody saw anything that could lead us to the shooter."

"But we know one of them was probably the shooter!"

"I'm aware of that, sir. Yet we have no clues, nothing on which to hold anyone or charge them. It's like they're covering for each other."

"And have you questioned all of them?"

"Yes. They've been here for twelve hours."

"If you have nothing against them, let them go. We have no choice. But tell them not to leave New York State."

"Do you have any news of Carolina, sir?" Betsy said.

"The operation's over. The surgeons removed two bullets from her body and tried to repair the damage to her organs. But she's lost a lot of blood and has had to be placed in an artificial coma. The doctors are not absolutely confident she will get through the night."

"Can you ask for the bullets to be analyzed as a matter of urgency, sir?"

"Of course. What are you thinking?"

"We have to know whether they could have come from a police weapon."

There was a long silence. Then the major got up from his chair and brought the meeting to an end.

"Get some rest," he said. "You look like zombies."

When Betsy got home she was shocked to discover Mark, her ex-husband, sitting on her porch.

"Mark? What the hell are you doing here?"

"We're all worried sick, Betsy. On T.V., all they are talking about is the shooting at the Grand Theater. You haven't answered our calls or our texts."

"I'm fine, thanks. You can go home now."

"When I heard about what had happened here, I was reminded of Sabar's jewelry store."

"Oh, please don't start on that!"

"Your mother said the same thing."

"Then you should marry my mother, you seem to think along the same lines."

Mark remained seated. He plainly had no intention of leaving. Betsy, exhausted, slumped down next to him.

"I thought you came to Orphea to be in a town where nothing happened," he said.

"That's true," Betsy said. "I did."

He made a bitter grimace. "Anyone would think you joined that intervention unit in New York just to piss me off."

"Stop playing the victim, Mark. Do I have to remind you that I was already in the N.Y.P.D. when you met me?"

"It's true. And I have to admit it was one of the things I liked about you. But have you ever, for a fraction of a second, put yourself in my place? One day I meet an amazing woman: brilliant, stunningly beautiful, funny. I'm actually lucky enough to marry her. And suddenly this stupendous woman puts on a bulletproof vest to go to work every day. And when she goes out through the door of the apartment, with her semi-automatic pistol at her belt, I wonder if I'll ever see her again. And every time I hear a police siren, every time there's an alert, every time the T.V. says there's been a shooting or an emergency situation, I wonder if she's been caught up in it. And when there's a knock at the door, is it a neighbor who wants to borrow some salt? Has she forgotten her keys? Or is it a uniformed officer who's come to tell me my wife died in the line of duty? And the rising anxiety when she's late home! And the nagging worry when she doesn't call me back after I've left her a string of messages! And the irregular hours, so that she goes to bed when I get up and vice versa! And the night calls and the going out in the middle of the night! And the overtime! And the canceled weekends! That's what my life with you was like, Betsy."

"That's more than enough, Mark!"

But he had no intention of leaving it there. "What I'm asking you, Betsy, is this: when you left me, did you take even a few moments to put yourself in my place and try to understand what I was going through? Like all those times we were supposed to meet for dinner after work, but then you would have a last-minute emergency and I would wait for hours before going home and going to bed without eating. And the number of times you told me 'I'll be right there' and in the end you didn't show up at all because something went on longer than you had anticipated. But for heaven's sake, out of the thousands of officers in that fucking N.Y.P.D., couldn't you just once have handed the case to one of your colleagues and joined me for dinner? Because while you were busy saving everyone, out of the eight million people in the city I felt like the eight million and first, the one who always came last! The police had stolen my wife!"

"No, Mark," Betsy said. "You lost me. You weren't able to keep me!"

"Give me a second chance, I beg you."

Betsy hesitated for a long time, and then said, "I've met someone. Someone nice. I think I'm in love. I'm sorry."

Mark stared at her for a long time in icy silence. He seemed broken. He finally said, bitterly, "Maybe you're right, Betsy. But don't forget, after what happened at Sabar's jewelry store, you weren't the same anymore. And it could have been avoided! That evening, I didn't want you to go! I asked you not to answer your fucking phone, do you remember?"

"Yes, I remember."

"If you hadn't gone to that jewelry store, if you'd listened to me for once, we'd still be together today."

It was the evening of September 21, 2012.

The evening when Sabar's jewelry store was held up.

I drove uptown in my unmarked car at breakneck speed, all the way to 57th Street, where the store was located. The immediate area had been sealed off.

My chief motioned me into the van serving as the command post.

"There's just one armed robber," he said, "and he's violent."

I was surprised. "Just one? That's unusual."

"Yes. And he seems nervous. Apparently, he took the jeweler and his two daughters, who are ten and twelve, from their apartment in the same building. He forced them downstairs to the store, presumably hoping they wouldn't be found until the next day. But some beat cops were passing, saw the lights on inside, became suspicious, and raised the alarm."

"So we have a hostage taker and three hostages?"

"Correct. No idea of the robber's identity. All we know is that it's a man."

"How long has this been going on?"

"Three hours now. The situation is beginning to get critical. He's demanding that we stay back, we have no visual, and the negotiator we called in is getting nowhere. Not even telephone contact. That's why I sent for you. I told myself you might be able to get somewhere. I'm sorry to have to call you while you're on leave."

"Don't worry, Chief, that's what I'm here for."

"Your husband is going to hate me."

"He'll get over it. How do you want to proceed?"

There weren't that many options. In the absence of a telephone connection, I had to make contact in person by approaching the store. I'd never done anything like that before.

"I know this is a first for you, Betsy," my chief said. "If you don't feel up to it, I'd understand perfectly well."

"I'll do it," I said.

"You'll be our eyes, Betsy. Everyone is switched to your channel. There are marksmen on the upper floors of the building opposite. If you see something, say it, so they can modify their position if need be."

"Alright," I said, adjusting my bulletproof vest.

He wanted me to put on my ballistic helmet, but I refused. You can't make true contact when you have a helmet on your head. I felt the adrenaline making my heart pound. I was scared. I wanted to call Mark, but I crushed the temptation. I only wanted to hear his voice, not unkind comments.

I went through a security rope and advanced alone, a megaphone in my hand, along the deserted street. Silence reigned. I stopped ten paces from the store and announced myself through the loudspeaker.

After a few moments, a man in a black leather jacket, wearing a balaclava, appeared at the door with one of the girls, a gun at her head. She was blindfolded and had adhesive tape over her mouth.

He demanded that everyone get away and that he be allowed to leave. He kept close to his hostage and moved all the time so as to complicate the work of the marksmen. In my earpiece, I could hear my chief giving authorization to shoot him down, but the marksmen couldn't get a lock on their target. The robber took a quick glance at the street and the surrounding area, no doubt weighing up his escape options, then disappeared back inside the store.

Something wasn't right, but it didn't strike me immediately. Why had he shown himself? He was alone. Why take the risk of being shot instead of making his demands by telephone?

Twenty minutes went by, then the door of the store opened abruptly, and the girl appeared again, still blindfolded and gagged. She advanced step by step, feeling her way with her feet. I could hear her moans. I wanted to approach, but suddenly the robber in the leather jacket and the balaclava appeared in the doorway, with a gun in each hand.

I let go of my megaphone, took my pistol out of its holster, and aimed it at the man.

"Put down your weapons!" I cried.

Hidden by the recess of the store entrance, he was not yet visible to the marksmen.

"Betsy, what's going on?" my chief asked over the radio.

"He's coming out," I said. "Shoot him if you have a visual."

The marksmen informed me they still had no visual. I continued to aim at his head. The girl was a few yards away from him. I couldn't figure out what he was doing. All at once, he made an abrupt movement in my direction. I pressed the trigger. The bullet hit him full in the head and he collapsed.

The shot echoed in my ears. My field of vision shrank. My radio started crackling. Immediately, intervention teams appeared behind me. I recovered my senses. The girl was at once hurried away. I entered the store behind a column of armed, helmeted officers. We discovered the second girl on the floor, bound and gagged, a blindfold over her eyes, but safe. We evacuated her, then continued searching the premises for the jeweler. We finally discovered him locked in his office, after we had broken the door down. He was lying on the floor, his hands tied with a hose clamp, adhesive tape over his mouth and eyes. I freed him and he writhed, holding his left arm. I thought at first that he was wounded, then realized that he was having a heart attack. I called the emergency services and in the minutes that followed the jeweler was taken to hospital and doctors attended to the two girls.

Outside the store, police officers were bustling around the body lying on the sidewalk. I joined them. And I suddenly heard one of my colleagues say in surprise:

"Am I dreaming or does he have the guns taped to his hands?"

"But . . . they're fake," another one said.

We took off the balaclava that was hiding his face. A thick piece of adhesive tape was stuck to his mouth.

"What the hell is going on?" I cried.

Overcome by a terrible suspicion, I took out my phone and tapped in the name of the jeweler in the search engine. The photograph that appeared on my screen left me dumbfounded.

"Fuck," one of my colleagues said, looking at my screen, "this guy looks a hell of a lot like the jeweler."

"It *is* the jeweler!" I screamed.

"If this guy's the jeweler," one of the other officers said, "then where's the hostage taker?"

That was why the robber had taken the risk of coming out and showing himself. So that I should associate him with a balaclava and a leather jacket. He had then forced the jeweler to put them on, had stuck the guns to his hands with tape, and had forced him outside, threatening to do something to his other daughter if he didn't go. Then he had gone into the office, locked himself in, tied his hands and stuck tape over his mouth and eyes, so that he could be taken for the jeweler and evacuated, his pockets full of jewels, to a hospital.

His plan had worked perfectly. When we arrived in force at the hospital where he had been taken for his supposed heart attack, he had disappeared from the examination room. The two police officers who had gone with him to emergency were waiting in the corridor, talking idly, with no idea of what had happened.

The robber was never identified, or found. And I had shot dead an innocent man. I had committed the worst sin for a member of a special unit: I had killed a hostage.

Everyone assured me that I had done nothing wrong, that they would all of them have done exactly the same. And yet I could not help replaying that scene in my head.

"He couldn't talk," my chief kept saying. "He couldn't make a gesture without moving his weapons in a threatening way. He couldn't do anything. He was a dead man walking."

"I think when he moved, he was going to throw himself to the ground to show he was surrendering. If I'd waited one second more before firing, he might have done that and he'd be alive now."

"Betsy, if the guy had been the real robber and you'd waited one second more, you'd have taken a bullet in the head."

What affected me most was that Mark couldn't understand or sympathize. Not knowing how to handle my distress, he simply went over and over the story, saying, "My God, Betsy, if you'd stayed home that evening . . . You were on leave! You didn't even have to answer your phone! But you always have to show willing." I think he was angry with himself for not making me stay. He could see I was distraught, and he was angry. I was allowed a period of leave, but I didn't know what to do with it. I stayed home, brooding. I felt depressed. Mark did try his best to cheer me up, he'd suggest I go for a walk, go running, go to a museum. But he couldn't get beyond that anger eating away at him. In the cafeteria of the Metropolitan, as we were having a cappuccino after a visit, I said to him:

"Every time I close my eyes, I see that man in front of me, holding his two guns. I don't notice the adhesive tape around his hands, all I see are his eyes. I have the impression he's terrified. But he doesn't obey. The girl's there in front of him, blindfolded . . ."

"Betsy, not here, please, we're here to cheer ourselves up. How can you move on from this if you never stop talking about it?"

"Shit, Mark," I cried, "this is my reality!"

Not only had I raised my voice, but in an abrupt gesture I had knocked over my cup. The customers at the other tables stared at us. I felt weary.

"I'll get you another," Mark said in a conciliatory tone.

"It doesn't matter. I think I need to walk. I need to be alone for a while. I'll go for a walk in the park, I'll see you at home."

I recognize with hindsight that Mark's problem was that he didn't want to talk about it. I wasn't interested in his opinion, and I wasn't looking for his approval. I just wanted someone to listen to me, whereas he wanted to act as if nothing had happened, or else as if everything was forgotten.

I had to talk freely. On the advice of the squad's psychologist, I talked about it with my colleagues. They were all attentive. I went for a drink with some of them, others invited me to dinner at their homes. These excursions did me good, but, unfortunately, Mark got it into his head that I was having an affair with one of my colleagues.

"It's funny," he said, "you're always in a good mood when you come back from your evenings out. It makes a change from the way you are when you're with me."

"Mark, don't be stupid, I just went for a coffee with one of the team. He's married and has two kids."

"Oh, that's a comfort to know he's married! Because married men never cheat on their wives, do they?"

"Mark, don't tell me you're jealous?"

"Betsy, you sulk all day when you're with me. You only smile when you go out on your own. And I'm not even talking about the last time we had sex!"

I couldn't explain to Mark that he was imagining things. Or maybe I didn't tell him often enough that I loved him. In any case, I was guilty of neglecting him, of dwelling too much on what was getting me down, of abandoning him. He finally found the attention he had been missing with a female colleague, who had been biding her time. The whole office knew about it, which meant so did I. The day I found out about it, I went to stay at Lauren's.

Then came the period of Mark's regrets, his excuses, his begging me to come back. He made honorable amends to my parents, who started pleading his case after he'd vented our whole life in their living room.

"Betsy, all the same!" my mother said to me. "Four months without sex."

"Mark told you that?" I said, aghast.

"Yes, and he cried."

I think the most difficult thing was not Mark's torment, but that, in my mind, the seductive, protective man, the one who saved lives in restaurants and charmed everyone, was now a whiner who complained to my mother about our sex life. I knew something was broken, and at last, in June 2013, he agreed to a divorce.

I was tired of New York, made weary by the city, its heat, its size, its unending noise, its lights that never went out. I wanted to settle somewhere else, I wanted change, and, as chance would have it, in the *New York Literary Review*, to which I subscribed, I came across an article about Orphea:

THE GREATEST LITTLE THEATER FESTIVAL
by Steven Bergdorf

Do you know this gem called Orphea, nestled in the Hamptons? A little paradise where the air seems purer and life gentler than elsewhere, which every year hosts a theater festival whose main production is always special and of high quality. [. . .]

The town itself is worth a visit. Its Main Street is a jewel of peace and quiet. Its coffee shops and restaurants are delightful and attractive, the stores enticing. Everything here is both dynamic and pleasant. [. . .] If you can, stay at the Lake Palace, a really superb hotel just outside the town, with a magnificent lake on one side and an enchanting forest on the other. It is like being in a film set. The staff waits on you hand and foot, the rooms are spacious and elegantly decorated, the restaurant sophisticated. It is hard to leave this place once you have experienced it.

I took a few days' leave while the festival was on, booked a room at the Lake Palace, and went to Orphea. The article hadn't exaggerated: I discovered there, so close to the city, a wonderful, protected world. I could immediately picture myself living there. I fell under the spell of its little streets, its movie house, its bookstore. Orphea seemed to me the

447

place I had dreamed about, the place where I could change my life.

One morning, when I was sitting on a bench in the marina, gazing out at the ocean, I seemed to glimpse in the distance the breath of a whale that had risen to the surface. I felt the need to share this moment with someone. The witness I chose was a passing jogger.

"What's happening?" he said.

"A whale, there's a whale over there!"

He was a good-looking man in his fifties. "We often see them," he said, amused by my excitement.

"It's my first time here," I said.

"Where have you come from?"

"Manhattan."

"That's not very far."

"So near and yet so far," I said.

He smiled and we chatted for a while. His name was Alan Brown and he was the town's mayor. I told him briefly about the personal difficulties I was going through and how I hoped for a new start.

"Betsy," he said, "I don't want you to get the wrong idea about what I'm going to say. I'm a married man and I'm not trying to hit on you. But would you come to dinner at our house tonight? There's something I'd like to discuss with you."

That's how it came about that I had dinner that night with Mayor Brown and his wife Charlotte. They were a lovely couple. She must have been a little younger than he was. She was a vet and had opened a small local clinic that was doing well. They didn't have children and I didn't ask any questions about that.

The mayor did not reveal the reason he had invited me until we got to the dessert course.

"Betsy, my chief of police is likely to retire in a year's time. His deputy is not the replacement I am really looking for. I have ambitions for this town and I'd like someone I can trust in that job. I have a feeling you're the ideal candidate."

As I was taking a moment to think, he added:

"I must warn you it's a quiet town. It isn't the city . . ."

"All the better," I said. "I need the quiet."

The next day, I accepted Mayor Brown's offer. And that's why, one day in September 2013, I moved to Orphea. In the hope of starting over. And above all of finding myself again.

JESSE ROSENBERG

Monday, July 28, 2014
Two days after opening night

Thirty-six hours after the opening night fiasco, with the Orphea theater festival long canceled, there was still an air of panic in the town. The national media had had a field day, accusing the police of failing to protect the public. Coming so soon after the murders of Stephanie Mailer and Cody Springfield, the shooting at the Grand Theater was one horror too many. A killer was on the loose in the Hamptons. Throughout the region hotels emptied and bookings were canceled as vacationers shelved their plans.

The governor of New York State was furious and made his displeasure known. Mayor Brown was abandoned by the community, and Major McKenna and the assistant D.A. were hauled over the coals by their superiors. In response to criticism, they decided to hold a press conference in the town hall that morning. In my opinion, it was the worst thing they could have done. We had no answers to give the media for the time being, so why further expose ourselves?

Up until the last minute, in the corridors of the town hall, Derek, Betsy and I tried to persuade them to give up on making any public statements at this stage, but it was to no avail.

"The problem is that right now you have nothing to tell the media," I said.

"That's because you haven't been able to find anything!" the assistant D.A. roared. "You haven't found anything since you started this investigation!"

"We need more time."

"You have had more than enough time! All I see is a catastrophe, two murders, one attempted murder, a community frightened out of its wits. You're a bunch of incompetents, that's what I'm going to tell the media!"

I turned to Major McKenna, hoping for his support.

"Sir, I don't think you can lay the whole responsibility on our shoulders," I said. "The security of the theater and the town was down to you and Deputy Montagne."

At this clumsy remark of mine, the major saw red. "Don't be insolent, Jesse. Not with me. I've been covering your ass since the start of this investigation. The governor called me last night, and my ears are still ringing! He wants a press conference, he'll get one."

"I'm sorry, sir."

"I don't give a damn if you're sorry, Jesse. Derek and you opened this Pandora's box, you're going to have to figure out a way to close it."

"Would you rather we'd covered everything up?"

The major sighed. "I don't think you realize the firestorm you've started by reopening this case. Right now the whole country is talking about it. Heads will roll, Jesse, and mine isn't going to be one of them! Why didn't you retire the way you'd planned, huh? You had all the professional honors you could have wanted, why didn't you go off and live your life in well-earned peace?"

"Because I'm a real police officer, sir."

"Or a real idiot, Jesse. I'm giving the two of you till the end of the week to wrap this thing up. If by Monday morning I don't have the killer sitting in my office, I'll get you thrown off the force without a pension. You too, Derek. Now go do your work and let us do ours. The reporters are waiting for us."

The major and the assistant D.A. headed for the press conference. Before he hurried after them, Mayor Brown turned to Betsy.

"I'd rather you learned it here, Betsy. I'm going to announce the official appointment of Jasper Montagne as Orphea's new chief of police."

Betsy turned pale. "What?" she said, choking. "You said he'd only be acting chief until I finished the investigation."

"With all the agitation here in Orphea, I have to replace Gulliver officially. And my choice has fallen on Montagne."

Betsy was on the verge of tears. "You can't do this to me, Alan!"

"I can, and I am."

"You promised me . . . That's the reason I came to Orphea."

"A lot of things have happened since then. I'm sorry, Betsy."

I tried to defend Betsy. "Mr Mayor, you're making a serious mistake. Deputy Kanner is one of the best police officers I've come across in a very long time."

"What's it got to do with you, Captain Rosenberg?" Mayor Brown said curtly. "Concentrate on your investigation instead of interfering in something that's none of your business."

The mayor turned on his heel and headed for the town hall.

*　　*　　*

At the Lake Palace, as in every hotel in the area, most of the guests were leaving, and the manager, ready to do anything to stop this hemorrhage, urged them to stay, offering exceptional discounts. But nobody wanted to be in Orphea, apart from Hayward, who was determined to help with bringing the investigation to a close, and who nevertheless seized the opportunity to keep his suite for a reduced price, now that it was no longer being paid for by the town. Ostrovski did the same.

Charlotte Brown and Samuel Padalin had left to go back to their homes the previous evening, while Bergdorf had returned to the city.

A few miles away, facing Central Park, in Mount Sinai Hospital, Jerry and Cynthia Eden were watching over their daughter, who was now in an I.C.U. The doctor came in to reassure them.

"Mr and Mrs Eden, you should both get some rest. We're going to keep Carolina in an artificial coma for the time being."

"But how *is* she?" Cynthia said, distraught.

"It's impossible to say for the moment. She came through the operation well, which is encouraging, of course. But we still don't know if there will be any physical or neurological after-effects. The bullets caused significant lesions. One lung was perforated, and the spleen was hit."

"Doctor," Eden said. "We need you to tell us: will our daughter wake up again?"

"If I knew for certain, I would tell you. As things stand . . . I'm sorry, but I just don't know. It is possible she won't make it."

* * *

Betsy, Derek and I were driving along Main Street, which was still closed to the public. Everything was deserted, in spite of the blazing sun. Nobody on the sidewalks, hardly anyone in the marina. The place was like a ghost town.

Outside the Grand Theater, a few police officers were still keeping guard, while municipal employees were collecting the remaining litter, including the souvenirs from the abandoned vendors' stands, the final testimony to the commotion that had taken place here.

Betsy picked up a T-shirt bearing the words I WAS IN ORPHEA JULY 26, 2014.

"I wish I hadn't been," she said.

"Me, too," Derek said with a sigh.

We entered the building and got to the auditorium, which was deserted. On the stage there was a huge area of dried blood like a lake on a map, as well as medical compresses and sterile dressing wrappings left there by the paramedics. One word came into my head: desolation.

According to the report that had been sent by the doctor who had operated on Carolina, the bullets had hit her from above, at an angle of approximately sixty degrees. That would allow us to determine the position of the shooter in the theater. We set about creating a small reconstruction.

"So, Carolina is center stage," Derek said. "Hayward is to her left, with Eden."

I took up position center stage, as if I were Carolina.

"I don't see how from the seats," Betsy said, "even from the back of the auditorium, which is higher than the front, the bullets could have struck her at that angle."

She walked pensively along the rows. I looked up and saw above me a technical gangway that led to the bank of spotlights.

I pointed. "The weapon was fired from there!"

Derek and Betsy searched for a way to get up to the gangway, and finally found a narrow staircase in the backstage area, near the dressing rooms. The gangway went all around the stage, as the lighting required. Once he was up there, Derek aimed at me with his fingers. The angle of fire looked to be right. And it was a relatively short distance. You wouldn't need to be a crack shot to hit your target.

"The theater was in darkness apart from the spotlights, which Carolina had full in her face. She could see nothing, but the shooter could see everything. There were no volunteers, no technicians apart from those handling the lighting, so he had all the time in the world to go up there without being seen, shoot Carolina at the right moment, then get out of the building through an emergency exit."

"To get up to that gangway, you have to pass through the backstage area," Betsy said. "And the only people who could do that had been accredited. Access was strictly controlled."

"So it must, after all, have been a member of the cast," Derek said. "Which means we have four suspects: Bergdorf, Ostrovski, Padalin, and Charlotte Brown."

"Charlotte ran to Carolina after the shooting," I said.

"That doesn't rule her out," Derek said. "She fires from the gangway, comes straight back down and runs to help Carolina. The perfect alibi!"

Just then, I received a call on my cell phone.

I sighed. "Shit, what does he want with me this time?" I picked up. "Hello, sir. We're in the Grand Theater. We've identified the place from which the shots were fired. A gangway that can only be reached through the backstage area, which means that—"

"Jesse," the major cut in, "that's why I'm calling you. I have the ballistic analysis. The gun used on Carolina Eden was a Beretta. And get this, Jesse: the same weapon was used in 1994 and two days ago."

Derek, seeing me turn pale, asked me what was happening.

"He's here among us," I told him. "The weapon that killed the Gordons and Meghan was also used to shoot Carolina."

"It's as if everything's cursed," Derek said.

DEREK SCOTT

November 12, 1994. One month after our terrifying car accident, I received the medal of valor. In the gymnasium at troop headquarters, in front of an audience of police officers, officials, journalists, and guests, I was decorated by the head of the State Police. He had made the journey for the occasion.

Standing on the platform, one arm in a sling, I kept my head down. I didn't want that medal, I didn't want the ceremony, but Major McKenna had assured me that a refusal on my part would not be well received by my superiors.

Jesse was at the back of the room. Keeping a low profile. He didn't want to sit in the seat that had been reserved for him in the front row. He seemed beaten. I couldn't even look at him.

After a long speech, the head of the State Police approached and solemnly put a medal around my neck, declaring: "Sergeant Derek Scott, for your bravery in the exercise of your duty, and for saving a life while endangering your own, I bestow this decoration on you. You are an example to your fellow officers."

Once the medal had been awarded, he saluted me in military style, and the brass band struck up a triumphal march.

I remained impassive, my gaze fixed. Suddenly, I saw that Jesse was crying and I was unable to hold back my tears either. I came down off the platform and made my way to the cloakrooms. I tore the medal from my neck and threw it angrily to the ground. Then I collapsed on a bench and sobbed.

JESSE ROSENBERG

Tuesday, July 29, 2014
Three days after opening night

This was the last great turning point in the case.

The murder weapon from 1994, which had never been found, had showed up again. The weapon that had been used to murder the Gordon family and Meghan Padalin had now been used to silence Carolina. This meant that Stephanie Mailer had likely been right: Ted Tennenbaum had not murdered either the Gordon family or Meghan Padalin.

That morning, at troop headquarters, the major summoned Derek and me, in the presence of the assistant D.A.

"I'm going to have to advise Sylvia Tennenbaum of the situation," he said. "The D.A.'s office will start a procedure. I wanted you to be warned."

"Thank you, sir," I said. "We understand."

"Sylvia Tennenbaum might decide to take action not only against the police as a whole," the assistant D.A. said, "but against the two of you."

"Whether or not he was guilty of those murders, Ted Tennenbaum was involved in a fatal car chase with the police, which would not have happened if he'd stopped when ordered to."

"But Sergeant Scott deliberately rammed his vehicle and pushed him off the bridge," the assistant D.A. said.

"We were trying to intercept him!" Derek said.

"There were other ways."

"Oh, yes? What other ways? If you're such an expert on car chases, tell me what other ways?"

"We're not here to blame you," the major assured us. "I took another look at the file. Everything pointed to Tennenbaum. There was the fact that his van was spotted at the crime scene a few minutes before the murders, the fact that he had a motive in the financial pressure being put on him by the mayor, confirmed in his bank statements, the fact that he purchased a gun of the same kind used in the murders, and the fact that he was a good shot. The evidence pointed only to him!"

I sighed. "And yet all that evidence has since been pulled to pieces."

"I know that, Jesse. But anyone would have gotten it wrong. You're not guilty of anything. Unfortunately, I'm afraid Sylvia Tennenbaum won't be satisfied with that explanation, and will do everything she can to obtain compensation."

We had come full circle in our investigation. In 1994, whoever had killed Meghan Padalin had also eliminated the Gordons as unwitting witnesses. Because Derek and I had followed the wrong lead about the Gordons and the weight of evidence convinced us of Tennenbaum's guilt, the real murderer had been sleeping easy these past twenty years. That was until Stephanie Mailer reopened the case at the instigation of Meta Ostrovski, who had always had his doubts, having himself seen that it was not Tennenbaum at the wheel of his van. Now that all avenues of inquiry were converging on him, the killer was eliminating those who might unmask him. He had started with the Gordons, and gone on to eliminate Stephanie, then Springfield, before trying to silence Carolina. The killer was right there, in front of our eyes, within reach. We had to act intelligently and quickly.

Once our conversation with Major McKenna was over, we took advantage of the fact that we were at troop headquarters to drop into the office of Dr Ranjit Singh, the medical examiner, who was also an expert criminal profiler. He had looked at the case file to help us flesh out the killer's personality.

"I was able to make a study of all the recorded elements of the investigation," he told us. "First of all, I think you're dealing with a male. Statistically, the probability of a woman being murdered by another woman is barely two percent. But in our case, there are more concrete factors: that impulsive side to the killer, the way he broke down the Gordons' door and murdered a whole family. And then the way he drowned Stephanie Mailer in the lake, and smashed Cody Springfield's skull. Violence of this kind is overwhelmingly seen in men. As I saw in the file, back then my predecessors also thought it was a man."

"So it can't have been a woman?" I said.

"It cannot be ruled out, Captain. There have been cases where the profile pointed to a man and the culprit turned out to be a woman. But the impression I get from the file makes me lean confidently toward a man. And this is an interesting case. The profile is quite an uncommon one. In general, someone who kills so many people is either a psychopath or a hardened criminal. But if this were a psychopath, there would not be any rational causes. In this case, though, it's clear he's killing for a very specific reason: to prevent the truth coming out. And he's definitely not a hardened criminal either. When he tries to kill Meghan Padalin, he misses her at first. That suggests he's nervous. He shoots her several times, with the last shot to the head. He isn't in command, he's lost control. And when he realizes the Gordons may have seen him, he slaughters everyone. He kicks the door down even though it's not locked and shoots three people at point-blank range."

"All the same, he's a good shot," Derek said.

"Yes, he's definitely a trained shot. I suspect he trained to shoot for the occasion. He's meticulous, but he loses it when he goes ahead with it. So he's not a cold-blooded killer, but rather someone who will kill reluctantly."

"Reluctantly?" I said in surprise.

"Yes, someone who would never have thought about killing, or would even disapprove of murder socially, but who must have made up his mind to do it, perhaps to protect his reputation, his status, or to avoid prison."

"Owning or acquiring a weapon, training yourself to shoot, that's quite a preparation," Derek said.

"I didn't say there was no premeditation," Dr Singh said. "What I'm saying is that the killer had to kill Meghan at all costs. It wasn't some petty motive, like robbery. Maybe she knew something about him and he had to keep her quiet. As for the choice of a gun, it's the weapon *par excellence* for someone who doesn't know how to kill. There's an element of distance, and an assurance that you will kill. One shot and it's all over. A knife doesn't allow that, unless you cut the victim's throat, but this killer wouldn't have been capable of that. This is something we often see in suicides: a lot of people find it's easier to use a firearm than to cut their wrists, throw themselves off a building or even take medications when they're not sure what effect they'll have."

Derek said, "If it's the same person who murdered the Gordons, Meghan Padalin, Stephanie Mailer and Springfield, and who also tried to kill Carolina Eden, why use a different M.O. with Stephanie and Springfield?"

"Because the killer was trying to cover his tracks," Dr Singh said, with conviction. "He didn't want anyone to make a connection with the murders in 1994. Especially after he had successfully hoodwinked everyone for so many years. I repeat: in my opinion you're dealing with someone who doesn't like killing. He's killed six people because he is trapped in a spiral of violence, but he is not a cold-blooded murderer, he is not your typical serial killer. He's someone who's trying to save his own skin at the cost of other people's. A reluctant murderer."

"But if he is a reluctant murderer, why didn't he get as far away as he could from Orphea?"

"That's an option he'll consider as soon as he can. He lived for twenty years thinking that nobody would discover his secret. He lowered his guard. That's probably the reason why he's taken such risks to protect his identity until now. He can't just pack up and light out: that would give him away. He's going to try to buy himself some time and find an excuse to leave the area for good without arousing suspicion. A new job, or a sick relative. You have to act fast. You're dealing with an intelligent, painstaking man. The likeliest way you're going to track him down is to find out who had a reason to kill Meghan Padalin in 1994."

WHO HAD A GOOD REASON TO KILL MEGHAN PADALIN? Derek wrote on the whiteboard in the archive room of the *Chronicle*, which had become the only place where we felt sufficiently at peace to continue our hunt, and where Betsy had joined us. In the room with us were Hayward—the deductions he had made in 1994 suggested he was a detective with considerable flair—as well as Bird, who had given up a great deal of time to help us in our search and had proved to be a valuable support.

Together we went over the elements of our investigation.

"O.K., Tennenbaum isn't the killer," Betsy said. "But I thought you had proof he bought the murder weapon in 1994?"

"The weapon came from a consignment being sold under the counter by a crooked soldier in a bar in Ridgesport," Derek said. "Theoretically, it's possible Tennenbaum and the murderer both bought a weapon from the same source at around the same time. It was definitely a place that was known back then to anyone wanting to acquire a gun."

"That would be quite a coincidence," Betsy said. "First Tennenbaum's van is at the crime scene, but he's not at the wheel. Then the murder weapon is bought from the same place as where Tennenbaum purchased a Beretta. Doesn't that seem odd to you?"

"Forgive my question," Bird said, "but why would Tennenbaum have bought a weapon illegally if he had no intention of using it?"

"Tennenbaum was being squeezed by a local gangster named Fold, who had set fire to his restaurant. He might have wanted a gun to protect himself."

"The same Fold whose name was in the script of my play that was found in Mayor Gordon's safe deposit box," Hayward said.

"Yes," I said. "The man we all think may have been driven off the road and left for dead."

"Let's concentrate on Meghan," Derek said, tapping with his fingers on the sentence he had written on the board: WHO HAD A GOOD REASON TO KILL MEGHAN PADALIN?

"O.K.," I said. "Is it possible Meghan knocked down Fold? And that someone connected with him—Costico, perhaps—wanted to avenge him?"

"Knocking a gangster off his motorbike doesn't tally with what we know about Meghan," Derek said.

"By the way," I said, "what happened to the analysis of the pieces of the car found by Special Agent Grace?"

"I hope to hear something tomorrow."

Betsy, who had been looking through the file, now took out an interview transcript and said:

"I think I've found something. When we questioned Mayor Brown last week, he told us he had received an anonymous telephone call in 1994. 'At the beginning of 1994 I discovered that Gordon was corrupt.' 'How?' 'From an anonymous phone call, around the end of February. It was a woman's voice.'"

"A woman's voice," Derek said. "Could it have been Meghan Padalin?"

"Why not?" I said.

"Are you saying Mayor Brown killed Meghan and the Gordons?" Bird said.

"No," I said. "In 1994, when the murders took place, Alan Brown was shaking hands in the lobby of the Grand Theater. He's right out of the picture."

"But it was that call which made Mayor Gordon decide to leave Orphea," Betsy sent. "He started transferring his money to Montana, then went to Bozeman to look for a house there."

"Mayor Gordon would have had a very good motive to kill Meghan Padalin, and his profile matches the one Dr Singh told us about earlier: a man without homicidal tendencies who, feeling himself cornered, or to protect his reputation, commits murder reluctantly. Gordon would certainly fit that description."

"Except you're forgetting Gordon also died," I said to Derek.

Hayward now spoke up. "I remember what struck me at the time was how well the killer knew Meghan Padalin's routine. He knew she went jogging every evening at the same time, and that she stopped to do her exercises in Penfield Crescent. Well, he may have been watching her for a while. But there's one thing the killer could not have known from his observations alone: the fact that Meghan wouldn't be attending the celebrations for the opening of the theater festival. It has to have been someone who knew the neighborhood would be deserted and that Meghan would be alone in the park, without witnesses. It was a unique opportunity."

"You mean someone close to her?" Bird said.

Just as we had originally wondered who could have known that Mayor Gordon would not be attending the opening night of the festival, now the question was: who could have known that Meghan would be in the park that evening?

We went back to the list of suspects, which was written in marker pen on the whiteboard:

> Meta Ostrovski
> Steven Bergdorf
> Charlotte Brown
> Samuel Padalin

"Let's proceed by elimination," Derek said. "Starting with the greatest likelihood that it's a man, that rules out Charlotte Brown for the moment. In any case, she wasn't living in Orphea back then and was highly unlikely to have any connection with Meghan Padalin, let alone the opportunity to spy on her and be aware of her routine."

"Based on what Dr Singh told us," Betsy said, "the murderer would have had no interest in the 1994 investigation being reopened. Which rules out Ostrovski. Why would he have commissioned Stephanie to look into the murders only to kill her later? Besides, he didn't have any connection with Meghan Padalin either, that we know of."

"That leaves Bergdorf and Padalin," I said.

"I've been wondering about Bergdorf," Derek said. "In 1994, just after the murders, he moves to New York, only to reappear suddenly in Orphea and get chosen to act in the play that's supposed to reveal the name of the murderer."

"And what do we know about Padalin?" I said. "Back then he was the grieving widower, and I don't think it occurred of us that he might have killed his wife. But before ruling him out, we'd have to know more about him, including why he auditioned for the play. Because if there's someone who was familiar with Meghan's routine and knew she wouldn't be going to the festival on opening night, it was him."

Bird had in fact done a little research into Samuel Padalin. "They were a nice, unremarkable couple, very well liked," he told us. "I talked to several people who were their neighbors back then. They're unanimous. Never any shouting, never any arguing. Everyone describes them as charming people who were clearly happy. By all accounts, Samuel Padalin was deeply affected by the death of his wife. One of the neighbors even told me he was afraid he might kill himself. Then he got back on his feet and remarried."

"Yes," Hayward said. "This confirms my impression at the time."

"Neither Bergdorf or Padalin would appear to have had an obvious motive to kill Meghan," I said. "So we come back to our original question. Why was she killed? If we can answer that question, we'll be closer to finding her killer."

We needed to know more about Meghan. We decided to pay a visit to Samuel Padalin in the hope that he might tell us a little more about his first wife.

When we arrived, he ushered us through to the living room, where we explained that it was Meghan, not the Gordons, who had been the target in 1994.

"Meghan?" Sameul Padalin said, incredulously. "What are you talking about?"

We were trying to judge his reaction, and so far it seemed sincere. Padalin was deeply shaken.

"We're telling you the truth as we now know it, Mr Padalin," Derek said. "We got it wrong about the target. It was your wife who was meant to be the victim, the Gordons were innocent bystanders."

"But why Meghan?"

"That's what we have to find out," I said.

"It makes no sense. Meghan was the gentlest person you could imagine. She was a considerate neighbor, a bookseller, loved by her customers."

"And yet someone hated her sufficiently to want to kill her," I said.

Stunned, Padalin fell silent.

"Mr Padalin," Derek said, "this question is very important. Were you being threatened? Or were you dealing with any dangerous people? People who might have wanted to attack you or your wife?"

"Not at all!" Padalin said, offended. "You really don't know us."

"Does the name Jeremiah Fold mean anything to you?"

"Never heard of him. You already asked me that question yesterday."

"Was Meghan worried about anything in the weeks before she died? Did she mention to you anything she felt anxious about?"

"Oh, no. That was not her life. What she loved was reading, writing, running."

"Mr Padalin," Betsy said, "can you, looking back on it—hard as that must be—think of anyone who might have known that you and Meghan were not going to the celebrations for the opening of the festival? The killer knew your wife was going to go jogging as usual that evening while the rest of the townspeople were on Main Street."

Padalin thought this over for a moment. "Everyone was talking about the festival. With our neighbors, when we were out shopping, with the customers in the bookstore, every conversation revolved around one subject: who had tickets for opening night and who would simply be mingling with the crowds on Main Street or at the marina. I know Meghan told anyone who asked that we hadn't managed to get tickets and that she didn't plan to get caught up in all that commotion downtown. Just like those people who don't celebrate New Year's Eve and take the opportunity to go to bed early, she'd say, 'I'm going to read on my porch, it will be my quietest evening in a long while.' Ironic, really."

He seemed at a loss.

"You say Meghan liked to write," Betsy said. "What kind of things did she write?"

"All kinds of things. She'd always wanted to write a novel, but had never been able to find the right plot, she said. But she did keep a diary, quite diligently."

"Have you kept it?" Betsy asked.

"I kept *them*. There are at least fifteen volumes."

Padalin left the room for a moment and came back with a dusty cardboard box perhaps exhumed from his cellar. Some twenty exercise books, all the same brand.

Betsy opened one at random: it was filled to the last page with thin, tightly packed handwriting. It would take hours to read it.

"Can we take them away?" she asked Padalin.

"If you like. But I doubt you'll find anything interesting."

"Have you read them?"

"Bits of them. After Meghan died, I had the impression that if I could read what she'd thought, she'd still be with me. But what I soon realized was that she had been bored. You'll see, from the way she describes her life: she was bored with everyday life, bored with me. She talks about her days in the bookstore, who bought which kind of book. I'm ashamed to tell you this, but I found it all a little pathetic. It wasn't a very pleasant impression, so I soon stopped reading."

This explained why the exercise books lived in a dust-covered box.

As we were about to leave, taking the box with us, we noticed some suitcases in the entrance.

"Are you going away?" Derek asked.

"My wife is. She's taking the kids to her parents in Connecticut. She's scared after all that has happened recently in Orphea. I'll probably join her later. At least, when I have permission to leave the state."

Derek and I had to get back to troop headquarters to see Major McKenna, who wanted to know where things stood. Betsy suggested that she take on the task of reading Meghan Padalin's diaries.

"Don't you want us to share the work?" I said.

"No, I'm glad to do it, it'll occupy my mind. I need that."

"I'm very sorry about the police chief job."

"That's how it is," Betsy said, making an effort not to break down in front of us.

Once back in Orphea, Betsy dropped by the police station. All the officers were gathered in the recreation room, where Montagne was giving an improvised speech about his new position as police chief.

Betsy did not feel up to staying and decided to go home and immerse herself in Meghan's diaries. As she came out of the station, she ran into Mayor Brown.

She stared at him a moment in silence, then said, "Why did you do this to me, Alan?"

"Look at the mess we're in, Betsy. Do I have to remind you that you're partly responsible? You were so eager to be involved in this case, it's time you owned up to the consequences."

"Are you punishing me because I did my job? Yes, I had to question you, and your wife, because the investigation demanded it. You didn't get a free pass, Alan, and that's what makes me a good officer. As for Hayward's play, if that's what you call that mess, let me remind you you are the one who brought him here. You're not owning up to your own mistakes. You're no better than Gulliver or Montagne. You thought you were a philosopher king, but you're nothing but an insignificant little despot."

"Go home, Betsy. You can quit the police force if you're not happy."

Betsy went home, seething with rage. No sooner had she gone inside than she sank down in tears in the entrance hall. She sat on the floor for a long time, huddled against the dresser, sobbing. She no longer knew what to do. Or whom to call. Lauren? Lauren would tell her she had warned her against moving to Orphea. Her mother? She would only lecture her for the umpteenth time.

When she had at last revived, her gaze fell on the cardboard box filled with Meghan Padalin's diaries, which she had brought with her. She poured herself a glass of wine, settled in an armchair, and started reading.

She began in the middle of 1993 and read through the last twelve months of Meghan's life, up until July 1994.

At first, Betsy was overwhelmed with boredom at such a tedious account of a life. She understood only too well what Meghan's husband must have felt wading through these pages.

But on January 1, 1994, Meghan described the New Year's gala at the Northern Rose Hotel in Bridgehampton, where she had met a man who had thoroughly captivated her.

Betsy read on to February 1994. What she discovered there left her shaken to the core.

MEGHAN PADALIN
EXTRACTS FROM HER DIARIES

January 1, 1994

Happy New Year to me. Yesterday we went to the New Year's gala at the Northern Rose Hotel in Bridgehampton. I met someone there. A man from outside the region. I've never felt anything like this before. Since yesterday, I've had a tingling sensation in my belly.

February 25, 1994

Today I made an anonymous call to the town hall. I spoke to the deputy mayor, Alan Brown. I think he's a good man. I told him what I knew about Gordon. Let's see what happens.

I told Felicity what I'd done. She flew into a temper. She said it was going to backfire on her. Well, she shouldn't have told me about it. Mayor Gordon is a son of a bitch, everybody has to know it.

March 8, 1994

I saw him again. We're going to meet every week from now on. He makes me so happy.

April 1, 1994

I saw Mayor Gordon today. He came to the bookstore. We were alone in the store. I told him everything: that I knew the whole story, and that he was a criminal. It came out all in one go. I've been brooding about this for two months. Obviously, he denied it. He needs to know what happened because of him. I'd like to tell the newspapers, but Felicity stopped me.

April 2, 1994

Since yesterday, I've been feeling better. Felicity yelled at me over the phone, but I know I did the right thing.

April 3, 1994

Yesterday, while jogging, I went as far as Penfield Crescent. I ran into the mayor, who was on his way home. I said to him, "Shame on you for what you did." I wasn't scared. For his part he seemed strangely uncomfortable. I feel like the eye pursuing Cain. Every day, I'll go there and wait for him until he gets back from work and remind him of his guilt.

April 7, 1994

Wonderful day with him in the Springs. He fascinates me. I'm in love. Samuel doesn't suspect a thing. Everything's fine.

May 2, 1994

Had coffee with Kate. She's the only person who knows about him. She says I shouldn't risk my marriage if it's just a fling. Or else I should make up my mind and leave Samuel. I don't know if I'm brave enough to make up my mind. The situation suits me fine.

June 25, 1994

Not much to tell. The bookstore is doing well. A new restaurant will be opening soon on Main Street. Café Athena. It looks nice. Ted Tennenbaum is opening it. He's a customer in the bookstore. I like him.

July 1, 1994

Mayor Gordon, who has not set foot in the bookstore since he found out that I know, came in for a long time today. He put on a strange act for me. He wanted a book by a local writer, and spent quite a while in the room we reserve for local writers. I'm not too sure what he was doing. There were customers and I couldn't really keep an eye on him. In the end, he bought Chief Hayward's play, "The Darkest Night". After he

470

left, I went and had a glance in the local writers' room, and noticed that the pig had left a copy of Steven Bergdorf's book about the festival all dog-eared. I'm sure he wanted to check if the stock he left us is selling so he could make sure we're paying him his share. Is he afraid we're robbing him? He's the thief.

July 18, 1994
Kirk Hayward came to the bookstore to get back his play. I told him it had sold. I thought he'd be pleased, but he was very upset. He wanted to know who had bought it. I told him it was Gordon. He didn't even want the ten dollars that were due to him.

July 20, 1994
Chief Hayward came back. He says that Gordon is claiming he wasn't the one who bought the play. But I know it was. I told Kirk again. I'd even made a note of it. See my entry of July 1, 1994.

JESSE ROSENBERG

Wednesday, July 30, 2014
Four days after opening night

That morning, by the time Derek and I got to our room at the *Chronicle*, Betsy had pinned photocopies of Meghan Padalin's diary to the wall.

"Meghan *was* the person who made that anonymous call to Alan Brown in February 1994, telling him that Mayor Gordon was corrupt," she said. "From what I gather, she found it out from someone called Felicity. I don't know what exactly this Felicity woman told her, but Meghan was very angry with Mayor Gordon. About a month or so after her anonymous call, on April 1, when she was alone in the bookstore, she finally confronted Gordon, who'd come in to buy a book. She told him she knew everything, and called him a criminal."

"Can we be sure she is referring to his corrupt business deals?" Derek said.

"That's what I wondered," Betsy said, going to the next page. "Because two days later, while she was out jogging, Meghan confronted Gordon in front of his house and hurled abuse at him. She writes in her diary: *I'm like the eye pursuing Cain.*"

"The eye pursued Cain because he'd killed," I said. "Did the mayor kill someone?"

"That's what I'm wondering," Betsy said. "In the months that followed, and up until her death, Meghan ran as far as Mayor Gordon's house every evening. She'd wait in in the park for him to get home and when she saw him, she would waylay him and remind him of his guilt."

"So the mayor would have had a reason to kill Meghan," Derek said.

"The perfect culprit," Betsy said, "if he hadn't died in the same shooting."

"Do we know any more about this Felicity?" I asked.

"Felicity Daniels," Betsy said with a smug little smile. "It took one call to Samuel Padalin to trace her. She lives in Coram now and she's waiting for us. Let's go."

Felicity Daniels was sixty years old and worked in a store selling household appliances in the mall in Coram, where we met with her. She had been waiting for us so she could take her break. We went to a nearby coffee shop.

"Do you mind if I have a sandwich?" she said. "Otherwise I won't have time for lunch."

"Go ahead," Betsy said.

Felicity ordered her sandwich from the waiter. My impression was that she was sad and tired.

"You said you wanted to talk about Meghan?"

"Yes," Betsy said. "As you may have heard, we have had to reopen the investigation into her murder and those of the Gordon family. Meghan was a friend of yours, wasn't she?"

"Yes. We met at the tennis club and hit it off. She was younger than me, by about ten years. But we had the same level in tennis. I wouldn't say we were very close, but from taking a drink together after matches, we got to know each other quite well."

"How would you describe her?"

"She was a romantic. A bit dreamy, a bit naive. Starry-eyed."

"Have you been living in Coram for long?"

"I came here with the kids just after my husband died. He died on November 16, 1993, his birthday."

"Did you see Meghan between the time you moved here and the time she died?"

"Yes, she'd come regularly to Coram, to say hello. She'd bring me cooked dishes, sometimes a good book. To tell the truth, I never asked her for anything. She kind of imposed herself, but she meant well."

"Was Meghan a happy woman?"

"Yes, she had everything going for her. Men liked her. Well, everyone swooned over her. Gossips will tell you it was thanks to her that the bookstore in Orphea did so well in those days."

"So she often cheated on her husband?"

"That's not what I said at all. She wasn't the kind of person to have affairs."

"Why not?"

Felicity Daniels frowned. "I don't know. Maybe because she wasn't brave enough. She wasn't the kind of person to live dangerously."

"And yet, according to her diary," Betsy said, "Meghan had a relationship with a man in the last months of her life."

"Really?" Felicity said in surprise.

"Yes, a man she met on December 31 at the Northern Rose Hotel in Bridgehampton. Meghan mentions meeting him regularly until the beginning of June 1994. After that, nothing. Did she ever talk to you about him?"

"No, never. Who was he?"

"I don't know," Betsy replied. "I was hoping you could tell me. Did Meghan ever mention feeling threatened?"

"Threatened? No way! You know, there must be people around who knew her better than I did. Why are you asking me all these questions?"

"Because according to Meghan's diary, in February 1994, you confided to her something about the mayor of Orphea, Joseph Gordon, which seemed to have really upset her."

"Oh, my God!" Felicity Daniels said, placing a hand over her mouth.

"What was it about?" Betsy said.

"About my husband Luke," Felicity said in a thin voice. "I should never have said anything to Meghan."

"What happened to your husband?"

"Luke was up to his neck in debt. He had an air conditioning business that went bankrupt. He had to dismiss all his workers. There was nothing he could do. For months, he hadn't told anyone. I only found out just before he died. After he died, I had to sell the house to pay off the debts. I left Orphea with the children and found this job as a sales assistant."

"Mrs Daniels, how did your husband die?"

"He committed suicide. He hanged himself in our room on the evening of his birthday."

* * *

February 3, 1994

It was early evening in the furnished apartment Felicity Daniels rented in Coram. Meghan had dropped by late in the afternoon to bring her a dish of lasagna and had found her in despair. The children were quarreling, refusing to do their homework, the living room was a mess, and Felicity was slumped on the couch, crying, no longer able to summon the strength to take the situation in hand.

Meghan intervened. She brought the children to order, helped them finish their homework, then sent them to shower, gave them their dinner, and put them to bed. Then she opened the bottle of wine she had brought with her and poured Felicity a large glass.

Felicity had nobody to confide in and she opened up to Meghan.

"I can't take it anymore, Meg. If only you knew what people are saying about Luke. The coward who hanged himself in his bedroom on his birthday while his wife and children were getting ready to celebrate it downstairs. I see how the other kids' parents look at me. I can't stand that mixture of judgment and condescension."

"I'm so sorry," Meghan said.

Felicity shrugged. She poured herself more wine. With the help of the drink, after a silence filled with sadness, she finally said:

"Luke was always too honest. Look where it got him."

"What do you mean?" Meghan said.

"Nothing."

"Oh, no, Felicity. You've started now, you'll have to finish."

"Meghan, if I tell you, you have to promise me you won't tell anyone else."

"Of course. You know you can trust me."

"Luke's business had been doing well in the last few years. Everything was fine with us, until the day Mayor Gordon asked to see him in his office. It was just before the start of the refurbishing work on the municipal buildings. Gordon told Luke he'd give him the contract for all the ventilation systems in return for a financial contribution."

"You mean a bribe?"

"Yes. And Luke refused. He said the accounts department would notice, and he might lose everything. Gordon threatened to destroy him. He told him the practice was common all over town. But Luke wouldn't give in. So he didn't get the municipal contracts. Or the ones after that. And to punish him for resisting, Mayor Gordon broke him. He did everything he could to make things difficult for him, bad-mouthed him, put people off working with him. Soon Luke lost all his customers. But he never said anything to me, he didn't want to worry me. I only found out just before he died. The company accountant came to tell me about the imminent bankruptcy, the workers having to be laid off. Poor fool that I was, I didn't know a thing. That evening I sat Luke down and asked him what was going on, and he told me the whole story. I told him we could fight it, and he said he couldn't do anything against the mayor. I told him he should report it to the police. He gave me a defeated look. 'You don't understand, Felicity, everyone in town is involved in these kickbacks. All our friends. Your brother, too. How do you think he got all those contracts in the last two years? They'll lose everything if we report them. They'll go to jail. We can't say anything, everyone has their hands tied.' The following evening, he hanged himself."

"Oh, my God, Felicity!" Meghan said, horrified. "And this is all Mayor Gordon's doing?"

"You mustn't tell anyone, Meghan."

"People have to know that Gordon is a criminal."

"Swear you won't say anything, Meghan! Businesses will be shut down, the bosses will go to prison, the workers will be out of a job . . ."

"So we're going to let the mayor go unpunished?"

"Gordon's very strong. Much stronger than he looks."

"He doesn't scare me!"

"Meghan, promise me you won't tell anyone. I have enough worries as it is."

*   *   *

"But she did tell someone," Betsy said.

"Yes," Felicity said, "she made an anonymous phone call to Deputy Mayor Brown. I was furious."

"Why?"

"Because people I liked might have been in big trouble if the police investigated. I knew what it meant to lose everything. I wouldn't wish that on my worst enemy. Meghan promised not to say anything more. But then, two months later, she called me and told me she'd had it out with Mayor Gordon in the bookstore. I screamed at her like I've never screamed at anyone. That was the last time I had any contact with Meghan. I just stopped talking to her. I was too angry with her. Real friends don't betray your secrets."

"I think she was trying to defend you," Betsy said. "She wanted there to be some kind of justice. She went every day and reminded the mayor that, because of him, your husband had killed himself. She wanted justice for your husband. You say Meghan wasn't very brave? I think she was. She wasn't afraid to confront Gordon. She was the only person who dared to do that. She was braver than all the other people in the town combined. And she paid for that with her life."

"You mean Meghan was the target of those murders?" Felicity said, astonished.

"We think she was," Derek said.

"But who could have done it? Mayor Gordon? He died at the same time as her. It doesn't make sense."

"Mrs Daniels," Betsy said, "can you think of any other friend of

Meghan's we could talk to about her? In her diary she mentions some-one named Kate."

"Yes, Kate Grand. She was another member of the tennis club. I think she was quite a close friend of Meghan's."

As they left the shopping mall in Coram, Derek received a telephone call from the bodywork specialist at the Highway Patrol.

"I was able to analyze the car debris you gave me. You were right. It's a piece of a right bumper, with blue paint around it, which means the car was blue, obviously. I also found on it streaks of gray paint, which, according to the police file you sent me, was the color of the motorcycle involved in that fatal accident of July 16, 1994."

* * *

In Mount Sinai hospital, Cynthia Eden ran out of Carolina's room and called a nurse.

"Get the doctor!" Cynthia cried. "My daughter has opened her eyes!"

* * *

In the archive room, helped by Hayward and Bird, we were studying the possible scenarios of Fold's accident.

"According to the specialist," Derek said, "and judging by the impact, the car probably came level with the motorbike and hit it, sending it off the road."

"So Fold was murdered," Bird said.

"Murdered in a way," Betsy said. "He was left for dead. Whoever hit him was a total amateur."

"A reluctant murderer!" Derek cried. "The very same profile that Doctor Singh drew of our killer. He doesn't want to kill, but he has to."

"There were surely a lot of people who wanted to kill Fold," I said.

"What if the name of Jeremiah Fold found in that copy of 'The Darkest Night' was an order to kill?" Hayward suggested.

Derek pointed to a photograph from the police file showing the interior of the Gordons' garage. There was a red car with the trunk open and suitcases inside. "Mayor Gordon had a red car."

"That's funny," Hayward said. "I seem to remember he drove a blue convertible."

At these words, a memory came back to me and I collected the case file from 1994. "We saw it at the time!" I said. "I remember a photograph of Mayor Gordon and his car."

I went frantically through the reports, the photographs, the transcripts of witness statements, the bank statements. And then I found it. The photograph taken on the fly by the realtor in Montana, showing Mayor Gordon unloading cardboard boxes from the trunk of a blue convertible outside the house he had rented in Bozeman.

"The realtor in Montana was suspicious of Gordon," Derek said. "He photographed him in front of his car so as to have a record of his license number and his face."

"So the mayor *did* have a blue car," Bird said.

Hayward was now peering closely at the photograph of the red car in Gordon's garage.

"Look at the rear window," he said. "There's the name of the car dealership. It may still be around."

We checked, and indeed it was. It was located on the road to Montauk and had been in business for forty years. We went straight there and were received by an elderly man in grease-marked overalls in his cluttered, insalubrious office.

"What can I do for the police?" he said amiably.

"We are looking for information about a car that was bought from you, probably in 1994."

He laughed. "1994? I can't really help you there. Have you seen the mess in here?"

"Take a look at the model," Derek suggested, showing him the photograph of the car in the garage.

The man glanced at it. "I sold heaps of that model. Maybe you have the customer's name?"

"Joseph Gordon, the mayor of Orphea."

The car dealer turned serious. "Now that's a sale I won't forget in a hurry," he said in a suddenly solemn tone. "Two weeks after buying his car, the poor guy was murdered, along with his whole family."

"So he bought it in mid-July?" I said.

"It must have been something like that. When I came to open up, I found him outside. He looked like someone who hadn't slept all night. He stank of alcohol. The right side of his car was ruined. He wanted a new one right away. I had three red Dodges in stock, and he took one without any argument. He paid in cash. He told me he had been driving drunk and had hit a stag, and that it might compromise his re-election in September. He gave me $5,000 and told me to take his car straight to the junkyard. He left in his new car and everyone was happy."

"Didn't it strike you as strange?"

"Yes and no. I see things like that all the time. You know the secret of my success in business, why I've been here so long?"

"No."

"I keep my mouth shut, and everyone around here knows that."

Mayor Gordon had good reason to kill Meghan, but he had killed Jeremiah Fold, with whom he had no connection that we knew of. Why?

Leaving Orphea that evening, Derek and I had questions going around in our heads. We drove back in silence, lost in thought. When I stopped outside his house, he didn't get out of the car but just sat there.

"What's up?" I said.

"Since I reopened this investigation with you, Jesse, it's been like a new life for me. I haven't felt so fulfilled in a long time. But it's also brought back the ghosts of the past. For the last two weeks, whenever I close my eyes at night, I find myself back in that car with you and Natasha."

"It could have been me driving. None of what happened is your fault."

480

"It was you or her, Jesse! I had to choose between you and her."

"You saved my life, Derek."

"And killed Natasha at the same time, Jesse. Look at yourself twenty years later, still in mourning for her."

"Derek, it wasn't your fault."

"What would you have done in my place, Jesse? That's the question I keep asking myself."

I didn't reply. We smoked together, in silence. Then we exchanged a brotherly hug and Derek went into the house.

I didn't feel like going home immediately. I wanted to see her again. I drove to the cemetery. At this hour, it was closed. I climbed over the low perimeter wall without difficulty and strolled down the quiet paths. I walked between the graves, the thick grass muffling my footsteps. Everything was calm and beautiful. I saluted my grandparents, who were sleeping peacefully, then came to her grave. I sat down and stayed there for a long while. Suddenly, I heard footsteps behind me. It was Darla.

"How did you know I'd be here?" I said.

She smiled. "You're not the only person who climbs over the wall to come see her."

I smiled, too. Then I said, "I'm sorry about the restaurant. It was a stupid idea."

"No, Jesse, it was a wonderful idea. I'm sorry about the way I reacted."

She sat down next to me.

"I should never have taken her in our car that day," I said. "It's all my fault."

"What about me, Jesse? I should never have made her get out of my car. We should never have had that stupid quarrel."

"In other words, we all feel guilty."

Darla nodded.

"Sometimes I have the feeling she's with me," I went on. "When I go back home in the evening, I find myself hoping to see her there."

"Oh, Jesse. We all miss her. Every day. But you have to move forward. You can't keep living in the past."

"I don't know if I'll ever be able to mend this crack inside me, Darla."

"But Jesse, life will mend it."

She put her head on my shoulder. We sat like that for a long time gazing at the grave in front of us.

NATASHA DARRINSKI
APRIL 2, 1968 – OCTOBER 13, 1994

DEREK SCOTT

October 13, 1994

Our car smashes through the guard rail of the bridge and plunges into the river. At the moment of impact, everything happens very fast. Instinctively, I unfasten my seat belt and open my window, as we were taught to do in the Police Academy. In the back seat, Natasha screams in terror. Jesse, who hasn't got his seat belt on, is knocked forward and hits his head against the glove compartment.

In a few seconds, the car fills with water. I yell at Natasha to unfasten her seat belt and get out through the window. I realize that her seat belt is stuck. I bend over her and try to help. I have nothing to cut through the belt, it has to be torn from its base. I pull on it like a madman, but in vain. We have water up to our shoulders.

"See to Jesse!" Natasha yells at me. "I'll manage."

I hesitate for a second. She yells again:

"Derek! Get Jesse out!"

The water is up to our chins now. I struggle out of the car then grab Jesse and manage to pull him with me.

We plunge into the water, the car sinks toward the bottom of the river, I hold my breath as much as possible, I look through the window. Natasha, completely submerged, hasn't managed to get free of her seat belt. She's trapped in the car. I have no more air. The weight of Jesse's body is pulling me down to the bottom. Natasha and I exchange a last look. I'll never forget her eyes on the other side of the car window.

Running short of oxygen, with the energy of despair, I manage to get up to the surface with Jesse. I swim laboriously to the riverbank.

483

Police patrol cars are arriving, I see officers running down to the water's edge. I reach them and hand Jesse over to them, lifeless. I want to go back and look for Natasha, I swim to the middle of the river. I no longer know where exactly the car went down. I can't see anything anymore, the water is muddy. I'm in total distress. I hear sirens in the distance. I try to dive back down. I remember Natasha's eyes, that look which will haunt me my whole life.

And this question that would pursue me: if I had kept trying to yank at that belt and tear it from its base instead of seeing to Jesse as she had asked, could I have saved her?

3

The Swap

JESSE ROSENBERG

Thursday, July 31, 2014
Five days after opening night

Time was not on our side, and yet that morning Betsy asked us to meet her at Café Athena.

"This really isn't the time for a leisurely breakfast," Derek said on the way to Orphea. We only had three days left to solve the case.

"I don't know what she wants," I said.

"Didn't she say anything more?"

"No, nothing."

"And Café Athena on top of everything else. That really is the last place I want to set foot, given the circumstances."

I smiled.

"What is it?" Derek said.

"You're in a bad mood."

"No, I'm not."

"I know you like the back of my hand. You're in a lousy mood."

"Come on," he said, "drive faster, I want to know what Betsy's up to."

He put on the flashing lights to make me accelerate. I burst out laughing.

When at last we got to Café Athena, we found Betsy sitting at a large table at the back of the room. Cups of coffee were waiting for us.

"Oh, there you are!" she said impatiently, as if we'd been dragging our feet.

"What's on your mind?" I said.

"I can't stop thinking."

"About what?"

"About Meghan. It's clear the mayor wanted to get rid of her. She knew too much. Maybe Gordon was hoping he could stay in Orphea and not have to run away to Montana. I tried to get hold of this Kate Grand, Meghan's friend. She's on vacation. I left a message at her hotel, and I'm waiting for her to call me back. But that doesn't matter. There's no doubt the mayor wanted to eliminate Meghan, and he did."

"Except that he didn't kill Meghan, he killed Fold," Derek said, not sure what Betsy was getting at.

"He set up a swap," Betsy said. "He killed Fold for someone else. And this someone else killed Meghan for him. They swapped murders. And in whose interest was it to kill Fold? Tennenbaum's, who had had enough of the pressure Jeremiah was putting on him."

"But we've only just established that Tennenbaum wasn't guilty," Derek said, irritably. "The D.A.'s office has started the official process to exonerate him."

Betsy was not to be deterred. "In her diary, Meghan says that on July 1, 1994, Mayor Gordon, who had stopped coming to the bookstore, dropped in to buy a play, a play we know he had already read and disliked. He wasn't the one who chose that script, it was whoever ordered the murder of Jeremiah Fold and put the victim's name in it, using a simple code."

"Why do that? They could just as easily have met."

"Maybe because they didn't know each other. Or they wanted never to have been seen together. They didn't want the police to be able to track them down later. Don't forget, Tennenbaum and the mayor hated each other, which makes for a perfect alibi. Nobody would have suspected them of being in cahoots."

"Even if you were right, Betsy," Derek said, "how could the mayor have known which book contained the code?"

Betsy had thought of this. "He must have gone through all the books there. Or maybe he had dog-eared it to mark the place."

"You mean dog-eared it the way Mayor Gordon did that day to Steven Bergdorf's book?" I said, remembering something that Meghan had mentioned in her diary.

"Right," Betsy said.

"Then we absolutely have to find that book."

"That's why I asked you to meet me here."

Just then, the door of Café Athena opened and Sylvia Tennenbaum appeared. She glared at Derek and me.

"What's going on?" she said to Betsy. "You didn't tell me they'd be here."

"Sylvia," Betsy said in a soft voice, "we have to talk."

"There's nothing to say," Sylvia Tennenbaum retorted. "My lawyer is about to sue the State Police."

"Sylvia," Betsy said, "I think your brother was involved in the murder of Meghan and the Gordon family. And I think the truth is in your house."

Sylvia was appalled by what she had heard. "You're not going to start, too, are you?"

"Can we discuss this calmly, Sylvia? There's something I'd like to show you."

Troubled as she was, Sylvia agreed to sit with us. I brought her up to date with the situation and showed her the extracts from Meghan Padalin's diary.

"I know you live in your brother's house, Sylvia. If Ted was involved, that book could still be there and we need to get our hands on it."

"I did a lot of renovation work," Sylvia said in a thin voice. "But I left his bookshelves as they were."

"Could we take a look?" Betsy said. "If we find that book, we'll have the answer to the question that's troubling all of us."

After a hesitation that lasted as long as it took her to smoke a cigarette out on the sidewalk, Sylvia agreed. We went to her house. This was the first time Derek and I had been back there since we had searched it twenty years ago. Back then, we hadn't found anything. Yet the evidence was there in front of our eyes. And we hadn't seen it. The book about the festival. The cover was still dog-eared. It was there on a shelf, among the works of the great American authors. It had not been moved in all that time.

It was Betsy who took it down. We gathered around her as she leafed through the pages, revealing a number of words underlined in ink. As with the script of Hayward's play, which had been found in the mayor's safe deposit box, the first letters of each of the underlined words, when put end to end, made a name:

MEGHAN PADALIN

*   *   *

In Mount Sinai Hospital, Carolina, who had been awake since the day before, was showing surprising signs of recovery. The doctor, who had come to check on her condition, found her devouring a hamburger her father had brought in.

"Hey, slow down," he said with a smile, "take time to chew."

"I'm so hungry," Carolina said, her mouth full.

"I'm pleased to see you like this."

"Thank you, doctor. It seems you're the one I owe it to that I'm still alive."

The doctor shrugged. "You owe it only to yourself, Carolina. You're a fighter. You wanted to live."

She lowered her eyes. The doctor checked the bandage on her chest. She had been given a dozen stitches.

"Don't worry," the doctor said. "We should be able to fix it and hide the scar."

"Definitely not," Carolina said in a low voice. "This scar is my way of fixing my life."

*   *   *

In Orphea, we went over to Springfield's bookstore to reconstruct what might have happened there on July 1, 1994, according to Meghan's diary. We had suggested to Bird and Hayward that they join us. They might help us to get a better idea.

490

Betsy placed herself behind the counter, as if she were Meghan. Hayward, Bird and I played the roles of customers. Derek took up position in front of the display of local books, which was in a section slightly removed from the rest of the store. Betsy had brought with her the article from the *Chronicle* from the end of June 1994, which she had found the day before Springfield was killed. She studied the photograph of Springfield standing by the display and said:

"At the time, the display was in a small space separated from the store by a partition. Springfield called it the Local Writers' Room. It was only later that he took down the partition to make more space."

"So at the time," Derek said, "nobody at the counter could see what was happening in that room."

"Exactly," Betsy said. "Nobody would have noticed what was being plotted in that room on July 1, 1994. But Meghan had been watching the mayor. She must have been suspicious of his presence here, given that he had not set foot in the store for months, and she kept an eye on him and noticed his little game."

"So that day," Hayward said, "there in the back room Tennenbaum and Mayor Gordon each conveyed the name of the person they wanted to get rid of."

"Two death sentences," Bird murmured.

"That's why Cody Springfield was killed," Betsy said. "He must have seen the murderer in the store and had finally put two and two together. The murderer might have been afraid that Meghan had spoken to her boss back then about the strange scene she had witnessed."

As far as I was concerned, this hypothesis stood up. But Derek was not convinced.

"Continue with your theory, Betsy," he said.

"The swap takes place on July 1. Jeremiah is killed on July 16. For two weeks, Gordon has been watching his every move. He has observed that Fold takes the same route every night to get home from Ridge's Club. Finally, he goes ahead with it. But he's not very good at this job. He doesn't kill him outright, he knocks his man off the road and leaves him at the side of the road when he isn't even dead. He picks up what broken bits he can, runs away, panics, and sells his car first thing the next day, taking the risk of being reported to the police by the car dealer. All total improvisation. Mayor Gordon only kills Fold because he wants to get rid of Meghan before she can report him to the police and bring him down. He's a reluctant murderer."

There was a moment's silence.

"Maybe," Derek said. "Let's assume all this holds up and that Mayor Gordon did kill Fold. What about Meghan?"

"Tennenbaum has been coming to the bookstore to watch her," Betsy went on. "She mentions his visits in her diary. He's a regular customer. On one of his visits, he must have heard her say that she won't be going to the opening night of the festival and he decides to kill her while she's out jogging, when the whole town will be on Main Street and there'll be no witnesses."

"There's one problem with your hypothesis," Derek said. "Tennenbaum didn't kill Meghan Padalin. Not to mention that he drowned in the river after we chased him and the murder weapon was never found, until it was used again last Saturday in the Grand Theater."

"Which means there is a third man," Betsy said. "Tennenbaum made sure the message was passed on for Fold to be killed, but it was also in someone else's interest. And today that person is covering his tracks."

"The man with the tear gas canister and the eagle tattoo," I said, and seeing Hayward's blank expression, I related what Miranda Bird had told us about the incident with Costico in the motel.

"What would his motive be?" Hayward said when I was done.

"Costico tracks him down thanks to the wallet he left in Mylla's room. And he puts pressure on him. Just imagine: Costico must have been furious to have been made to look ridiculous like that in the parking lot, in front of all the hookers. He would have wanted to take his revenge on the man, by threatening his family and turning him into one of Fold's lackeys. But the man with the tattoo wasn't the kind to let these things be done to him, and he knew that in order to regain his freedom he had to eliminate not Costico but Fold."

We badly needed to get our hands on Costico, but he had disappeared without a trace. The missing persons bulletins brought no results. Colleagues from the State Police had questioned those with any known connection to him, but nobody could explain why he had vanished into thin air, leaving behind his money, his cell phone, all his things.

"I think this Costico is dead," Hayward said. "Like Stephanie, like Springfield, like everyone who could have led us to the murderer."

"Then Costico's disappearance is proof that he's in league with the murderer. It's definitely the man with the eagle tattoo we're looking for."

"It's pretty vague as a description," Bird said. "What else do we know about him?"

"He's a customer of the bookstore," Derek said.

"Someone who lives in Orphea," I said. "Or at least he lived here back then."

"He was connected to Tennenbaum," Betsy said.

"If he was as connected to Tennenbaum as Tennenbaum was to the mayor," Hayward said, "then we need to cast our net wide. At the time, everyone knew everyone in Orphea."

"And he was in the Grand Theater on Saturday evening," I said. "That's what'll allow us to track him down. We thought it might be a cast member, but it could be someone else with special access."

"Then let's make a new list," Betsy suggested, taking up a fresh piece of paper.

She wrote down the names of the cast members.

> Charlotte Brown
> Carolina Eden
> Steven Bergdorf
> Jerry Eden
> Meta Ostrovski
> Samuel Padalin

"You should add me," Bird said, "and Kirk. We were there, too. Although speaking for myself, I don't have an eagle tattoo."

He lifted his T-shirt and showed us his back.

"I don't have a tattoo either, dammit!" Hayward said, taking off his shirt.

"We've already eliminated Charlotte from the list of suspects because we're looking for a man," Derek said. "And Jerry Eden, too."

This left three names on the list:

Meta Ostrovski
Samuel Padalin
Steven Bergdorf

"We can rule out Ostrovski," Betsy said. "He had no connection with Orphea, he only came here for the festival."

"That leaves Padalin and Bergdorf," Derek said.

The vise was tightening inexorably.

That afternoon, Betsy was contacted by Meghan's friend Kate Grand, calling from her hotel in North Carolina.

Betsy explained why she urgently needed her help, and then said to her, "I discovered from her diary that Meghan Padalin had an affair with a man at the beginning of 1994. She says she spoke to you about it. Do you remember anything?"

"Yes, it's true, Meghan did tell me. I never met the man, but I remember how it ended—badly."

"Meaning what?"

"Her husband Samuel found out and gave her a beating. That day, she came to me in her nightdress, with bruises on her cheeks, her mouth still bleeding. I let her crash at my place for the night."

"Samuel Padalin was violent toward Meghan?"

"Well, he certainly was that day. She told me she feared for her life. I advised her to report him to the police, but she didn't. She left her lover and went back to her husband."

"In other words, Samuel forced her to end it and stay with him?"

"It's possible. After that episode, she became quite distant toward me. She said Samuel didn't want her to see me anymore."

"And did she obey him?"

"Yes."

"Mrs Grand, forgive me for asking you this question straight out, but do you think Samuel Padalin might have killed his wife?"

Kate Grand was silent for a moment, then said:

"I was always surprised that the police didn't take a look at his life insurance."

"His life insurance?"

"One month before his wife died, Samuel took out a big life insurance policy for the two of them. It was for a million dollars. I know that because my husband dealt with it all. He's an underwriter."

"And did Padalin get the money?"

"Of course. How do you think he was able to pay for his house in Southampton?"

DEREK SCOTT

Early December 1994, at troop headquarters.

In his office, Major McKenna reads the letter I have just brought him.

"A transfer request, Derek? Where the hell do you want to go?"

"Just put me in administration," I suggested.

"A desk job?" the major said in a choked voice.

"I don't ever want to be out in the field again."

"For Chrissake, Derek, you're one of the best police officers I've ever known! Don't ruin your career on a whim."

"My career? What career, sir?"

"Listen, Derek," the major said in a kindly voice, "I understand how upset you are. Why don't you see the shrink? Or take a few weeks' leave?"

"I've had enough of being on leave, sir. I spend my time going over the same images in a loop."

"Derek, I can't put you in administration, it would be a waste."

The major and I stared at each other for a moment, then I said, "You're right, sir. Forget that letter."

"Now you're talking."

"I'll resign."

"Oh, no, not that! O.K., you can have a desk job. But only for a while. Then I want you back here as a detective."

The major assumed that, after a few weeks of boredom, I'd reconsider my decision and ask for my old job back.

As I was leaving his office, he said, "Any news of Jesse?"

"He doesn't want to see anybody, sir."

*

At home, Jesse was busy sorting through Natasha's things.

He had never envisaged living a day without her. Faced with the deep void that he could not fill, he alternated periods of clearing things out with periods of reassembling memories. Part of him wanted to turn the page, immediately, to throw everything out and forget it. At those times, he started filling cardboard boxes with all the objects that had a too powerful connection with her, intending them for the garbage. Then it took just a moment's pause, an object attracting his attention—a photograph frame, a pen without ink, an old university notebook—and everything would lurch and he would move on to his curator phase. He would take the object in his hand and look at it for a long time. He would tell himself that maybe it was better not to throw everything away, that he should keep a few souvenirs, to recall all that happiness, and he would put the object down on the table in full sight to preserve it. Then he would start taking back out of the cardboard box everything he had put in it. You're not going to throw this away, are you? he would ask himself. Or this? Oh, no, you're not going to do without the cup you bought at MoMa that she drank her tea in! Jesse ended up taking everything out of the boxes. And the living room, which had briefly been swept clean of all these objects, took on the appearance of a museum devoted to Natasha. Sitting on the couch, his grandparents watched him, eyes overflowing with tears, murmuring, "That's shit."

*

By mid-December, Darla had emptied the whole of Little Russia. The neon sign had been taken down and put in a dumpster, all the furniture sold off to pay the last few months' rent and allow the termination of the lease.

The removers took away the last chairs to deliver them to the restaurant that had bought them, while Darla watched, sitting on the sidewalk, in the cold. One of the removers came and brought her a cardboard box.

"We found this in a corner of the kitchen, we thought you might want to keep it."

Darla examined the contents of the box. There were notes made by Natasha, ideas for menus, her recipes, all the souvenirs of what they had been planning. There was also a photograph of Jesse, Natasha, Derek, and her. She took the photograph in her hands and looked at it for a long time.

"I'll keep the photograph," she said to the remover. "Thanks. You can throw away the rest."

"Really?"

"Yes."

The remover nodded and walked back to his van. Darla, devastated, burst into tears.

Everything had to be forgotten.

JESSE ROSENBERG

Friday, August 1, 2014
Six days after opening night

Had Meghan threatened to leave Samuel Padalin? Maybe Padalin hadn't taken it well and had killed her, pocketing his wife's life insurance in the process.

He was not at home when we arrived that morning. We decided to go to see him in his place of work. Advised of our arrival by the receptionist, he led us without a word to his office and waited until he had closed the door behind us before exploding.

"Are you crazy, coming here unannounced like this? Do you want me to lose my job?"

He seemed furious.

"Are you a man who loses his temper easily, Mr Padalin?" Betsy said.

"Why do you ask me that?"

"Because you used to beat your wife."

Padalin was aghast. "What are you talking about?"

"Don't pretend to be surprised," Betsy said.

"I'd like to know who told you."

"That hardly matters."

"Listen, about a month before she died, Meghan and I had a big argument, that's true. I slapped her, and I shouldn't have. I went off the rails. I have no excuse. But that was the only time."

"What was the argument about?"

"I found out that Meghan had been cheating on me. I wanted to leave her."

*   *   *

499

Monday, June 6, 1994

That morning, as Samuel Padalin was finishing his coffee and getting ready to leave for work, his wife joined him in her robe.

"Aren't you going to work today?" he said.

"I have a fever, I don't feel well. I just called Cody and told him I wouldn't be coming in today."

"Good idea," Padalin said, gulping down the rest of his coffee. "Go back to bed."

He put his cup in the sink, kissed his wife on the forehead, and set off for work.

He probably would never have known a thing if he hadn't had to return home one hour later to pick up a file he had taken home to study during the weekend and had left on the living room table.

As he got to the street, he saw Meghan coming out of the house. She was wearing a beautiful summer dress and elegant sandals. She was smiling and seemed in a good mood, nothing like the woman he had said goodbye to an hour earlier. He stopped and watched her as she got in her car. She hadn't seen him. He decided to follow her.

Meghan drove to Bridgehampton, unaware that her husband was a few cars behind her. After driving along the main street of the town, she turned onto the road to Sag Harbor, then, after another two hundred yards, turned into the sumptuous property of the Northern Rose Hotel. It was a highly regarded but discreet little hotel, much appreciated by celebrities from New York City. When she got to the majestic building with its colonnades, she entrusted her vehicle to the valet and went into the hotel. Samuel did the same, giving his wife a head start in order not to be seen. Once in the building, he couldn't find her either in the bar or in the restaurant. She had gone directly upstairs. Obviously to join someone in a room.

That day, Padalin did not go back to work. He waited for his wife in the hotel parking lot for hours. When she did not reappear, he returned home and hurried to look at her diaries. He discovered to his horror that she had been meeting with this guy at the Northern Rose Hotel for several months. Who was he? She said she had met him at the New Year's gala. They had been there together, so he must have seen him. It might even be someone he knew. He felt like throwing up. He went back to the car and drove for a long time, not knowing what he should do.

By the time he got back home, Meghan had returned. He found her in bed, in her nightdress, pretending to be ill.

"My poor darling," he said, trying very hard to keep his voice steady, "aren't you feeling any better?"

"No," she said in a thin voice, "I haven't been able to get out of bed all day."

Padalin could contain himself no longer. He exploded. He told her that he knew everything, that he had been to the Northern Rose, that she had joined a man there in a room. Meghan did not deny it.

"Get out!" Padalin screamed. "You disgust me!"

She burst into tears. "Forgive me, Samuel!" she begged him, ashen-faced.

"Get out of here! Get out of this house! Take your things and get out, I never want to see you again!"

"Samuel, don't do this to me, I beg you! I don't want to lose you. You're the only man I love."

"You should have thought of that before sleeping with this man you met."

"It was the biggest mistake of my life, Samuel! I don't feel anything for him!"

"You make me sick. I read your diaries, I saw what you wrote about him. I saw all the times you met with him at the Northern Rose!"

"You've stopped caring about me, Samuel! I don't feel important! I don't feel looked at. When he tried his charms on me, I liked it. Yes, we've met regularly. Yes, we've flirted. But I've never slept with him!"

"Oh, so it's my fault now?"

"No, I'm just saying that sometimes when I'm with you I feel alone."

"I read that you met him at the New Year's Eve party. So you did it right under my eyes! Does that mean I know the guy? Who is he?"

501

"It doesn't matter," Meghan sobbed, no longer sure if she should talk or keep quiet.

"*It doesn't matter?* I can't believe this!"

"Samuel, don't leave me, I beg you!"

The tone became more heated. Meghan reproached her husband for not being romantic, for neglecting her, and Padalin, exasperated, finally said to her:

"I don't excite you? Do you think you excite me? You have no life, you have nothing to tell, apart from your dull little stories about the bookstore and all those things you imagine in your head."

At these words, deeply hurt, Meghan spat in her husband's face, and he instinctively gave her a violent slap. Shocked, Meghan bit into her tongue. She felt blood fill her mouth. She was stunned. She grabbed her car keys and ran off in her nightdress.

*   *   *

"Meghan returned home the next day," Padalin told us in his office. "She begged me not to leave her, she swore to me that this guy had been a terrible mistake, and because of him she'd realized how much she loved me. I decided to give my marriage a second chance. And you know what? It did us the world of good. I started paying her much more attention, she said she was happier. It transformed our relationship. We were more in tune than ever. We had two wonderful months, we were full of plans . . ."

"What about her lover?" Betsy said. "What became of him?"

"I have no idea. Meghan swore to me she had broken with him completely."

"How did he take it?"

"I don't know."

"And you never found out who he was?"

"No, never."

There was a moment's silence.

"So that's the real reason you never looked at her diaries again," Betsy said, "and why you kept them hidden away in your basement. Because they reminded you of that painful episode."

Padalin nodded, unable to speak. His throat was too knotted for him to utter another word.

"One last question, Mr Padalin," Derek asked. "Do you have a tattoo on your body?"

"No," he said.

"Can I ask you to lift your shirt? It's only a routine check."

In silence, Padalin removed his shirt. No tattoo.

What if the jilted lover, unable to bear losing Meghan, had killed her?

We could not rule that out. After our visit to Padalin, we drove to the Northern Rose Hotel in Bridgehampton. Obviously, when we told the receptionist that we were trying to identify a man who had booked a room in 1994, he laughed in our faces.

"We would like to see a record of all the reservations from 5 to 7 June and we'll study the names ourselves," I said.

"You don't seem to understand," he said. "You're talking about 1994. We still had handwritten registration in those days. There's no database I can use to help you."

As I was negotiating with the receptionist, Derek was walking up and down the lobby of the hotel. His gaze came to rest on the wall of honor, on which hung photographs of famous guests: actors, writers, directors. Suddenly, he took down one of them.

"Sir, what are you doing?" the receptionist said. "You can't—"

"Jesse! Betsy!" Derek cried. "Look at this!"

What he was holding was a photograph of Meta Ostrovski, twenty years younger, in a tuxedo, posing, all smiles, beside Meghan Padalin.

"When was this photograph taken?" I asked the receptionist.

"At the New Year's Eve party in December 1993. That man's the critic Ostrovski and—"

"Ostrovski was Meghan Padalin's lover!" Betsy said in an undertone.

We went straight to the Lake Palace. We ran into the manager as we entered the lobby.

"Already?" he said in surprise. "But I only just called."

"Called whom?" Derek asked.

"Why, the police. It's about Mr Ostrovski. He's just left the hotel, apparently called back urgently to the city. It was a chambermaid who informed me."

"Informed you of what, dammit?"

"Follow me."

The manager took us up to Suite 310, where Ostrovski had been staying, and opened the door with his passkey. We entered the room and discovered, stuck to the wall, a multitude of articles on the 1994 killings, Stephanie's disappearance, our investigation, and photographs of Meghan Padalin everywhere.

4

The Disappearance of Stephanie Mailer

SATURDAY, AUGUST 2 – MONDAY, AUGUST 4, 2014

JESSE ROSENBERG

Saturday, August 2, 2014
Seven days after opening night

Was Ostrovski the third man?

We had lost track of him since the day before. We knew only that he had gone back to the city. N.Y.P.D. surveillance cameras had filmed him as he drove his car across the bridge into Manhattan. But he had not gone home. His apartment was empty. His cell phone was off. His only family was an elderly sister, who likewise could not be traced or reached. So Derek and I had been staked out in the street next to his building for nearly twenty-four hours. It was all we could do for the time being.

All leads led to him. He had been Meghan Padalin's lover from January to June 1994. The Northern Rose Hotel had been able to confirm to us that he had stayed there quite regularly during that six-month period. That year, he had not come to the Hamptons only for the theater festival in Orphea. He had been there for months. That must have been for Meghan. So he had not been able to take it when she left him. He had killed her on opening night, along with the Gordon family, unwitting witnesses of the murder. He had had time to get there and back on foot and be in the theater for the beginning of the play. He had then been able to give his opinion of the performance to the newspapers so that everyone would know he had been in the Grand Theater. It was an impressive alibi.

A little earlier in the day, Betsy had been to see Miranda Bird, taking with her a photograph of Ostrovski, hoping that she would identify him, but she had been quite vague.

"It might have been him," she had said, "but it's hard to say for certain after all these years."

"Are you sure about the tattoo?" Betsy had asked. "If not, we need to know."

"I don't remember now," Miranda had said. "Maybe I was confused."

While we were waiting for Ostrovski in New York, Betsy, in the archive room of the *Chronicle*, had been going over everything in the file with Hayward and Bird. They wanted to make sure they had not neglected anything. They were tired and hungry. They had eaten almost nothing all day apart from the candies and chocolate bars that Bird would fetch at regular intervals from the drawer of his office upstairs, where there was apparently an unending supply.

Hayward couldn't take his eyes off the wall covered with notes, images, and press clippings. He finally said to Betsy:

"Why is the woman who could identify the killer not named? All that's written on the list of witnesses is: 'The woman in the motel on Route 16'. All the others are named."

"That's true," Bird said. "What's her name? It might be important."

"It's Jesse who's dealing with that," Betsy said. "You'll have to ask him. Anyway, she doesn't remember anything. Let's not waste time on it."

But Hayward would not let go.

"I looked in the State Police file from 1994. This witness isn't there. Is this a new element?"

"You'll have to ask Jesse," Betsy said again.

Since Hayward kept insisting, Betsy asked Bird if he could fetch some more candies. Once he had left the room, she took advantage of his absence to sum up the situation to Hayward, hoping he would understand how important it was to not mention that witness again in front of Bird.

"Oh, my God," Hayward said in a near-whisper. "I can't believe it. Michael's wife worked as a prostitute for that bastard Fold?"

"Keep your mouth shut, Kirk," Betsy said. "If you don't, I swear I'll kneecap you."

Betsy already regretted telling him. She could see him blurting it out. Bird came back into the room with a bag of candies.

"So, what about this witness?" he said.

Betsy smiled. "We're on to the next point. We were talking about Ostrovski."

"I can't see Ostrovski wiping out an entire family," Bird said.

"We should never trust appearances, you know," Hayward said. "Sometimes we think we know people and then we discover incredible secrets about them."

"Never mind," Betsy cut in, glaring at Hayward. "We'll know exactly where we are once Jesse and Derek have laid their hands on Ostrovski."

*

It was 8.30, outside Ostrovski's building.

Derek and I were about to abandon our stakeout when we saw Ostrovski coming along the street, walking at a steady pace. We leaped out of our car, guns at the ready, and hurried to intercept him.

"You're crazy, Jesse," Ostrovski complained as I pinned him to the wall and handcuffed him.

"We know everything, Ostrovski!" I cried. "It's over!"

"What everything do you know?"

"You killed Meghan Padalin and the Gordons. As well as Stephanie Mailer and Cody Springfield."

"Are you sick or something?" Ostrovski said.

A crowd of onlookers was forming around us. Some were filming the scene on their cell phones.

"Help me!" Ostrovski called to them. "These two aren't police officers! They're crazy people!"

We were forced to show our badges to the crowd. We pulled Ostrovski inside the building to be somewhere quiet.

"I'd like you to tell me what's wrong with you," Ostrovski said. "How could you think I killed those poor people?"

"We saw the wall of your suite, Ostrovski, with the press clippings and the photographs of Meghan."

"There's your proof right there that I didn't kill anyone! I've spent the last twenty years trying to understand what happened."

"Or it could be you've spent the last twenty years trying to cover your tracks," Derek said. "That's why you commissioned Stephanie, isn't it? You wanted to see if it was possible to trace the crimes back to you, and when it looked like she was doing precisely that, you killed her."

"Oh, goddammit! I was just trying to do the job you two incompetents should have done in 1994."

"Don't take us for idiots. You were Jeremiah Fold's slave! That's why you asked Mayor Gordon to get rid of him for you."

"I'm nobody's slave!" Ostrovski spat at me.

"Enough of this bullshit," Derek said. "Why did you leave Orphea so suddenly if you have nothing to hide?"

"Since you ask, my sister had a stroke yesterday. She had to have an emergency operation. I wanted to be with her. I spent all night and all day in the hospital. She's the only family I have left."

"Which hospital?"

"New York Presbyterian."

Derek contacted the hospital to check. Ostrovski wasn't lying to us. I immediately removed his handcuffs.

"Why are you so obsessed with those killings?" I said.

"Because I loved Meghan, dammit!" Ostrovski cried. "Is that so hard to comprehend? I loved her and she was taken from me! You can't know what it is to lose the love of your life!"

I stared at him for a long time. There was a terribly sad light in his eyes. I finally said:

"I know it only too well."

Ostrovski was out of the picture. We had wasted time and precious energy, and now we had only twenty-four hours left to solve the case.

If we didn't hand over the killer to Major McKenna by Monday morning, it would be the end of our careers.

We had one remaining option: Steven Bergdorf. We had allowed him to return home to his family in New York City on condition he did not leave the state. Once the editor of the *Orphea Chronicle*, and formerly Stephanie Mailer's employer, he had left Orphea soon after the 1994 killings, then had come back to take part in the play that was supposed to reveal the name of the murderer. We went to his apartment in Brooklyn. We drummed for a long time on his door. No answer. As we were thinking of breaking it down, a neighbor appeared on the landing and said:

"No point knocking like that, the Bergdorfs have left."

"Left?" I said in surprise. "When?"

"Day before yesterday. I saw them from my window, getting into his car."

"Steven Bergdorf, too?"

"Yes, Steven, too. With his family."

"But he's not supposed to leave New York State," Derek said.

"That's not my problem," the neighbor replied. "No doubt they went somewhere in the Hudson Valley."

Derek and I issued a missing persons bulletin for Steven Bergdorf, then decided to return to Orphea. I informed Betsy and we set off.

In the archive room, Betsy hung up.

"That was Jesse," she told Bird and Hayward. "Apparently, Ostrovski has nothing to do with any of this."

"Just as I thought," Bird said. "So what do we do now?"

"We should grab a bite to eat. It looks like it could be a long night."

"Let's go to the Kodiak Grill," Bird suggested.

"Great," Hayward said. "I'd die for a good steak."

"No, we'll have to go without you, Kirk," Betsy said, afraid that he could not be trusted to be discreet. "Someone has to stay here on call."

"On call?" Hayward said. "Why?"

"You're staying here and that's it."

She and Bird left the building by the back door and the alleyway and got in Betsy's car.

Hayward cursed at finding himself alone once again. He thought of the months he'd spent in the basement of the police station. He searched through the documents scattered on the table in front of him and plunged into the police file. He helped himself to the remaining candies.

Betsy and Bird were driving down Main Street.

"Do you mind if we swing by my place?" Bird said. "I want to say goodnight to my daughters before they go to bed. I've hardly seen them this past week."

"Gladly," Betsy said, veering in the direction of Bridgehampton.

When they got to the Birds' house, Betsy saw that all the lights were off.

"Isn't there anyone in?" Bird said, surprised.

Betsy parked outside the house. "Maybe your wife went out with the children."

"They must have gone for a pizza. I'll call them."

Bird took out his cell phone and cursed on seeing the screen: no bars.

"There's been bad reception here for a while," he said.

"I don't have any coverage either," Betsy said.

"Wait here a minute. I'll run inside and call my wife from the land-line."

"Do you mind if I come in at the same time and use your bathroom?"

"Of course not. Come."

They went into the house. Bird showed Betsy where the bathroom was and picked up the phone.

*

Derek and I were approaching Orphea when we got a radio call. The operator informed us that a man named Kirk Hayward was trying desperately to reach us but didn't have our cell numbers. The call was passed on to us by radio and we suddenly heard Hayward's voice echoing in the car.

"Jesse, the keys are here!"

"What keys?"

"I'm in Bird's office at the *Chronicle*. I found them."

We couldn't figure out what Kirk was talking about.

"What did you find, Kirk? Speak clearly!"

"I found Stephanie Mailer's keys!"

Hayward explained that he had gone upstairs to Bird's office to look for more chocolate. Rummaging through one of the drawers, he had come across a bunch of keys attached to a yellow plastic ball. He had seen it before somewhere. Searching his memory, he recalled being in the Beluga Bar with Stephanie Mailer as she was leaving, when her purse had fallen on the floor. The contents of the purse had scattered. He had picked up her keys to give them back to her. He remembered that key ring perfectly.

"Are you sure they're Stephanie's keys?" I said.

"Yes, in fact there's a car key with them. A Mazda. What kind of car did Stephanie drive?"

"A Mazda. They're her keys. Don't say anything, just do everything you can to keep Michael there."

"He's gone. He's with Betsy."

*

In the Birds' house, Betsy came out of the bathroom. Everything was quiet. She walked across the living room. No sign of Bird. Her gaze fell on some framed photographs arranged on a chest of drawers. Photographs of the family, over the years. The births of the daughters, vacations. Betsy noticed a photograph in which Miranda Bird looked especially young. She was with Michael, it was Christmas time. In the background was a fir tree with decorations, and through the window you could see snow outside. In the bottom right-hand corner of the picture was the date, as all photographs had in the days when they were developed in stores. Betsy moved her face closer: *December 23, 1994.* She felt her heart start to pound. Miranda had told her she had met her husband several years after the death of Fold. She had lied.

Betsy looked around. The house was silent. Where was Bird? Anxiety took hold of her. She put her hand on the grip of her gun and headed cautiously for the kitchen. There was nobody there. Everything seemed inexplicably deserted. She took out her gun and entered a dark corridor. She pressed the light switch, but the light didn't come on. Suddenly, she received a blow across her back that threw her to the floor and made her drop her gun. She tried to turn over, but her face was immediately sprinkled with some kind of asphyxiant. She screamed in pain. Her eyes were burning. She received a blow on the head, which knocked her out.

She sank into a black hole.

*

Derek and I had put out a general alert. Montagne had dispatched men to the Kodiak Grill and the Bird residence. But Betsy and Michael were nowhere to be found. When we finally got to the house, the officers on the scene showed us fresh bloodstains.

Just then, Miranda Bird got back from the pizzeria with her daughters.

"What's going on?" she said when she saw the officers.

"Where's Michael?" I cried.

"I've no idea. He called me earlier and said he was here with Betsy."

"And where were you?"

"With my daughters, we went for a pizza. What the hell's going on, Captain?"

When Betsy came to, her hands were cuffed behind her back and there was a bag over her head that stopped her from seeing anything. She forced herself not to panic. From the sounds and vibrations, she realized that she was lying on the back seat of a moving car.

She deduced that the car was driving along an untarred road, presumably of earth or gravel. Suddenly, the vehicle stopped. Betsy heard a noise. The back door opened abruptly. She was lifted and dragged out onto the ground. She could see nothing. She didn't know where she was. But she could hear frogs: she was near the lake.

*

In the Birds' living room, where the smell of tear gas was still evident, Miranda was finding it hard to take in what she was being told.

"How can you possibly think Michael was involved in any of this? It may be his blood you found here!"

"Stephanie Mailer's car and house keys were in his desk," I said.

Miranda refused to believe it. "You're making a mistake. You're wasting precious time. Michael may be in danger."

I joined Derek in the next room. He had a map of the area open in front of him, and was talking with Dr Ranjit Singh on the telephone.

"The killer is intelligent and methodical," Singh said over the loudspeaker. "He knows he can't go very far with Betsy, and he won't want to risk running into police patrol cars. He's a very cautious person, remember. He wants to limit the risks and avoid a confrontation at all costs."

"So you think he's still in the Orphea area?" I said.

"I'm sure of it. Within a radius he's familiar with. A place where he feels safe."

"Could he have done the same thing with Stephanie?" Derek said, studying the map.

"Probably so."

Derek circled with a marker pen the beach close to where Stephanie's car had been found.

"If the killer arranged to meet with Stephanie in that place, it means he was planning to take her somewhere near there."

With my finger, I followed Route 22 as far as Stag Lake, which I circled in red. Then I took the map to show Miranda.

"Do you have another house in the area?" I said. "A family house, a cabin, a place where your husband could take shelter?"

"My husband? But—"

"Answer my question!"

Miranda examined the map. She looked at Stag Lake and then pointed to a nearby stretch of water: Beaver Lake.

"Michael likes going there," she said. "There's a landing stage with a boat. You can get over to a lovely little island. We often picnic there with the girls. There's never anybody there. Michael says you can be alone in the world there."

Derek and I looked at each other and, without needing to speak, ran to our car.

*

Betsy had been thrown into what she thought was a boat. She pretended to be still unconscious. She felt the movement of the water and heard the sound of oars. She was being taken somewhere, but where?

Derek and I were driving flat out along Route 56. We soon had Stag Lake in view.

"There's a turn-off on your right," Derek said, cutting the siren. "A dirt track."

We only just spotted it. I turned onto it and accelerated like a madman. I soon saw Betsy's car parked by the water, beside a landing stage. I hit the brakes and we got out of the car. Despite the darkness, we made out a boat on the lake, heading toward the island. We took out our guns. "Stop! Police!" I shouted, and fired a warning shot.

In response, we heard Betsy's voice from the boat, calling for help. The figure holding the oars struck her a blow. Betsy screamed. Derek and I plunged into the lake. We just had time to see Betsy being flung overboard. She went straight down, then tried, just with the strength in her legs, to come back up to the surface for air.

Derek and I swam as fast as we could. In the failing light, it was impossible to make out the figure in the boat, who was going around us, back toward the cars. We couldn't stop him: we had to save Betsy. We gathered our remaining strength to reach her, just as Betsy, exhausted, let herself sink to the bottom of the lake.

Derek dived down to the bottom. I did the same. Everything was opaque around us. At last, Derek touched Betsy's body. He grabbed an arm and managed to bring her up to the surface. I came to his aid and somehow we dragged Betsy to the shore of the little island and pulled her onto dry land. She coughed and spat out water. She was alive.

On the other shore, the boat had pulled up to the landing stage. We saw the figure get into Betsy's car and drive away.

*

Two hours later, the attendant at an isolated gas station saw a man covered in blood come into the store, in a panic. It was Michael Bird, his hands bound with a rope. "Call the police!" he cried. "He's coming, he's after me!"

JESSE ROSENBERG
Sunday, August 3, 2014
Eight days after opening night

In his hospital room, where he had spent the night under observation, Bird told us how he had been attacked at his house.

"I was in the kitchen. I had just phoned my wife. Suddenly, I heard a noise outside. Betsy was in the bathroom, so it couldn't have been her. I went out to see what was going on, and was sprayed with tear gas before receiving a violent blow full in the face. I blacked out. When I came to, I was in the trunk of a car, with my hands tied. The trunk suddenly opened. I pretended to be unconscious. I was dragged along the ground. I could smell earth and vegetation. I heard a noise, like someone digging. I half opened my eyes. I was in the middle of a forest. A few yards away was a guy in a hood, digging a hole. It was my grave. I thought about my wife, my daughters. I didn't want to die like that. With the energy of despair, I stood up and started running. I ran down a slope, and ran as fast as I could through the forest. I could hear him behind me, running after me. I managed to get some distance from him. Then I came to a road. I followed it, hoping to see a car, but finally spotted a gas station."

Derek, having listened carefully to Bird's story, said, "Enough of this bullshit, Michael. We found Stephanie Mailer's keys in your desk drawer."

Bird looked amazed. "Stephanie Mailer's keys? What are you talking about? That's completely absurd."

"And yet it's the truth. A whole bunch of them, the keys to her apartment, the newspaper offices, her car, and a self-storage facility."

"That's quite simply impossible," Bird said, seeming genuinely astonished by all this.

"Was it you, Michael?" I said. "Did you kill Stephanie?"

518

"No, Jesse, of course not! I mean, it's ridiculous! Who found those keys in my desk?"

We would rather he hadn't asked that question. Since the keys had not been found by a police officer in the course of an official search, they had no value as evidence. But I had to tell him the truth.

"It was Kirk Hayward."

"Hayward? Hayward searched my desk and just happened to come across Stephanie's keys? That makes no sense! Was he alone?"

"Yes."

"Listen, I don't know what it means, but I think Hayward is pulling the wool over your eyes. Just as he did with that play of his. So what's happening? Am I under arrest?"

"No."

Stephanie Mailer's keys were not valid evidence. Had Hayward really found them in Bird's desk as he claimed? Or had he had them with him from the start? Unless it was Bird who was trying to pull the wool over our eyes and who had staged the attack on himself? It was Hayward's word against Bird's. One of them was lying. But which one?

The wound to Bird's face was serious and had required several stitches. Blood had been found on the front steps of his house. His story held up. The fact that Betsy had been thrown onto the back seat of her car was also consistent with Bird's version, since he claimed he had been put in the trunk. In addition, we had searched his house as well as the offices of the *Chronicle* and had found absolutely nothing.

After our visit with Bird, Derek and I went to see Betsy in a nearby room. She, too, had spent the night in the hospital. She had pulled through quite well. She had an ugly bruise on her forehead and a black eye, but she had escaped the worst. The little island had been searched and Costico's decomposing body had been found buried in a shallow grave. He had been shot.

Betsy had not seen her attacker, nor heard the sound of his voice. All she remembered was the tear gas that had blinded her and the blows that had knocked her out. When she had come to, she had a canvas bag over her head. As for her car, in which there might possibly be finger-prints, it had still not been recovered.

Betsy was ready to leave the hospital and we offered to drive her home. In the corridor, we told her Bird's version, and she seemed doubtful.

"The attacker left him in the trunk of the car while he rowed me to that island? Why?"

"Maybe the boat wouldn't have taken the weight of three people," I suggested, "and he was planning to make two trips."

"When you got to the lake, did you not look in the car?"

"No," I said. "We dived straight into the water."

"So we can't do anything to Bird?"

"Nothing without cast-iron evidence."

"If Bird's blameless," Betsy went on, "why did Miranda lie to me? She told me she met Michael a few years after Fold died. But in their living room, I saw a photograph from Christmas 1994. That's just six months later. By that time, she was back with her parents in New York. She could only have met Michael when she was working for Fold."

"You think Bird could be the guy from the motel?" I said.

"Yes, I do. And what's more, I think Miranda made up that stuff about the tattoo to throw everyone off the scent."

Just then, who should we see but Miranda Bird, who had just arrived at the hospital.

"My God, Betsy, your face!" she said. "I'm sorry about what happened. How are you feeling?"

"I'm feeling fine."

Miranda turned to us. "You see, Michael had nothing to do with it. Poor man, what state is he in?"

"We found Betsy in the very place you suggested," I said.

"It could have been anyone! Everybody in the area knows Badger Lake. Do you have any evidence?"

We had nothing concrete. I felt as if I was reliving the investigation into Tennenbaum in 1994.

"You lied to me, Miranda," Betsy said. "You told me you met Michael several years after Jeremiah Fold died, but that's not true. You met him when you were in Ridgesport."

Miranda said nothing. She seemed disconcerted. Derek spotted an empty waiting room and suggested we all go in there. We sat Miranda down on a couch.

"When did you meet Michael?" Betsy insisted.

"I don't remember," Miranda said.

"Was Michael the man in the motel, the one who defied Costico?"

"Betsy, I—"

"Answer my question, Miranda. Don't force me to take you to the station."

Miranda's face fell apart. "Yes," she said. "I don't know how you found out about that incident at the motel, but yes, that was Michael. I met him when I was a hostess at the club, at the end of 1993. Costico wanted me to trick him into going to the motel, like all the others. But Michael wouldn't let himself be caught in the trap."

"So when I talked to you about it," Betsy said, "you made up that story about a tattoo to put us off the scent. Why?"

"To protect Michael. If you had found out that he was the man in the motel . . ." Miranda broke off, realizing she had said too much.

"Go on, Miranda. If we'd found out that he was the man in the motel, what else would we have discovered?"

A tear ran down Miranda's cheek. "You would have discovered that Michael killed Jeremiah Fold."

We were coming back to the same point: Fold, who we knew had been killed by Mayor Gordon.

"Michael didn't kill Jeremiah Fold," Betsy said. "We're sure of that. It was Mayor Gordon who killed him."

Miranda's face lit up. "It wasn't Michael?" she said, as happy as if this whole story was just a nightmare.

"Miranda, why did you think Michael had killed Fold?"

"After the incident with Costico, I saw Michael again a few times.

We fell in love. And Michael got it into his head to free me from Fold's clutches. All these years, I thought . . . Oh, God, I'm so relieved!"

"You never talked about it with Michael?"

"After Jeremiah died, we never talked about what had happened in Ridgesport. We had to forget everything. It was the only way to mend things. We wiped it all from our memories and we turned to the future. We succeeded. Look at us, we're so happy."

*

We spent the day in Betsy's house, trying to pull together all the elements of the case.

The more we thought about it, the more obvious it was that everything pointed to Bird. He was close to Stephanie Mailer, he had had special access to the Grand Theater and could have hidden the murder weapon there, and he had followed our investigation closely from the archive room of his newspaper, having himself offered to put it at our disposal. This had allowed him to eliminate all those who might bring him down as the investigation advanced. Despite this bundle of clues, without concrete evidence we could not touch him. A good lawyer would easily get him free.

Late that afternoon, we were surprised to see Major McKenna pull up outside Betsy's house. He was there to remind us of the threat hanging over Derek and me since the start of the week.

"If you don't bring this case to a conclusion by tomorrow morning, I'll be obliged to ask for your resignations. That's what the governor wants. This has gone on too long."

"Everything indicates that Michael Bird could be our man," I said.

"I don't want indications, I want evidence! Cast-iron evidence! Do I need to remind you of the Ted Tennenbaum fiasco?"

"We found the keys—"

"Forget the keys, Jesse. They aren't legal proof, as you know perfectly well. No court would admit it. The D.A. wants a cast-iron case, nobody wants to take risks. If you don't close this case, it'll be closed for you. It's gotten worse than the plague. If you think Michael Bird is the culprit, get him to talk. You need a confession, however you get it."

"But how?" I asked.

"Put pressure on him. Find his weak spot."

"If Miranda thought Michael had killed Fold to free her," Derek said, "that means he's ready to do anything to protect his wife."

"What are you getting at?" I said.

"That we shouldn't be focusing on Michael, but on Miranda. And I think I have an idea."

In the late evening, I had a call from Chief Montagne who reported that a Highway Patrol officer had arrested Steven Bergdorf in the Adirondack Mountains. I thanked Montagne and asked him to ensure that Bergdorf called the station in Orphea without failure the following afternoon.

JESSE ROSENBERG

Monday, August 4, 2014
Nine days after opening night

We got to the Birds' house at seven in the morning. Bird had been allowed home the previous evening.

It was Miranda who opened the door to us. Derek immediately handcuffed her.

"Miranda Bird," I said, "you're under arrest for lying to a police officer and obstructing a criminal investigation."

Michael came running from the kitchen, followed by his children. "You're crazy!" he yelled, trying to get between us.

The children started crying. I didn't like doing what we were doing, but we had no choice. I reassured the children, trying to keep Bird at a distance, while Derek led Miranda away.

"The situation is serious," I told Bird, in a confidential tone. "Miranda's lies have had serious consequences. The D.A. is furious. She'll be lucky to get away without a prison sentence."

"But this is a nightmare!" Bird said. "Let me talk to the D.A., there must be some misunderstanding."

"I'm sorry, Michael. There's nothing you can do, unfortunately. You'll have to be strong. For your children."

I left the house to join Derek in our car. Bird ran after us.

"Let her go!" he cried. "Let my wife go, and I'll confess everything."

"What do you have to confess?" I said.

"I'll tell you if you promise to leave my wife alone."

"It's a deal."

Derek removed the cuffs from Miranda's wrists.

"I want a written agreement from the D.A.," Bird said. "A guarantee that Miranda is under no risk."

"I can arrange that," I said.

One hour later, in an interrogation room at troop headquarters, Michael Bird read a letter signed by the D.A. exempting his wife from all prosecution for having deliberately misled us in our investigation. He signed it and confessed, with something like relief in his voice.

"I killed Meghan. And the Gordons. And Stephanie. And Cody Springfield. And Costico. I killed them all."

There was a long silence. After twenty years, we finally had a confession. I urged Michael to tell us more.

"Why did you do it?"

He shrugged. "I've confessed. That's all that matters, isn't it?"

"We want to understand. You don't fit the profile of a murderer, Michael. You're a kind family man. How does a man like you end up killing seven people?"

He hesitated for a moment.

"I don't even know where to begin."

"Begin at the beginning."

Searching deep in his memories, he said, "It began one evening at the end of 1993."

* * *

Early December 1993

It was the first time Bird had been in Ridge's Club. This wasn't at all his kind of place. But a friend of his had urged him to come with him. "There's a singer there with an amazing voice," he had said. But when they arrived, it wasn't the singer who captivated Michael, but the hostess on the way in. That was Miranda. It was love at first sight. Michael was under her spell. He started going regularly to Ridge's Club, just to see her. He was besotted.

At first, Miranda rejected his advances. She made it clear to him that he wasn't to approach her. He thought she was just playing hard to get. He didn't see the danger. Eventually, Costico noticed him and told Miranda to entice him into a trap at the motel. She refused at first. But a session with the bowl of cold water persuaded her to agree. One evening in January, she arranged to meet Michael in the motel. He joined her there the following afternoon. They both got undressed and only then did Miranda, lying naked on the bed, say, "I'm underage, I'm still at school, does that turn you on?" Bird was stunned. "You told me you were nineteen. You're crazy to have lied to me. I can't stay in this room with you." He tried to get dressed but then he saw a huge man coming out from behind a curtain: it was Costico. There was a struggle, and Bird managed to get out of the room, naked, but with his car keys. Costico rushed out after him to the parking lot. Bird had time to open the door of his car and reach for a canister of tear gas. He neutralized Costico and escaped. But Costico tracked him down without difficulty and gave him a regulation beating in his own home, before bundling him into a car and driving, in the middle of the night, to Ridge's Club, which had by then closed. Bird found himself in the office. With Fold. Miranda was there, too. Fold told Bird he would have to work for him from now on. He was his slave. "As long as you do as you're told, your girlfriend here will be safe." At this point, Costico grabbed Miranda by the hair and dragged her over to the bowl of cold water. He plunged her head in the water for several seconds, and repeated this until Bird promised to cooperate.

*　　*　　*

"And so you became one of Jeremiah Fold's slaves," I said.

"Yes," Bird said. "I was even his favorite slave. I couldn't refuse him anything. If I ever seemed unwilling, he'd take it out on Miranda."

"And you didn't think to go to the police?"

"It was too risky. Jeremiah had photographs of my entire family. One day, I went to see my parents, and there he was, in their living room, drinking tea. I was afraid for Miranda, too. I was crazy about her. And it was mutual. At night, I would come to see her in her motel room. I wanted to persuade her to run away with me, but she was too frightened. She said Fold would track us down. She said, 'If Jeremiah finds out we talk, he'll kill both of us. He'll dispose of us, and nobody will ever find our bodies.' I promised her I'd get her out of there. But things got complicated for me. Fold had set his sights on Café Athena."

"He had started to put the squeeze on Tennenbaum?"

"That's right. And guess who he entrusted with the task of collecting the money every week? Me. I knew Ted a little. Everyone knows everyone in Orphea. When I told him it was Fold who'd sent me, he took out a gun and stuck the barrel to my forehead. I thought he was going to kill me. I told him everything. I told him the life of a woman I loved depended on my cooperation. That was the one mistake that Fold made. He was always so meticulous, so attentive to details. He never imagined that Ted and I would join forces against him."

"The two of you decided to kill him," Derek said.

"Yes, but it was complicated. We didn't know how to go about it. Ted liked a fight, but he was no murderer. And besides, Fold had to be alone. We couldn't attack him in front of Costico or anyone else. So we decided to study his habits. Did he go for walks alone sometimes? Did he go running in the woods? We had to find the right moment to kill him and dispose of his body. But we soon discovered that the man was untouchable. He was more powerful than Ted and I could have imagined. His slaves spied on each other, he had an impressive intelligence network, he was in league with the police. He knew everything."

*   *   *

May 1994

Bird had been staked out for two days in his car near Fold's house, watching him, when suddenly the car door opened, and, before he could react, he was punched full in the face. It was Costico, who pulled him out of the car and dragged him to the club. Fold and Miranda were waiting in the office. Fold was furious. "You're spying on me," he said. "Are you planning to go to the police?" Bird swore he wasn't, but Fold wouldn't listen to him. He ordered Costico to beat him up. When they had finished with him, they started in on Miranda. The torture seemed interminable. Miranda was messed up so badly, she couldn't go out for weeks.

After that episode, and afraid they were being watched, Bird and Tennenbaum went on meeting in the greatest secrecy, in unlikely places a long way from Orphea, so as not to risk being seen together.

"It's impossible to kill Fold ourselves," Tennenbaum said. "We have to find someone who doesn't know anything about him and persuade that person to do it."

"Who would agree to do something like that?"

"Someone who needs a similar favor. We'll kill someone in return. Someone we don't know either. The police will never trace it back to us."

"Someone who's done nothing to us?" Bird said.

"Believe me," Tennenbaum said, "I'm not happy about suggesting this, but I don't see any other way out."

On reflection, Bird thought it was probably the only way to save Miranda. He was ready to do anything for her.

The problem was to find a partner, someone who had no connection with them. How to do that? They could hardly place a small ad.

Six weeks went by. In mid-June, just when they had despaired of finding someone, Tennenbaum contacted him.

"I think I've found our man."

"Who is he?"

"It's best you don't know."

*   *   *

"So you didn't know the identity of the partner Tennenbaum had found?" Derek said.

"That's right," Bird said. "Tennenbaum was the go-between, only he knew who the two killers would be. That way we'd cover our tracks. The police couldn't trace anything back to us since we didn't know each other's identity. Apart from Tennenbaum, but he had guts. To be sure we had no contact, Tennenbaum and this partner had agreed on a method for swapping the names of our victims. He had said to him something like, 'We mustn't speak again, we mustn't meet again. On July 1, go to the bookstore in Orphea. There's a room there where no-one ever goes, with books by local writers. Choose one, and write the name of the person in it. Not directly. Circle the first letters of words to spell out the name. Then turn down the corners of the pages. That'll be the signal."

"And you wrote the name Jeremiah Fold," Betsy said.

"That's right, in Hayward's play. Our partner had chosen a book about the theater festival. In it was the name Meghan Padalin. The nice bookstore assistant. That was who we were supposed to kill. We started watching her movements. She went running every evening as far as Penfield Crescent. We thought we'd knock her down in a car. We still had to figure out when to do it. Our partner clearly had the same idea as us. On July 16 Jeremiah died in a traffic accident. But things might have gone badly. He had taken a long time to die, and might have been saved. That was the kind of pitfall we had to avoid. Ted and I were both good shots. My father had taught me to use a rifle when I was very young. He told me I had a real talent. So we decided to shoot Meghan. It was safer."

*　　*　　*

July 20, 1994

Tennenbaum met with Bird in an empty parking lot by the beach.

"We have to do it, my friend. We have to kill that girl."

"Can't we just drop it?" Michael said with a grimace. "We got what we wanted."

"I'd like to, but we have to keep our end of the bargain. If our partner thinks we've fucked him around, he could come after us. I heard Meghan talking in the bookstore. She's not going to the opening of the festival. She'll be jogging, same as every evening, and the neighborhood will be deserted. It's the perfect opportunity."

"So we'll do it at the opening of the festival," Bird murmured.

"Yes," Tennenbaum said, covertly putting a Beretta in his hand. "Here, take this. The serial number is filed off. Nobody will trace it back to you."

"Why me? Why don't you do it?"

"Because I know the other guy's identity. It has to be you, it's the only way to cover our tracks. Even if the police question you, you won't be able to tell them anything. Believe me, the plan is perfect. And besides, you told me you were a good shot, right? You just have to kill that girl and we'll both be free of everything at last."

*   *   *

"So on July 30, 1994, you went ahead with it," Derek said.

"Yes. Tennenbaum said he'd come with me and asked me to meet with him at the theater. He was the duty fire officer that night. He'd parked his van outside the stage door so everyone noticed it and he could use it as an alibi. We went together to the Penfield neighborhood. Everything was deserted. Meghan was already in the park. I remember looking at my watch: 7.10. On July 30, 1994, at 7.10, I was going to take the life of a human being. I took a deep breath, then ran like a madman toward Meghan. She didn't realize what was happening. I fired twice, and missed. She ran toward the mayor's house. I got into position, waited for her to be in my sights, and fired again. She fell. I went to her and put a bullet in her head. To make sure she was dead. I felt almost relieved. It was unreal. At that moment, I saw the mayor's son looking at me from behind the living room curtain. What was he doing there? Why wasn't he in the Grand Theater with his parents? It all happened in a fraction of a second. I didn't think. I ran to the house, in a state of panic. The adrenaline made me feel ten times stronger. I kicked the door in and found

530

myself face to face with the mayor's wife, Leslie. The gun almost went off by itself. She collapsed. Then I aimed at the son who was running to hide. I fired several times, and at the mother again, to be sure they were dead. Then I heard a noise in the kitchen. It was Mayor Gordon, who was trying to escape through the back door. What could I do except kill him, too? By the time I came out, Ted had gone. I went back to the Grand Theater to mingle with the opening night crowd and be seen. I still had the gun on me, I didn't know where or how to get rid of it."

There was a long silence.

"And then?" Derek said. "What happened after that?"

"I had no more contact with Ted. The police said the mayor was the target and Meghan was an innocent bystander. The investigation was going in another direction. We were in the clear. There was no way to trace it back to us."

"Except that Charlotte had borrowed Tennenbaum's van without his permission and gone to see Mayor Gordon just before . . . you got there . . ."

"We must have just missed her. It was only when a witness recognized the vehicle outside Café Athena that everything went wrong. Ted started to panic. He contacted me again. He said, 'Why did you kill all those people?' I said, 'Because they'd seen me.' That was when he said, 'Mayor Gordon was our partner! He was the one who killed Fold! He was the one who wanted us to kill Meghan! He and his family would never have talked!' Ted told me how, in mid-June, the mayor had become his ally."

* * *

Mid-June 1994

That day, Tennenbaum went to see Mayor Gordon to talk about Café Athena. He wanted to bury the hatchet. He could not bear the endless arguments anymore. Mayor Gordon received him in his living room. It was late afternoon. Through the window, Gordon saw someone in the park. From where he was, Tennenbaum could not see who it was. It was then that Gordon said in a somber tone:

"Some people shouldn't live."

"Like who?"

"It doesn't matter."

At that point, Tennenbaum sensed that Gordon might be the kind of person he was looking for. He decided to tell him of his plan.

* * *

"Without knowing it," Bird said, "I'd killed our partner. Our brilliant plan had turned into a fiasco. But I was convinced the police would never trace it to Ted, since he wasn't the murderer. I didn't know you'd track down the man who sold the Beretta, which would lead you to him. He hid for a while in my house. He gave me no choice. His van was in my garage. It would be discovered eventually. I was scared to death. If the police found it, I was done for, too. I finally threw him out, threatening him with the gun, which I had kept. Half an hour later, the police were chasing him. That was the day he died. The police were sure he was the killer. I was in the clear. I met up again with Miranda, and we've been together ever since. Nobody ever knew about her past. As far as her family was concerned, she had spent two years in a squat before returning home."

"Did Miranda know you'd killed Meghan and the Gordons?"

"No, she didn't know a thing. But she did think I had killed Fold."

"That's why she lied to me when I questioned her the other day," Betsy said.

"Yes, she made up that tattoo story to throw you off the scent. She knew the investigation was focusing on Fold, and she was afraid that would lead you to me."

"What about Stephanie Mailer?" Derek said.

"She showed up in Orphea one day and told me she was writing a book about the murders. She asked if she could look through the paper's archives. I offered her a job on the *Chronicle* so that I could keep an eye on her. I hoped she wouldn't discover anything. After all, nobody else had. For several months, she didn't get anywhere. I tried to put her off the track by disguising my voice and calling her from phone booths. I pointed her in the direction of the volunteers and the festival, which was a false lead. I would arrange to meet her at the Kodiak Grill and not show up. I was buying time for myself."

"And you tried to point us in the direction of the festival, too," I said.

"Yes. But Stephanie tracked down Kirk Hayward, who told her it was Meghan who was the target and not Gordon. She passed that on to me. She wanted to tell the State Police, but not before she had seen the case file. I had to do something, she was going to uncover the whole story. I made one last anonymous call, telling her there'd be a great revelation on June 23, and arranging to meet her at the Kodiak Grill."

"The day she came here to headquarters."

"I didn't know what I was going to do that night. I didn't know if I should speak to her, or run away. But I knew I didn't want to lose every-thing. She came to the Kodiak Grill at six o'clock, as agreed. I was sitting at a table at the back. I watched her all evening. Finally, at ten, she left. I had to do something. I called her from the phone booth. I told her to meet with me in the parking lot on the beach."

"And you went there."

"I said I was going to explain the whole thing, I was going to show her something very important. She got in my car."

"Were you planning to take her to the island on Badger Lake and kill her?"

"Yes, nobody would have found her there. But as we got to Stag Lake she realized what I was getting ready to do. I don't know how she knew. Instinct, I guess. She threw herself out of the car and ran through the forest, and I ran after her and caught up with her on the shore. I drowned her. I pushed the body in the water, and it went straight down. I went back to my car. Just then, a motorist passed on the road. I panicked and drove off. She had left her purse in the car. Her keys were in it. I went to her apartment and searched it."

"You wanted to get your hands on her research," Derek said. "But you didn't find anything. So you sent yourself a text message, using Stephanie's phone to make it look like she'd gone away for a while and to buy time. Then, although it wasn't discovered until a few days later, you faked a burglary at the newspaper offices to get her computer."

"That's correct," Bird said. "That night, I disposed of her purse and her cell phone. I kept her keys because I thought they might come in useful. Then, when you showed up in Orphea three days later, Jesse, I panicked. That evening, I went back to Stephanie's apartment, and searched it thoroughly. But then you arrived, although I thought you'd left town. I had no other choice but to attack you with tear gas and get away."

"And then you made sure you were closely involved with the play and the investigation," Derek said.

"Yes. And I had no choice but to kill Cody Springfield. I knew he'd told you about Bergdorf's book. It was in a copy of that book that Mayor Gordon had written Meghan's name. I started to imagine that everyone knew what I'd done in 1994."

"And you killed Costico, too, because he might have led us to you."

"Yes. When Miranda told me you had questioned her, I reckoned you'd go and talk to Costico. I didn't know if he would remember my name, but I couldn't take the risk. I followed him home from the club, to find out where he lived. I rang at his door, and pulled my gun on him. I waited until nightfall, then forced him to drive me to Badger Lake and row over to the island. Then I shot him and buried him there."

"And then it was the opening night of the play," Derek said. "Did you think Hayward knew your identity?"

"I wanted to be prepared for anything. I snuck my gun into the Theater the day before opening night. Before the search. Then I watched the performance, sitting on the gangway above the stage, ready to shoot at the cast."

"You shot Carolina, thinking she was about to reveal your name."

"I had become paranoid. I wasn't myself anymore."

"And what about me?" Betsy said.

"On Saturday night, when we went to my house, I really did want to see my daughters. I saw you come out of the bathroom and look at that photograph. I realized you had discovered something. After I managed to escape from Badger Lake, I left your car in the forest. I hit myself on the head with a stone and tied my hands with a length of rope I had found."

"And you did all this to keep your secret?" I said.

Bird looked me straight in the eyes. "When you've killed once, you can kill twice. And when you've killed twice, you can kill the whole world. There are no more limits."

*

"You were right, after all," Major McKenna said to us on the way out of the interrogation room. "Tennenbaum really was the murderer. But he wasn't the only one. Congratulations!"

"Thank you, sir," I said.

"Jesse, is there any chance you'll stay a while longer on the force? I have made your office available. As for you, Derek, if you want to come back to homicide, there's a place waiting for you."

Derek and I said we would think it over.

As we were leaving headquarters, Derek said to Betsy and me:

"Would the two of you like to come over for dinner tonight? Darla's making a roast. We can celebrate the end of the case."

"That's kind of you," Betsy said, "but I promised my friend Lauren I'd have dinner with her."

"That's a pity. And what about you, Jesse?"

I smiled. "I have a date tonight."

"Really?" Derek said, surprised.

"Who with?" Betsy asked.

535

"I'll tell you some other time."

"You're a dark horse," Derek said.

I waved to them and got in my car to go home.

*

That evening, I went to a little French restaurant in Sag Harbor that I particularly liked. I waited for her outside, with flowers. Then I saw her arrive. Betsy. She was radiant. She embraced me. With a gesture full of tenderness, I placed my hand on her bandaged face. She smiled and we kissed, for a long time.

"Do you think Derek suspects?" she said.

"I don't think so."

And I kissed her again.

2016

Two years after the events

In the fall of 2016, a little theater in New York City put on a play called "Stephanie Mailer's Darkest Night", written by Meta Ostrovski and directed by Kirk Hayward. The two men are currently touring the country with it.

Steven Bergdorf's article about the Orphea Festival and his role in 'The Darkest Night' did indeed revive the fortunes of the *New York Literary Review*. It went viral on social media and was syndicated nationwide.

Alan Brown did not stand again in the mayoral elections of September 2014. He left with Charlotte for Washington, where he joined the staff of a senator.

Sylvia Tennenbaum was elected mayor of Orphea. She is greatly liked by the townspeople. A year ago she started a spring literary festival which is enjoying a growing success.

Carolina Eden began studying literature at New York University. Jerry Eden resigned from his job at Channel 14. He and his wife Cynthia left Manhattan and settled in Orphea, where they took over Cody Spring-field's old bookstore, renaming it Carolina's World. Its reputation has spread throughout the Hamptons.

As for Jesse, Derek, and Betsy, after the conclusion of their investigation into the disappearance of Stephanie Mailer, they were decorated by the governor.

Derek, at his request, was transferred from administration to homicide.

Betsy left the Orphea police and joined the State Police with the rank of sergeant.

Jesse, having decided to continue in the police, was offered the post of major, but refused. Instead, he asked to be able to work in a threesome with Betsy and Derek. Thus far, they are the only team in the State Police working in this way. Since their formation, they have solved all the cases entrusted to them. Their colleagues call them the 100 Percent team. They take precedence when the most difficult cases are assigned.

When they are not in the field, they are in Orphea, where all three now live. If you need them, you're sure to find them in a lovely restaurant at 77 Bendham Road, where there used to be a hardware store until it was put out of business by a fire at the end of June 2014. The place is called Natasha's, and it is run by Darla Scott.

If you go there, say you've come to see the 100 Percent team. It will amuse them. You will find them at the same table, at the back of the establishment, just beneath a photograph of Jesse's grandparents and a portrait of Natasha looking forever beautiful—three spirits that watch over the restaurant and its customers.

It's a place where life seems sweeter.

DRAMATIS PERSONAE

JESSE ROSENBERG: captain in the New York State Police
DEREK SCOTT: sergeant in the New York State Police
BETSY KANNER: deputy chief of police in Orphea

DARLA SCOTT: Derek Scott's wife
NATASHA DARRINSKI: Jesse Rosenberg's girlfriend

JOSEPH GORDON: previous mayor of Orphea
LESLIE GORDON: Joseph Gordon's wife

ALAN BROWN: mayor of Orphea
CHARLOTTE BROWN: Alan Brown's wife

RON GULLIVER: current chief of police in Orphea
JASPER MONTAGNE: deputy chief of police in Orphea
KIRK HAYWARD: former chief of police in Orphea
MAJOR McKENNA: major in the State Police
SEAN O'DONNELL: police officer in Orphea

MEGHAN PADALIN: victim of the 1994 murders
SAMUEL PADALIN: Meghan Padalin's husband

BUZZ LAMBERT: director of "Uncle Vanya" in the 1994
    Orphea Festival
CODY SPRINGFIELD: owner of the Orphea bookshop
TED TENNENBAUM: former owner of Café Athena
SYLVIA TENNENBAUM: his sister, current owner of Café Athena

MICHAEL BIRD: editor of the *Orphea Chronicle*
MIRANDA BIRD: his wife

STEVEN BERGDORF: editor of the *New York Literary Review*
TRACY BERGDORF: his wife
SKIP NALAN: deputy editor of the *New York Literary Review*
META OSTROVSKI: critic for the *New York Literary Review*

JERRY EDEN: C.E.O. of Channel 14
CYNTHIA EDEN: his wife
CAROLINA EDEN: their daughter

TARA SCALINI: childhood friend of Carolina Eden
GERALD SCALINI: her father

JEREMIAH FOLD: bar owner in Ridgesport
COSTICO: Jeremiah Fold's henchman

JOËL DICKER was born in Geneva in 1985, where he studied Law. *The Truth about the Harry Quebert Affair* was nominated for the Prix Goncourt and won the Grand Prix du Roman de l'Académie Française and the Prix Goncourt des Lycéens. *The Baltimore Boys*, at once a prequel and a sequel, was published in English translation in 2017. *The Truth about the Harry Quebert Affair* is now a major SkyWitness series starring Patrick Dempsey.

HOWARD CURTIS is an award-winning translator from the French, Italian and Spanish. His previous translations include works by Georges Simenon, Jean-Claude Izzo, Luigi Pirandello and Luca D'Andrea.